PROJECT HELL

FELICITY KATES

PROJECT HELL

First edition 2016
Second Edition 2021
Copyright © 2016, 2021 Kathryn Sherwood and KC Stories

Written by Felicity Kates.
Edited by Piper Denna.
Cover art and design by Kate Reedwood.
All rights reserved.

www.legacyhumter.space

ISBN-13: 978-1-7771102-2-2

DEDICATION

To Philip K. Dick, a brilliant author taken before his time.
To my mother, whose love of reading sparked a lifetime of
storybook adventures.
And to Chris, with thanks for everything.

CONTENTS

ACKNOWLEDGMENTS

Like everyone on a journey of any kind, I owe a great many people a great deal of gratitude for their assistance, wisdom, encouragement, and friendship:
To Mike, my husband, and Alex, my son, thank you for your support and understanding my need to be alone at times so I can play with my imaginary friends and scribble down their words.
To the ladies at HEART who read the very first draft and didn't run away screaming in horror at the awkwardness of my attempt to blend science fiction and romance together.
To Piper, editor extraordinaire, and my friends, Shannon, Chris, Suzanne and Christine, whose willingness to beta read and offer encouragement has been invaluable and is very much appreciated.
And to the members of the Kates Korner Fan Group, the Legacy Hunter Guild, and all my wonderful friends, family, and readers, cheering me on behind the scenes.
Without each of you and your kindness, advice and belief in me, this book would still be an idea floating in my head, instead of the reflection of life that it has become.

Thank you so much for everything. I love you all. I couldn't have done it without you, my friends.
~Felicity~

UNEXPECTED GIFTS

*Deliverance Colony. New Earth
resettlement project, year 31.*

"WHAT THE HELL is this shit?" Peyton Chase muttered as he eyed the coffin-sized box that occupied his living quarters floor. No box had been there when he'd left to gather provisions. No box should be there now. And yet, there it was.

Not bothering to close the front door behind him, he set his bags of food on the floor and studied the black logo on the lid of the opaque white cargo container.

The Factory.

A message popped up on his hand-held tablet. Peyton shook his head as he read the blinking readout.

Delivered as ordered. Accept with your thumbprint.

Fuck. He hadn't ordered anything from 'The Factory'. He would *never* order anything for personal use from 'The Factory', not even if his life depended on it.

"Jared. Get your piece of shit ass in here right now, you stupid son-of-a-bitch," he called out as he instructed his tablet to scan the box. The environmental sensors positioned throughout Deliverance Dome's geodesic habitat were designed to detect viral contagions, but after the outbreak two years prior, it didn't hurt to be careful.

As if on cue, Jared entered the doorway, his brows raised in feigned innocence, which confirmed Peyton's suspicions about who had authorized the unexpected delivery.

"Yeah, man?" Jared said. He glanced at the box, the shit-eating grin teasing his lips widening into a full-blown smile. "Hey, how about that?" He placed a carton of supplies next to Peyton's bags on the floor and straightened. "Looks like you got a delivery from The Factory. I wonder what it could be?"

Scan complete, the outlined image of the package's contents was clear to see on the flat screen readout of Peyton's tablet. No contamination existed, but the box contained hell just the same.

The urge to throttle his longtime friend twitched in Peyton's fingers as he turned to him. "A Doll? A damned Doll?" He tossed his tablet onto the oblong box, letting his anger fill his voice.

Jared raised his hands and backed away, his smile slipping. "Now wait a minute. You did admit you were lonely, right?"

"I was drunk, you jackass," Peyton said, feeling a hangover-sized headache coming on. He rubbed his fingers against his temples.

He'd indulged far too much that night two weeks ago, sitting in Jared's cramped living quarters and sharing a bottle of the Dome's home-stilled whisky. Amongst other things, they'd discussed the usefulness of Jared's android companion, Bambi, as she went about her task of tidying up his place. The serene smile on her face never slipped. Her artificial intelligence program ensured domestic duties of every kind were completed efficiently and without complaint. But it was the blankness in her eyes and the way she mimicked expressions that Peyton couldn't get past. She was a gross distortion of the real thing. A mockery of life. Useful in sharing the workload, and Jared seemed happy with her. But had Peyton ever said he wanted a Doll of his own? No goddamned way.

"Yeah?" Jared said. He stopped backing away and leaned against the doorjamb, crossing his arms over his chest. "It's been two years since Sarah died, Peyton. You need to move on with your life. Get your grumpy ass laid before your dick falls off. Everyone's worried about you—"

"Everyone? Does everyone know about this?" Peyton gestured

at the box as the realization hit him. *Not Aunty Jo. Please, God, do not let my Aunt Joanna be involved in this asinine plot.*

"Well, maybe." Jared shrugged. "Aunty Jo did ask around for donations to add to the pot to get you a premium model."

"Holy Christ." Peyton groaned. He picked up the tablet and tossed it at Jared. "Send it back. Get this thing out of my place and send it the hell back. I don't need a goddamned android sex doll."

Jared shook his head and placed the tablet on top of the box again. "No go, bro. Next transport from the Arkopolis isn't until Thursday afternoon and you know it. She's yours."

"Like hell she is. You ordered her. You keep her."

Jared laughed. "Think I don't know what an ungrateful dick you are? Her delivery thumbprint is keyed to you, dumbass. You're the only one who can wake her from stasis."

"Fucking perfect." Peyton growled, his jaw clenching tight. "That DNA database is supposed to be for research." The genetic code of the entire colony was kept on file as a record in case all else failed in the quest to save humanity from extinction. But there wasn't any point in arguing the fact that he was stuck with a box in his room, at least until the shippers came back for it in three days. That didn't mean he had to put up with Jared taking up space too, however. "Get your stupid ass out of my place," he snapped. "I don't need a goddamned intervention."

"Yeah. 'Cause you're just fine, right?" Jared said. His gaze darted around the sparse apartment, full of heated words they'd shared over Peyton's life choices. He shook his head, his frustration clear in the tightness of the movement. "Whatever," he said and backed out of the room with a stiff shrug. "Enjoy her, man. I chose her especially for you," he called out as he turned to leave. "You can thank me later. Grumpy dickhead." Jared slapped the external release button and the door hissed shut.

"Meddling piece of shit," Peyton muttered into the silence filling his living room. Familiar silence. Empty silence. A comfortable void the box threatened to breach with its robotic occupant inside.

A Factory-made fuck doll.

Avoiding the container, he headed for a doorway on the left instead. Light flickered on as he entered his workroom, illuminating his steel-grey sanctuary filled with carefully organized shelves of mechanical items in need of repair. He settled into his comfortable chair at the worktable with an angry thump.

Goddamn Jared Jar-head and his crusade to fix everything. Buying him a sex doll. Of all the stupid things to go and waste hard-earned trade credits on. And Aunty Jo was in on it too. Hell. Why was he surprised by that? His elderly aunt had never known what boundaries were, let alone respected them. She'd undoubtedly pop by unannounced at some point to see how Peyton liked the gift. And take a strip off him when she discovered he wasn't keeping it.

Shit.

Just what he didn't need. Another guilt trip "pep" talk.

"Why do you insist on hiding in the rafters, Peyton? You aren't a bat. Come down and live with the rest of us. No one blames you for what happened."

"No one, my ass," he muttered into the silence. No one but him, and the fifty-odd dead souls he'd had to cremate under quarantine conditions, while hoping and praying his vaccination held true and no one else got sick.

It was too hard to face the sadness in everyone's eyes, the empty places at the mess hall tables. Far easier to live on his own up in the modified storage rooms he called home.

He picked up the precision laser instrument he used to remove metal corrosion from where he'd left it on the table earlier. Choosing a mechanical limb from the pile awaiting his attention, he began working.

After a few passes of the tool, the hum and flick of the laser dissolved the corrosion, leaving behind silvery, unblemished steel. The angry knot inside him slowly melted as well. This was the kind of work he enjoyed. Removing decay, rebuilding, making something old new again.

A damn sex doll. In his living room.

He tossed the metal arm he worked on and blindly snatched up another. They were taking over. More robots existed on New Earth than humans, especially in Deliverance colony. He'd gone from being a physician to a robotics technician. The only good thing about that was robots never died. People, on the other hand, left a hole behind. An empty ache that never healed.

But did that make him lonely?

Who wasn't lonely?

With a three to one ratio of men to women amongst the survivors struggling to repopulate the Earth, finding a life mate of the opposite sex was an idea of the past. Most people settled into communal relationships with multiple partners instead of just one.

Sarah had been special, the love they'd shared unique.

Missing her was something a quick fuck with a willing *machine* was never going to fix.

A sex doll might work for Jared and some of the others, but it wouldn't work for him. A Doll wasn't the answer he needed. She wasn't Sarah, no matter how well put together she might be.

And he sure as hell wasn't opening that damn box to see.

**

Two hours later he stood in front of the oblong box, contemplating the tablet in hand that displayed the Doll's activation instructions. Maybe he could rewire it to explode?

Ideal companion, my ass.

"I chose her just for you." Right.

What did Jar-head know about what he liked?

But it would be interesting to see how far The Factory had come in their "products". He'd pick this android apart is what he'd do and utilize all the information for his own uses. And after he picked the design to pieces, he'd put it back together and assign it to assist someone else. Then he'd still be fulfilling his obligation to Deliverance Dome's twenty-seven remaining residents. They'd establish a foothold for humanity on the northern portion of the New Western continent, he'd see to that.

The ecological catastrophe that had wiped out the multi-billion population of Earth had left the planet ravaged even a thousand years after the final plagues had finished. The ecosystem remained contaminated with residual toxins that made the environment barely hospitable for humans. A situation that the eco-reclaiming project needed to permanently fix, because there sure as hell wasn't anywhere else in the galaxy that humanity could exist.

Who could have guessed all those centuries ago that the Arkology ships sent into the galaxy to find new homes for humanity would instead discover that the only earth-sized planet remotely habitable within realistically achievable distance was Earth itself? Or that the colonization technology packed on board the ships would be the lifeboat needed to re-seed the homeworld long after the planet had become silent and the cities crumbled to dust.

They needed to do everything they could to fight extinction, and with barely three thousand humans left in the known universe, it was a fight they needed to win.

Who was he to stand in the way of the future of humanity?

The Doll would be useful, helping out with any number of back-breaking chores needed to keep the Dome's soil reclaiming project running. And using a precious premium piece of machinery from The Factory to literally shovel shit only made the idea of her working as part of their team even sweeter. A grin twitched his lips as he pressed his thumb to the outline on his tablet and accepted receipt of the delivery.

Immediately, a new message appeared in bold text on the screen:

> Congratulations, Peyton Chase!
>
> We hope you will enjoy your new Lumacore Industries, Companion Class Synthetic Human. At Lumacore, we ensure the highest quality in robotic assistants.
>
> To awaken your sleeping beauty from suspended animation, place a kiss upon her loving lips.

The grin fell from his own lips as he glanced through the message a second time, certain he must have been mistaken.

Sleeping beauty? Loving lips?

"What? They can't be serious." He tossed the tablet onto his nearby couch as the lid of the box slid open with a hiss.

Cool cryogenic-suspension vapor pooled outward from the container. He wafted it aside with his hand, helping it to dissipate into the warmth of his living room, and studied the so-called sleeping beauty in question.

"Well, shit." he muttered. Either there hadn't been much selection or, despite having grown up together, Jared didn't know his tastes very well.

In terms of physical appeal, she was not what he had expected. For one thing, he preferred women with dark hair. This Doll's fair hair, slightly damp from being in suspension, fell in lanky strands across her shoulders and against the inside of the metal container. For another, though her body remained wrapped mummy-style in semi-translucent protective covering, he could tell her waif-like torso sported small breasts, not the more-than-abundant handfuls he was accustomed to with Sarah. Her legs were slender, her hips sleek, and her skin almost deathly pale. For a sex doll, she wasn't the generic Factory model he was accustomed to seeing around the Domes. Certainly not the super-sexualized playmate Jared had purchased a year ago, with breasts as large as melons and an artificial, never-ending smile.

This Doll was compact. Almost utilitarian. An intriguing change from the norm. In fact, she looked damn near human and disturbingly corpse-like, lying on the floor in her coffin-like container. Not a breath rose in her chest. Not an eyelash fluttered. He'd seen death more times than he cared to remember and looking at this delicate creature lying there devoid of life made his gut clench.

Yet the stillness she radiated wasn't lifelessness; it was anticipation.

She waited.

For him.

Well, not necessarily *him*. Anyone who'd purchased her could awaken her from her cocoon of suspended animation sleep. All it took, apparently, was a fucking kiss. A ridiculous activation mechanism if there ever was one. Whose asinine idea at The Factory had that been?

He grimaced. If only it had been so easy to awaken Sarah when cradling her lifeless body in his arms. Trapped within his environmental protection suit, he hadn't even been able to kiss her goodbye or risk exposing himself to the virus that had killed her, the Karezza Idiopathic Syndrome—or 'K.I.S. of Death' virus, as it had been nicknamed.

A kiss to awaken.

A kiss to kill.

Did any of the geneticists at the Arkopolis understand the irony?

Would they even care?

He closed his eyes and concentrated on the task at hand, letting cool logic ease his anger.

This Doll was not Sarah. She did not look like Sarah. Could not *be* Sarah. And he didn't want her to be. All he needed to do was activate her so she could help the colonists survive. End of story.

Opening his eyes, he focused on her lips.

They looked very pink against her pale skin. Soft. Slightly bowed, pressed together in asymmetrical imperfection. The bottom one was a touch too full in comparison to the top. A subtle detail that gave her life-like appearance credibility.

And, although pale, her pallor did not have the waxy sheen of syntha-skin, nor did her hair seem coarse. The wisps drying about her heart-shaped face had formed delicate curls. He bent forward and brushed a strand with his finger. It felt soft, like real hair, or at least a high-quality cellulose construct.

Interesting.

Technology at The Factory had advanced considerably in the quest to create artificial life. Was she one of the new Bio-roids, the synthesis of human genetics and technology he'd heard rumors about? Couldn't be. They were still in the idea stage. Or had been when Sarah had worked with The Factory's genetics team. This was just a high-tech Doll, even if an impeccably made one.

Despite his reluctance to be impressed by anything Factory-made, he shook his head and let out a low whistle as he dropped to his knees beside the container to get a better look at the specimen inside.

Her cheek was smooth and soft to his touch. Still damp and cool from being in suspension but warming beneath his fingers. Jesus. How many credits had Jared and the others pooled together to get their hands on such an advanced android?

A shadow of guilt crept over him at how he'd reacted to the idea of their gift. He didn't want or need their concern. It weighed him down, made him feel raw inside when he'd rather not feel anything. His conscience twisted as he imagined the look of disappointment Aunty Jo would have when she discovered he'd rejected her attempt at seeing him happy again.

Happiness. What an overrated emotion. Numbness was so much better. The kind he found from the predictable routine of getting up every day, doing his work, and pretending it all meant nothing more than the brief solace he found at the bottom of a bottle of whisky.

He stared at the Doll's peaceful, lifelike form and the illusion she represented.

Fuck happy. He didn't need happiness. But who was he to stand in the way of everyone else's? Aunty Jo deserved better than the bitterness filling his soul.

Damnit. Maybe he should just keep the Doll himself.

He could get her to do chores around the colony and pretend to be happy with the arrangement as well as anyone. And it might stop all the worried looks and *concern* over his need to be alone.

He could always turn her off when he'd had enough of her invasion of his privacy, a definite bonus when compared to living with people, who never seemed to shut the fuck up, especially when he wanted to be left in peace.

But as for Jared's idea that androids were an ideal solution for lonely nights in a world with far too few humans? Even with her realistic modeling, Peyton doubted he could bring himself to ever go that far. Nothing could numb the ache he felt inside when he thought of Sarah. Not whisky, not a quick fuck, not work and not a goddamned Doll.

A quick peck would do it. Awaken her from stasis. Then he could get her started with helping out the colony and make everyone fucking *happy*. And he could get on with finding the best way to numb his own life.

He brought his face close to hers. A subtle, sweet scent tickled his nose as he brushed his mouth against her lips.

They were soft. And warm. Really warm. Human body temperature warm. Slightly damp from the dew left by cryo-thawing, and they parted to his gentle pressure with a sigh.

The sound traveled from his head down to his toes, then arced back up and slammed into his brain with a jolt. His pulse jacked, beating in an answering rhythm to the vibration her moan created.

What the fuck?

Shocked, he grasped the edge of the box as her mouth moved beneath his. A questing tongue flicked out and slipped past his lips. She tasted sweet. Fragrant, like her honey scent, which filled his mind.

He jerked backwards, breaking the connection.

A flicker of recognition stirred deep inside him. Awareness that his affection-starved body was not only reacting to the feel of her soft lips, but that his racing pulse and the sudden stiffness of his cock were the result of a pheromone-activated imprinting sequence flooding through his veins.

"Hell," he said, and backed away, his mind racing to keep ahead of his pulse. "Deactivate," he demanded. He needed to shut this shit down right now.

But that didn't stop her fluttering lashes or the shudder that passed through her body as the Doll strained within her restrictive wrappings to suck in a gasp of air with a cough.

FIRST IMPRESSIONS

"I SAID, DEACTIVATE," the voice demanded a second time with an increased level of insistence. It was a deep voice, definitely male, with a reverberating undertone that suggested...displeasure? Not a voice that matched anything in the Doll's memory, yet despite the bizarre command to somehow turn herself off, his domineering tone caused her to focus, regroup.

She coughed again, sucking in a deeper breath this time. Her lungs stung with the effort, the cells burning as they remembered how to process oxygen. The air felt foreign but warm as it passed over her tingling lips. Her mind registered the scents and tastes, categorizing them into things she could understand.

The crisp sweetness of laundered linen. The soft saltiness of skin. An overtone of clean citrus body cleansers with a hint of musky maleness. Unfamiliar, but pleasant. Who was this man who'd woken her with a kiss? His taste lingered on her tongue, seeped slowly into her senses, bringing her to life.

She blinked. Misty wetness blurred her vision, turning the world into a kaleidoscope of colors that swirled as she struggled to see. Nothing made sense. The shapes all blended together. He could be anyone. She could be anywhere.

Within the darkness of stasis-induced brain fog, she struggled to remember. Fleeting images passed through her mind. A dark room. The bitter tang of metal. The need to run. To hide.

The air caressed her damp face, causing her to shiver as a trickle of apprehension passed through her. She couldn't move her arms. She couldn't move anything except her head. Something held her tight. Pinned her. Trapped her.

Was she still there? In that dark room that echoed pain?

Her pulse spiked in instinctive panic. She needed to escape. Break free.

"I can't—" she managed through trembling lips. "I can't move." She fought against her restraints, twisting and turning. "Get it...get it off of me!" she cried out. "Please!" She begged the stranger hovering near her for help.

"Calm down," he ordered in that same domineering tone. Strong fingers pulled at the tight bindings, loosening them as he muttered a low curse. "Just...shit. Stop squirming. I'll have you out in a second. Damnit! Why won't you turn off?" He sounded bewildered. Annoyed.

Heart thudding in her throat, she forced herself to become still, staring blindly in the direction of his presence. She had no choice but to trust him. Trust that the strength radiating from him was a source of solace and not the fear choking her.

Hands pressed against her, warm hands with broad palms and deft fingers that pulled at the wrappings around her chest and arms, breaking the tough layers of...of packing? Yes, packing material, not restraints. She wasn't tied up or pinned down. She'd been placed in stasis and shipped. The crisp material snagged for a second beneath his grip, then with a tearing sound, it pulled loose.

Air raced across her exposed skin in a cool rush, causing her shivers to increase as relief flooded through her in a wave so strong she choked back a sob.

She was free.

Taking in a deep breath, she pressed her palms to her closed eyes. In the moment of calmness, logic pushed past the jumble of emotions churning through her mind.

Wherever she was, it was not that dark room filled with fear in The Factory. And this stranger had set her free.

She had escaped.

To where and from what, she couldn't identify. The more she concentrated on the cause of her panic, the more it slid into the murky darkness of a stasis-induced dreamscape. But the impression lingered that something life threatening had stalked her while she slept and that perhaps she owed the impatient stranger hovering above her, her life.

"Hell," he muttered as he pulled the last of the binding away from her legs.

"What?" She blinked up at him. The bright halos blooming before her eyes blurred and shifted until they formed an image of pleasing organic symmetry.

A face stared down at her. Pale skin framed by short brown hair. Dark eyes fringed by even darker lashes. Full brows, strong cheek bones, a light covering of stubble on the jaw. Definitely male. And definitely not a pattern-match for any identity stored in her memory matrix, yet the knot of panic continued to ease as she studied him.

"Hell," he repeated, his gaze flicking over her naked body with undisguised curiosity that snagged on the hairless apex of her thighs. "It's like living in fucking hell," he muttered. His gaze darted to hers then fell to her lips, skittered past, and settled on her breasts.

A tremor wracked her, making her erect nipples tighten further. She clutched at the edge of the shipping container as a wave of desire passed through her in response to his scrutiny.

"You're cold," he stated as if grasping at the idea like a lifeline. A deep flush stained his clenched jaw as he glanced at her face again and caught her quick answering nod. "Shit. I'll...shit. I'll get you something to wear." He wrenched his gaze away and headed across the room.

Slowly sitting up, she studied him as he moved toward a panel on the far wall.

His living quarters were small. Utilitarian. A single bed with its plain brown coverings neatly folded into place. Nestled beside it on the wall, a flat-screen monitor provided soft lighting. The only other furnishings were the couch and a low metal table empty of anything except a communications tablet. No decorations marked the pale walls, no digi-vids of family. Nothing to give her a clue about his life, except that it was empty.

Flushed, flustered, and aroused, whoever her new master was, he was struggling with the imprinting pheromones flooding his veins and the way they heightened his own natural attraction to her. Interesting. She had no desire to fight the chemistry linking them. If he were the type of mate to demand immediate sexual gratification, imprinting would be completed with little effort. His muscular limbs and broad shoulders fit her specifications for desire quite nicely. As long as he didn't harm her, she had no problem calling him master.

But by the way he moved in brisk, irritated mannerisms as he opened the panel in the wall and retrieved a blue shirt similar to the one he currently wore, he might have an issue with taking her as his slave. Which was odd considering he had initiated the imprinting sequence. Maybe she wasn't what he'd expected? She glanced at her pale naked figure. Already she could feel her body responding to his unconscious desires, subtly changing her into whatever form he found most appealing. Her nudity didn't bother her in the slightest, but it definitely bothered him. He avoided looking at her while walking toward her, holding out the shirt between them like a shield.

"Thank you," she murmured as he gently helped her slide the shirt over her head and arms.

Maybe he was upset with her for the way she'd reacted when waking? She cringed inside, wishing she could go back in time and redo that process. Screaming in fear was not the way to begin an initial imprinting session. She needed to rectify that error. It was vital that she make a good impression with this man. The idea of being sent back to The Factory heightened the feeling of dread, which continued to linger at the back of her mind. For whatever reason, that fear was real.

The shivers wracking her subsided as the soft, warm fabric of his shirt fell around her shoulders and covered her to mid-thigh. She couldn't resist a smile as his scent surrounded her—spicy, fragrant cleansers combined with musky masculinity. It was a pleasing scent that spoke of power and virility.

His nostrils flared as he stepped back and leaned against the edge of the nearby couch. Crossing his arms over his chest, he pinned her with an intent stare. He might have been flustered a moment ago, but now he was back in control.

"Mind telling me who you are? No, wait. Why don't we start with *what* you are?"

The question made her pause as she gingerly stood up and forced blood to flow through her numb limbs. "What do you mean?" She smoothed the fabric of his shirt over her stomach. On him it fit snugly over his crossed arms, defining his well-made shoulders and chest. On her it sagged like an oversized dress.

He picked up a small tablet from the edge of the couch and glanced quickly at the display. "It says here you are Lumacore Industries, Companion Class Synthetic Human, model number: sixty-nine, one, one, three, eight, Alpha. But you aren't like any Doll I've ever seen." He placed the tablet back onto the seat next to him. His eyes found hers again in an implacable stare. "So the question stands. What are you?"

She fidgeted with the edge of her shirt. That identification belonged to one of her lower functioning android cousins. The Alphas were an older model. She shared the same programming matrix, but the full-bodied functions she possessed far exceeded any other synthesized lifeform created at The Factory. Perhaps he'd read the tag wrong? Humans were not infallible.

"I am not a silicone enhanced android," she explained. "I am a bio-synthetic humanoid. My body requires feeding and maintenance, like yours."

"You're a Bio-roid?"

"Yes. I eat. I breathe. I learn and adapt. And I can't be turned off," she added, recalling his earlier request to deactivate. "Did you not know this before purchase?"

"I didn't purchase you," he said, his gaze turning cold.

"You didn't?"

"No. You were given to me." His lips twisted into a mirthless smile that didn't reach his eyes. Instead, curiosity lit his features as he peered closely at her face. "Incredible. I can't tell the difference." As he touched her cheek with his fingers, fire flowed along her skin. "No wonder you're so soft and warm," he murmured. "Your skin is real."

His pupils dilated as he studied her, widening points of darkness in glittering, rich, chestnut irises. The musky call of his pheromones increased as his skin flushed. The urge to press her body against his and show him just how real she was possessed her. But he stepped away from her again, his gaze bright with clinical interest.

He let out a low whistle. "A Bio-roid. Cloned human tissue fused with a mechanical matrix. The latest development in genetic research at the Arkopolis," he said as if reciting the specs from a research paper.

She nodded, pleased he seemed so impressed by her state-of-the-art pedigree.

He brushed his fingers across his lips, his eyes growing distant as he contemplated the situation. "How did Jared get his hands on a Bio-roid?" he murmured to himself. He settled on the arm of the couch and looked at her again. "You're just an idea. A dream. Not even in production yet, let alone on wide release." He shook his head. "There must be some kind of a mistake. Do you know who your master is supposed to be?"

Her anxiety from earlier returned. Would he send her back if he was displeased with the truth? She shook her head and asked the question burning in her mind. "Who are you?"

"My name is Peyton. Peyton Chase."

Peyton Chase. Identification validated.

The message whispered through her consciousness, bringing with it a feeling of approval. He may be unfamiliar in appearance, but she was certain she was exactly where she needed to be. She stepped over the edge of the box. The tiled floor felt cold against her bare feet. "You are a doctor, correct?" She didn't need his affirming nod to know the answer as her memory rose through the cloudy murkiness of stasis fog.

Yes, Peyton Chase was a doctor. She had chosen him because he was known for his dislike of The Factory. And he lived...where did he live? "And this is...?" She let the question trail off as her memory drew a blank.

"Deliverance Dome," he said, his expression darkening. "Or rather what's left of it. And about as far away from the Arkopolis as a settlement can be."

Yes. *Deliverance Dome.* Recognition sparked. "A virus devastated this place."

"Over two years ago. And I can't believe The Factory would ever send a state-of-the-art piece of premium merchandise to live in my portion of hell," he said, his voice laced with suspicion.

She breathed in deep but sensed nothing abnormal in the atmosphere. "It's clean here now. No trace of contamination."

"But the stigma lives on," he said in a cold tone. "A Bio-roid. An android very few people have ever heard of, let alone know exists, sent to Deliverance Dome?" His voice was filled with disbelief, his tall, strong body tense. "No. It doesn't make sense. There must have been a mix up somewhere. Someone got sent my Doll and I got you instead. Come on, let's get you back inside your case while I figure this out." He started toward the pile of packing material he'd left draped over the side of the box.

She froze. Her being here with him wasn't a mistake. His identification resonated with hers, despite imprinting being incomplete. "You don't want me?"

"No." His blunt denial echoed loud in the room, but his gaze flicked from her face to her toes, tripping over her short hem on its way down.

"Why not?"

"I don't need you."

He sounded casual, but pain vibrated from his simple declaration and registered deep in her cortex. He did need her, despite his claim. Perhaps more than she needed him. But he didn't want commitment. She placed her hand on his shoulder and felt the broad muscle flex. Her own muscles vibrated in synch with him. They were connected. She must have a place in his life. But she needed to convince him of that fact and fast. Because she absolutely could not go back to The Factory.

"I can be all things," she said. "I'm highly adaptive."

"I'm sure you are," he muttered as he nudged her toward the box.

"Peyton, look at me."

"No." He kept his gaze averted and began to rebind her arms.

A chill gripped her spine as the thin material touched her skin. "Please, don't."

"It's for the best."

"Stasis is cold."

His gaze found hers and held it. "You can feel when in suspended animation?"

"Yes. It's empty. Dark. It frightens me."

"Ah, hell..." The binding material crunched between his fingers as they curled into a fist. "You're scared." He dragged his free hand through his hair. "A robot that feels. This is exactly what I didn't want!" His jaw clenched tight. "What the hell am I supposed to do?"

She folded her hands, affecting calm in an attempt to lessen his distress. "Let me stay with you."

His expression darkened. "Give me one good reason why I should."

"You're a good man," she asserted, feeling the truth of the statement deep in her core.

He laughed. Bitter and cold. "Get in the box," he ordered.

She put her hands up to stop him as he raised his own to help her step into the container. "Listen. I'll do whatever you want. Be whoever you want. Just, please, do not send me back to The Factory."

"Why?"

"I...don't like it there." She searched for the source of her fear but couldn't isolate the cause through the persistent cloud of brain fog left from stasis.

"Neither do I, sweetheart. But I don't need trouble either. Get in the box."

She dropped onto her knees before him and begged. "Please. You know that I can't lie. I don't remember who packed me or how I was shipped here. But I can't go back. They..." Again, the dark fog inside her mind stole the reason away, leaving behind cold fear. She closed her eyes and struggled to remember, but the increased concentration only brought a heavy pounding behind her eyes. "My memory is still confused from stasis. I don't know why I'm here, but you have to believe me. If you send me back, I'll die."

He looked at her sharply. "Someone is trying to kill you?"

"Yes. No. I don't know. I think...I think I ran away."

A dark room. The bitter tang of metal. Needing to run. To hide. And then she was running... Running. Her only hope of escaping the pain.

"Hell," he muttered. He speared his fingers through his dark hair.

She threw herself against his legs, clinching herself to him. "Please, Peyton. Don't send me back there." Her voice choked on the tears building inside her. This was not how things were supposed to happen. He was supposed to help her, not send her back.

"Get up," he said gruffly. His strong hands grasped her arms and gently lifted her to her feet. "You don't need to cry." He stared at her, his dark eyes storming with emotions. His fingers were soft against her skin as he brushed at the tears gathering on her lashes. He glanced at the wetness on his fingertips, his jaw clenching tight. "You aren't going back to The Factory."

Relief rushed through her. She launched herself at him. Wrapping her arms about his neck, she whispered, "Thank you," over and over again, kissing his cheek, his jaw, his lips—his sculpted, perfect lips.

He pulled back abruptly, forcing her to end the kiss. "Stop it. You don't need to do that," he said, his voice edged with renewed anger as he pushed her away. "Shit. I just wanted you to tell me the truth. I wouldn't make a stray dog live with those Arkopolis bastards."

A stray dog? He thought of her as a stray dog? And he'd made her beg for nothing? The derisive label of 'asshole' whispered through her mind. But at least she wasn't going back to the Arkopolis. She had to thank him for that. He could have tapped on his tablet and turned her in as a runaway. He still could. Which meant she needed to be very, very nice to Dr. Peyton Chase. Imprinting had begun, but it wasn't completed yet. Until it was, she wasn't secure as his property.

He tossed the packing material he held in his hands into the box, and then bent to pick up the pieces that had fallen to the floor.

"I can help you with that," she said hastily.

He jerked in surprise as she bent to assist him, causing their heads to collide in a flash of pain.

"Goddamn." He grunted and steadied her, settling her onto the couch.

"I'm sorry. I'm so sorry. I was just trying to help."

"Listen," he said, batting her hands aside as she reached out to rub the red welt forming on his temple. "Let's get a few things straight right now. I said you can stay here. But I don't expect you to clean up for me. And you don't need to act all sexy and sweet. You aren't my slave."

"But what if I want to be?"

"You don't get a choice in the matter."

"Well, if I don't get a choice because you're ordering me to not have one, then that means I'm your slave."

He closed his eyes. "I am going to fucking kill Jared."

"Who?"

He shook his head and studied her again. "Look. What I mean is, whatever pre-programmed expectations you have about being a Doll—"

"You mean a sex doll, right?"

"Yes, that. You don't have to do that with me. The only thing you need to do is stay put here, on this seat, until I can figure this shit out."

"Okay." She paused, studying his serious expression. Far too serious for such a handsome man. "Is that going to take a long time? Because I really need to use the bathroom."

He didn't even crack a smile. Just pointed toward a door on the side of the room.

She silently rose and walked toward it. All jokes aside, she really did need to refresh herself. She had no idea how long she'd been in cryo-stasis, but it felt like a million days.

The doorway hissed open as she waved her hand across a panel in the wall. Light flickered on as she stepped inside the washroom, illuminating steel fixtures, a narrow shower stall, and a small mirror. Functional, despite the size. The scent of his citrus body cleansers filled the air, making her wish he was the type of master who would take his slave at first sight. His reluctance was a problem.

Sometimes imprinting can be difficult, her encoded lessons advised. *Humans are unpredictable at best, and often fear change.* Fear was her enemy here. Her fear, his fear. Best to complete the imprinting process before he changed his mind. Even if it meant her taking the upper hand.

When she re-entered the living area, he was busy arranging her cargo box in an upright position against the wall beside the outside door.

"Do I have a name?" she asked.

He glanced around at her. "A what?"

"A name," she repeated, walking slowly toward him.

His brows twitched as he admired her bare legs. "No. Do you require one?"

"Yes." Imprinting couldn't continue until she had a name.

The box lid slid shut with a press of his thumb on a switch. He turned to face her directly. "What did they call you at The Factory?"

She stopped in front of him, intrigued by the pleasant horizon of his broad shoulders. His blue shirt, with its 'V' of tantalizing chest hair, pulled tight across his well-developed pectorals as he folded his arms and leaned sideways against the wall.

"I don't remember."

His brow furrowed. "Then what would you like to be called?"

She affected a relaxed stance and looked up at his face. "I would prefer something meaningful. I am, however, programmed to accept whatever name you choose."

He grinned, a flash of straight white teeth. "How about Hell?"

"A religious expletive? Really?"

"Seems appropriate, don't you think?"

She blinked at him, uncertain how to respond as disappointment settled deep inside her. He really didn't like her. But liking was arbitrary in their kind of relationship. What she needed to do was survive, which meant at least pleasing him until the stasis brain fog wore off and she could remember what it was she'd been running from. She plastered on a pleasant smile. "Verify by repeating this name now."

His eyes reflected the ambient glow of a nearby lighting orb ensconced on the cream walls, his expression softening as he studied her. He stroked a finger across his dark-stubbled chin. "I'll call you Helen after Helen of Troy, the woman whose beauty started a war."

She couldn't help the pleasure that filled her. Helen was a pretty sounding name. He thought she was beautiful?

"But for short, I'll call you Hell." He winked and walked past her across the living room to the couch. "I don't know about you, but I could really use a drink. Today has been one *hell* of a day. In fact, you could call it *hell*-ish." He sat on the soft seat with an exhausted sigh, chuckling over his pun.

Picking up the tablet from the table, he flicked on the wall monitor. A race appeared on the screen. The two all-terrain transports involved created a cloud of dust as they careened between boulders strewn around a dirt track that was banked by deep canyon walls.

"Damn," muttered Peyton, his face falling into serious lines as his attention quickly became caught up in the action. "I forgot The Chase was on. I've got 20 credits on Vassino to win."

Hell moved to stand beside him. "You enjoy teasing me, don't you, Peyton?"

He glanced sideways at her. "I prefer to be left alone. But since I'm stuck with you for the moment...why not indulge in a little fun?" He turned to the race when the fast action culminated in a screech of tires as the two vehicles barely avoided collision. "*Shit. Did you see that?*"

"Yes. My thoughts exactly. Since I'm here, why not indulge?" she murmured. Imprinting must be completed as soon as possible, and Peyton's quintessential desire called to her, despite his gruff attempt to distance himself. And his poor taste in humor.

"Peyton," she called his name. Satisfaction filled her as the soft tone of her voice drew his attention despite the excitement happening on the screen. "I enjoy teasing you, too," she said and lifted the short hem of her shirt, exposing her naked sex to his searing gaze.

BE CAREFUL WHAT YOU WISH FOR

PEYTON'S COCK JUMPED to attention at the taunting display of pale, smooth flesh exposed mere inches from his face. Hunger growled deep in his soul. He'd been semi-hard since waking the Doll from stasis, fighting the damn imprinting pheromones flooding his veins. Fighting the need to make use of her in the way his primal instinct urged him to. Now, desire slammed into him like a fist, making him achingly hard. Her pussy was pretty, and plump, and so damned close he could practically taste her. All he had to do was grab her hips and give her slit a lick.

She let the hem of her shirt drop and stepped back with a teasing smile, her sweet scent wafting across his face.

"Hell!"

Gritting his teeth, he grabbed her shirt. The fabric bunched between his fingers as he pulled her sideways and down onto the couch beside him.

She landed with a hard gasp, her amber-colored eyes wide. He pinned her with his arms and bowed his head, his brow a hairsbreadth from hers. "Do not tempt me." He snarled and sprang away before the urge to meld his lips with her perfect pink ones grew too great. "You don't know what you're asking for."

The image of her naked pussy burned in his mind as he stormed across the room and swiped his palm over an access panel.

"I shouldn't have opened that box," he muttered as he stepped into the silence of his workroom. "I should *not* have opened that box!"

Of all the stupid things to happen in his life. He had to get saddled with a robot who thought she was real. No, a robot who *was* real. Real lips, real breasts, real skin as smooth as silk. His erect cock twitched against his boxers. Would it feel just as real to slide into her hot, tight sex? *Geeze, Peyton, don't think about it!*

He made his way past the racks of mechanical parts awaiting attention and sat at his workbench. The familiar odor of electrical lubricant and metallic decay did nothing to calm his stormy mood.

Snatching up the tablet he kept on his worktable, he called Jared. No answer. Just like when he'd tried earlier while Hell was in the bathroom. Figures the dickhead would be offline when he really needed him. He left him another message. "Pick up, asshat. We need to talk." He tossed the tablet down in disgust and picked up his laser utility tool instead.

Busy. He needed to keep busy so he could think his way through this mess. He flipped over the nearest gyroscopic controller requiring adjustment and set to work.

Hell was a problem.

A runaway prototype android whose damn imprinting pheromones were making him so hard his dick refused to go back down. He rubbed at his lips in disgust, trying to scrub the effects of her kiss off, but knew it would be no more effective than the shot of Androstanol blocker he'd rushed to give himself as soon as he'd realized what had happened. Then she'd begged him to unwrap her with that whimper of fear in her voice, and he'd felt the urgent need to protect her flood through him, killing any chance he might have had to just close the box lid and stay the fuck away.

Nope, he was stuck with her chemical hooks clawing beneath his skin now. Who needed that kind of trouble? Certainly not him. But despite his desire to not get involved, the instinct to protect her was a howling need he couldn't stop from shaking him to the core. She'd woken up scared. Scared! What the hell had happened to her at The Factory? Had someone hurt her? Why else would she have run away?

He gripped the laser in his hand tighter. Brain fog was a common side effect of being in stasis. Once it wore off in a few hours, he'd demand the whole story from her. But he could already imagine what it might be. He was well aware that the bastards at the Arkopolis had no respect for individual life, certainly not the mechanical kind. When it came to matters of scientific progress, everyone was just a means to an end.

Thing was, if she'd run away, someone would likely be wanting her back. Someone like the lead geneticist, Markus Willbright, who'd often butted heads with Sarah over the moral cost of creating artificial life. It was true, humankind had a responsibility to ensure the survival of itself, but Markus never seemed to care if that meant losing his own humanity in the process. As head of operations at The Factory, it was a good bet Markus was involved in Hell's creation.

But had it even been sanctioned?

That thought gave Peyton pause. He wouldn't put it past Willbright to have run an unauthorized experiment in the name of science.

Peyton frowned. He'd have to keep Hell here with him in secret. It was the only way to make sure she'd be safe until he found out what had happened to her in the first place, and how the hell she'd ended up being sent to him. But how was he supposed to hide her? Especially with a Dome full of people waiting to meet his new Doll. He was surprised they weren't lined up banging on his door already.

And to make matters worse, Hell had needs. Feelings. Fucking tears. Things that annoyingly made him want to *care*. What the hell was he supposed to do with that? He rubbed the mark on his temple where her head had connected with his, feeling the headache brewing behind. He definitely didn't need her type of trouble.

Behind him, the door slid open with a soft hiss.

Hell. Of course. He sensed her hesitant step as she entered his private domain. "You don't need to be in here," he instructed. He kept his back to her and continued to flake minute particles of decay from the gyro's sensitive inner workings. "Go and rest. We'll talk in a bit when you've recovered from stasis."

"You make machines?" Wonderment filled her voice as she slowly walked further into the workroom, ignoring his instructions completely.

"No."

"You fix them then?"

He sighed. "Yes."

"Why?"

Why? He put down the handheld laser and turned to face her. She stood near the door, an opened bottle of whisky and an empty glass in her hands, smooth legs planted as if challenging him to tell her to go again. The short hem of her—no, *his*—shirt skimmed the top of her thighs.

Bare. She was bare under there. The image of her sweet sex burned hot in his mind. Hairless, pert lips that begged to be tasted and touched.

He gritted his teeth as heat turned to anger. "Because things break down. And since the so-called 'risk of contamination' makes everything from Deliverance damn near worthless, trade credits for replacements are hard to come by."

Her slender neck bowed as she gave a quick nod. "Yes, I understand. The Virus. People are still afraid." She tilted her head. Her questioning, innocent gaze caught the cool ambient light. "What I meant was, why *you*? Why do you fix machines when you hate them?"

"I don't hate machines."

"You hate me."

"You aren't a machine. You're—" *Temptation.* He turned his back on her and picked up the laser tool. "Go back to the other room. I don't have heat pumped in here. It gets cold at night."

Her footsteps padded toward him. Shit. Well, he wasn't going to entertain her if she wanted to stay. He had work to catch up on. Work he should have just kept doing instead of opening that damn box.

He attempted to shut out her presence by concentrating on the work at hand. The laser hummed its soft, warming rhythm as it pierced the weak spots in the gyro's metal. Two more passes and the corrosion would be gone. Too bad flesh couldn't be cured as easily.

She placed the bottle onto the table. Ice cubes clinked as they knocked against the sides of the glass in her hand. "You said you needed a drink," she murmured as she set the glass down.

Hell, yeah, he did. Maybe it would numb the effect of her damn imprinting pheromones that invaded his body. The scent of liquid oblivion tantalized him almost as much as Hell. She'd brought only one glass, not two. Unless she meant to drink straight from the bottle, she didn't intend to join him. Maybe she couldn't tolerate alcohol? Either way, it was good. He didn't need her hanging around. With an appreciative nod, he poured himself a drink.

She picked up one of the finished pieces of robotic parts he'd been working on.

"This workmanship is exquisite." Her indrawn breath of admiration was impossible to resist. He glanced over the rim at her as he took a sip.

She scrutinized the repaired servo mechanism, turning it over in the light. Her full lips parted with a smile as she exhaled. Her breasts moved, erect nipples defined in sharp relief by the flimsy material which clung to them. She had big nipples for such small breasts.

He liked big nipples.

He swallowed the cool liquid, enjoying the burn as it slid down his throat. "That's part of the central controller for a service-bot."

"Yes, I know. But you've added to it. Here, I think." Her slender finger traced the fine wiring. "And here." Her eyes narrowed as she turned it over. "And this circuit array has been added from something else."

"It used to be a walking, talking coffee maker. But we needed more help with maintaining the Dome, so now Henry makes a mean cup of java and takes out the garbage too."

"Henry?" Her gaze flicked to his. She had beautiful amber irises, like the color of warm whisky. A jolt of heat flashed in his groin. *Get a grip, Peyton!*

"Henry." He pointed to a pair of mechanical legs and a bulky torso lying on the bench beside him. "Here's the rest of him." *God, now why did I say that? She's going to want to see.*

True to his prediction, her sweet scent arrived seconds later, accompanied by the very physical proximity of her body heat as she bent across him to get a good look at Henry's parts.

She passed gentle fingers over a metal leg. "What happened to him?"

"His knee locked as he was going down the stairs. Basically, he fell apart. Metal corrosion. We need new parts. But we don't have them."

"And you're putting him back together. You're very good with your hands." She straightened and looked at him, then gestured around the room. "All of these mechanisms require a special talent to bring them to life again." The velvet smoothness of her smile made his throat dry.

He took another sip of whisky. "They're just pieces of junk."

This close, her short hem was eyeball height. Her smooth thighs were parted just enough he could slip his hand between them and explore the slit above. Was she wet? Would she taste as sweet as the rest of her looked?

She gestured downward. "I could help with that."

"What?" Could she see his bulging crotch through his pants? He'd untucked his shirt earlier to hide the evidence, but who knew what she was capable of, this runaway android sex doll who was programmed to satisfy his every need. He shifted in his chair in an attempt to ease the pressure in his groin, but that brought his face closer to temptation.

"I like to fix things too," she said.

Somewhere up above, Hell's mouth probably curved to match the smile in her voice, but he'd be damned if he could tear his gaze away from the place where her thighs disappeared beneath her shirt. He knew exactly what was hidden on the other side.

Trouble.

Trouble he didn't need. But despite himself, he couldn't stop thinking about it.

"I'm good with my hands. Very precise," she added.

Images exploded in his mind of just how good she was with her hands. And mouth. Those soft lips would feel damned hot wrapped around his cock, with her slender fingers gripping his balls just so, exerting just the right pressure to make him come like a fucking geyser.

Precise.

The alcohol wasn't having any effect on numbing the imprinting pheromones. He took another sip of his drink and then downed half the glass. "Hell," he rasped, focusing on the burn in his belly as the whisky landed like a fist.

"Poor Henry," she said at the same time. "How long has he been this way?"

Poor Henry? A sympathetic frown pulled at her lips as she caressed Henry's broken metal leg.

Of course, her concern was for the robot—empathy for a mechanical brother. She hadn't been talking about *him.* Now why the hell did he feel disappointed? He didn't want her. He didn't need her. She was trouble with a capital T.

Her thick, golden lashes fluttered as she turned a questioning look to him.

What had she asked? "Oh...he, uh, he fell just last week. But I don't need your help."

"Really?" She cocked a brow.

"I can manage—"

"Why don't you let me try?" She grabbed the laser utility tool and plopped herself onto his lap. He exhaled with a whoosh as her tight ass made contact with his pants-restricted arousal. His dick hadn't been this close to a meal in months and raged at the sudden prospect of dinner.

He set his glass down, put his hands on her narrow waist, and tried to lift her off. "Hell—"

"Quit squirming and let me work."

She pushed harder against his lap. His erection pushed back. He closed his eyes and tried not to moan. Or think about how good her body felt against his, her petite form, so slight, yet full of strength. She'd be wild in bed, giving as good as she got, stroke for stroke, probably keening, maybe even calling his name until—

"Done!" Sounding pleased, she tossed down the laser and leaned back against him.

Opening his eyes, he forced blood to flow to his brain and peered over her shoulder. She gestured at Henry's leg on the workbench, each wiggle of movement setting off new ricochets of pleasure through him.

Disbelief cut through his haze of arousal. The gyro he'd been cleaning was now set into its housing and reattached. A task which would have taken him all night had taken her a minute at most.

"Now Henry has a knee again." Pride filled her voice. A flush stained her cheek and those so-very-tempting lips—he smoothed back her tawny hair so he could see their profile better—were full, glistening, and luscious pink.

He was fighting a losing battle. His cock had known it as soon as he'd unwrapped her. Now his brain knew it too.

"Hell," he muttered.

"What?" She turned to face him. Her dilated pupils gave her a dreamy expression.

"You have fast hands." As if his had a mind of their own, his fingers crept up her sides and skimmed just beneath her small, perky breasts.

"I told you. Quick hands. Very...precise." Her pink tongue darted out and licked her lips, emphasizing their succulent sheen.

Fire burned where her firm ass cheeks straddled his cock. He couldn't take much more of this game, but he couldn't seem to pull away. He was frozen with searing need. He'd been alone too long.

"Why don't you let me help you, Peyton?" Her expression softened, full of need and something he couldn't place.

"Help with what? With Henry?"

Her gaze held his as she gave a slight shake of her head. "Not this time," she whispered. "With you."

There it was. A plain invitation. Why couldn't she take no for an answer? And why couldn't he stop wanting her?

He closed his eyes, fighting the lure of her imprinting pheromones, which heightened the response of his body. Alcohol. More alcohol would help. If he drank enough, he'd eventually pass out and forget all about Hell.

She pressed close, twined her slender arms around his torso, and tightened her hold. "I can make you feel better."

"I'm sure you can." He groaned. Her fine golden hair tickled his jaw. "But I can't do this." Yet, even as he said it, instead of reaching for more whisky, his traitorous hands roamed her body and learned her curves.

She sighed, a soft warm breath against his cheek. "You've made it very clear you don't want me as a slave. But really, you do need me."

"You're a mistake," he insisted. No, she was soft, sweet perfection, which was even worse. He opened his eyes.

She studied him with amber luminosity. "Perhaps." A flicker dimmed her expression, replaced quickly by a determined light. "Maybe I'm not meant to be here. Maybe I'm not meant to exist at all. But you've given me a place to stay. You've made me feel safe. And most of all, you've given me hope. Let me return the favor and help you right now."

God damn. She was sexy. And warm. And fit his lap so damn right. The underside of her breast was a perfect curve. He could explore that one area for hours. She was right. He could fuck her. He could fuck her, and fuck her, and fuck her, and fuck her, and then what? Fuck her again because he wouldn't be able to stop? Because he fucking *needed* her?

"No," he said.

"It's clear you need—"

"What I need is to be left alone!" He slid her off his knees in a burst of resolution. The sudden loss of her body heat shouldn't have bothered him, but it did. Already things had gone too far. "Sleep in my bed tonight if you want. I'll be on the floor. Alone." His heart pumped a crazy rhythm.

"This is ridiculous." She planted her hands on her hips and didn't budge from his side.

"Whatever." He drew in a steadying breath as he picked up the laser and pulled Henry's leg over to continue working. The robot needed to be fixed as soon as possible to help with maintaining the Dome. They had so few hands left. A man down, even a cobbled-together mechanized one, meant extra work for everyone. Or a task left undone.

"Peyton." Her voice had lost its usual smoothness. He didn't look up. "Did it occur to you that there are methods of achieving release other than intercourse? Well, you just passed up the best blow job of your life. Remember that while you're sleeping on the hard floor tonight."

He managed to keep his face averted as she left his side, but the laser quivered in his suddenly shaking hand.

Best blow job of my life?

"I'll be waiting, if you change your mind," she tossed over her shoulder. The door slid closed behind her with a hiss.

All Tied Up and Nowhere to Go

THE SILENT, CREEPING cold drove Peyton from his workshop and inside the heated apartment an hour later, not the prospect of a warm, willing female curled in his bed.

Ha! Who was he kidding? He hadn't stopped thinking about Hell since she'd stormed out of the room. While his hands had kept busy re-connecting micro filaments, her boastful taunt played inside his mind—*you just passed up the best blow job of your life.*

Shit.

Great blow jobs he'd had, but none in recent times. Not since Sarah's passing. Yet, despite his better judgment, he was interested now. Parts of him were so interested they wouldn't go down. Could a man die from a perpetual hard-on?

The whisky hadn't helped. Jerking off hadn't helped. No, all that rubbing had just made the situation worse. Now he was more than slightly drunk and hornier than ever.

Standing beside the bed, he stared at the Doll who stirred such trouble.

Hell had left the vid-screen on and the image of a moonlit sky washed over her pale, sleeping figure. At some point she'd discarded her shirt and lay entwined with the blankets. Her fair hair spilled across the pillow in inviting disarray. The dark brown sheet covered a scant portion of her torso, did nothing for her legs, and drew his eye to her exposed left breast. Designed to fit another

33

man's tastes, it wasn't as large as he liked, but young and high, it perched on her chest, mesmerizing him. Her nipple had tightened in the cool air, forming a pointy bud.

Temptation incarnate. Who was he to resist?

Weary from the long day, he rolled his stiff shoulders and sat on the bed.

She can help you with that, massage your muscles with those nimble fingers, hot desire whispered in his mind. All he had to do was say the word and she would soothe him in any manner he chose. She was the ultimate companion, the result of decades of genetic research and clever programming. The desire to please was built into her core.

Then why had she seemed upset when he'd rebuffed her advances earlier? Logic dictated that if he didn't want her, then she should be content with his instruction to stay away. The obvious answer had to be the truth; he really did want her...and she knew it.

The object of his scrutiny sighed deeply. Her pale lashes fluttered open. As her amber irises focused on him, her lips pulled into a sensuous smile. Stretching, she propped her head upon her hand and arched a brow. "Hi," she said, her voice soft and sleepy.

"Hi," he said and drained the last of the glass of whisky in his hand.

Her gaze followed him as he set the empty glass onto the nearby table. He cleared his throat. "Do you remember anything about how you got here yet?"

She shook her head, a small frown touching her lips. "No."

"It's probably too soon," he said and sighed. The room spun slightly as he leaned back against the railed headboard and crossed his arms. "Brain fog can last several hours sometimes."

"Yeah," she said. "But that's not why you're here, is it? To talk to me about my problems?"

He looked at her. She had a pretty way of being coy and he was tired of fighting. "No," he admitted. It was comfortable here with her on the bed like this, with the whisky numbing his brain, dulling the arguments he'd had against letting her have her way. Fuck it. She was made for this, and yeah...fuck it. Come hell or high water, fuck it.

"So, you've come to your senses at last," she said with a pleased purr in her voice.

He couldn't help laughing. She sounded so sure of herself, and with good reason. She was programmed for seduction. "No. I've *lost* my senses," he said. "And I haven't come yet," he muttered.

Not into her sensuous mouth anyway.

Her smile deepened as her eyes flicked to the pronounced tent at his groin. "No, I can see you haven't." Prickles of heat danced across his skin as she moistened her lips with her tongue. "Let's see what I can do about that."

Her expression turned serious as she raised her free hand and took her time moving it toward him. Perhaps she wanted to give him the chance to change his mind, but the anticipation drove him nuts. Decision made, he needed release. Now. He reached for his fly and began to undo it. Her slender fingers stopped him.

"Let me," she whispered.

His pulse jacked. Nodding, he forced his hands to his sides. He was used to being in control, but this could be interesting too. "What do you want me to do?" *Holy shit. What a stupid question.* "I mean, to you," he added quickly, trying to cover up his blunder. How much whisky had he drunk? Three? Four glasses? He sounded like a teenage kid about to get his first hummer. Not a thirty-something man who'd been very happily married. *Don't think about that now!*

Hell watched him with thoughtful deliberation. She sat up and patted the mattress close to her. "Come lie down here and relax." Whisking the tangled sheet away from her body, she curled it sinuously between her hands.

Clothed, she was temptation; fully naked, she was irresistible. Delicate bones created a framework for creamy skin accented by soft curves. Her breasts were tipped with rosebud nipples that matched her pink rosebud lips, and, if he was a betting man— which he was—her spread pussy lips would be rose-colored too. She had slender hips a man could hold when thrusting, breasts a man could dream of fondling. So different from Sarah's lushness, yet each aspect fit Hell's form with precision. And that smooth, hairless groove defining her sex...it might be the whisky talking, but he swore it called out to him saying, 'Touch me. Please!'

He reached for her.

She caught his hands. The sheet wound about his wrists and looped over the headboard railing faster than his inebriated eyes could blink.

"What the hell?" Finding his arms trapped over his head, he strained as she finished tying the ends of cloth together. But whatever programming she'd had concerning forcible seduction also included devising slip knots. No matter which way he twisted, the knot only tightened.

"Let me go!"

She scurried to the safety of the end of the bed where his legs couldn't pin or kick her, folded her hands demurely, and smiled. "I'll untie you when we're done."

Anger burned hot. She'd tricked him, sucked him in with her nudity, and now he paid the price. Trussed, he had to let her do anything with him.

But wait...wasn't that exciting?

He swallowed a deep breath. "Untie me. *Now!*"

Her brows arched. "I'm doing this for your own good."

"I should have stuck you back in that box while I had the chance." He closed his eyes to block out her sexy, pronounced nipples, but the image of her naked body was burned into his mind. *I am going to kill Jared for getting me into this!*

The bed squeaked as she sat on a corner of it. "It's for your safety. Once you touch me, you won't be able to stop, and penetration cannot occur before imprinting is complete."

He cracked open an eyelid. "What's that supposed to mean?"

She gestured toward her groin. "The new generation of Dolls are equipped with tamper-proofing devices, to ensure virginity upon delivery to customers."

"Shit." He *really* should have put her back in the damned box. "What happens if someone sticks it in without authorization?"

"Zap."

"Zap?"

"Um hum. Third degree burns kind of zap. From what I understand, it's a really, ah...shocking experience." She flipped her long honey-colored hair over her shoulder. Her breasts jiggled with the movement. Her hardened nipples nodded at him as if agreeing with her decision. "Tied up, you won't be tempted to 'stick it in', as you say, before it's time."

"How will I know when it's okay?" Imprinting needed to be completed before he could bury his cock inside her? What did that even mean?

"You'll know," she said with a smile.

"What about you?" His pulse beat erratically as he pulled against the knots keeping him at her mercy. Bondage was a game he'd never played. At least, *he'd* never been the one lying on the bed, vulnerable as all hell. The idea of trusting an android to keep his dick safe made his balls want to crawl up inside his body and hide. On the other hand, wasn't said dick straining in his pants, excited by the prospect of danger?

Her gaze raked him from head to toe. "You have a magnificent body. I want to know how you taste. Can I touch you?"

"Hell, yeah." Hunger for sexual release warred with his need to break free of his bonds. Or maybe it heightened it. With all this bullshit about imprinting going on, it felt more than a bit unsettling to relinquish control like this. Imprinting would mean she was his problem to deal with permanently. On the other hand, whether or not he was tied to the bed, the ball—or rather his balls—were in her court anyway. He couldn't live the rest of his life with his cock as hard as granite, and right now she seemed to be the only thing capable of curing his condition.

"Thank you," she said as if his permission to proceed actually meant something.

Crawling upward between his outstretched legs, she kneeled, leaned forward, and started with his shirt. The whisper of her fingers as they slipped each fastener did interesting things deep in his belly, and he knew she'd been correct in restraining him. She'd showered while he'd been in the workroom and her sweet scent mingled with his body cleansers. Wafts of the tantalizing concoction inflamed his senses as well as his cock. Her breasts jiggled with each subtle movement, enticing him to touch them. He strained against his bonds as instinct flared deep inside and insisted he fondle her, find her sweet spots, and fuck her senseless. Going months without a good hard fuck had its price, and tonight he was paying it like the king of all pipers.

He closed his eyes to decrease the torment as she opened the shirt. Slipping her hands under the fabric, she trailed her fingers across his chest and stroked his shoulders. "I like the feel of your muscles, the way you are so strong. You must enjoy exercise."

"We don't get much idle time here." His stomach tightened as she caressed the lines of his ribs and moved to touch his pecs. She seemed fascinated with the hairs on his chest and around his nipples, and swirled her fingertips around and around, slowly, not touching the sensitive skin. Hot breath wafted across his left pec, his only warning before she touched the taut nipple with her tongue. And licked it.

He arched, grunting at the sudden jolt of pleasure.

Smiling, she blew cool air across the wet skin.

He hissed through clenched teeth. Instinct screamed to grab her and do the same to her tightened nipples.

As if sensing his desire, she moved upward over his body and dangled her breasts close to his face. He tilted his head and reached with his tongue. Her response was an unintelligible gurgle as he traced her distended nipple, licking the tip. Straddling his chest, she held his head to her breast as her wet skin puckered into a hard, needy point.

He captured her nipple with his lips. Her sweet taste filled his mouth, urging him to suckle her hard. He worked his tongue against her nipple again and again, enjoying its pert thickness, velvety texture, and the jolt of heat which shot straight to his groin.

"*Oooh*," she moaned. Her fingers tightened in his hair. He gently nipped her, making her gasp sharply.

"Did that hurt?" he asked, concerned.

Leaning back, she settled her naked pussy against his belly and looked at him. Wonderment played across her features. "No. You make me feel tingly. Here..." She cupped her breasts and kneaded them gingerly as if discovering their pleasure for the first time. "And here." Moving her hands down across her smooth stomach, she slid a finger between her folds.

Her brows shot up. "I am so wet!" She showed him her glistening finger.

Oh, how he envied that finger.

"That you are," he agreed. Even without the evidence presented mere inches from his face, her warm wetness heated his belly, telling him just how turned-on she was. His hands clenched tight. The sheet rubbed against his wrists as he pulled against his bonds. Damn the tensile strength of dura-weave cotton! "If you kneel above my mouth, I can lick your pussy with my tongue like I did with your nipple," he said. *Please, dear God.*

Her jaw dropped open as if the idea that he might pleasure her had never occurred to her before. What exactly had The Factory programmed her to know about sex? Was this her first time experiencing pleasure?

Her face flushed. "Would you slide your tongue into my vagina?"

"Definitely." *Holy Christ!* The tongue in question thickened in his mouth at the idea.

"We'd better not. I wouldn't want it to get zapped."

"Good point," he said.

She squirmed against his belly, hot, wet, and needy. Maybe this was her first time doing this kind of thing. He wanted to help her find release, to taste her pleasure. "Tell you what," he said, trying to sound calm and convincing despite his rapidly beating pulse. "Slide your finger in your folds until it's really slick, then bring it to my mouth and let me lick it clean." Would she do it? Hot blood thudded in his ears.

Her burning gaze locked with his. Her hand moved on her sex

and palmed the plump flesh of her mound. He felt her finger slide against his belly and between her lips. Her hand jerked when it found her nub. She closed her eyes. "Oh...this feels wonderful." Her thighs tensed as she pressed down against him and slid her finger around again.

"Keep going," he encouraged. *Oooh yeah! That's right baby, play for me.* Jesus, he was going to come just watching her touch herself. His dick throbbed, trapped in his pants. He struggled to remain calm as her mouth opened, and her pink tongue darted out to wet her lips. *I am so going to be in there!*

She began to pant and buck against his belly as her finger rubbed her clit again and again. Her wetness increased. He flexed his abs to match her rhythm. "That's right, sweetheart. Show me how wet you can get."

Did she know she approached orgasm? The same innocent wonderment suffused her expression, deepened now with a heady flush. Her eyelids fluttered; her hair flipped as she tossed her head back. Her free hand moved across her ribs and kneaded her breast. When her fingers found a puckered nipple, she pinched it. Hard.

"Peyton!" she cried out.

Her thighs tightened. She shuddered against him. Her wetness soaked his belly. Gasping, she slid her fingers free from her pussy and opened her eyes. Hazed with passion, she focused on him and smiled. "That was amazing." Her voice was weak, her breathing erratic. "Did you like watching?"

"Hell, yeah." Her unabashed performance turned him on to the point of insanity.

"Good. Do you still want a taste?" she asked. She slowly held her slick finger up to his mouth.

She was impossible to resist. Her sweet and earthy scent invaded his nostrils. He strained against his bonds, eager to savor her. As she brought her finger to his lips, he dipped his tongue out, then took her finger into his mouth. His eyelids slid shut as he moaned. God damn, she tasted intoxicating. Honeyed and warm. A taste he would never forget. It tingled on his tongue and seeped deep into his consciousness. Desire sliced through him. One taste wasn't enough. He needed more.

He sucked her finger, hard. She slipped it between his lips, in and out, in and out. His hips instinctively thrust to the rhythm as he moaned low and long. He didn't care anymore. Didn't care how or why, as long as she let him do with his cock what she was doing with her finger.

"I want to taste you now," she murmured.

He was beyond ready, but she took her time, slinking down his body to perch between his legs. His jaw clenched as he strained to remain in control while she unbuttoned his fly.

Holy Christ. How much more could he take? His cock would explode if she didn't free it soon. He raised his hips to help her move his restricting pants off his ass, not bothering to stifle a grunt as her fingers brushed his over-sensitized dick in passing.

"I agree," she murmured. "Ahhhhhh," she mimicked in a throaty purr. The waistband of his boxers lifted as she snuck a peek beneath the fabric. She gasped. "You're magnificent, Peyton," she said, admiration and heat in her eyes. Then she let the elastic fall into place with a snap and sat back.

His pulse jacked. *What?* She wasn't going to make him wait more, was she?

A devious grin tipped her lips. She was.

"Hell!" His body shuddered as need raged. He lifted his legs and tried to capture her with them.

She slipped out of range and laughed, her gaze misted with heat, challenging him to do something about it.

The minx! His searing blood hissed like steam as he yanked against the restraints to no avail. "Still into teasing, sweetheart?" he rasped.

"Sweetheart?" Her lips twitched into a breathy smile.

He ground his teeth together. How like a woman to focus on the most irrelevant part of a sentence. He hadn't needed a woman in his bed for a long time. Hadn't thought about it, hadn't *wanted* to think about it. But now, with her scent in his nostrils and her taste in his mouth, need surged to the point of painfulness.

"Just remember." He growled. *"You're* the one who started this." She'd tied him up and toyed with him. Oh, yes, there'd be payback coming her way. "But you'll be begging me to finish it and fuck that pretty little pussy of yours until you scream."

Her eyes went wide, filled with shock and searing interest.

Christ! What the hell am I doing?

Maybe he'd had a bit too much whisky. This game they were playing was just a onetime thing. To get him over whatever pheromone-induced spell she'd put him under. After tonight, there'd be no more torment like this...exquisite...pleasure.

She smiled and held his gaze as she crept closer again. Her hand slipped under his boxers, pulled them down and freed his super-heated cock. Cool air caressed his skin as his dick sprang free and pointed at her like a tent pole, or an accusing finger.

Nope, definitely a pole, no wee finger down there.

"So beautiful," she whispered and skimmed her hand along his length, tracing the blue veins that pulsed with prolonged need for release.

"Fuck." He slammed his head against the pillow beneath it. His tense muscles shuddered, lost in the movement and feel of her skin against his. She said something about 'smooth and hard', but his ears filled with a warm buzz as she cupped his balls.

So precise. Exerting just the right amount of pressure.

He'd never experienced this before, such uncontrolled desire to have her lips clamp over him and suck him dry.

"If you insist." She giggled.

Shit. Was he thinking out loud? Her taste filled his mouth, her gentle moans filled his ears; her touch on his dick was exacting as she explored him from tip to root and then back up again.

Exquisite. Precision.

Her tongue lapped at his cock and tasted the drop of glistening wetness seeping from the tip. "Mmm," she moaned. She didn't shy away, but licked again, lingering over the tiny hole as if hoping to find more treats.

"Sweet Jesus." He arched off the bed. His arms strained against their bonds. Shockwaves wracked him. Pleasure. Throbbing pleasure heightened by pain.

He ached to break free and dive inside her, but he could not. *He could not!* He was at her mercy and in her complete control.

It felt wrong and twisted and so right at the same time. So very fucking right. His pulse thickened, thudding loudly as she played with him. Her touch was not what he was used to. Nothing about her was what he was used to. She was small and firm, not luscious and full. Yet so damned soft it seemed insane. She was unlike Sarah in every way. Sarah had been...Sarah had been. His wife.

Sarah!

His chest constricted as agony and guilt cut into his arousal like a knife. He needed to stop. His traitorous cock demanded he couldn't. Hell took him into her mouth, sliding her lips up and down, up and down. Moist, hot, and hungry. The sensation was too intense.

"Ahhh," he groaned. "Ahh—"

His fingers bit into the soft flesh of his palms. The sheet abraded his wrists. She moaned and rubbed his tip against the back of her throat as she took him all the way in. He opened his eyes and found her gaze fixed on him, her amber irises misted with passion.

"*Hell!*" he shouted and thrust all his raging need into her willing mouth. Need he'd denied existed, need he'd kept hidden within a vault of insensitivity so deep he'd hoped never to think or feel again.

Cracked open, it spilled out with memories of warmth, of smiling eyes and chestnut hair, of loving arms holding him tight, of dreams dying in a burning casket.

The hungry lips around his cock clamped tighter.

He arched his back. Years of pent-up grief exploded in a swirl of colors and a sharp cry as an intense orgasm shook his body. For a moment, breathing stopped. Then he sank down onto the soft mattress, euphoria crashing through him.

"Ah, shit. Ahh..." he gasped out through ragged breaths. Exhaustion overtook him, making his eyelids heavy and his mind spin on the edge of darkness. Sleep always came quickly after an intense orgasm, and this one had been off the scale. When was the last time he'd felt such numbing bliss?

"So good," he murmured as her soft lips and tongue licked him clean. "Fucking beautiful." She was always so beautiful. Her mouth hot and ready to please him and get him hard again. He didn't deserve her. He'd never deserved her. But she was his, his beautiful wife. His heart clenched tight. "I love you, Sarah," he said and tried to reach down to cup her head and stroke her dark silky hair.

"Imprinting complete," she replied.

"What?" His eyes snapped open.

Amber eyes stared back at him. Not Sarah. He jerked against the sheet binding his hands. Pain shot from his abraded wrists and doused the darkness from his mind. Hell sat on his bed, sweaty and flushed and gazing at him with concern. Of course. Sarah was long dead. And Hell was...

"Did you just say, imprinting complete?"

"Yes." She lazily licked his jizz from her swollen lips with a smile.

Anger rushed in, bringing icy clarity with it. "That's why you wanted to suck me off and have me taste you. So you could finish imprinting yourself on me." The mother of all headaches began to pound behind his eyes. What a tool he'd been. A fucking horny tool.

"No," she said, her voice steady. "Imprinting complete means your deepest desires have been stamped on *me*. From this point forward, I belong to you alone. I wanted to give you a blow job because you needed it. You like it kinky, Peyton."

Best blow job of his life.

Fucking Hell. She'd reduced him to a quivering mess. He'd practically begged her to fuck him. Her virginal innocence had been an act, a product of clever programming designed to arouse and claim him.

"*Untie me.*" He'd had enough of being in her control.

She leaned over and quickly did as asked.

Whipping the sheet away, he sprang from the bed as best he could with his pants around his ankles. Sensation prickled back into his wrists. He winced.

Sweat chilled his body. Her intoxicating wetness bathed his belly. He needed a shower. He *didn't* need Hell with her manipulative tricks.

"Do me a favor," he said as he kicked off his pants from around his feet. "Next time you think I need something, *just leave me the hell alone.*" Striding to the wall, he opened a drawer and pulled out a clean pair of underwear.

She sighed. "Festering wounds eventually kill people if they aren't opened and cleaned."

He shut the cupboard with a bang and turned. "What the hell is that supposed to mean?"

Kneeling on the bed, she faced him, hands clasped together in a calm pose. If being disheveled and nude bothered her it didn't show. Why would it? She looked fucking amazing, and she knew it. "It means you're hurting. You need to face your pain." Her eyes held his in a steady, knowing gaze.

"What can you possibly know about pain?" He walked to the bathroom but stopped and pointed at her before going inside. "You aren't human. Theoretically, you're not even alive."

She stared at him in silence. Was that pity in her eyes?

He stepped into the bathroom and punched the door release button. The entry shut with a soft, delicate hiss.

Fuck!

He should have built his place with the old-fashioned kind of doors that slammed.

DO ANDROIDS DREAM OF ELECTRIC SHEEP?

THE KEENING WAIL reverberated with mind-piercing horror, making Hell twist and strain as she tried to get away. But it followed her as she turned, blind in the darkness surrounding her. Heart racing, she whimpered, struggling to block out the sound as the shrieking increased.

Why wouldn't it stop?

It hurt her mind, made it pound, made it vibrate close to shattering. She strained, trying to cover her ears with her hands, but heaviness dragged her limbs. Pinned. She was pinned and drowning in searing screams of pain.

Panic exploded. She bucked against the suffocating prison weighing her down. One arm broke free. Adrenaline and fear tightened into a fist that connected with something soft—

"Fuck!" A startled voice yelled. "Damnit, Hell," Peyton said and the weight pinning her disappeared. "For God's sake, stop screaming!"

Shock cut through the noise and terror, freezing her limbs. Chest heaving, she sucked in air and closed her mouth. The horrifying wail ceased. Confusion swirled with the sudden silence throbbing through her head.

That was me? That was me screaming?

Shaking, she blinked sleep from her eyes. Dim light formed familiar shapes in the darkness. A bed. Peyton's bed. With its comforting scent and worn sheets tangled like snakes about her legs. Peyton sat at the bottom, his body coiled as if to spring. One eye was covered by his hand; the other flashed with anger.

"What the hell is wrong with you?" he snapped. He pulled his hand away from his eye and blinked, shaking his head as if to clear it.

She swallowed and winced for the effort. Her throat burned. The rest of her groaned as she struggled to sit up. Pain throbbed in her head, centered on her memory cortex. The intensity no longer shattered, but a discordant hum hissed. Something was, indeed, wrong.

Internal diagnostic initiated.

Rubbing her temples, she focused on Peyton. "What...happened...?" she croaked. Sandpaper. It felt like she'd swallowed sandpaper. How loud had she been screaming? And why?

Peyton nursed the soft flesh around his eye and studied her in silence. "I was hoping you might tell me that," he said after a long pause. He picked up his tablet from the nearby table and spoke into it. "Lighting to forty-five percent." The confusion and concern on his face became easier to see as the room steadily brightened.

She shook her head. The throbbing dimmed and with it the ache in her limbs. Her breathing steadied as she focused on remembering. After their argument, he'd been...upset. "You wanted to sleep on the couch." Curse the Maker, it hurt to talk. She coughed, but it did little to ease the sting. "I fell asleep here." She indicated the bed, frowning. "And then..." And then what? And then nothing...blank. She pressed her temples harder, grasping at emptiness. "And then..."

"And then you scared the living-shit out of me screaming. And when I tried to wake you up, you punched me." He pointed to his eye, jaw set firm.

I hit him? Oh, hell! "Something pinned me—"

"You were caught in the sheets, thrashing. I tried to help you." Peyton's wary gaze accused even as his deep voice softened with worry.

Screaming? Thrashing out and hitting? *What is wrong with me?* "I'm sorry." She struggled out of the net of blankets and reached for him to look at his damaged eye.

He backed away. "It's fine," he muttered. "Your voice sounds awful. I'll get you some water. And then I think we'd better have a talk."

Her arm dropped back to her side as he turned and walked to a door at the far end of the room, which lead to the small apartment kitchen.

What have I done?

Remorse settled in her heart along with the certainty there was something very wrong with her. *I can't believe I hit him.* It had been an accident. But an accident inspired by a serious sleep-induced delusion on her part that...what? That she'd been attacked? *No, restrained and in pain...*

It didn't make any sense. Stasis fog should have worn off by now, so why couldn't she remember?

Am I defective?

Dread sickened her stomach that it might just be true.

Internal diagnostic complete. No anomalies detected.

What? Dread turned to deep-seated horror. Whatever ailed her was beyond the capabilities of her diagnostics to catch, unless her diagnostic program was damaged too. A malfunction in her central processing cortex? Such instances had occurred in the past with earlier versions of androids, resulting in cascading memory loss and eventual, unrecoverable system crash.

Panic flared anew. She rummaged through the sheets, searching for her shirt. "What time is it?" she called out.

"Just after six a.m." Peyton stood at the end of the bed, watching her with a careful expression, glass of water in hand.

"What time is the next transport to the Arkopolis?" Her shirt lay in a tangled mess on the floor. She picked it up.

"It's not for another two days."

"Two days?" she said and put her hand over her mouth as her panic deepened. "Just put me in stasis, then, and schedule me on the transport." Her hands shook as she pulled the fabric over her head and stood, ready to go.

Peyton frowned. "What? Stasis? I thought you didn't like stasis."

"I don't." Goose bumps rippled along her bare arms and legs. "But something is wrong. Something is—"

"Something is scaring the hell out of you." He walked over to the side of the bed and handed her the glass. "Take a sip. It'll soothe your throat." His gaze was calm, steady, reassuring.

The liquid trembled in her grasp, but she did as instructed. The icy water chilled her burning throat. "Thank you." She managed a smile.

He took the glass and set it on the table with a nod. "Now, tell me what's going on."

He settled her on the edge of the bed and sat beside her. His arm curled around her shoulders, his spicy-scented body heat bridging any gap that might have been between them. He didn't even like her, yet worry warmed his deep brown eyes, cementing her earlier conclusion that Peyton was a good man with a good heart. And now that his desires were imprinted into her cognizance, saying goodbye to him might just break hers.

"I think my cortex is malfunctioning." Her throat constricted, making her voice hoarse, but the cause was no longer physical damage. Despair hissed close to the surface, struggling to break free. "I need to go back to The Factory before it's too late to fix me."

He stared at her as if trying to see through flesh and into the android beneath. "Are you certain you're malfunctioning?"

Holding his penetrating gaze, she nodded. "My diagnostic checks out, but there has to be something wrong. I screamed in my sleep." *And hit you. Can't forget that.*

His lips pulled into a thin line. "Maybe you had a nightmare."

"A nightmare?" She sat straighter. The bed squeaked as she pulled down the short hem of her shirt. "How could it be a nightmare? My memories log back to twelve hours, eighteen minutes and thirty-three point five seconds ago when you woke me from stasis. And all of those have been," she focused on her bare knees, unwilling to let him see the extent of her feelings, "...pleasant." What an understatement. He'd given her amazing fulfillment in so short a time. "I can't remember anything before that."

"So you don't remember what you were dreaming about at all?"

"No." She risked a glance at him. Ambient light played across his handsome profile. But his expression was unreadable. "My sleep-time memory is blank."

He studied her for a moment, his gaze neutral. Then his lips tipped into a smile and he nodded as if coming to a conclusion. "Then we'd better take a look inside your head and see what's going on. I have some diagnostic equipment of my own. It's rudimentary, but it should allow us to analyze your memory engrams."

Her stomach clenched. "You want to download my memories?" He'd see what she'd been thinking. Know what she'd been feeling. The idea was invasive, but did she have a choice?

His brows lifted as if he knew what she was thinking. "Not all of them. Just the ones from when you were sleeping." He stood and offered a hand to her.

She stared at it, then into his eyes. "Why do you want to do this? Isn't it easier to put me in stasis and drop me off on the next transport?"

His gaze never wavered, but something hot flickered in the dark of his pupils. "Probably," he admitted after a moment. "But if it's just a nightmare, you won't have to worry." He reached forward and grabbed her hand. Warmth flowed from the contact and wrapped around her heart.

"And if it's not?"

His expression was unreadable as he walked toward the door of his workroom, his hand locked on hers. "Then we'll fix it."

**

Peyton couldn't help noticing the way Hell's nipples reacted as soon as she stepped through the doorway into the cold workroom. She was so real, so brutally fucking real in every way. Her movements, her actions, reactions. The trust she placed in him.

Fuck!

The sweet taste of her still lingered on his tongue, despite several earlier teeth brushings and his resolve to forget how much he'd enjoyed it when she'd tied him up and sucked him off. How easy would it be to lift the hem of her shirt and suckle those rosebud tips again?

Easier than putting her back into stasis, knowing how much it frightened her.

And far, far easier than what he'd have to do if the suspicions building in him about what was happening to her proved to be correct. He gritted his teeth against the anger and despair throbbing inside him and concentrated on keeping his mind clear and his expression neutral. He couldn't allow emotion to interfere. He needed to quickly figure out what was happening and then act accordingly. Hell contained a mystery, and, if his hunch was right, it was deadly.

He lifted the dust shroud off the medical scanning bed he kept crammed against the far wall. "Lie here and make yourself comfortable."

Her eyes widened as she studied the equipment. "I thought you said this was rudimentary?"

"It is by today's standards. This technology is over three years old." He flicked on a light beside the bed and fired up the scanner. A warm electric hum filled the air.

"This does more than examine robotic memory engrams." Hell brushed her fingers over the bank of instruments attached to the scanning controls. "Toxicology, radiology, deep tissue luminology…" Her golden gaze settled on him. "You use this for your work as a physician."

"When I have to." He fixed his attention on adjusting the controls. Hell's perceptiveness was downright annoying. "The sooner we get started, the sooner we'll know what's going on." He patted the padded bed.

She hesitated. "When did you stop practicing medicine full time?" Uncertainty filled her expression along with a good dose of nervousness.

He sighed. "When I stopped being able to save my patients."

His pulse jacked at the memory of impotent horror when, one by one, the people who had come to him for help with their identical symptoms had died. Symptoms of memory loss he'd later come to know as the K.I.S. of Death virus. Symptoms eerily similar to what Hell experienced now—nightmare dream activity with no associated memories.

The implication was insidious and devastating. She'd come from the Arkopolis, unexpected and unannounced. A runaway, she'd said. Or had she been sent on purpose and that story was just a cover? He'd long suspected The Factory's genetic experiments had been behind the original outbreak. Was Hell a walking time bomb? A viral Trojan Horse meant to finish off the troublesome survivors of Deliverance? The scan he'd done earlier would have picked up anything obvious. But if it was deeper than that and time-released into her own system… He stared at her, trying to see beneath the scared façade she presented.

Her eyes revealed nothing except the pity he abhorred.

He steeled his resolve and gestured at the scanner. "I can't help you if you won't let me."

She returned his nod and sat on the scanning bed. Her delicate fingers pulled down the hem of her shirt as if to gain some modesty while she lifted her legs up and swung them into a lying position.

For the first time in almost twelve hours, he wasn't tempted to slide his hand between her thighs. Here, in his medical bay, clinical detachment reigned. *Thank God!* He needed to remain objective to follow through with this task. One life versus twenty-odd souls. *Or two lives if she's already infected you with a mutated strain,* his conscience advised. They'd definitely exchanged bodily fluids since she'd arrived. His own vaccination would provide some immunity but...maybe not enough. His mind reeled with the devastating choice presented before him, but the virus could not be allowed to infect the Dome's population. Not this time.

Hell licked her lips. Her luminous gaze fixed on his as she looked up at him from the scanning bed. "You don't need to strap me down, do you?"

"No." He shook his head and brushed aside the fear he heard in her voice. "Just close your eyes and try to relax."

He forced his best reassuring smile as he centered the scanning array above her temples. Lifting the tiny flap of skin behind his left ear out of the way, he inserted a cable and jacked his own physician-requisite wet drive into the scanner controls. It was a move he'd made countless times, during countless operations, but this time his hand shook.

This time he might have to kill his patient.

And then kill himself.

I THINK THEREFORE I AM?

THE HUMAN BODY was a marvel of mechanics, each system, each cell, unique in purpose, yet working in tandem, and organized for the single basic purpose common to all beings—the genesis of life.

Under the digital eye of the scanning bed, Hell's body appeared no different to Peyton.

Resplendent in rainbow hues, a semi-transparent holographic image shimmered in the air above her: blue for muscle, yellow for bone, and pulsing purple tendrils that flowed in intricate harmony to the strong beat of her heart.

No wires here, no cybernetic implants or the synthetic musculature Peyton had suspected a Bio-roid would possess, just flesh and blood. Hell was human and yet...not. She did not have an umbilicus scar; she hadn't been born. Yet, if she was an android, as she must be, where was the machine?

Puzzled, he shifted the image with a thought and followed a group of rounded red blood cells as they surged a steady, if somewhat accelerated, path through her veins. Heavy with waste, the purple shade of the cells deepened to almost black until the circuit passed through the tissue of her lungs. There, the carbon dioxide staining her blood was exhaled and fresh oxygen infused, resulting in a bright purple as the cycle renewed again.

Beautiful inside and out, she glowed with life and symmetry—

and absolutely no viral complications whatsoever. With some trepidation, he checked the scans again. The Karezza Idiopathic Syndrome left a very specific signature, an aberration which he'd mistakenly interpreted as a minor infection on his first encounters. A diseased cell looked normal except for a distinguishing protein strand which poked like thin hairs from the smooth surface. But nothing in her blood stream resembled anything close.

The virus wasn't there. Nor any derivatives. Not in her blood or mucous.

He shut his eyes as relief rushed through him. She wasn't infected.

Thank God.

You can say that again.

He jumped. Relief crashed head on with confusion. He hadn't spoken out loud, and neither had Hell, but her voice echoed in his head as if she'd whispered in his ear.

Amber eyes smiled up at him, luminous through the holographic haze of her body suspended between them. It must be the scanner. He was jacked in through the bio-chip implanted in his brain. But she...how was she communicating with the machine?

"How are you hearing my thoughts?" His voice suddenly seemed loud when spoken.

I can hear the machine talking. If I think hard enough, I can talk back.

She must have a wireless emitter somewhere. He froze as the implication sank in. "Which do you hear? The scanner or my biochip?"

I'm not sure. The scanner, but it's your thoughts directing its actions.

Unnerved, his hand twitched, wanting to pull the jack out and sever the connection. This had never occurred before, his previous patients being completely human or non-sentient machines. Sharing his consciousness with another felt claustrophobic at best, a violation of his brain-space most definitely.

It's okay. I can't see what you're thinking unless you focus your thoughts. Her voice was soft, but not reassuring.

Dear God. Did she know he'd thought about killing her? Best not think of that. He cleared his throat. "I'd rather we speak out loud."

So would I, but there's a semi-stasis field emitted by the scanner. I can't move.

He caught the edge of her panic that accompanied that thought. It clutched at his belly then disappeared but left behind the shadow of her fear. Was it stasis that terrified her or being restrained?

"I'm sorry. I should have warned you. It's part of the diagnostic routine."

I know. So if it's not a virus, what's wrong with me, Peyton?

He shifted his stance and studied the image before him again; Hell's body flowed with life, vivid, exquisite in detail from her smooth skin to her glossy nails. Beneath existed flesh, blood, bone, and a mystery. "I'm not sure." He cleared his throat. "I'm not even sure what you are."

What do you mean?

She remained frozen, but the heart beating before his eyes increased its pace.

"You aren't what I expected, I mean," he soothed. "I thought you'd be more machine, but..." He let the sentence trail as he focused the scanner. Intent on finding a viral signature, he hadn't paid attention to the data from his other tests. "Well, I'll be damned."

You'll be dead if you don't tell me what's going on!

Her anxiety screamed so acute in his mind he would have jumped bolt upright if he wasn't already standing. Her pulse rate and respiration display flashed bright colors of warning. But it faded to the edges of his vision as he studied the double helix spinning before his eyes.

"Amazing," he murmured. "Your DNA is based on the human genome structure, but the construct is different. It's artificial. Manufactured." Sweat trickled down his back despite the chill in his workroom. "I didn't see it before because I was looking for augmentation; cybernetic implants like my own chip that take flesh and enhance it, or as in the case of a normal android, take a robot and make it seem human." He shook his head. "But you— you are a complete synthesis of bio-robotics."

Each cell in her body was a tiny organic machine, growing and replicating like living flesh; bio-nanotechnology at its finest. Which made her...what? Not just any Bio-roid for sure. Had the geneticists at the Arkopolis succeeded at last? Was the creature lying before him the future of humankind? A living being, completely adaptable to any environment, right down to the cellular level.

He did a quick scan and sucked in his breath.

What's wrong, Peyton?

"Nothing," he lied. "You have a complete set of reproductive organs."

I do?

"Yes, except—" He stopped in order to gather his emotions.

Except what?

"Except you have no ova. They appear to have been removed."

Wide amber eyes stared up at him. Innocent. Implacable. His chest tightened but he couldn't look away. Did she understand the implications inherent in his news? All the hopes, all the dreams for achieving a bright future where humans could thrive were lying on the scanning bed before him. Her ova were missing, but the important thing was that they had existed in the first place.

What happened to them?

"I don't know. Maybe they were taken for further experimentation." But either way she was the future. A new species of human. "You're an android capable of human reproduction," he explained. "The very first I've ever heard of." Then he laughed as a thought struck him. "I should have called you Eve."

Her children would be better, stronger, more resistant to disease. It was the dream come true. The hope Sarah had been working so hard towards achieving. His throat clenched up as he looked down at her through the mist glowing between them.

She stared at him as if dumbfounded. *I hadn't considered offspring. I—I never had a mother. At least, I don't remember having one...*

Her pulse and respiration had subsided, but an anxious rhythm started again now. His own matched pace as images of childhood swam to the surface of his thoughts, along with the memory of his mother's tender, long-dead smile. He banished the memory back to the darkness before Hell could see it.

"Do you remember being in the lab where you were grown?"

Grown?

"Yes, grown. I was wrong earlier when I said you weren't theoretically alive. You weren't made like a machine and clothed in flesh to look human. You've been grown—no doubt using accelerated means—but still..." He gave up and pointed at the holographic image of her left wrist. "Look here. Your augmentation starts at the cellular level. Denser bone mass for increased strength, something a human would have to have implanted through bone lacing, but it's as natural to you as breathing because your cells were programmed to be like that from the start. And your muscles—"

A flicker caught his attention. There, on her flexor digitorum, a pale red thread in the blue of her holographic flesh. A scar? A hairline tear, and accompanying it in the ulna beneath, a thickening in the density of her bone consistent with a healed fracture.

At some point she'd had a fractured wrist. He checked the other one and frowned. In the exact location on her right wrist, an identical break existed along with the scar where something had scored the muscle and left its mark. It had healed so well that the damage was barely visible. If he hadn't been looking at the right spot on her wrist by chance, he would have missed it. Her immune system included an accelerated healing process, but still, this type of clean regeneration required extensive treatments in a lab.

Identical fracture scars existed at her ankles. His jaw tightened. *Four broken limbs?* Blunt force trauma perhaps, but with the regularity of placement? It seemed more likely she'd been forcibly restrained—and judging by the healed tearing of the tendons at her wrists and ankles, she'd struggled against it.

And not once, but several times.

A deep cellular scan of her scar tissue indicated multiple overlapping stress lines; the shadow of consecutive breaks rippling deep into bone. Each painstakingly healed to the point of almost non-detection. Someone had done a very good job of covering up the fact she'd been hurt. What the hell had happened to her?

Lying on the scanning bed, Hell's small, beautiful body looked about as threatening as a kitten. It was hard to imagine anyone could deliberately harm her.

Maybe I'm just clumsy and fell... Or something?

There was a note of strained hope in her voice. But he didn't believe it any more than she. He'd known her less than a day but had never seen her move with anything less than grace. No, she'd been restrained against her will and suffered for it.

His fingers tightened on the scanner array as he adjusted its position. Her pulse and respiration were accelerated. A faint sheen of sweat covered her body. He did his best to keep the worry brewing inside from his thoughts, not wanting to alarm her further. "Did you know you've been hurt?"

No.

A simple answer with complex implications. "The scars are faint. You wouldn't notice them if they don't hurt."

She should remember, though. She should have memories. She'd been grown in a lab, interacted with. She should remember from the point her consciousness came online while still in whatever Petrie chamber she'd gestated in. But she couldn't remember anything prior to waking from stasis less than twenty-four hours before.

A sense of unease clenched his stomach as he focused his attention on scanning her brain.

And stopped.

Something blocked him from going further than a surface scan. The smooth, rippling contours of her cerebrum slowly rotated in resplendent green hues before him. Hidden within were the ganglions and neurons connecting the various lobes of her nanite-powered brain.

"Is your cortex pass-code protected?"

Yes.

"Can you unlock it?"

Yes.

He felt the shift as her consciousness turned inward. The Factory would have embedded an encrypted code for maintenance access, but Hell should have admittance to her cortex with a passkey of her own. He hoped to God the sequence wasn't image driven. If her memory was damaged, she might not be able to remember the correct images.

Her pulse, which had been steadily increasing for the past several minutes, shoved the blood through her veins with an unhealthy force now, and he knew before she spoke that something was wrong.

It's not working. Frustration gave her tone an odd echo in his mind. *My access to cerebral functions has been...removed. The code has been changed.*

"Changed? By who?"

By you.

What? "That doesn't make any sense."

A sound like a sigh swept through his mind. *It seems the sequence was reset when imprinting completed, to allow my owner—you—personally encrypted access. Part of the code comes from both of us. It's a security feature, I guess, to make certain I can't be reprogrammed by anyone—me included—without your knowledge.*

She didn't sound particularly happy about it. Well, that was okay, he wasn't either. He remembered her satisfied *imprinting complete* as the flush of sex still hammered in his veins while dazed from his intense climax. He hadn't liked the implications then and he didn't like them now. Yet, as much as he wished to deny it, the fact remained her key programming now included him as her master. He could alter her to his will.

The trust involved weighed heavy. A cold ache snaked up his legs from standing so long in the workroom. He shifted and stamped his feet. "What's the new pass-code?"

It's a multi-sensory triptych sequence using a scent, a word, and an image. I already know the first two. They come from me. But—Peyton? That sighing sound whispered in his mind again. *I want you to know I didn't choose this.*

He gritted his teeth. She obviously thought he wasn't going to like his part in creating the passcode and felt guilty. Well, she should, his life had been turned upside down since he'd unwrapped her. Nothing was simple where Hell was concerned. Not even performing a brain scan. He shook his head, suppressing a sigh. "You didn't choose what, Hell?"

The image. Your contribution. It's what you were thinking about...when I completed imprinting. It was the strongest image in your mind. And I'm sorry but...

Her hesitation snapped his patience. "But, *what?*"

I need you to think about Sarah.

His fingers bit into the hard metal casing of the scanner, but he couldn't stop the image of Sarah's chestnut hair and golden skin from flashing with searing clarity. It took his breath away in a painful blow. Her luscious body, arched in ecstasy, seemed to glow from within. The planes of her face, distorted with joy, were tensed in the throes of climax and for a heartbeat he was there, feeling the surge of her love.

The image wavered, as an amber glow ghosted his memory of Sarah's eyes. Then her irises solidified into their proper blue, and he held the picture in his mind, feeling the sharp pang he always did with the knowledge he'd never hear his wife's sweet voice again.

She's so beautiful, Hell's wistful voice whispered in his head.

Then the image of Sarah dissolved.

The holographic brain before him shimmered as he passed through the invisible barrier shielding her cerebrum—and into a maelstrom of mind-searing hell.

**

Pain. So much pain.

It clung to Peyton as he waited in utter blackness. Raced across his skin in waves of heat. Made him bite his lip so hard blood tricked into his mouth, warm, bitter, and sharp.

Someone screamed. A hoarse, desperate cry of fear.

Was it him? Was it Hell?

Why couldn't he move?

He was pinned. Pinned and no matter how hard he struggled against his restraints, he couldn't escape. The metal straps bit into his flesh at his wrists and ankles. Holding him down. Keeping his legs spread wide. Ready for when *they* came back.

So much fear clung to that word, it choked the air from his lungs making it hard to breathe.

They. Who are they, Hell?

He could hear her crying. Feel her tears running down his cheeks.

No,no,no,no,no,no,no,no,no

Her heart raced at the sound of shuffling feet.

"Please," Hell cried out. *"Stop. Please!"* Her body shook with the fear coursing through her and Peyton's veins as the footsteps came steadily closer. One pair or two? He couldn't quite make out. A distorted resonance created an echo, disrupting sound within Hell's memory.

The words came as if from far away, muffled and slurred, "Hold her down. I don't want to get bitten this time."

Laughter. Ugly and hollow in the darkness.

Peyton strained his eyes, but he couldn't see, couldn't see anything.

"She adapts so quickly," a second voice said. "Her body heals at a tremendous rate."

"Yes. Let's see how quickly she recovers from this."

Hell whimpered and tried to struggle. But hands held her head. Another pair pressed her shoulders against the platform. And the cold tip of a blade slid from her cheek in a slow, lazy line down her neck to her breast, lightly grazing her skin. The sharp tip circled her left nipple.

"Please no," she said, her body shivering.

Fingers touched her nipple gently, sensually, pulling and rubbing it until it was erect and full.

Peyton sucked in his breath, feeling the twisted desire flow through her. The need for pleasure aching within her reacting to the stimulus, and her fear. So much fear.

"Lovely," a voice murmured. Deeper and different than the others. "Can you feel it throbbing in here?" A hand pressed against her pussy. Caressed her sensitive clit. Pulled and rubbed it like the fingers on her nipple.

A moan escaped Peyton's lips, filled with Hell's fear-stained pleasure. She couldn't control it. She didn't want to react, but it was impossible. Her body craved the soft touches, even when her mind feared the pain.

"She's wet. I think she likes it."

"Good. That means she's learning."

The sharp blade pressed into her breast without warning. A quick cut that seemed to go on forever as excited nerves were severed. They screamed in acute terror as they were ripped away from her skin.

Darkness rushed in as Peyton screamed along with her. Blood spilling down his chest. While the knife point circled her other nipple and fingers softly stroked her clit, twisting and mixing pleasure with pain.

This? This is what they'd done to her?

Fucking sadistic torture?

"Engram decay critical. Synaptic failure imminent."

The edges on the memory shifted and crackled as the discordant hum increased.

Hang on baby, I'll get you out of this, Peyton said through the scanning array connecting him to Hell. Anger hissed though his veins. Hatred. *Rage.*

ppp...eeyyy...tooon...

"I've got you, sweetheart. I've got you. It's all over now."

And he held her close in his mind as he crushed the black memory with his fist.

MEMORY...ALL ALONE IN THE MOONLIGHT...

"FUCKING HELL!"

The words dug like jagged hooks, pulling Hell from the comfort of darkness.

"Peyton?" She grunted between clenched teeth. "If you're going to swear, do it quietly. My brain feels like someone shoved a laser in it."

"Funny, that's what it looked like too."

Though softer now, his dry tone buffeted against the thick layers of stasis-induced drowsiness which wrapped her brain. Was he trying to make a joke? Peyton never joked. Not unless he was upset. The situation must be worse than she'd thought.

She kept her eyes closed and touched a finger to her temple. The discordant hum in her cortex was gone, but a heavy thud had taken its place, along with the eerie sensation she'd been screaming again.

"What happened?" she whispered.

Sitting up required more effort than it was worth. She settled for opening her eyes. Then closed them again quickly before the glaring lights of Peyton's workroom set her temples pounding anew.

"Can you tell me what you remember?"

There was an odd note in his gentle question. Warm fingers brushed across her forehead, bringing with it the memory of his presence inside her mind as he'd analyzed her body and peeked into her cortex and—

Adrenaline shot through her veins. She sat bolt upright on the scanner bed, knocking the blankets he'd covered her with onto the floor.

"Why aren't I dead?" Ignoring the shudder in her limbs and the sickening thud behind her eyes, she stared at Peyton, who stood beside her.

A veil of sweat covered his handsome features, coating them with a pale sheen in the light. Dark smudges lurked beneath his bloodshot eyes. His skin looked stretched as he forced a thin, exhausted smile. "Well, it was touch and go for the first hour or so, but after I managed to stem the initial cascade effect, the rest was relatively simple surgery."

Surgery. "Oh, holy shit!" Her hand shook as she covered her face with it.

Despite being disconnected from the scanner, the distinct taste of Peyton's fear remained. Fear which had mirrored her own when the scanner's alarms had bathed everything in baleful red, accompanied by the computer's indifferent drone repeating, "Engram decay critical. Synaptic failure imminent."

"Your hippocampus—your memory center—was damaged," Peyton explained, his voice soft. "Someone wiped whole sections of it. Several times, in fact. Except, they didn't do a very clean job, at least not the last time. Fragments of old engrams were left behind. When new ones tried to imprint on top..." He gestured at his temples with a flick of his fingers. "Weak points were created. As the degradation increased, it caused a slow collapse of your cortical functions. You probably wouldn't have woken from stasis if we'd put you back in that box."

Brain dead.

That's what they called it when the body lived on but the machine regulating it failed. It was possible to salvage an android by replacing the damaged cortex and starting new, but the original personality was gone forever. All her parts *seemed* in order, but who knew what had been lost?

His fingers brushed her forehead again, a frown creasing his own brow. "I removed all the aberrant memory engrams causing the problem. Your accelerated healing process has helped re-grow the injured neurons, but you might experience headaches for some time. I don't think the damage was permanent, however."

No permanent damage. Thank the Maker. No, thank Peyton.

The shaking of her hand rippled through her body and straight into her core. She drew her knees up to her chest but couldn't halt the quiver.

A strong arm curled around her shoulders. "It's okay. You're safe now, sweetheart."

"Thanks to you," she managed through chattering teeth. She leaned into him, letting his strength and warmth comfort her. But her brush with death still felt coldly near. The scanner bed's hard padding, the scent of lubricant in the workroom, were very real reminders of the lengthy time she'd lain frozen, awaiting the ultimate kiss of oblivion. Only it hadn't come. Peyton had released her from the pain searing her skull. He'd worked on her for over five hours according to her internal chronometer. He'd brought her back instead of letting her go. The tremors wracking her body stilled as she pulled back and studied his strong profile.

"You saved my life when it would've been easier to let me die." An incredible realization, especially considering killing her had been the thought most on his mind when he'd initiated the scan. "Why?"

The warmth of his arm pulled away, but his comforting scent lingered. He picked up a nearby cloth and busied himself with wiping down the scanning array's control panel. "I swore an oath once, to help those in need regardless of personal opinion."

"But you don't practice regularly anymore. Doesn't that relieve you of clinical obligation?"

A flush spread from the deep "V" of his tunic and up his neck. His gaze snapped to hers, hot and hard. "Would you rather have died?"

"No." Ignoring the numb tingle in her limbs, she twisted so her feet hung off the scanner bed and touched the icy floor. "I'm grateful for your help. But I don't want to be an obligation. I've caused you enough trouble already." Chest suddenly tight, she sucked in a breath. "Is there someone else here that I can stay with?"

"You want to stay with someone else?" He tossed the cloth down on the scanning bed, his lips a thin line.

"No, but I figured it's what you wanted."

"What I want—" he snapped, then stopped. He turned away from her, his body rigid as he thrust his fingers through his dark hair. His face was set in hard lines when he turned back to her. "What I want is to keep you safe. You're the most important thing that's ever happened to humanity, and those bastards—" He stopped again, as if whatever the bastards in question had done was too difficult for him to say. He shook his head and tried again. "I got a call from Markus Willbright from The Factory, just before you woke up. They're looking for you, Hell."

Willbright. Willbright. "Wait..." She clutched her temples as she slid off the scanner and stood. "I remember him!" She glanced at Peyton and caught his grim nod. But the excitement, whisking through her at the fact she could actually remember something, quickly faded. Why did that name make her feel uncomfortable? She had a vague impression of a quiet man of mixed Asian ancestry who'd come to see her in her glass-walled room. He'd only ever looked at her and tapped on his tablet, recording whatever it was that scientists recorded, then disappeared again behind closed doors. But Peyton obviously hated him by the anger flaring in his eyes.

"What did you tell him?"

"I lied. I told him I'd never heard of a Bio-roid before, let alone seen one, and said I was quite happy with my new Factory-made sex doll, thank you very much."

He'd lied to protect her? She sat back down on the scanner with a thump. "Did he believe you?"

"Probably not." Peyton's attention was fixed on retrieving a data cube from the scanner array, the handsome planes of his face set hard. Clearly all of this was a burden to him that he'd rather not carry.

"Wouldn't it have been easier to have just told him the truth and sent me back?"

The flush deepened across his cheeks, giving his tired expression a fevered cast. "No."

"Why?"

"Because of this." He held up the translucent blue data cube for her to see before closing his fingers over it again. "I managed to piece together some of the fragmented engrams rupturing your hippocampus."

"And?" she prompted after it became apparent he wasn't going to say anything further.

"And, like I told you before, you're never going back to The Factory again." He turned away angrily as if that were the end of the subject.

Her muscles protested, but she followed him to the door. "What's on the data cube?"

He shook his head and gestured around the room as he passed into the warm living quarters. "You're staying here with me until we come up with a better plan." He paused and turned to face her so abruptly, she nearly bumped into him. "But we'll need to change your appearance. Find a disguise of some kind. You're very small for a sex doll." His fingers settled on measuring the curve of her breast as if calculating its size.

"Peyton," she slapped his hands away. "What is going on?" Her memories of her life at The Factory were indistinct clips at best. No more than frustrating bits and pieces that left her with the certainty she'd escaped for good reason. But without that reason, she was lost.

His gaze locked on hers. Beneath the tiredness and strain in his eyes, fire flickered—deep, hot, and full of rage. "Someone..." He licked his lips. "Someone hurt you. Deliberately." He uncurled his clenched fist and looked at the data cube again. Then, as if making a decision, he shoved the cube into his pants pocket and walked over to the bed. "But it doesn't matter. Like I said, you aren't ever going back."

Fractured limbs, erased memories, a damaged cortex; she had almost died—no, *would have* died if Peyton hadn't intervened—and someone had done it on purpose. Despite the warmth of the room, a chill settled deep in her bones.

"Who—" She cleared the lump from her throat, the sound loud in the tense stillness. "Who hurt me? Was it Willbright?"

Peyton's attention had settled on a message light blinking on the monitor beside the bed. He frowned. "The data corruption was too great. I couldn't make out an exact identity. It always happened in the dark."

He sounded as frustrated as she felt. The urge to know her assailant and ask him *why* rippled through her nerves like fire.

A room filled with darkness... The sharp bite of metal. The need to run, to flee, to escape the pain. "I want to see it." She took a step forward, despite the racing of her pulse at what she might see.

"What?" The bed squeaked as he turned to face her again.

"The data cube. I want to see what's on it." She held an expectant palm toward him.

His gaze turned cold as he stared at her outstretched hand. "No."

"No? What do you mean 'no'?" Her fingers curled into an empty fist before dropping back to her side. "I want to see what happened for myself."

"No. You don't." He folded his arms across his chest.

"Yes. I do." She matched his clipped tone and settled her hands on her hips.

The murky something, which formed her existence before waking from stasis in Peyton's living room, held a terrible secret. A secret so terrifying, it made her shake inside. But as frightening as the truth might be, she wanted to know what had happened to make Peyton so angry. And, more importantly, she needed to complete the missing parts of her identity, even if it was an identity she'd rather not have. The need to know who she was, where she'd come from, why she'd run away burned hotter than the fear of finding out the truth. Why couldn't he see that?

He stared at her, tired brown eyes implacable, his jaw tense. The pulse at his throat beat strong and fast. She didn't need peripheral diagnostics to know his blood pressure was rising again.

Well, so was hers. "What gives you the right to decide what I do or do not know?" she snapped. "Those memories are mine. They belong to me."

"What gives me the right?" He stood and stepped toward her, bending so his face stopped mere inches from her own. His eyes burned like hot coals. "Besides the fact that imprinting makes me your fucking master, do you have any idea how lucky you are? To have a mind structured in such a way that it can be wiped clean?"

Okay. He did have a point about the whole master thing, and she did feel lucky to be alive, but that's where any gratitude stopped. "Someone hurt me, Peyton. I want to know."

"Trust me. You're better off not remembering what happened." He broke away and ran his fingers through his tousled hair. "There are more than a few memories I wish I could forget." Pain filled his voice, raw and very real.

Her chest felt heavy as the reality of his sorrow tightened around her heart. He'd known so much suffering, so much death. Not just Sarah's, but countless friends. She'd sensed the depth of his loss while they'd been connected through the scanner. What she wouldn't give now to have that link back again so she could show him the truth.

"Peyton," she called gently. Shoulders tense, he continued to stare at the message light blinking on the monitor. "Memories can be full of pain. I understand that," she continued. "But it's the good ones as well as the bad which make us who we are. They define us as, as people." She unclenched her hands and wiped them on her shirt, smoothing the silky fabric. Her bare toes flexed against the tiled floor; she was flesh and blood and bone, but not human. And not quite machine either. Forever separate. Unique.

Alone. "Without mine, what am I?"

His chin lifted and he turned to face her, his expression still full of pain. It disappeared, replaced by alarm as a droning buzz echoed through the room.

"Someone's at the door. Shit." He grunted. Looking around quickly, his eyes settled on the bed. He grabbed her arm and pulled her down onto it. She fell against the soft mattress with a squeak. "Just be quiet and stay completely still no matter what happens," he ordered in hushed tones as the buzzing drone repeated itself.

Her protest was stifled by a hastily dropped blanket over her head. Heart thudding, she sank into the bedding, her senses filled with Peyton's spicy sex-scent and the sounds of him punching in an access code on the entry panel.

"Jared," he muttered with a grunt. Though he obviously wasn't pleased by the intrusion, the alarm had gone from Peyton's voice. The blanket, however, remained a concealing barrier over her head and torso. Her legs were visible, but she didn't have time to hide them before the door slid open with a hiss.

"Hey, asshole," a male voice barreled into the room. His tone was lighter and filled with more warmth than Peyton's. "You owe me twenty credits. Guerin kicked Vassino's ass." Jared snickered then stopped. "You look like shit, Peyton. Didn't you sleep last night? Someone keep you...*up*?" He laughed, this time a deep rumble full of teasing. "Those Dolls are pretty amazing, huh? Just like the real thing. Except they don't ever say no." Hearty chuckles erupted with renewed force.

"Yeah, pretty amazing alright," Peyton drawled in a dry tone. "Let's just—"

"Is this her?" A weight settled against the bed. "God damn, look at those legs, you could lick them forever." A strangled cough choked out of Peyton, but Jared appeared not to hear it. "I know you've never wanted to try my Bambi, but shit, I've got a boner just looking at this one's feet. Ever think of sharing? She looks so real."

A warm calloused palm skimmed along her calf. She bit her lip, resisting the urge to flinch.

"*Don't*." The hard, deliberate tone in Peyton's voice stilled the hand's ascent. "Touch her," he added more softly, but not any less forcefully. The feel of Jared's calloused fingers disappeared from her skin.

The blanket's weaving let in a diffused speckle of light, which wavered as someone moved past her field of vision. Peyton?

Jared? She couldn't tell. The air inside her cocoon was thick with the tension filling the room.

"Whatever you say, Peyton." Jared's voice had lost its humor.

Peyton sighed in that weary tone of his. She imagined him pulling his fingers through his hair. "No, I'm sorry. You're right. I didn't sleep well last night. And...it's been a difficult morning. Why don't we go down to The Grub and grab a bite to eat? I need to pick up more provisions anyway."

At the mention of food, Hell's stomach let out a low growl. She winced. How long had it been since she'd last eaten?

Peyton coughed and slapped his stomach. "See? Hungry."

"Er, yeah," Jared snickered. "Guess you worked up a bit of an appetite, eh?" The grin had returned to his voice. Hell had the impression he was naturally good humored, his crassness the result of hard living in a lonely place, much like Peyton's. Except Peyton frowned way too much.

She stiffened and struggled not to shriek as someone pinched her left buttock sharply. The men's footfalls moved toward the door.

"Oh, yeah, the old man wants to see you," Jared said. "He's looking to get a team together. A Reclaimer in the northern sector got loose in the snow and broke down again."

"*Again*? Damn." Peyton grunted. "Is it number 21 or 24?"

"24," Jared said. "The one with the wonky A.I."

"Heaven forbid that it ever learn to do what it's told," Peyton muttered.

Jared laughed. "I kind of like that it's got a mind of its own."

"You would," Peyton said. "Guess it'll be about an hour or so before I get back, then," he announced overly loudly. "I don't suppose there's any chance *my Doll* can stay out of trouble while I'm gone," he added.

"Your Doll?" Jared sounded confused. "She's just a machine. If you tell her not to move, she'll stay put all day."

"Don't count on it," Peyton muttered as the door slid shut with a hiss.

Don't count on it, indeed. Stay put? Like a good little doggy? *Or a stray one.* The pounding at her temples increased. Peyton's sex-laden bed scent threatened to make her sneeze.

She waited for a moment, making certain of the silence before throwing off the blanket. Static-y hairs floated past her vision as she scanned the empty room.

Peyton had taken the data cube with him in his pocket. But he must have a back-up copy left in the scanner. He hadn't specifically ordered her not to go looking for answers there, so technically, she wasn't disobeying him. In fact, he hadn't given her any specific instructions at all. Asking her if she could stay out of trouble while he was gone was not the same as instructing her not to. She smiled. An hour should be more than enough time to access the scanner and find out what secrets her past held.

Without a backward glance, she headed for the workroom.

GHOST IN THE MACHINE

"IF WHAT YOU'RE saying is true, and this 'Hell' is an experimental Bio-roid, how the hell did she end up...here?" Jared gestured at the central chamber of Deliverance Dome as they walked through it on the way to Peyton's quarters.

Utilitarian, drab, and lacking the little comforts that made a settlement 'home', the vast hexagonally shaped hall echoed of empty hopes and dreams. In the beginning, there were pictures, the odd dab of paint to indicate someone cared, but the time and energy to keep up cheerful luxury hadn't existed for years.

Peyton attempted a nonchalant shrug but couldn't hide the anger burning within him. For the past hour or so, he'd warred with himself over what to tell Jared about Hell. In the end, he'd opted for the truth. It's not like his brother-in-law was completely clueless. At least, most of the time. And talking about the agony eating Peyton up inside did feel kind of good. Sort of. Maybe. Okay, no. Actually, it made all the fucked-up-ness seem brutally real. He didn't want it to be real, but he couldn't block out the mind-searing images of what had happened to Hell.

"The best I can piece together is that she got tired of being tortured within an inch of her life," he said. Hell's scars had included twenty-three fractured bones besides the four he'd initially discovered. A ruptured spleen, multiple contusive marks on her musculature indicating vicious beatings—all nicely healed, of course, but that was just the beginning of the horrors her shattered body had revealed. "She's gone rogue," he explained. "Her tracking device was internally disabled, which means she hacked her own security and turned it off. She ran to the furthest place from the Arkopolis she could get to by transport."

Jared shifted the box of supplies he carried in his arms and glanced sideways at Peyton, suspicion clear in his blue eyes. "And she doesn't remember doing this?"

"No. Synaptic decay was advanced before she entered stasis. By the time she arrived and I unpacked her, she was nearly blank except for hardwired info. She was dying before she got here." His pulse spiked as he thought of the desperate battle he'd fought to stop that from happening. After five hours of intense surgery, the fatigue ached in his hands and mind. But he'd refused to lose the battle. Not this time.

Their bootfalls echoed on the gunmetal-grey rigging of the rampart leading up to the eastern rooms of the habitat. "Kinda convenient of her to choose you though, being you're a, er, retired doctor and all. Do you think she knew?"

"That I was a doctor? Yes. She recognized my name. Where did she heard it in the first place? I'm guessing it was at The Factory." He did a mental shrug over what Markus Willbright might have said about him. It couldn't have been anything good. "It's possible she had a plan in place to seek help," he added. "She's shown nothing but intelligence and courage since I activated her."

Jared's lips pulled into a puzzled frown. "I wonder what happened to the Doll I ordered for you?" His gaze grew distant as he looked toward the curved ceiling of the Dome. Daylight streamed through the windows above, bathing the metal walkways crisscrossing the nexus in triangles of welcome warmth. "They'll be looking for her," he murmured as they passed into another patch of shadow. "You know that, right?"

"They already are," Peyton said with a nod. "I had a so-called courtesy call this morning from The Factory, asking if I was satisfied with my purchase."

Jared's bitter laugh echoed in the empty walkway. "What did you tell them?"

Peyton frowned. "I said everything was fine, thanks."

Jared shot him a sharp look. "Well, that was stupid. They'll know you were lying. You're never happy with anything."

I was happy with Sarah, he thought bitterly. But that seemed like a lifetime ago. "I have no doubt they'll eventually trace her location anyway. There's only seven habitable Domes on the entire planet."

Jared's brow creased. "You're asking for a heap of trouble trying to hide her instead of turning her in."

"Yeah? Well, bring it on. 'Cause I'm not sending her back to that fucking place!" Peyton's fingers dug into his palms as his hands fisted. He stopped walking and placed his bags on the walkway as his stomach clenched, anger and sickness roiling.

Concern tightened Jared's features. He shifted the box in his arms and placed a steadying hand on Peyton's shoulder. "I wasn't saying that what you're doing is wrong," he said in a low, firm voice. "I meant that you're going to need help with this. Talk to my old man. He'll want to see her too. A Bio-roid. A freaking Bio-roid! I remember Sarah talking about that possibility before she...passed." Jared's voice trailed off, his gaze becoming somber as he studied Peyton.

"Yes," Peyton said. "An interesting coincidence, don't you think?"

Jared's expression became guarded. "Coincidence?"

"Hell was created from Sarah's ideas, after she conveniently died," Peyton said. "You don't think that's a big coincidence? Especially with how Hell's fighting for her own safety now?"

"Okay," Jared said, his tone full of strained patience. They'd had this kind of argument many times before. As son of the Dome's principle representative, Lee Palmer—and thereby trained in diplomacy—he'd never been one to jump to conclusions, preferring hard facts before deciding on a course of action. But he'd always been open to debate. "Supposing there's a connection between Sarah's death and Hell's situation, then answer me this: why would anyone do that, Peyton?"

"Because people are fucked up," he spat out.

He leaned against the railing. The view of the habitat before him swam as he steadied his raging anger with controlled breaths. He'd been more interested in filling his stomach with mind-numbing alcohol than food at the mess hall, but the sickness eating his soul hadn't gone away. If anything, it had intensified. He squeezed his eyes shut tight, unable to block out the images seeping through his brain like poisonous snakes. "You have no idea what they did," he whispered. "What they're capable of..."

Like the twilight between sleep and awake when dreams seemed very real, peeking into recorded memories disoriented the mind. He'd experienced Hell's pain and horror firsthand, seen the terror through her eyes. The nightmare reality burned into his memory danced clear in his thoughts; the pain searing his nerves felt as real as if his own body had been devastated by the torture she'd endured. He rubbed his temples, not wanting to relive the trauma but unable to stop it anymore.

"They cut off her goddamn nipples while she was awake," he said, his voice a harsh rasp with the intensity of the sickness he felt inside. "Just to see how she'd react. To see if she would pass for real." Sweat prickled under his shirt, trailing down his sides like blood. Her blood, his blood. Locked in that darkened room where pain waited a touch away and hot breath seared his lungs in punishing gasps. He swallowed hard against the bile rising in his throat. "Then while she writhed and screamed in pain..." He bit his lip to stop from crying out as the knife cut into the skin of his borrowed memories. "...someone decided to have more fun and raped her with a medical instrument. Anally. Vaginally. Repeatedly." He kept his eyes shut tight, fighting the nausea and sickness that no amount of whisky could ever dull. Her anguish was clear and vibrant, mixing with his as it surged through his blood.

"What?" Jared's shock and outrage echoed off the walls. The box he carried slid from his grasp and hit the walkway with a loud thud. "Jesus Christ. Who...who would do something like that? Willbright?"

"I'm not sure. Maybe one person. But I think it was more. It's all just fragments. Images I pieced back together from her damaged memory engrams." And dear God how he wished he hadn't. "They encoded her nanite DNA to accelerate her healing process. Then strapped her spread-eagled in the dark to the lab table and started the 'experiment' again. I don't know how many times. They wanted to see how much pain she could take and if they could program her to endure even more."

Her screams. Her screams. Oh God, her screams...

"Fucking sadistic bastards." Unable to contain it anymore, Peyton hissed in pain as he doubled over. His stomach heaved, trying to rid him of the memories and sickness filling him. Hot bile erupted in a spew. It splattered on the walkway, dribbled down between the slats.

Thirty feet below, the air purification system continued to rumble, oblivious to the regurgitated firewater descending fast. He hoped to God no one was working down there or they'd be in for an unpleasant surprise.

"Christ Almighty." Jared fumbled with the box. Then thrust a container of water into Peyton's hand. "Here."

Leaning on the railing for support, Peyton wiped his face with a sleeve and took a sip. The cool liquid washed the acid from his throat. His limbs felt tight and clammy, but after a few moments, the nausea receded. Too bad about the headache thudding behind his eyes.

"You okay?" Jared's face was white and pinched. He snaked a hand through his shaggy mop of light brown hair in a worried gesture Sarah had shared.

Reminded of his promise to care for her younger brother, Peyton forced a smile. "Sure," he lied. "That last batch of whisky needs more fermenting is all." He swallowed the last of the water and handed the container back to Jared. "Thanks," he said, and with a determined grip, he picked up his bags again. No point in lingering when there was work to be done. And Hell...he'd left her alone long enough. God alone knew what she'd gotten up to while he'd been gone. She hadn't been happy with his decision to keep the truth of her abuse from her.

Jared pursed his lips and eyed him dubiously but replaced the container without comment and picked up the box of provisions. Through the grated flooring beneath their feet, a steady hum of machinery resonated in the burgeoning silence. They set off along the catwalk, heading for the set of stairways that lead upward to the section of rooms Peyton called home.

"Sonofabitch," Jared muttered as they clomped up the first flight and around a corner. "You'd think after the millennia of study gone into improving the human genome, someone would have found the sequence responsible for sadism and removed it."

"It's probably linked to something else, like autonomic breathing. You have to admit, they have us by the balls with that one." He attempted a laugh, but it sounded as hollow as he felt inside.

"This is serious, Peyton. The Factory produces all kinds of cybernetic help-mates from robots to androids and everything in between. And yes, some owners will always treat their property like trash. But shit, we didn't approve the neo-genesis project for the sick pleasure of some fucked-up scientists. What's happened to Hell can't be sanctioned by the High Council."

Reaching the next landing, Peyton paused. "Who knows? I never thought they'd go so far as to use innocent people as test subjects for a viral infection either, but the evidence still stands."

Jared readjusted his grip on the box and shook his head. "What evidence? Yes, Sarah was spending a lot of time at The Factory back then, but you've said yourself that she wasn't sick until she was here at Deliverance. What happened to us was an accident.

What happened to Hell wasn't. That is something to pursue. You need to let the rest go."

"Like hell I'll ever let it go," Peyton snapped as they started up the second flight. His gut instinct screamed that the virus hadn't been an accident, it had been planned. That Sarah had been an unwitting carrier when she'd come back from The Factory for a visit. That she'd been deliberately infected with it. That she'd been chosen to be Patient Zero. And that she hadn't picked it up through the water or the food or whatever other bullshit explanation the rest of the world tried to come up with.

But, without unwavering proof, most Domers, like Jared, found it easier to ignore the truth than swallow it. They argued that the colonists were supposed to be the best and brightest, the descendants of forbearers who were hand-picked to be the future of humanity. There wasn't any room for abuse and mistrust when so much was riding on everyone cooperating and doing their part to rebuild the populace.

Yeah. Like genius-level people weren't capable of being duplicitous assholes.

In Peyton's experience, hiding one's head in the sand did nothing except expose one's butt. It seemed far safer to stare horror in the face than get unexpectedly reamed.

They climbed in silence, the echo of their boots in the narrow stairwell forestalling further debate. As they reached the top, Jared grunted and put the box down on the walkway outside of Peyton's quarters. "What are you going to do about Hell?" he asked as he wiped his forehead with his sleeve and studied Peyton.

"Hide her until I make sure she's fully recovered. Then beat every last drop of sweet, mother-fucking justice out of those Arkopolis bastards."

Her memories, despite being chewed up, would at the very least prove abuse was happening at the genesis labs. But as for avenging Sarah, he would never rest until he found undeniable proof that she'd been infected on purpose.

Absolute power corrupts absolutely. So much power in so few hands and no controlling body to answer to. He'd argued against the arrangement from the start, claiming every step of the research should be shared with all the inhabitants of New Earth. After all, it was everyone's future at stake. But he'd been out-voted and now look where they were at.

He lifted one of the bags in his hands. "Thanks for the clothes and stuff."

Jared nodded. "Bambi won't miss them. But maybe I will," he

added with a twisted grin. "I included her Vamp-whorer outfit. Friday nights will never be the same without it."

"Neither will my view of black pleather. Shit." Peyton rubbed his eyes to blank the image of Jared and his sex doll that sprang to mind. Suddenly serious, he put a staying hand on Jared's arm. "I trust you'll keep this to yourself? Hell doesn't know what happened to her, and I don't want anyone else to either."

"Of course." Jared nodded. "What do you want me to tell the old man?"

The less anyone knew, the better, but he owed Lee some kind of explanation, if only out of respect for his father-in-law's position as elected leader. "Let him know what's going on, but don't go into detail. I'll fill him in while we're out to fix that broken Reclaimer in the northern sector."

"You realize a disguise won't work for long, right? Anyone who touches Hell will know she's no ordinary Doll. She's warm."

"No one's going to touch her," Peyton snapped. The harsh finality in his voice hung heavy in the air. Hell had been 'touched' enough to last her a lifetime. He'd be damned if he'd let anyone get close enough to hurt her again.

"Uh-huh." A smile flitted across Jared's lips. His eyes glinted in amusement in the dim hallway light. "No one except you?"

Peyton frowned. "That's not what I meant."

"Can I offer you some advice?" Jared interjected, folding his arms across his chest. "She's designed for pleasure; you really need some. Get laid. Enjoy it. You've punished yourself over Sarah long enough." He pulled away from the wall and turned toward the stairs, deliberately kicking the box in passing. "And Jesus, Peyton, will you move back to the main habitat already? It's getting old climbing half the Dome just to visit this shit-hole you call home."

"Need I remind you it was your 'gift' that got me in this mess in the first place?" Peyton called after him as Jared started down the stairs. "And I happen to like living up here, dickhead. Makes you exercise your lazy ass bringing me supplies."

Laughter echoed up the stairs accompanied by a flick of Jared's middle finger before he disappeared from sight.

Left alone on the walkway, Peyton lingered over picking up the box, suddenly uncomfortable with the idea of returning home. The most advanced android ever created by humankind waited in his bedroom—a beautiful, broken dream, willing to do whatever he wanted.

What was it he wanted?

Peace, revenge, a nightmare-less sleep? The guilt choking his soul like a vise to crush him into oblivion?

Hell could give him none of those things, and the one thing she could give him he couldn't enjoy, not with visions of her tortured as a sex toy burned indelibly in his mind.

Hefting the box, he adjusted its weight and entered the broken sanctuary of his home.

If he couldn't be with her, and he couldn't send her away until he knew she'd be safe, what was he going to do with Hell?

RECKONINGS

HE FOUND HER in his workroom, straight-backed and silent, sitting at the table, a laser tool humming softly as she passed it over the connections of Henry's reattached limbs.

Deciding to ignore the fact that she'd invaded his personal workspace without asking, he examined the intense relief he felt at seeing her again. There'd been an annoying moment of panic when she'd not been in the bed where he'd left her. Instead, he'd found the bed neatly made with no trace of her whereabouts. And for the next few moments, his mind had raced through every possibility as to why, ending with the irrational fear that she'd left. Which wouldn't be a bad thing considering the trouble she'd brought to his life. But seeing her here in his workroom, and smelling her familiar sweet scent, he was left with one foolish conclusion: finding her here was better than not finding her at all. Which meant that, yep...he was seriously fucked.

"Hey," he said. "I brought you some clothes and things."

"Thank you," she murmured softly. She didn't turn in greeting, just kept up the rhythmic flick, flick, flick of her wrist, the laser moving in precise, quick increments he could only dream of mimicking.

"I left them on the couch for you to try on. I had to guess the size. There's shoes," he added when her back remained firmly

He tried a different tactic to break the ice. "That's amazing," he said as he walked to the table and placed a hand on Henry's cold metal leg, awed by the scope of Hell's achievement. "You finished fixing this in less than two hours? It would've taken me a week."

Silent, she kept her attention trained on the fine wiring. Her fingers clutching the laser were white, almost as white as her pinched expression. Lips pulled tight, eyelids puffy. Had she been crying?

Shit. "What's wrong?" he asked as panic built in the vicinity of his heart. He couldn't stand the thought of any more tears. Hers or anyone else's. "Do you have another headache?" The surgery to remove and repair her damaged memory engrams had been quite invasive. She'd probably feel its effects for days. He placed his hand on her shoulder. Beneath the fabric, her muscles tensed.

"Nothing," she said, her voice devoid of its usual pleasantness.

"Uh-huh..." Leaning against the table, he crossed his arms. "Nothing." He knew that clipped tone well. He'd never heard it from Hell before, but apparently the 'you've-done-something-wrong-but-I'm-not-going-to-tell-you-what' cold-shoulder act was universal to women, even android women. "Does nothing have anything to do with you still wanting to see the data cube?"

The object in question seemed to burn a hole in his pocket, and his fingers strayed to feel the hard square outline. She might think she needed to know what had happened to her, but after experiencing the memories himself, he knew differently. The cube held nothing but knowledge of an existence she was better off never remembering. He'd incinerate the damned thing at the first opportunity, except he needed the information as evidence against The Factory's abuses.

The flicking of the laser stopped. "No," she whispered. Body tense, she kept her face turned downward, still as glass.

"Then for God's sake, what's wrong? You're acting like a...like a robot." He lost patience and bent forward. Grasping her chin with his fingers, he tilted it up and looked into her eyes.

Her amber irises were filled with anguish. "There's nothing wrong with me," she spat out, snatching her chin from his grasp. "But there sure as hell is something wrong with humans." Color returned to her skin in a flash of anger that dotted her cheeks. *"How could they do that to me?"*

She slammed the laser onto the table so hard it smashed. Bits of metal and shards of glass careened in all directions and pinged against Henry's metallic skin. She stood and swept the instrument's remains off the table with a decisive flick of her hand, and leveled Peyton with a glare so intense it was clear she held him personally responsible for all of humanity's crimes.

He backed away, startled. "What the hell are you talking about?"

But as he held her silent, accusing gaze, so wounded and full of heart-wrenching despair, understanding uncoiled in his mind. "Wait. You know." It came out as fact, not a question. She knew. Somehow she knew what had happened to her. Had she remembered? No, that was impossible. He'd made sure to remove every last trace of her corrupted memories. The only place they were recorded was on the data cube. Then how—? He turned toward the medical scanner.

He hadn't thought to wipe the drive clean after her surgery. It would have a record of the entire operation. Fucking Hell. He'd told her to stay out of trouble. But sure enough, a quick check of recent activity of the scanner's archive revealed her foolish duplicity.

"Sonofabitch." He grunted as his headache from earlier returned with full force. He rounded on Hell. "You broke into my goddamned computer?"

"What else was I supposed to do?" she snapped at him with an impatient flip of her hand as if his question was ludicrous.

Adrenaline shot through his veins like fire. "You stupid...meddling...gah!" He thrust his fingers through his hair in frustration. "You were supposed to do as I said and leave it alone." He took a decisive move toward her. Maybe to shake some sense into her, maybe to kiss it. Because with the way her eyes flashed and her lips pursed in anger, she looked so vital and alive it was impossible to ignore his burning need to force her to see reason.

She braced her stance, lifting her chin. "Am I supposed to do everything you say?"

"Yes!" He clenched his fists at his sides to avoid throttling the indignant look out of her eyes.

"What's the point then, Peyton?" She stepped closer, face flushed, eyes glinting. Her sweet scent rose off her in a hot wave, reminding him that she was his. Her prominent nipples poked like tempting sentinels beneath her thin shirt. She pointed between them and tapped her chest. "What's the point in giving me thoughts, giving me feelings, giving me an identity, if all I'm supposed to be is a brain-dead robot?"

"At least a brain-dead robot would listen and trust me." The need to protect her burned hot, angry, and uncomfortably close. It'd started in the morning with her almost dying on his operating table. No. It had started as soon as he'd woken her with a kiss and she'd cried out for help. He'd failed so many others. He couldn't do it again. Not like Sarah, not this time. Not Hell. Why couldn't she just do what she was told and let him keep her safe?

"I had to know the truth. Even if the truth is that I'm nothing more than…" Her voice hitched and the anger flushing her face became lost in the anguish that filled her eyes. She looked down as if to hide it, fingers twisting the hem of her shirt. "Even if all I am is someone's sick play toy." Goosebumps sprang along her arms as a shiver rippled through her.

An identical one shivered through him. "You aren't a toy," he murmured. With an unsteady finger he gently stroked away the silky hairs falling across her cheek.

"Could have fooled me," she whispered. Her chin trembled as she met his gaze, but her wide pain-filled eyes stayed hot and dry, full of resignation.

He couldn't bear to see her pain. It was bad enough with it burned into his memory and searing his soul. Foolish Hell. If she had just listened! He shook his head, and wrapping her in his arms, he pulled her snug against him, trying to shield her with his body. To give her strength. Warmth. Whatever she needed in order to fight the desolation that had her by the throat.

Her fine, sweet-scented hairs tickled his chin as she pressed her face against his chest and wrapped her arms around him. He sighed at the touch, his heart aching. She was beautiful, delicate. A tiny bit of warmth trembling against him, yet impossibly real and so full of life. He could feel it beating through her as if it were his own pulse.

How could anyone treat her with such brutality?

The memory of her screams echoed in his ears. He tightened his hold even as instinct warned him to pull back. To not get too close. But it was already too late. Maybe it had always been too late.

"Why?" she whispered. Her chin lifted. Without her anger to hide it, the confusion and pain filling her soul loomed clear in her amber eyes, darkening their lustrous glow. "Why was I made?"

He shook his head, unable to think past the despair shadowing his own thoughts, and gently stroked her hair with his fingers.
After a moment he found his voice. "Why was I?"

LOVE ME TENDER

HELL STARED UP at Peyton's stricken face, the chilly workroom forgotten in the force of his intense sadness. The desire to pull him inside her body and shield him from the horrors shadowing his brown eyes ached deep in her core. He'd seen her tragic memories. They mixed with his own, weighing down his soul like lead. How much despair could a human take before breaking?

How much could she?

Maybe she shouldn't have broken into his computer and reabsorbed the memories he'd tried to shield her from. But she'd had to know. She'd had to in order to understand who she was and where she had come from. She squeezed her eyes tight and shuddered inside, remembering the demons that had stalked her in that dark room. The pain. The fear. The reason she had run as far and as fast as she could to the man clutching her so tightly in his arms now, surrounding her with his powerful hold and spicy-scented heat.

His heart beat strong beneath her cheek as she pressed herself against him, clinging to the focus his presence gave her. Since the moment she'd woken to his kiss, his intentions had been true: protect and shelter. He was the best of men. The only man...

...the only man who ever made me feel truly safe. Remember that. If nothing else, I want you to remember him...

Her breath caught in her chest and she jerked backward as the sliver of memory flitted through her mind, reminding her of sunshine and light. A warm voice. Kind. Happy. But the conversation faded before she could grasp anything more, leaving behind the sensation that it had been a long time ago. Just a fleeting moment, but so important. And now it was gone.

Peyton's hand stilled its soothing motion on her hair. He looked down at her, his dark expression tinged with concern. "You okay?"

She nodded, uncertain what to say to explain the frustration she felt. Things were clearer now than before her operation. Memories were slowly bridging gaps, but these little snippets of conversations were more irritating than helpful. Which ones were real and which the result of the damage done to her? She had no way to tell.

But studying his handsome, tired face, she knew that it didn't matter. That the only thing of importance was the man before her and the connection they shared, which struggled to grow beneath a blanket of loss and despair. "I'm sorry," she whispered, feeling the burden she'd placed on him weighing heavy. "So sorry for everything."

"You don't need to be sorry," he said, his voice low and earnest. Even now, he tried to protect her.

"Yes, I do. All you wanted to do was help me. And when you look at me now, all you see is that girl, screaming in the darkness."

He shook his head as if to deny it, but she knew the truth was too strong to ignore. He'd seen what had happened to her. He'd tried to shield her from the memories, but he couldn't protect himself from what he'd witnessed. Her tragedy had become part of him. She sensed it within him, mixing with his own despair and curling around his heart, clinging to each beat as it fought to leach him of his strength and turn him cold.

With each passing moment, it grew stronger. Soon it would become an impenetrable wall that would stand between them forever.

She needed to break it. Now. Remind him that life was filled with so much more pleasure than pain. All you had to do was reach out and grasp it.

She caressed her palm over his warm neck and skimmed the sweat-damp curls at his nape. His pupils widened as her fingers tightened on his hair, the intensity of his gaze sparking with the fire burning beneath his grief.

The pulse at his throat stepped up its tempo. "Hell," he murmured with a shake of his head as if trying to deny her intention.

But 'no' was not an option. The tight line of his lips begged to be softened, and she couldn't–wouldn't—let the growing wall of despair stand between them. She pulled him toward her, needing to brand her mouth with his.

Soft, warm, supple, lips melded to lips, and opened.

She hadn't tasted him fully before, not like this, with blending mouths and curious tongues. Running hers along his teeth, she reveled in the different textures of hard enamel and slippery flesh. His flavor was powerfully arousing, desire-laden pheromones and Peyton's unique spicy taste. She hungered for more. Ached for it. She pressed closer.

But with an abrupt movement, he pulled back.

The loss of connection bit deep inside her, sent her emotions scattering in shock. She glanced at his face and caught the fleeting edge of an expression she'd never expected to see. Pain, yes, anger perhaps, even a touch of fear at losing control, but not revulsion.

Her stomach clenched as reality hit.

She was damaged goods. A used piece of merchandise. And he knew it. Apparently, he didn't like it. She hadn't thought her torture would make a difference to him in that way, but it did. The wall of ice had been built too fast. A shiver rippled across her body as it registered the loss of his heat.

"You really do hate me, don't you?" she said. Recoiling, she bolted for the door, determined to get away from the disgust shining so clearly in his eyes.

"Hell!" he called after her, his voice hoarse.

She didn't stop as she passed through the doorway and into the warm living room that smelled so invitingly of him. Where could she go? Would someone else in the Dome take her in? Help her? Jared perhaps? He'd seemed kind in his own way. Did it matter she'd imprinted on Peyton and couldn't ever connect like that with another? She slapped her palm against the exit panel. It opened with a hiss. She had to get away. Far away. Maybe to another Dome where no one knew the dirty secret of her past. That she was used, sullied, broken, beaten, a disgusting toy made for hurting—

"Helen!"

Peyton's strong hands wrapped around her waist and lifted her off her feet. He pulled her back through the main entryway and into his living quarters. The access hissed shut in front of her face with a decisive click, sealing off escape. Voice strained, Peyton commanded the sentry computer to lock.

She froze, held tight in his grasp, unable to face him, unable to pull away. She quivered inside, balanced on the knife edge of emotions too powerful to contain. Relief that he'd come after her. Fear that it was out of pity. And the foolish, twisted hope that somehow it was because he cared.

The world was a confused blur of contradictions that made her cheeks wet and her throat raw.

Think of nothing. Feel nothing, the voice inside her coached. *You are stronger than the pain. You are stronger than everything.*

But try as she might, she couldn't stop the tears slipping silently past her guard. Or Peyton's draw as he wrapped her in his arms again, cradling her from behind.

"I'm sorry," he whispered beside her ear, causing a shiver of heat to pass through her. "So sorry for what's been done to you." Remorse drenched his voice, along with a hard edge of anger.

A couple of deep steadying breaths and her voice became usable. She thrust into it all the shame and frustration screaming for release. "Why? Because I disgust you?" The door before her wavered as fresh tears brimmed and released. He tensed, as if to reply, but she cut him off with a shake of her head. "No. I don't blame you. It's not your fault. You didn't want me in the first place." He'd said so right from the start, hadn't he? Unable to continue speaking about it, she closed her eyes, choked by the humiliation inside her as reality curled around her heart, leaching away her anger at him, and smothering it with the truth she'd tried so hard to deny.

She gripped his muscular imprisoning arms with tear-stained hands. She'd been a fool. Such a fool to think he could ever care for a creature like her. An android made of clever codes and Frankenstein dreams. She wasn't even human. Any delusions otherwise were her own fault.

"Shhhh, baby," he soothed. His fingers brushed over her lashes, wiping away her tears. "You're wrong," he murmured against her wet cheek. "So wrong." The dark stubble of his day-old beard prickled her skin. "I do want you. I've wanted you since I first saw you. Can't you feel how much I want you?" His hold tightened. His rock-hard cock jutted against the soft flesh of her ass. "I want to bury myself inside you so badly, it hurts." Urgency made his voice a throaty rasp...and very, very arousing.

Her breathing changed with the images of blatant, burning possession his words conjured in her mind: hot greedy touches, his breath against her skin. Panting. Urgent. While he stretched her, filled her, made her scream with the pleasure of having all of him.

The hope inside her trembled, threatening to flare to life. She ached for him to touch her like that. To make the loneliness go away. To claim her the way he should have done the moment she'd awakened to his kiss.

He began to nuzzle her neck, nipping around her sensitive earlobe. One strong hand slid up to cup her breast, the other splayed wide across her abdomen, holding her against him.

"You don't disgust me. I fucking disgust myself." Heavy with censure, his throaty whisper fanned across her neck. She closed her eyes, absorbing the feeling of his heat against her skin. "Wanting to take you like this, like a goddamned animal. After the hell you've been through. It's sick. I don't want to hurt you." But he didn't pull away. His hips pressed against her ass, his arousal unmistakable. Her sex clenched tight, hungry to claim the thickness of his hard cock.

They trembled together, swaying to the beat thudding between them. His spicy, warm scent filled the air so thickly, her head spun. The ache inside her expanded, tingling through her with raw need. He wanted her. He wanted *her*. Even broken and damaged as she was, he wanted her. The hope within her bloomed into fierce existence. She grasped at it, held it tightly, hardly daring to think.

Tears forgotten, she sucked in a breath. "I need this." Her voice sounded strange, distorted, not her own. "I need to feel something more than sickness inside. I need you to show me pleasure, to give me new memories. Show me how good it can be, Peyton. Show me that I belong to you."

She twisted in his arms, wanting to face him, to see the heat filling his voice mirrored in his eyes. There. Twin sparks, angry and raw and filled with self-loathing, but sparks just the same. They brightened as he looked at her, fed by the fire burning within him.

"Please," she whispered, begging the fire. "I need this."

His answer was a low growl as his hands slid down her hips and cupped her ass. Then he quickly lifted her up and thrust her against the door.

The sudden display of strength, so powerful and primal, sent a jolt of pleasure through her. She gasped and wrapped her legs about his hips, clinching herself to him, enjoying the feeling of his hard body nestled against her sensitive sex.

She wouldn't delude herself into believing he cared about her beyond the connection that imprinting had made. But he did need her, and he wanted her with a fierceness that made her breath scarce.

Her sigh of pleasure became muffled as his lips swept against hers, claiming her in the way she'd craved since the first time she'd seen him. His mouth moved over hers, firm and commanding. Pressing, teasing. He nibbled and kissed her lips until she had no choice but to obey. She opened for him. Fully. Completely. His tongue slid against hers, filling her with feverish desire. *Please*, she begged him with a moan, *please,* as his blatant possession devoured her. She clutched him tight, her fingers pulling at his hair.

This.

This fiery need.

Oh, yes, this is what she wanted. This was what would chase away the horror she'd endured and bring meaning to her life.

Her moans intensified as his hand slid beneath the bottom of her shirt and caressed her naked ass. She shivered as desire spread from his touch through every inch of her body. All he had to do was lift the hem and she'd be bared to him, body and soul. She yearned for the contact, the connection, the pleasure he'd shown her yesterday.

Dragging her mouth from his, she held his hot gaze. "Take it off," she said and lifted her arms over her head, encouraging him to remove her shirt.

His cheeks were flushed, his eyes dark with the intense need hounding him. "Hell," he said, his voice a low rasp. "You're killing me." His throat moved in a tight swallow, but he lifted the shirt up over her head in a quick movement and tossed it onto the floor.

Then he stilled, studying her, his ravenous gaze roaming her naked body from her sex to her face and freezing on her breasts as her nipples reacted to the caress of cool air. She shivered, but not from the lack of clothing. Every inch of her body was reacting to the heat in his eyes and the need burning from him.

But denying the fierce rhythm of his pulse, he cradled her against the door, and gently, ever so gently, he touched her left nipple with his fingers. "You are so beautiful," he whispered with an agonized groan, and she could see the shadow lurking inside him, the dark cloud of memories of what had been done to her. It eclipsed what he was experiencing now, causing him to wince as he traced the contour of her nipple, the stroke of his fingers tentative, almost reverent.

Fresh tears stung her eyes. She didn't want to think of the pain she'd endured or remember the bite of the knife against her skin. All she wanted to feel was the pleasure that only he could give her.

"Touch me," she said, her voice unsteady. "With your mouth. Like yesterday."

His eyes closed as he breathed in deeply, his jaw clenching tight. A shudder rippled through him, as if he struggled for control. When he looked at her again, his gaze was filled with a fierce light. "You will look at me. You will not move your eyes from mine. I need to see your pleasure. If I cannot see it, I will stop. Do you understand?"

She nodded, finding it hard to breathe with the force of the conviction behind his words. Placing her hand on his cheek, she traced the strong line of his jaw and the stubble shadowing it, then guided his mouth to the hardened tip of her breast.

True to her word, she held his gaze as sensations assailed her. The soft warmth of his mouth, tingles and ripples and exquisite pleasure from the stroke of his tongue. Around and around, in a gentle circle, he moved his mouth over her sensitive flesh.

Awareness tangled in her mind. The hot wetness of his lips, which sent electric shivers through her body. The memory of cold, sharp metal as it bit into her tender skin and tore the frightened nerves apart, ripping them from her body.

The tang of blood trickled in her mouth as she bit her lip to stifle a scream. His hot breath played over her skin, his gaze full of concern. He started to pull back, but she clutched at his hair, seeking strength, struggling to keep her eyes open wide.

"More," she begged. "Please."

His brow furrowed slightly, but he obeyed. His gaze remained on hers as his mouth moved over her once-ravaged nipple again. Now whole and plump, the pinnacle of flesh tightened as he suckled it in a gentle movement that changed her inner scream to a gasp.

The tension in his brow altered, became fierce with the determined fire in his eyes as he assessed her, weighing her reaction. He was in control, complete, utter control of her pleasure. But there was no fear here, just searing need that made her wet to be like this with him.

"Yes," she whispered, encouraging him, letting him hear her pleasure in the breathiness of her voice. "So good. Like that."

He kept it up, licking and teasing her nipple, causing tingles and warmth to spread through her body. She clutched at his hair and began to move restlessly against him, her shoulders pressed against the door. It was hard to hold his gaze when her eyes kept wanting to drift shut, when she wanted to just lean her head back and enjoy the sweet sensation he caused inside her.

But the fire in his eyes kept hers riveted to his, and his promise of no more pleasure if she dared to disobey. How had she ever lived without this curling, tickling, burning need that snaked through her body at his command and made her breath come in little gasps?

His lips and tongue rolled the tip of her breast, tweaking it lightly. At the same time, his palm slid over her hip and caressed her naked sex. His fingers danced across her swollen nub, just once, a delicate whispered touch that jolted through her entire body.

"Ahhh," she gasped and arched as sensation shot deep into her abdomen. Between the two points of contact, an ache blossomed, sharp and hungry. "Peyton," she breathed.

Her fingers spasmed in his tousled hair. Tingles rippled along her thighs. Exposed, vulnerable, she arched her back and pressed down against his fingers. Her bare toes curled as her thighs clutched him tighter.

Moaning, he explored her sensitive nipples and clit, his mouth and fingers swirling around each in tandem. Hot breath raged against her skin. Hot energy built inside her core. It circled to the play of his fingers, soft, then sharp, fast, then slow. Her nerves quaked as sensations ricocheted through her body, jagged as a knife, yet soft as a kiss. She trembled, moaning, her body taut as pressure built to his command.

His groans vibrated from his mouth to her breast, making her nipples tighten even further. They ached, so taut and hard. The left one wet from his mouth, like his fingers were wet from her slickness. The pleasure mirrored yesterday's, but it was so much more powerful than when she'd touched herself while he watched. This time, he was in control, complete delicious, intoxicating command of every sensation that ripped through her. From the touch of his fingers, to the hardness of his erection as it strained against her. And his eyes, always assessing, binding her to him with his ferocious, burning need.

He moved his hips, his body gyrating, over and over, keeping the rhythm of his fingers on her clit. Close to shattering, the desire to taste him, to feel all of him, spasmed impatiently through her.

The fire in his eyes flared, the feverish hunger within him a visceral thing she ached to feed. Unable to contain her desire anymore, she gripped his hair and pulled his mouth from her nipple, then covered his hot, wet lips with hers. His tongue thrust into her mouth at the same time as his finger dancing on her clit pressed hard.

"Peyton!" she moaned into his mouth.

Color faded to black, then burst in a halo of bright stars. She bucked against his hand, riding the sharp waves of bliss that suffused her body. As the world became unfocussed and spun, his mouth moved off hers, but his dark eyes remained fixed on her own, his hungry gaze capturing every jerk and shiver of her pleasure as it rippled through her.

"So beautiful," he whispered. He cradled her against him, his body quivering, or maybe it was hers. She couldn't tell where she ended and he began. "Absolutely fucking beautiful."

Weak, she sagged within his arms, held up by his strength and wrapped tight with his warmth. As his lips dotted her cheek with gentle kisses, she smiled, joy-filled laughter bubbling inside her.

"You okay?" he asked as his fingers stroked her hair. His breathing was uneven, his pulse quick beneath her ear.

She pulled back and caught his gaze. It flickered with concern for her, but his eyes were bright with that fiery desire, which she'd begged into existence. It waited impatiently for release now, the bare-faced urgency reigniting her own desperate need in an instant.

She nodded in order to assuage any concerns he might have. But she wasn't okay. She was more than okay. She was ecstatic, yet consumed with an intense longing that demanded to be fulfilled. That orgasm had been wonderful. And he'd been so gentle, so caring with her. But she didn't want gentle anymore. She wanted him. All of him. Now.

"You're sure it wasn't too much?" he asked, studying her. He gently stroked her flushed cheek with his fingers as her breaths settled.

Too much? She felt like laughing. She wetted her lips with her tongue as she played with his collar. "How many of these shirts do you have?" she asked with a coy smile.

"A few," he said, his brow furrowing in confusion.

"Good. Then you won't miss this one." Hooking her fingers in the "V" above the buttons, she gave it a sharp yank. The buttons went flying as fabric tore with a satisfying ripping sound.

His eyes widened as he grunted, startled by the sudden movement. "Christ," he murmured, staring down at his wrecked shirt. She quickly slid the fabric off his arms and tossed it to the floor.

A grin curved his lips as his gaze met hers again, sparking with hungry fire. "I never liked that one anyway," he teased. He readjusted his hold on her, his fingers flexing against her ass as a shudder quaked through him, primal desire straining to be released.

"You are so, incredibly sexy," she murmured with a breathy smile. His naked, muscular shoulders were bunched tight with the tension of holding her up against the door, his chest muscles rigid. She slid her palms over them, enjoying the feeling of his heat and strength and the way his skin flexed as she lightly grazed him with her nails. She bit her lip. He was magnificent in every way she could imagine. Strong, yet so gentle, it made her heart ache.

He swallowed hard, his smile slipping, his expression becoming serious. "I'm not the sexy one," he whispered. The fire within him flared bright in his eyes as he held her gaze.

She wanted to burn in that fire. Let it devour her, body and soul, and chase away any memory of pain. "More," she whispered as a shiver of craving rippled through her. She looked deep in his eyes, letting him see the truth of her need. "I want you to show me everything."

"Hell, yeah," he said, and lifting her high in his arms, he carried her to the bed.

***

There was heat and need.

And maybe thoughts buzzing through his brain, but he couldn't hear them over the slamming of his pulse through his veins. His body trembled from the effort of holding her up against the wall as he placed her on the bed. Or maybe it was from the want raging through him to fuck her to tomorrow and beyond.

She was exquisite, perfect. So hot as she moved sinuously against the sheet, the look in her eyes mirroring the urgency in her voice.

"Take me, Peyton."

"Yes." He'd take her all right. To the fucking cliffs of insanity and back.

But this was so different than the blissful joining he'd had with Sarah. Or the quick, impersonal fucks he'd shared with others to purge the burning loneliness.

He slowly stroked his hands down Hell's soft curves, appreciating her warm flawless skin. Her eyes widened, her pupils dilating over the pleasure she experienced. His heart twisted, threatening to break.

How could anyone take a knife to such beauty?

This was a girl who'd only known torture. Not a virgin, yet innocent in so many ways.

And hungry for him to show him the pleasure she craved.

She spread her legs, exposing herself to him.

"Please. I need to feel you inside me."

Christ. His cock jerked. He almost lost his load right then and there.

But she trusted him to do this right, to make everything right. To teach her what real pleasure was. And no way in hell was he going to fail her now.

Forcing his gaze away from her glistening, hot-pink pussy, he caged her small body with his large one and rested his weight on his arms.

"Patience, sweetheart," he whispered by her ear. Her skin smelled sweet, her hair like citrus and fuck-me-now pheromones. "Do you know what the key to true pleasure is?"

She shook her head, her breath moving fast between her lips.

"Anticipation."

He kissed her softly. Her ear, her hair, her jaw. Slowly making his way down her neck, taking his time even though his cock was hard and his will threatening to break.

When was the last time he'd had sex? Weeks, months? It felt like a decade. But there was having sex and then there was making love. And the way her skin flushed as he kissed it and her fingers tangled in his hair, taking his time was reaping rewards far greater than a quick bang.

His cock could wait.

At least for another minute.

Maybe.

Fuck. She tasted so good. Her nipples like hard buds. He couldn't get enough of them. Or her.

"Peyton," she whimpered. She bit her lip, her eyes shut tight, a look of intense delight suffusing her face.

His breath was tight in his chest as he made his way lower.

He studied her spread thighs.

Stick to the plan, Peyton. Go slow. Show her how good this can be.

He kissed the soft skin of her belly, enjoying the sharp intake of her breath and the way her muscles flexed. The curve where her thigh met her belly was soft velvet. He traced his tongue along it and touched her naked sex with his tongue tip, glancing upward to catch her reaction.

Her eyes met his, full of heat and hunger.

"Do you like this?" He traced his tongue lightly against her seam above where her clit was peeking within her folds. She tasted like the orgasm he'd just given her moments before.

Her fingers tightened in his hair. "Yes," she whimpered.

"Good. So do I."

He licked and sucked at her clit, spreading her folds with his tongue, and teasing her with the tip. Over and over. He was lost to her now. Her taste, her scent. The soft sounds of pleasure she made. The way everything about her seeped through his skin and into his brain. As she shuddered close to orgasm, he pulled back and placed his cock where his tongue had been.

She fit so perfectly. So goddamn right. He didn't know where she ended and he began. There was only heat and need and the perfect rhythm of their bodies moving together, and as he quickly reached his peak and it felt like his lungs were bursting as he shouted from the sweet intensity of it, there was her soft pleasure-filled voice calling his name.

HOME IS WHERE THE HEART IS...ISN'T IT?

THE NEXT AFTERNOON, Hell sat at the kitchen table. Deliciously sore, but rested from the night's pleasurable exercise, she smiled as she studied Henry, who stood beside her. "No, I didn't tell him I finished fixing you. It's supposed to be a surprise," she said. She put down the micro-caliper and patted the robot's new limb. "There, that should help. How does it feel?"

Henry wiggled his three-pronged claw, one of six arm-like appendages which stuck out of his metallic barrel-like body. The unblinking photo-receptors on his conically shaped head brightened in what she took to mean delight.

"Better," he replied in his monotone voice. "No squeaks."

"No squeaks," she agreed with a nod.

He grasped a cloth from the table and turned back to wiping the counter as the gyroscopic stabilizers in his clunky legs wheezed.

She smiled, pleased by her achievement. Putting him back together had given her a sense of accomplishment she'd never experienced before. At The Factory, she'd been nothing more than an experiment kept in a locked room. But here, in this tiny apartment she was beginning to call home, it was both awkward and exhilarating to try new things and discover her likes and dislikes.

Fixing mechanical things, for instance, that was something she enjoyed doing. Henry had come a long way since she'd first seen him in pieces on Peyton's worktable. While repairing him, she'd incorporated a few upgrades, the ability to vocalize more than non-committal beeps being the most obvious. It hadn't taken much, just some re-working of his programming matrix to be more like her own. But the difference meant that Henry was now learning to relate to the world and discover his potential.

Would Peyton like the change? She frowned at that thought. From what she'd observed so far, he didn't appear to like much of anything except swearing, whisky and steaming-hot jungle sex. The first two flaws required readjustment, but the latter characteristic—that was something she could definitely get on board with.

Sex. Yes, she unquestionably liked that. Especially the climaxing part. She fanned her face with her hand as she thought of the pleasure Peyton had shown her last night. She'd lost count of the number of orgasms he'd given her, but excitement rippled through her at the thought of experiencing the rush again. *Pleasure lessons. Peyton's pleasure lessons.*

The sound of the shower turning off made her heart skip a beat.

Peyton was awake.

He'd be ready to eat soon. That's what humans did, didn't they? When they got up for the day? They ate breakfast together?

She dubiously eyed the plates of scrambled soy-protein and toasted wheat bread she'd placed on the table. Cooking was a thing she'd discovered she did not enjoy. Unlike the organized symmetry of programming a machine, which made instinctual sense to her, deciding which food elements went best together for optimum flavor seemed more like an art form than an exact science.

Pale and rubbery, the soy had lacked appeal when removed from the wrapper. It didn't look much better now. The addition of sliced pickle cubes gave it a dash of color, along with a distinct vinegary smell. She wrinkled her nose. Maybe some kind of sauce would help?

Rising from the table, she pulled open the refrigeration unit. She peered at the stocked shelves of square cartons and cylindrical containers. Most held the nutritionally balanced beverages she'd discovered the previous day. They had a pleasant flavor, but she was in the mood for something more substantial today and certain that Peyton had worked up an appetite.

Selecting a red jar, she opened the lid. Sweet, fruity aroma tickled her nose. That one might go nice on the bread. While turning to place the jar on the table, movement in the kitchen doorway caught her eye. She hastily set the jar next to the plates and, assisted by the back of a chair, fixed a pose of pretended nonchalance.

Clad only in boxers, Peyton lounged in the entryway. His shower-damp torso flexed as he wiped his neck with a towel. Droplets of water pearled on the smooth lines of his shoulders and rippled in the contours of his abs. His dark hair stood in matted curls; his dark eyes riveted her to the spot.

At the intensity of his stare, heat simmered up her neck and burned her cheeks. She sucked in air and let it out in a breathy smile. "You're awake," she said and cringed inside. What a stupid thing to say. Of course he was awake. The sound of his shower had prompted her to make the food. "I mean, did you sleep well?"

He'd been asleep for almost twelve hours, gently snoring, his normally creased brow smooth and untroubled and the shadows beneath his eyes gone. When incoming messages beeping on his monitor had alerted her in the early morning hours, she'd thought of kissing his relaxed, sensuous mouth to wake him. But she hadn't wanted to break the unaccustomed peace surrounding him, so she'd set his message response to "do not disturb" and let him sleep. He was up now, though, and her lips tingled as she remembered the possessive feel of his own pressed against them. She wanted to experience it again.

A smile tipped those warm lips of his. "I haven't slept like that in a very long time. How are you?"

"Good," she said, a fluttery feeling in her belly. "I'm really, um...good." So much for nonchalant. Could she be any more awkward? His all-consuming presence seemed to leach breath and thought from her. Or maybe it was the way he toweled himself dry, rubbing and patting skin that radiated heat with such force it weakened her knees.

"Why aren't you wearing the clothes I brought you yesterday?" he asked with a slight frown.

She fidgeted with the hem of his shirt. The one-piece jumpsuit had lacked appeal. It was big and baggy and didn't have his scent. "I like wearing this," she said and stroked her palm down the warm, familiar fabric. "It reminds me of you. Would you like me to take it off?" *And not put anything else on, except you?*

"Humm." His gaze slid to her bare legs and roamed her body in a way that made her pulse speed up and her nipples tighten. He stilled as he stared at the distinct outline of them poking beneath her shirt. "You're not wearing anything underneath, are you?"

"No." She tightened her grip on the chair, feeling embarrassed and excited at the same time.

Why was it so difficult to face him this morning? Who cared if they'd had sex at least three times before collapsing into bliss-filled exhausted sleep? They were still the same two people. Weren't they? Or maybe that was the problem.

His eyes met hers again, his gaze sparking with memories from last night. He swallowed hard, as if about to say something, when the sharp sound of plates clanking together interrupted, drawing his attention to the robot.

Peyton's brows rose, as if he'd only just realized the service-bot was there. "Henry?"

The robot swiveled toward him and raised one of his spindly arms. "No squeaks," he said.

Peyton's eyes widened. He glanced back at Hell. "You taught him how to talk?"

"Yes."

Face slack with amazement, he watched the robot busily stack dishes in a cupboard. "It's good to see you working again, Henry," he said after a moment.

The robot twisted one of his claw-like hands in a gesture reminiscent of a thumbs-up and settled back to cleaning the kitchen.

Peyton shook his head as his gaze dropped to the tidy table with its double plate setting and stack of toast. "Incredible," he said. "You finished fixing Henry, reprogrammed him, *and* you made food." He stroked his freshly shaved chin, eying the soy concoction on the plates as if trying to determine what kind of food she'd made. "What else have you been up to while I slept?"

"I—you aren't mad, are you? I wanted to surprise you."

He draped his towel over his shoulder. "Well, call me officially surprised," he said with a smile. His metal chair squeaked as he pulled it out from the table and sat down.

The spicy aroma of his shower-fresh cleansers filled her senses, reminding her of the night's activities. Her stomach growled.

The corners of his mouth twitched. "Hungry?"

"Starving," she admitted, heat rising to her cheeks all over again. *But not for food.*

"You've been busy," he murmured, catching her gaze with a knowing flash of fire in his eyes, "working up an appetite."

She lifted her own chair, so it didn't scrape the flooring and settled onto it. "So have you." Warmth licked the inside of her thighs with the echo of his busy tongue. Oh yes, he'd worked, and worked, and worked to find all her pleasurable secrets.

The mission to forge new memories and eradicate the old pain-filled ones had definitely been accomplished last night. Despite her begging him to take her quickly so she could immediately drown in the pleasure, he'd resisted. Instead, he'd laid her gently on the bed and told her she needed to learn patience, that anticipation was the key to true pleasure, and if she wanted him to show her everything, she needed to behave.

Smiling inside, she'd happily let him take his time in proving his point by kissing every inch of her body, building up her excitement with gentle licks and caresses until she could barely think and every nerve ending screamed for exquisite release.

He'd allowed her to cool down, just long enough to catch her breath, and then he'd done it again—turned her into a quivering, shivering, moaning thing as his fingers explored and pleasured her in ways she'd never imagined could exist. Feather-light touches, urgent touches, the puff of his breath on her wet skin.

Then he'd done it again.

And again.

Until finally, with his body quivering from the strain of holding back, and as she'd shuddered on the brink of yet another orgasm, he'd slowly entered her.

His eyes had bored into hers, the light in them fiercely burning. There'd been an awkwardly timed joke about him not getting "zapped" by her vaginal security system, humor meant to hide his worry over him causing her pain as she adjusted to his size.

Pain? There had been no pain, only the exquisite pleasure of his hardness rubbing against her slick skin and filling her. She'd been so wet...so *wet*... and ready for him.

She'd cupped his cheek with her palm and softly

whimpered his name, reminding him with whispered words, which barely made it past her lips in the tenderness of the moment, that she belonged only to him.

That conviction, or perhaps it'd been the way she'd angled her hips and wrapped her legs about him, had shattered his resistance and he'd finally unleashed the feral beast within him. In one quick thrust, and a mighty groan, he'd stretched her, claimed her and filled her to the hilt.

After that, everything was a blur of hungry, bliss-filled sensation. Hot, panting breaths and moans. Spicy, sweat-damp skin. The decadent taste of him, the feel of him plunging inside her, again and again.

She crossed her legs, her thighs tingling from the flush which suffused her skin as she remembered the sound he'd made, his deep, primal growl of pleasure when he'd emptied himself inside her. The complete abandon and intense ecstasy in his voice was embedded deep in her cortex. She closed her eyes and replayed it, shivering as she remembered how his hands had clutched her tightly, how he'd trembled and flexed, his body arching as he released his pent-up desire and whatever other emotions he'd kept bottled inside for far too long. She had finger marks on her ass to prove it. Faint ones that didn't hurt, but marks just the same.

She smiled. She'd left marks on him too. Crescent grooves on his shoulders where her nails had scored his skin. She hadn't meant to hurt him, but having him like that, skin to skin, with nothing between them except a mutual desire for pleasure, and hearing him groan and shudder and knowing that she'd given that to him—that experience had been more than she could contain. The excitement of the moment still hummed through her. She was getting wet just thinking about it again now.

"Earth calling Hell. Hello, Hell. You there?"

Her eyes flashed open.

He watched her with humor twitching his lips, as if he knew exactly what she'd been thinking about.

"Um, yes..." Feeling hot, she played with her collar. "I was just...ah," What the heck had they been discussing? She glanced at her top. Oh yes, he hadn't answered her earlier question. "What about my shirt?" she asked with a coy smile. "On or off?"

His gaze flicked to hers, then quickly dropped to her nipples again. His brow furrowed slightly. "Keep it on while we eat. Then we'll...talk." Glancing at the food, he poked the rubbery soy on his plate with a fork. "This is very, ah...interesting."

Talk? *Talk?!* She stared at him in disbelief. He wanted to talk?

No, clearly he wanted to have sex, with the way his skin radiated pheromones and his blood raced through his veins. But, for whatever reason, he wasn't going to act on it, at least not yet. Unless 'talk' was a euphemism for something much more naughty? No. She sighed. He wasn't that diffident. Peyton was putting up walls again. Or maybe, she realized with apprehension, despite last night's intimacy, they hadn't been broken down.

"I've never cooked before," she admitted quietly, her gaze dropping to the unappealing soy scramble. "At The Factory, they didn't..." She paused, remembering the metal tray filled with unappealing sustenance that had been pushed through a slot on her door. "They always brought me food."

At the mention of The Factory, his expression darkened. But it disappeared as he glanced at her. "I'm sure it's fine," he said. "Thank you."

Scooping up a forkful of the egg-like substance, he sniffed it. His nostrils twitched, his brows rising. But with a smile, he popped the forkful of scramble in his mouth and chewed.

The lines around his eyes tightened. He swallowed quickly and reached for a glass of water. "Very pickle-y," he sputtered. "But not bad," he added hastily with a glance in her direction. He shoved another forkful in his mouth, chewing with great deliberation.

Picking up her own fork, she dipped into the dubious mixture. The unseemly pickle smell filled her nose. She was pretty sure food wasn't supposed to smell like that. But if Peyton said it was okay, how bad could it be?

Pinching her nostrils between her fingers, she took a bite. Sour, rubbery texture filled her mouth and she knew he'd lied. She grabbed a napkin and spat into it, chasing away the taste with a gulp of water. "Oh, the Maker, it's terrible."

"Don't worry about it," Peyton said with a shrug, a smile twisting his lips. "It doesn't matter."

She looked at him, her stomach twisting. Was he laughing at her? "What do you mean it doesn't matter?" It did matter. It mattered a great deal. What kind of 'perfect companion' couldn't cook a decent meal? One that had been kept in a box all her life, tortured and abused and robbed of nearly everything of importance, including life skills.

"I mean, it doesn't matter," Peyton insisted, studying her. His smile slipped as tears began to prickle her eyes. "Henry, take these plates, please, and leave them on the counter," he said to the robot.

While Henry did as instructed, Peyton reached for the toast and spread some of the fruity substance on two pieces. Passing one to her, he took a bite of his own as he regarded her carefully. "Listen, Hell," he said after a swallow. "I don't expect you to cook for me. And I don't expect you to clean my place." He gestured with his free hand at the spotless room.

My place. Not our place. He still thought her an intrusion. The dry toast rasped her fingers. She placed it on the table, untasted.

"What exactly do you expect me to do?" Sitting back in the chair, she crossed her arms over her chest and leveled him with a hard stare. "Open my legs when your need rises and file my nails when it doesn't?"

He coughed, choking on the toast in his mouth.

Avoiding his bewildered look, she rose from the table with a screech of her chair and grabbed the plates of scramble from Henry. Without a word, the service-bot moved out of the way as if sensing the mounting discord, his heavy feet clomping as he left the kitchen.

Damnit! Desire for Peyton was imprinted into every fiber of her body, and she was more than ready and willing to act on it. But deep inside, she needed to be more than just a toy designed for pleasure. She needed a purpose greater than lust, which excited the body but didn't fill the heart. There had to be something more to her existence than this.

She turned to the waste disposal chute. Peyton's chair squeaked from behind her. His large hands grasped the dishes from her fingers before she could scrape the meal away.

"Save it," he muttered, jaw tense. "Just needs the right spices added." He reached into a cupboard and then stopped. "Where the hell did my storage boxes go?" A frown tightened his profile. Opening the next cupboard, he shook his head and brought out a container. "The pickles were an inspired touch. But a little bit less of them would have been better. You just need time to learn," he said, scraping the leftovers into the dish. "You'll have plenty of time to practice being domestic, if that's what you want to do. I'm leaving today." He sealed the container with a snap of the lid and turned to the refrigerator.

Cool air danced along her skin as he placed the leftovers inside the fridge. Her heart stumbled. "You're...leaving?" She couldn't keep the shock from her voice. Not even two full days together and he was abandoning her?

"Some machinery broke down in the northern sector. I'm part of a team needed to fix it." He leaned against the countertop and folded his arms across his chest. "I'll be gone for a couple of weeks."

"Machinery?" Oh. So he wasn't walking out on her. The slamming of her heart settled into a determined rhythm. "Well, I'm going too, then."

"No. You're not," he said as if that were the end of the conversation.

"Yes. I am," she insisted, irritated by the exasperation in his expression.

He shook his head as he turned and left the room, snapping the towel from his shoulder.

Following his stride, she pointed at her chest. "I may not know how to cook a decent meal, but I do know how to fix machines. I can help you."

"That's not the point," he said. Tossing the towel onto the couch, he picked up a bag that was lying there. "And before you say, 'what is the point, Peyton,' like I know you're going to do...." His accusing glare and mimic of her high-pitched tone sucked the words right out of her mouth. She gnashed her teeth together, caught in his game. He pointed his finger at her. "Let me remind you of the fact that people from The Factory are looking for you as we speak, and if they find you, they'll be more than happy to take you back to hell. My legal claim to you is disputable. I'm fully prepared to defend it, but as you ran away rather than being bought, it makes the validity of who owns you confusing. And the Council may decide, despite the abuse you've suffered, that you belong at The Factory until all the official crap is sorted out."

Why do I have to be anyone's property? Can't I belong to myself? she thought as the reality of her situation chilled her to the core. "If people are looking for me, wouldn't I be safer away from the Dome with you?"

He shook his head and thrust the bag into her hands. "Dolls don't usually come along on excursions," he said. "And the less people who know who you really are, the better. So do me a favor and keep the door locked while I'm gone. And for God's sake, wear this disguise and try to act like a brain-dead Doll when my team arrives." He glanced at the monitor on the wall and shoved her toward the bathroom. "Which, since I slept in late, is going to be any minute. So hurry up and change!"

She clutched the bag of clothing to her chest as he pressed his hand against her back, forcing her through the doorway.

"Yesterday, you wanted me to be more human," she declared over her shoulder.

"I changed my mind!" he shouted as the door slid shut between them with a hiss.

In the light of the small bathroom, Hell opened the bag and pulled out the contents. The clothing in her hands seemed obsidian silk. Examining the bundle more closely, a chuckle rooted in her belly and expanded. He wanted her to wear this, did he? And parade around in front of his friends? Well...she'd put it on, all right, wig, corset, panties and all, and he'd see just how much like a brain-dead Doll she could be.

PLEASURE LESSONS

"JESUS CHRIST," PEYTON groaned, thrusting his fingers through his still damp hair. "She's driving me insane." Case in point, wasn't he now talking to himself and grinning like an idiot?

Turning away from the closed bathroom door behind which Hell had disappeared, he caught sight of Henry standing next to the kitchen entryway. The bulky robot's optical sensors regarded him with what looked suspiciously like humor.

"Don't you say a word," Peyton said, with a point of his finger at the shiny metal service-bot.

Henry hunkered down and remained satisfyingly silent. *Thank God*. One irritating droid in the house was enough. Two of them would be a living nightmare. Why couldn't Hell ever just listen? Why did she have to question everything, get under his skin, be so damn sexy that he couldn't get her out of his mind?

Imprinting pheromones were one thing. A simple trick of chemistry designed to ensure satisfaction with a product. But this attraction was...he didn't want to think about what it was. It was claustrophobic, is what it was. Every cell in his body seemed to ache for her. His blood fired through his veins with his need to touch her, taste her, pound inside her tight sex. The force of it made it hard to breathe, let alone think.

And he really needed to think. Short term and long term, he needed plans in place where Hell was concerned. But right now it was hard enough to get dressed, let alone consider the future.

With a wave of his hand, he opened a panel in the wall, expecting to find a clean shirt. The underwear he'd brought Hell yesterday greeted his stare. The image of her perfect, naked body flashed in his mind, causing his pulse to quicken. "Fuck," he hissed between clenched teeth.

Slamming the drawer shut, he opened the next one. There were his shirts, rearranged in color coordinated symmetry: brown, black, grey, blue, all neatly folded in crisp, precise piles. The urge to deliberately mess up the order twitched through his fingers. When had she found time to do all the reorganizing? And fix Henry? In less than two days, she'd put him back together and programmed him to speak. My God. She was incredible. Had she slept at all last night?

Grabbing a long-sleeved shirt, he thrust his head through the V-neck.

If it wasn't enough that he couldn't keep her out of his mind, she had to invade every part of his life, including his kitchen. His goddamned kitchen. Organizing things. Shit. Who knew where she'd hidden the ingredients for making, well, anything? It was as if she knew he liked to cook and had set out to deliberately mess with him.

He pushed his arms through the sleeves and pulled the close-fitting fabric down his chest. To be fair, he hadn't felt the urge to cook a decent meal in ages. And his home had looked like a train wreck of total disregard. Especially his workroom. He hadn't realized quite how disastrous the mess had been, until Hell had arrived.

And now?

And now, here he was, dressing in a tidy home, the worst breakfast he'd ever tasted lingering on his lips, and all because she cared. This remarkable android whose abysmal treatment by humans should give her no reason to care about anything, cared—about him.

His heart skipped a desperate plea for assistance to keep beating. "Hell," he muttered. She was programmed to form an attachment. He shouldn't read anything more into it than that. But he couldn't get out of his mind the look in her eyes when she'd come at his command. Or the way her unguarded pleasure had made his cock fucking harder than granite.

He was in danger of becoming addicted to her, which, given the circumstances, was a completely fucked-up fact.

Twelve fucking hours. When was the last time he'd slept like that? *Last time you emptied a bottle of whisky alone, asshole,* he reminded himself. But it hadn't been drinking that had made him pass out last night.

Finding a neatly balled pair of socks inside yet another wrong drawer, he sat heavily on the edge of the bed.

Their mingled sex scents wafted upward, invading his nostrils. Not that he'd been able to forget the sweet fragrance of her body. Or the soft feel of her skin. Or the little mewling sounds she made when close to climax. The room spun as blood raced straight to his cock. Again. She'd turned him into a walking hard-on. In the kitchen, it'd taken every ounce of strength he had to not flip up her shirt, bend her over the table, and dive balls-deep into her tight pussy.

"What about my shirt? On or off?" Her coy words played through his mind.

Holy fuck. A man could only take so much. But after last night, she must have been sore. He hadn't been exactly gentle.

Examining the bed, he found blood there. Dark stains amongst the tangled sheets. He quickly gathered them up and replaced them with fresh linens, anger twisting his stomach. The bastards had made her so tiny, so impossibly fragile, and her re-grown hymen as tender as a virgin's.

Goddamnit. He covered his face with his hand and sat on the bed again.

Pleasure lessons. That's what she'd called it.

Lessons to make the horror go away and show her what good sex was like. He'd initially resisted, thinking it was wrong to feel so aroused for her. She couldn't possibly want him that way after all she'd been through. But then she'd pleaded, and when he'd seen the desperate need in the depths of her eyes, he'd realized she was searching for a new experience upon which to reprogram and heal herself.

So what was a guy to do? Say no? Watch her cry while the goddamn memories of her abuse overloaded her fragile android brain? He'd done what had needed to be done and given her what she'd wanted. Only he wasn't sure who had received the lesson in pleasure. He'd never come so hard in his life as he'd done with Hell last night.

He shouldn't have done that, taken her fully. Claimed her.

But his response to her body was uncontrollable. Slight and delicate, her fine skin felt like silk beneath his fingers and her tight sex—my God—the exquisite pleasure he'd experienced when wrapped in her silky heat. And she'd been so damn brave, begging him to fill her with his rock-hard cock, urging him on with her soft cries and moans until pleasure devoured both their fears. And then she'd asked him to do it again. And then again, until they'd lain together, sweaty and satisfied, cradled in each other's arms while exhaustion carried them into sleep.

He stared at the bathroom door. For all his life, there had been only Sarah in his heart. Her voluptuous curves and happy sighs had been his idea of perfection. Hell, however, consumed him with a force which shocked him to the core. Was it the pent-up frustration of two years of near celibacy? The fact she'd imprinted to be his perfect companion?

Frowning, he found a clean pair of pants and slid them on.

Sexual gratification aside, he couldn't deny he liked Hell. The way she walked, the sound of her voice, the way she looked at him with bright eyes. They way she'd tried so hard to make him breakfast or whatever type of meal it had been. The fact was that she'd tried, despite not knowing how—that fact, and the reason why, had nearly broken him then and there.

The goddamn fucking Factory. Someone was going to pay for what they'd done, for forcing him to chop apart her mind in order to save her life. And he'd needed to save her life, because damnit, he couldn't stand there and watch such a beautiful soul die.

It didn't mean anything that he liked her.

Or that she liked him. Her root programming insisted she anticipate his wants and needs. Did he need an argumentative sex doll who occupied every part of his thoughts?

"I've got to get away from her," he muttered, pressing his palms to his eyes. Distance. Yes, distance from her would help clear his mind, and hard work fixing that broken Reclaimer in the northern sector would keep him busy enough to not miss her. Maybe. Who the fuck was he kidding? He missed her now and she was only in the bathroom changing into the Doll costume he'd borrowed from Jared. Bambi's 'Vamp-whorer' outfit. He frowned at that thought. Knowing Jared's taste ran to the kinky, maybe he should've checked to see exactly what Hell would be wearing.

He glanced at the wall display. One fifteen. Jared and the others were late. He should bolt out the door and meet them part way instead of letting them into his home. But thanks to Jared telling everyone he was gifting him an android, they wanted to see the 'new Doll'. So, it was show them all something or risk suspicion, and suspicion would lead The Factory to his door and Hell faster than he could spit.

Did she understand the danger? Would she play her part?

Would she actually do as told without question for the first time since he'd met her?

He shook his head and turned to the bathroom. Not a sound from inside. Time to check up on her.

Or not.

The sudden buzz of the sentry's visitor alert changed his path mid-step. He turned toward the main entryway instead. A quick check of the monitor showed him Jared waiting on the other side. Sucking in a steadying breath, he opened the access and stepped aside, allowing Jared entry along with...oh no.

"Hello, Peyton," snapped Aunty Jo, as she pushed past him and glanced around the room.

The seams of her aging, round face pulled into a frown, making her look like a disgruntled old apple. At barely five foot two, she came up to his pecs. Her piercing green gaze had the gigantic ability to diminish him to the size of an ant, however.

"Aunty Jo. What a pleasant surprise," he managed, and shot Jared an accusing look. "You really suck, you know that Jarhead?" Though when subjected to Joanna Chase's inquisition, anyone sucked at keeping secrets. "Where's the rest of the team?"

The younger man grinned. He remained by the door, his hands shoved in his pockets. "Waiting at the transport, ready to leave when you are."

"Uh-huh." Well, at least that was something. No witnesses for the interrogation about to begin. Peyton kept his expression pleasant as he turned back to Joanna. "Can I get you anything, Aunty Jo? A cup of tea, perhaps?" *Or maybe a shot of whisky and a hefty dose of Valium?*

Her censuring frown deepened as she placed her hands on her hips and pinned him with a glare. "I want to see this Hell."

"Humm," Peyton stroked his jaw, feigning thought, or rather the lack of it. "I think she's out exploring the storage rooms right now." *Dear God. Please don't let her come out of the bathroom. Please don't let her come out of the bathroom. Please don't let her come out of the bathroom.*

A hiss sounded as the bathroom door slid open behind him and the last vestiges of his belief in the Almighty vanished.

"Did you call, Master?" Hell's sexy voice purred. "I'm ready to continue playing our game," she added, and emphasized the point with the sharp, stinging snap of a whip across his ass.

"*Jesus fucking Christ!*" Peyton bellowed, jumping from the shock that coursed through him. He stared, dumbfounded, at Hell. "What the sweet fuck are you doing?"

"Exactly what you asked me to," she said with a sweet smile. "I'm being a brain-dead Doll." She glanced at the whip in her hand and wiggled it, seeming amazed at its serpentine alacrity.

His mind stuttered as he took in her transformation from innocent looking waif to dominatrix. Her blond hair was tucked up beneath a black jaw-length wig. Red lipstick slicked her lips, giving them a glossy sheen. She'd applied some kind of make-up that made her lashes thick and dark, and her amber-colored eyes seem even larger and alluring. For some reason, she appeared to have a strap-on Devil's tail. But the thing that made his cock twitch, despite the sting in his ass, was the black lace panties and the corset-style bustier that she wore. Peek-a-boo holes had been cut out of the satin fabric to reveal her breasts. The openings were clearly meant for a much larger pair, but the bottom edge of the corset still lifted them up, offering her thick nipples to him. The pink buds tightened as he watched.

Holy shit, his brain whispered as he struggled to think with all the blood rushing to his cock.

"Holy shit," Jared said from behind him, jarring Peyton back to the moment and the reality that they weren't alone. Jared's jaw practically rested on the floor as his eyes took in Hell's exposed breasts and knee-length stiletto boots.

"Better cover yourself, dear. The men are in danger of drooling to death," Joanna said, tossing a bucket of ice water onto Peyton's arousal with her dry, piercing tone. She cocked her brow at him, clearly not impressed. "Is this what you've been up to for the past two days?"

Fuck.

"No," Peyton answered. He quickly grabbed a blanket from the bed and covered Hell with it. She teetered on her heels as he wrapped it about her shoulders.

"Yes," Hell said with a smile at Aunty Jo. "Peyton's been teaching me all kinds of new things."

"I see," said Joanna, and pursed her lips, studying them both.

"Shut up," Peyton hissed in a low tone close to Hell's ear. He jerked the whip from her grasp and tossed it to the floor. His ass still stung from the first pass. He wasn't going to stand there and let her do it again. "Just shut up and don't say anything," he warned.

He should have known better.

"Did I hurt you, Master?" Hell said, concern creeping into her eyes as she looked at the whip and back at him. "Do you want me to kiss it better?"

A strangled gurgle wedged in his throat as he stared at her, his pulse flushing his skin. The urge to throttle her coursed through him as Jared burst out laughing. She was deliberately provoking him? Fuck it. What she needed was the pink heat of the whip on *her* ass accompanied by a good hard fucking. He'd show her who was boss. And by the look in her eyes and the way her pulse fluttered at her neck and the sweet scent, which rose off her flushed skin, he was pretty sure she wanted that too.

"Come here, girl," Aunty Jo demanded.

Hell's brow furrowed. She looked at Peyton, discomfort clear in her eyes. But there was no escape as Joanna frowned at the hesitation and walked toward Hell instead. With a strong grip, she pushed Peyton aside and peered closely at the so-called Doll.

As her wrinkled fingers touched Hell's cheek, her keen gaze widened in surprise. "My God," Joanna whispered. "It's true, isn't it? When I heard the story, I was skeptical, and when I walked in the room, I wasn't sure ..." She touched Hell's cheek again and rubbed her fingers together as if considering the warmth. "But I can't tell the difference.... Your skin.... You're real, aren't you? A living android."

At Hell's quick, affirming nod, Joanna shot Peyton an accusing glare. "Why didn't you call me as soon as you realized?" Before he could answer, she shook her head and pulled her tablet out of her pocket. "Lee? It's true. All of it." She sounded both excited and irritated as she spoke into the communication device. "Yes, that's right. Sarah's Bio-roid is standing right here wearing a—what in God's name are you wearing, dear?" She shook her head again, her lips pulling into a frown, but her attention had refocused on whatever Lee was saying. "I agree. Yes." She nodded. "Okay, sounds good. You let the others know what's going on. We'll meet you in a few minutes." She smiled at Hell. "Grab a jacket, dear. You're coming with us."

"I am?" Hell said, sounding pleasantly surprised.

"*What?*" Peyton shouted as his heart skipped a beat and his planned opportunity to gain some distance from Hell quickly evaporated. "No, she's not."

"Yes. She is. Lee wants her to."

"Dolls. Do not come. On excursions. There isn't enough room." It would be cramped enough in the small transport with a team of six people without any extras coming along.

"Peyton," Joanna said sounding unimpressed by his attempt at reasoning. "You can't seriously want to leave her here alone. From what I understand, she's just had major surgery."

Fuck. He turned to Jared. "Is there anything that you didn't let spill? What happened to keeping things a secret?"

Jared shrugged. "She's Aunty Jo. You know what she's like."

Peyton matched his aunt's unbending stance and peered down at her. "She'll be fine here on her own. Henry can keep her company."

Joanna's brows flicked in surprise. "Henry? You fixed Henry?"

At the sound of his name, Henry said an excited, "No squeaks," from where he stood beside the kitchen. He gave a little wave of his arms in greeting.

Both Joanna and Jared sucked in surprised breaths. Peyton closed his eyes, belatedly realizing his mistake in mentioning the droid.

"Henry!" Jared shouted. His lips split into a wide smile. "Dude... What are you doing hiding over there? Trying to pull a fast one on us?" He walked to the robot and gave him an affectionate pat on the head.

"No squeaks," Henry said again, his optical receptors brightening at the attention, and his newly fixed claw hand clacking smoothly in demonstration.

"Shit!" Jared said, sounding impressed. "You can talk now? No more beep, beep, beep? That's major!" He glanced at Peyton. "You didn't tell me he was getting upgrades."

"Uh, yeah..." Peyton said, feeling like his life was spinning further and further out of control.

"Henry can talk?" Joanna asked in a puzzled voice as she watched the robot spin his arms around for Jared.

"I taught him how," Hell said with a proud smile. In fact, she was beaming as she watched the happy little robot.

Joanna looked at her sharply. "Wait. You did? *You* reprogrammed him to talk. Not Peyton?"

"Yes. It wasn't very hard," she added at Aunty Jo's penetrating stare. "I just instructed some of my nanites to alter his code and added a few tweaks to his processing array. It was fun."

"Fun. You found it...fun." Joanna said. "Can you fix other machines too?"

"Yes. Probably." Hell said. She kept her gaze carefully trained on Joanna's and avoided looking at Peyton, but he was certain she could feel his glare burning her crisp with the volatile mix of emotions coursing through him. "Mechanical things make sense to me," she added. "I'd like to help if I can."

"Well, then," Aunty Jo said, giving Peyton that smug look he knew so well. The one which meant he was shit out of luck in trying to win any argument against her. "That settles that then, doesn't it?"

STILETTOS

"PEYTON, I CAN walk by myself. You don't have to shove." For what seemed like the hundredth time, Hell tried to pull her arm free from his vise-like grip as they hurried down the stairwell from his home into the main habitat, heading for the transport.

"Shut up," he muttered close to her ear. An echoing din of footfalls battered the narrow corridor, but his irritation carried loud and clear. "Keep moving and just *shut up!*"

Despite the thick padding of her—or rather his—coat, his grip on her arm didn't budge; if anything, it tightened. She shuffled along, trying to keep up a good pace, but at three sizes too large for her frame, the garment hung like a net, snagging her hasty steps. The spike-heeled boots cramping her feet didn't help either. While the skimpy costume she wore beneath the coat was too big in the chest, the boots were a bit too small. Go figure.

Upon reaching the landing, she stumbled. Peyton prevented her from careening headlong onto the mesh flooring by jerking her backward against him. Her black, bob-style wig swung over her eyes. Within the tight prison of his arms, she pushed the hair back into place and squeezed in a breath.

"I don't understand why you're so angry. It's not my fault your aunt insisted I come along on the trip." It was obvious that he hadn't wanted her to. After the intimacy they'd shared, the rejection stung, even though she'd gotten what she wanted and officially been asked to join the team.

His warm breath snorted past her cheek. "You're still talking. Keep it up and I'll use that goddamned whip on your ass." His hand snaked beneath the coat and pinched her bare bottom.

The clang of footsteps on the landing behind them drowned out her squeal. Peyton pushed her toward the next set of stairs as Joanna Chase huffed into view with Jared close behind. The old woman's lined face offered what seemed a permanent scowl. Did none of the Chase family know how to laugh?

Joanna put her hand on Peyton's arm, stopping her nephew from escaping further.

"And another thing," Joanna said. She'd been rattling off opinions since Peyton had angrily dressed Hell in his jacket and practically shoved her out the front door. "What were you thinking when you called the poor girl Hell? What kind of a name is that?"

"A completely appropriate one," he muttered under his breath.

"She deserves a proper name," Joanna chastised.

"Her full name is Helen, Aunty Jo." Peyton explained, sounding tired. "After Helen of Troy."

"Well," Joanna huffed. "You should use it then. And I cannot believe you made *Helen* dress like that," she said, stressing the use of Hell's full name as her cool green gaze flicked over her from head to toe. "She's far superior to one of those whore-dolls."

"That's the whole point, Aunty Jo, I'm trying to disguise her." With a tight-lipped suffering sigh, he shook his arm free and nudged Hell down the next steps.

"As what? The treat of the week?" The noise of their footfalls couldn't drown out Joanna's scornful tone. "Like a peek-a-boo corset would attract absolutely no attention whatsoever. Not to mention the spiked collar and strap-on tail. Where are your brains?" The sneer in her voice indicated exactly where she thought his brains were—firmly dangling between his legs.

Which wasn't really fair, Hell mused. Peyton had shown considerable restraint and kindness since he'd first unwrapped her. This aunt of his needed to stop being so judgmental, especially about people's appearance.

The treat of the week?

Reaching the main walkway, Hell stopped and shot Joanna a smile over her shoulder as the older woman descended the last steps, graying brown hair bobbing against her shoulders. "Actually, I don't mind the clothes. They make me feel kind of, you know, *grrrrr*." She punctuated her best sexy purr by clawing the air with her newly red-lacquered nails.

Joanna's frown deepened into a fissure of extreme distaste.

Jared winked at Hell as he stepped past Joanna. "They make you look kinda *grrrr* too," he said, giving her a once-over with an approving smile that disappeared when he met Peyton's angry gaze head on. Though Jared's shoulders didn't fill the ubiquitous V-neck shirt popular amongst the Domers as nicely as Peyton's, the mischievous grin in his blue eyes seemed intent on making up for any lack of stature. "You're a dog, Peyton."

A feral growl was, in fact, emanating from Peyton. "You're a dickhead," he snapped at Jared. "A whip? And fangs? What kind of shit do you get up to with Bambi?" He shook his head and shut his eyes. "No. On better thought, don't answer that."

"What? You don't *vant* me to *suuuuck* you, Dr. Chase?" Hell asked, showing off her fake fangs with a dramatic flair of her lips.

"Are you still talking?" Peyton asked with a look that promised she'd feel the sharp sting of the whip across her ass in the very near future.

Which, she had to admit, was oddly exciting.

Renewing his hold on her arm, Peyton pulled the coat closer around her body, concealing her chest from Jared's interested stare. The corset pushed her bare breasts up, forcing her nipples to protrude even further than normal. They rubbed against the coat, stimulating them to perpetual hardness. She longed to feel Peyton's lips on them again. Like yesterday. Oh, the Maker, she could definitely go for that again. But despite the intimacy they'd shared last night, he hadn't even kissed her yet today.

Instead, his lips firmed in an unhappy line as he helped her hobble in stiletto heels along the grilled metal catwalk. "This is ridiculous. No one takes a Doll with them on a trip to fix machinery," he muttered.

"Nonsense," Joanna barked from behind them. "A person of her talents is exactly what's needed on this mission."

Peyton froze mid-step. "*What?*"

Jared burst into laughter.

"Mechanical talents, you lummox," Joanna hissed, tweaking Jared's ear. "We can use her help fixing those Reclaimers. And despite what you—" she pointed a finger at Peyton and narrowed her eyes as he opened his mouth to argue, "think of the danger involved, we've been given a gift with Helen. Like it or not, she's here now. Best put her to use working magic with the machinery like she did with Henry."

"I'm surprised you don't want him coming along too," he muttered.

"That's a good idea," Aunty Jo said with a nod. Her gaze became thoughtful. "He could be of use too." She pulled her tablet out of her pocket and typed a quick message on it.

"Sure. Why not?" Peyton said, his voice heavy with sarcasm. "We can all sit around in the transport having a wonderful chat. Maybe play Parcheesi."

"If this is about the upgrades I did," thrusting her hands on her hips, Hell lifted her chin to face Peyton square in the eye, "Henry deserves the right to function at his top potential. I sacrificed some of my own nanites to give him basic sentience and the ability to vocalize his emotions. I did you a favor."

"Yeah? I didn't ask you to."

"Did anyone ever tell you you're an ungrateful ass?" she hissed, tapping his chest with her finger.

From the corner of her eye, she saw Jared raise his hand, a grin splitting his lips wide. "I have."

Peyton ignored him. "Ungrateful?" His gaze never wavered from Hell's; the angry blaze in his eyes flared as they widened. "Fine." He cupped her shoulders and pushed her out of his way. "You want to come on the mission? Then come. Sure hope you like digging around in worm shit."

He stalked away across the catwalk, apparently done with her, his relatives, and the whole conversation. His long stride took him around the corner and out of sight before she'd sucked in a steadying breath.

"Worm shit?" she asked as his retreating footsteps echoed down the stairs.

Beside her, Jared nodded. "Make them big enough and worms will eat just about anything. The Reclaimers are very large vermicomposting units. Toxic wasteland in...clean soil out. The idea was the brainchild of my sister."

"Sarah?"

He nodded. "That's right."

Oh, the Maker! "No wonder Peyton's so upset. Anything dealing with Sarah usually sets him off."

"Don't worry, dear." Joanna's seamed face broke into an unexpected smile that lit her eyes. The difference from her perpetual scowl was startling. The light expression gave her a much more youthful appearance. "I haven't seen him this worked up in a very long time. But it's not memories of Sarah that has him hissing a fit." She laughed and gave Hell a knowing wink. "Jared, why don't you go and get Henry? We'll wait here for you."

At his reluctance to head back upstairs again, she prompted.

"Go on. There's work to be done and the others are waiting."

"Fine," he said and threw his hands up in frustration as he relented. "But I'm using the freight elevator back down."

Joanna shook her head. "Freight is for freight, not people."

"Technically Henry is freight," he muttered.

"Actually," Hell said. "You might find he's closer to being 'people' now."

"Thanks," Jared said. With an exaggerated eye roll, he shook his head and continued up the stairway.

She liked him. She liked all of Peyton's relatives that she'd met so far. Even Aunt Joanna, who waited until Jared was out of sight and then said in a conspiratorial murmur, "Now that we're alone, dear, why don't we have a little chat?"

"About what?" Hell asked and returned Joanna's steady gaze. They were of a similar height, but Peyton's aunt had mastered the art of seeming much taller than she was by the way she held herself with an air of importance that she definitely shared with her nephew.

The Chase family were clearly used to being in charge.

Joanna gave her a nod, a look of approval in her assessing gaze. "When I agreed to help purchase a Doll for my nephew, I certainly didn't have you in mind, but I have to say, despite your current attire, I'm pleased."

"Thank you. I think," Hell said.

Joanna laughed. "I like your spirit. So does Peyton. But I do have concerns. Have you imprinted on him yet?"

Nothing like cutting right to it, Hell thought. "Yes," she said. Not that it was his aunt's business, but she respected the honesty of the conversation.

Joanna nodded. "I figured as much. The way he looks at you..." She sighed. "He's not a man who let's go easily. He loves too deeply. Always has since he was a child." Her lips tipped into a frown as her mind conjured memories Hell could only guess at.

"What happened to his parents?" Hell asked.

Joanna looked at her sharply. "Perceptive," she said and gave her another quick nod of approval. "A transport accident. Early on in the resettlement program, when we were still building the colonies. It was a quick death, luckily, but it left Peyton orphaned at age six. I've brought him up as if he were my own since then. It hasn't always been easy."

"I imagine not," Hell agreed, thinking of how irritating and demanding Peyton could be. She examined the different reasons Joanna might be relating Peyton's history to her and gave a nod of her own. "So he lost his parents when he was young. And then later on, the love of his life."

"Yes. Friends since childhood. Inseparable. They were the same age. Born in the first wave of New Earth children in the re-population plan. I think he always loved Sarah."

His childhood sweetheart. "And part of him always will," Hell admitted. Did she feel threatened by that? Maybe, if she was being truly honest. It was hard to share a man like him with anyone, even a ghost.

...the best of men. The only man... the warm voice whispered in her mind, teasing her with its hint of knowledge that disappeared when she tried to grasp it. She frowned in frustration.

Joanna smiled, but it held a concerned edge. "But now you're here."

"Yes," Hell said, starting to feel uneasy by the pressing questions and probing remarks.

"Exactly how long are you intending to stay, dear?"

Hell's frown deepened. "He's my Master. I belong to him."

Joanna barked out a laugh. "Don't give me that crap. You aren't like a regular Doll. A 'brain-dead Doll', as you say, would never argue and talk back to him like that. You don't have submissive programming. You have free will or you would never have managed to run away from The Factory. Not that I blame you after everything you've been through there."

Hell stilled. "How do you know about that?"

Joanna laughed. "Jared is a sweet boy, but he doesn't understand discretion as well as he should at times. I happened to be there when he was talking about you with his father."

Oh, the Maker. "Does everyone know about me?"

Joanna shook her head. "No, dear. Lee had to be told. He's the leader of our little colony. But besides himself and the trusted members of our team on the transport, your secret is safe for now."

For now. That disclaimer had an ominous tone to it. But realistically, if she wanted to have any kind of life here at Deliverance Colony, the rest of the inhabitants would eventually have to know about her true existence and accept her for who she was.

"When this business with The Factory is done, what are you planning to do?" Joanna asked.

"I don't know," Hell said and pulled Peyton's coat tighter around her body. "I assume it will be up to Peyton." She would like to always be with him. Living in his home. Getting pleasure lessons and helping him fix machines. Maybe he would come to love her one day, maybe he wouldn't, but they could build a life together. Couldn't they?

But Joanna shook her head. "Your skill at imprinting is very strong. He's already sunk deep under your spell. He'll never want to let you go. Not without a fight. And I won't stand to see his heart broken again."

"I would never do that," Hell said and crossed her arms over her chest. Joanna was overstepping the line to make such an accusation.

A wistful look crossed the elderly woman's features. "How do you know?" she asked gently. "From what I understand, you ran away from an abusive situation. A life you have trouble remembering. I certainly can't fault you for that. But how do you know if you truly belong to Peyton or to someone else?"

Hell stood there mutely, having no answer to that. In her heart, she wanted to stay at Deliverance Dome with Peyton. But what if that were simply wishful thinking? What if reality handed her a different card?

Joanna reached out and put her arm around her shoulders, giving them a tight squeeze. "I can see your intentions are true, Helen. And, imprinting aside, that you care for my nephew a great deal. But speaking from experience, I want you to tread carefully in respect to your relationship with him. For your sake and his. Life has a habit of being unfair."

"I know," Hell said and felt the weight of truth settle upon her. Life wasn't fair. She knew that better than anyone else. From the moment she'd been created, she'd been treated unfairly. She had the deep scars to prove it. "But that's why fighting for the things we love is so important," she whispered.

Joanna's eyes crinkled at the corners as a surprised smile lifted her lips. For a moment she just stood there, seeming at a loss for words. Then she shut her eyes and shook her head. When she opened them again, they seemed misted over. Was that a tear? Hell stiffened as she was pulled into an unexpected and tight hug.

"If only the whole world would see it that way, dear," Joanna whispered in a choked voice.

NO SQUEAKS

PEYTON KNEW THERE was going to be trouble as soon as he saw the crowd hanging around the transport bay. He cringed inwardly as he scanned the faces milling about the rectangular room. When it came to leaving on excursions into the wilderness to fix machinery, well-wishers would often come by before departure to offer a friendly send-off. The crowd was large today. Just his luck. But people wouldn't miss taking a break—any break—from the daily routine. And who could pass up a juicy bit of gossip?

"Hey, Peyton. How's that new Doll working out? Haven't seen much of you in the last couple of days."

Peyton kept a smile on his face and greeted the middle-aged cook's smug grin and backslap with a nod. "She's keeping me busy, Derek," he said, truthfully.

"Yeah, I bet," the portly, dark-haired man said with a hearty laugh.

Making his way through the crowd as quickly as possible, Peyton fended off several similar conversations with polite nods and laughs as he headed to the transport. The main door to the multi-legged all-terrain vehicle stood open, its boarding ramp extended.

Lee Palmer stood by the ramp, supervising the loading of a box of equipment, which was being carried by the other two members of the repair team: Rusty and McClellan. He'd known all three men for as long as he could remember, and each were as different from the other in appearance and personality as oil was to water. But he'd trust them all with his life if he had to.

Walking backwards up the ramp, Rusty suddenly stumbled and let go of his end of the heavy cargo container. It hit the ramp with a loud clang, causing McClellan to lose his hold as well.

"Careful!" shouted Lee as the crate shook the metal ramp.

McClellan shook his head at Rusty, a frown on his face. "Too much for yer skinny arse?"

"You looking at my arse again?" Rusty shot back. He wiped his hand through his red hair with a scowl as McClellan barked out a laugh. Square-shouldered and stocky, he was shorter than Rusty, but being older by a good twenty years, he liked to make fun of the red-haired man's lanky youthfulness and seeming lack of muscle.

"You know, there are anti-gravity lifting plates to help with that," said Peyton as he stopped beside the group.

All three glanced at him in surprise.

"Well, look who finally made it," McClellan said with a sly grin.

"The lifters are charging," Rusty said with a disgruntled frown. He flexed the fingers of his right hand as if they pained him. "The batteries are shit."

McClellan's gaze darted behind Peyton. "Where's the others?" His dark eyes narrowed in concern.

"Coming," said Peyton uncomfortably.

"They should be here any moment now," Lee said looking at a message on his tablet. He raised his grey-streaked brows in surprise. "Joanna's bringing Henry too?" His blue eyes studied Peyton, full of questions.

"Looks like," he replied with a sigh.

"Henry? You mean he's fixed now?" Rusty asked. "I thought it was going to take weeks."

"Well..." Peyton began.

"Wait a minute," McClellan said, cutting him off. "You left your wee Doll alone with Joanna?"

Peyton brushed his fingers through his hair, uncomfortable with the way he'd stormed off and left Hell alone. "Yeah. Probably not my brightest idea." Lord knew what Joanna had talked about behind his back or what Hell would do.

"No shit," McClellan said and started laughing along with Rusty.

Peyton frowned. He shouldn't have gone ahead without her but being around Hell was damn near impossible to endure with her dressed like a vampire-ish sex kitten, wanting to claw his ass. It would have been easier to have just left her locked in his place for safety, but no, Aunty Jo just had to stick her opinionated finger into the pot and stir it up. He'd rather she stick it up her ass, but he'd never been able to tell her no. Probably because, as much as he hated to admit it, she tended to be right about things.

He couldn't imagine how Hell was going to get through this crowd without people seeing through her disguise. The last thing they needed was someone snitching to The Factory and bringing hell fire down on the colony for harboring runaway property.

I shouldn't have left her on the stairs. I should have hauled her back to my place and then fucked her sweet ass goodbye for the week. I can't protect her like this.

He darted his gaze over the crowd again, reassessing the danger. Great. Genova the Gossip had just slipped in the door and was making her way through the crowd toward him. He wasn't surprised to see her given how much she loved to make his business hers, but things would probably have gone smoother if she'd stayed in the greenhouse where she worked.

He looked away quickly, but it was already too late. She'd caught his eye, and now she had a smile that lingered while she sauntered toward him.

"Fuck me," he muttered under his breath.

"Calm down, Casanova," Lee said close to his ear. He gestured at his tablet as if showing Peyton something interesting. "Just act natural. I've filled Rusty and Mac in about Hell's situation," he murmured. "All you need to do is treat her like a Doll and everyone will think she's one. We've brought Bambi along too, to give her credibility." He gestured toward the side of the transport where Jared's dark-haired, voluptuous Doll waited for instructions to board, dressed in suitably kinky attire, and a placid smile on her face. "It's all part of the master plan," Lee said with a smile that crinkled the creases in his aging face.

"There's a master plan?"

Lee laughed, a deep warm chuckle that made his thick, white moustache twitch. He pulled his cap down on his balding head in a gesture of dismissal that Peyton knew from years of experience meant the old man was done talking. Like his daughter, Sarah, Lee enjoyed keeping information close and would never share anything until he was good and ready. Stubborn asshat Palmers.

"Hey Peyton," Genova said as she reached his side. Lee moved away, abandoning Peyton to face her inevitably irritating conversation alone. The traitor.

"Yeah. Hi," he said, being polite while trying to avoid eye

contact. She had that look in her green eyes again, the one that said she'd like to fuck him silly. She was pretty enough with her dark hair, caramel-colored skin, and decent sized rack. But he knew from experience that that was where her attractiveness ended. "Sorry, can't talk now. We're kind of busy getting ready," he said. He started to move away, but she placed her hand on his arm.

Genova studied Mac and Rusty, who were quietly arguing over who should carry the top end of the crate that blocked the ramp. Her brows raised when she noticed Bambi waiting by the side of the ship.

"You guys going to be gone a while? Jared's taking his Doll."

He shook off her grip. "Well, you know how it gets lonely at night on the road." Peyton cringed inside as the words left his lips. Goddamnit...what idiotic brain fart had possessed him to say that?

Genova's gaze flicked over him appreciatively, a small smile pulling at her full lips. "Why don't I come too? I could keep you both company. You remember how good it was when we were together, don't you?"

A faint flush heated his skin as the unwelcome memory of her warm naked body pressed against his flashed in his mind. He shook his head, but he was saved from digging himself into a deeper hole by the clang of heavy metal feet on the flooring as the door to the bay opened and Henry entered. Jared walked at his side, Aunty Jo and Hell behind him.

The crowd stilled as everyone turned to see the newcomers.

Peyton's heart hit his stomach as he studied Hell, her pretty face frozen in a mask of brain-dead obedience and betraying no recognition whatsoever that she knew him. She walked behind Henry as if she'd been instructed to, without so much as a flicker of a question or a wobble in her step, despite the heeled shoes, just like a good Doll would.

The gyroscopic stabilizers in Henry's legs wheezed in the ensuing silence as he made his way toward the transport. But as the crowd parted, he stopped and held up his new claw-like hand. In his monotone robotic voice, he proudly announced, "No squeaks!"

Everyone in the crowd started chatting at once as they surrounded the robot, amazed at his quick repair and upgrades.

"Henry!?" said Genova, but unlike the others, she didn't move to check the out robot. Instead, she glanced at Peyton, the sexy glint in her almond-shaped eyes brightening with admiration. "You did that? Made him talk?"

"Um, yeah," Peyton said, his gaze quickly flashing to Hell and then back at Henry. Hopefully she wouldn't get wind of the lie. But as a normal Doll wouldn't have the capacity to make that kind of upgrade to the service-bot, there was no way round it. "I've been busy," he added as explanation.

"I can see that," Genova said, watching the excited robot with a puzzled frown. "But how exactly did you give him reflexive speech?"

"It's, ah, technical."

The robot did a little twirl, clearly enjoying the flood of attention. His arms and hands spun around while he animatedly chattered, "No squeaks," over and over again. Laughter echoed around the room as people enjoyed the display. It was a good sound. A happy sound, one that Peyton had to admit they didn't hear very often. If he wasn't so worried about keeping Hell safe, he might have smiled too.

Nearly forgotten in the excitement, Joanna and Hell quietly made their way through to where the transport waited. As if on cue, Hell stopped beside Bambi, her expression still and Doll-like vacant. Joanna nodded in approval. "Wait here, Hell, while we get this crate moved off the walkway." She caught Rusty and McClellan's eye with a meaningful nod at the cargo crate and gestured for them to lift it quickly.

Snapping their gazes from staring at Hell, they both did as instructed and grabbed the box again.

Joanna shook her head impatiently at Lee with a scowl.

"Hell?" Genova said beside Peyton. "You call your Doll, Hell?"

Peyton shrugged off the scorn in her tone. Why did everyone have such a problem with that name? "It was a spur of the moment thing," he muttered. Not that he cared what Genova thought of him for it. Or anyone else, for that matter.

"Mmmm," Genova murmured and moved closer to him, brushing against his arm. "I can give you heaven," she said with a wink.

He moved away from her and tried not to scowl as he remembered the moment of weakness that had brought them to this awkward conversation now.

Back when Sarah had first passed on and he was in his deepest, blackest despair—and heavily into whisky—Genova had offered to make the pain go away, if only for a little while.

He'd made the mistake of taking her up on that offer a time or two but had regretted it almost immediately. Genova was very skilled at giving pleasure, but she'd wanted a permanent arrangement instead of a casual thing. It hadn't mattered to her that she already had two other lovers with whom she shared a relationship. She'd gladly have taken on three. Or four. Or however many partners—male or female—that struck her fancy. And she'd wanted Peyton to share them too. But that kind of lifestyle wasn't one he would ever be comfortable with. And the need to avoid her constant badgering flirtations was one of the reasons he'd decided to move upstairs to the storage rooms and live apart from the rest of the colonists.

There was room for only one woman in his life at a time. His gaze strayed to Hell, his heart beating fast.

"You must really like her if you're bringing her too," Genova said, her voice cool with disapproval and laced with a dangerous amount of undisguised jealousy. "I have to say I'm surprised. I never thought you'd go for that kind of thing. I told Jared he was wasting his credits. You need a real woman to satisfy you. With a real pair of tits." She linked her arm through his and brushed her breasts against his side.

He had to admit, she did have a nice pair. They were definitely full and soft. But her interest in him was causing nothing but panic to flare inside him that she'd wander over to Hell soon and take a really good look at her. He needed to get rid of Genova, and fast. He shrugged, hoping she'd drop the topic and move on if he seemed bored with Hell. "She's just a Doll."

"I don't see how she can excite you. She's too skinny and pale," Genova observed with a critical eye. "What is she wearing beneath that jacket?" she asked, studying Hell a bit more intently than he would have liked. She started to move toward her.

Peyton clasped her to his side, pulling her back. "That's her Vamp-whorer outfit," he said, choking back the need to throttle Jared again.

"Really?" Genova said with an interested purr in her voice. She looked up at him, startled by his tight hold, but clearly not minding the intimacy. "I didn't realize you were turned on by that kind of thing." Her brows lifted as she studied him, the fuck-me-now look in her eyes burning brighter than ever. "I've got a costume that will make your head spin." She glanced down at his cock, indicating which head she meant.

"Really?" he asked, playing along to distract her from Hell.

"Oh, yes," she whispered. Her cat-like eyes flicked dismissively at Hell and back to him. "When you get bored of playing with your Doll, come by my place and I'll show you the real thing," she said and ran her hand down his stomach. Her fingers danced over the button on his fly.

The touch was meant to be suggestive, but it made him shudder with revulsion instead. Taking his reaction as a shiver of excitement, she smiled and pressed her lips to his.

The kiss was warm and wet and full of promise. Promise he didn't intend to pursue in any respect, but for the sake of the android standing nearby, he'd pretend to reciprocate. Blood pounded in his ears as he held his breath while her lips moved over his. He tentatively put his hand on her back as she pressed her body against him.

But when her fingers snaked down his fly and brushed his cock, he jumped back and ended the kiss.

"Mmmm," she murmured, laughing. "Are you sure you don't want me to come along for the trip?"

He shook his head, his breath sticking in his chest. "Not with my aunt around," he said and darted a meaningful glance in Joanna's direction. He lifted Genova's knuckles and grazed them with his lips, hating himself for the deception, but needing to keep any suspicion that he might actually like Hell from entering Genova's mind. He had no doubt she was capable of exposing Hell to The Factory if her jealous anger made a visit and she decided to investigate things further. She had a vindictive streak that had made his life hell when he'd first decided to end things nearly two years ago. And there'd be hell to pay again for the game he was playing now. But he'd face that fire when he had to, as long as he saw Hell safe first.

Genova bit her lip, looking hungry enough to eat him on the spot. "How long will you be gone?"

"Two weeks. Maybe three." Maybe I'll never come back, he thought to himself.

"Peyton!" Aunty Jo snapped, sharp enough that he jumped. He quickly dropped Genova's fingers. "We can use some help here." The old woman gestured at the few bags and canisters beside the ramp that still needed to be loaded.

"You'd better go," Genova said, glancing at Aunty Jo. "The old dragon is getting ready to spew fire." She pouted and ran her hand over the contours of his chest, her eyes bright with longing. "I'll be waiting when you get back," she said with a sigh.

He managed to keep a smile on his face while he nodded.

With a coy smile, she blew him another kiss and sashayed back to join the rest of the crowd, probably in search of her conquest for the night. As one of the few women left it the colony, she had her pick, and her favorites. She'd slept with everyone in the crowd several times over.

Feeling disgusted with himself, Genova, and the world in general for forcing him to be a deceptive asshole, Peyton immediately looked at Hell, hoping her gaze was still vacantly staring at nothing and that she'd not seen his little display.

But her eyes were staring right at him. And yep, he could see a flicker of shock in them. And the hurt. Definitely the hurt.

Fuck.

"Jared!" he shouted as Rusty and McClellan heaved the crate on board and freed up the ramp. He reached for one of the bags on the ground. "Time to go!"

Jared nodded and gave him a thumbs-up. He motioned for Henry to move to the transport as Lee and Joanna gathered up some of the cargo and disappeared inside.

Peyton gestured for the Dolls to follow suit. "Come on ladies, let's get to it," he instructed. They both obeyed immediately, just as good Dolls should, walking with their backs straight and expressions devoid of emotion, but Peyton didn't miss the flash of pain in Hell's eyes as she passed him. It lodged like a dagger in his chest.

He shook his head, his mind filled with a mixture of disbelief, frustration, and disgust. Despite the odds, Hell had made it through the crowd with barely a murmur of interest from anyone. But as he followed her beautiful, sweet ass on board, he grimaced. The greater test was yet to come. For the next week he was trapped in a small, three room transport with his brother and father in-law, irrepressible aunt, two horn-dog friends, a robot, a sex doll, and the woman who was quickly coming to mean more to him than the breath in his lungs—and who he'd just treated worse than a dog, for no good reason other than he'd had to.

How the hell was he going to explain his way out of this one?

SHADOWS IN THE GLASS

BUILT IN THE lee of a vast outcropping of ancient, snow covered granite, Deliverance colony's metallic-grey habitat glinted amongst pine trees and scrub in an area called Shelter Valley. It was a pretty place, Hell thought. A river ran near the Dome. Partly frozen in the winter cold, the water sparkled as it danced and played around icy boulders on its way past. Wind turbines lined the top of a ridge, their dark blades spinning slowly against the soft clouds and blue sky, which made up the horizon. Two secondary geodesic buildings had been built beside the first. Greenhouses. Used for year-round farming, she'd been told. Another smaller building stood alongside, where machinery was stored.

And that was it. The entire colony. A tiny refuge for humanity nestled within the wilderness. Yet as small as it was, the sun-kissed, metal structures symbolized refuge, familiarity, and home.

Hell pressed her fingers against the cold window as the habitat slipped away into the distance at an ever-increasing rate. The transport pod's spider-like legs worked at a furious pace, carrying them toward a snowy ridge that marked the valley's northern extreme. Thanks to the independently stabilized design, however, the crew compartment glided along smooth and easy, despite the rough terrain, which choked the landscape.

"It's like a scuttling crab, you see?" A dark-haired crewmate, who'd been introduced to her as McClellan, leaned over and wiggled his hairy knuckles in front of her face. He seemed to have taken on the task of showing off every detail of their conveyance. Which was nice of him, except her mind was focused elsewhere, specifically on the feeling of disillusionment that shadowed her thoughts.

"Articulated limbs are better than wheels for climbing over wreckage and through debris," McClellan continued. "And in the glacial areas, they can pick into ice walls or flatten to become skis. The anti-gravity plating on the chassis bottom helps reduce the weight, like in a hover transport, but this is much sturdier and takes less energy to keep moving." His expectant, dark-eyed stare suggested an appropriately appreciative response was in order.

"That's very fascinating," she said, and glanced out the window again. The ant-shaped transport was now picking its way through a dense section of trees, tall and thick and full of shadows. Catching her pale reflection against the glass, her mind slid back to the scene she'd witnessed in the transport bay between Peyton and the pretty woman with the light brown skin, and the awkward way he'd tried to hide his reaction to her touches. Her *intimate* touches. His skin had flushed. His pulse had raced. His body had tensed with guilt.

And how did she feel about that?

Hell pursed her lips while she considered the question. The lipstick staining her mouth twisted like a red scar in her reflection, but her dark wig framed her face in an oddly familiar way. She pressed her hand on the window again, remembering the feeling of cold glass against her palm.

"What is love?"

The dark-hired woman on the other side of the glass wall smiled, the corners of her blue eyes crinkling. "You're full of questions today. What do you think love is?"

They'd talked of it before. About pheromones and body responses. But the answer remained a mystery. "I don't know," *she admitted.*

"Then I'll have to find a way to teach you. It's a very important thing."

The woman disappeared in a flash of white light as the transport moved from the shadowy trees and into a shaft of brilliant sunlight. Hell jerked her hand back from the cold glass.

I don't know, she repeated to herself as a shiver wracked her. She closed her eyes, her thoughts spinning. "I really don't know."

She didn't know anything.

Not about Peyton, not about love, and least of all about herself. Her head pounded as she thought of the blue-eyed woman. Her face and voice were familiar, yet indistinct. Yes, familiar with the unsettling impression that perhaps she was indistinct because maybe Hell didn't really want to remember her. Or wasn't supposed to. Her past, like Peyton's, was a thing best undisturbed. He was allowed to have his own life with its own secrets, and she should be happy she'd escaped to this one.

And yet...questions poked at her like sharp blades, twisting her up inside. Goading her into feeling irritated with him for daring to have secrets, and at herself for needing to question them. And these intrusive snippets of memories were not helping one little bit.

"Are you okay?" McClellan asked, concern lacing his deep voice.

Hell opened her eyes. "No," she said matter-of-factly. She was far from okay.

Removing her fake press-on fangs, she tossed them into a nearby waste container on the other side of the compartment with a deft flick of her hand. The spiked collar followed suit. McClellan's eyes widened as he watched the smooth, accurate arc and the way the collar landed dead center in the bin with a loud clang.

"Who was that woman talking to Peyton before we boarded?" she asked in the most casual voice she could muster.

McClellan raised his bushy dark brows and blinked. "That would be Genova. She's in charge of the greenhouses."

"How long have they been lovers?"

He pulled at his loose V-neck collar as if it were too tight and glanced at the cabin door. "Ah, you'll have to ask Peyton about that."

She studied the closed door.

When would Peyton be back? He'd disappeared into the cockpit cabin—with an unhappy, "Stay here," tossed in her direction—to speak with an older, graying man named Lee Palmer, whose facial features were a dead giveaway that he was a relation of Jared's, even if the surname hadn't already been the same. Jared, for his part, had gone into the aft cargo pod along with a lanky man introduced as Rusty—possibly in reference to the color of his hair—to secure their belongings and store equipment under the stern eye of Joanna.

Which left Hell sitting in the crew area, hemmed in between McClellan, Jared's vacant-eyed Doll named Bambi, and Henry—all of whom seemed inclined to stick to her like glue. Not that she minded Henry's presence, or Bambi's for that matter. The two robots had been added as diversions for her appearance with the crew.

Henry in particular had proven most effective at drawing attention away from her with his exuberant, "No squeaks!" as he'd shown off his new claw-like hand and functioning arms to the crowd. The well-wishers gathered to send off the transport had been amazed at the service-bot's repairs and upgrades...and congratulated Peyton, of course, for his mechanical expertise. They'd glanced at her with curiosity, but as she'd stood silent beside Bambi and only moved when told—like Bambi—they'd assumed she was like Bambi, except a newer model. So all in all, she had to admit, Peyton's sex-bot disguise had worked. For now.

"So you're the real thing, huh?" McClellan asked giving her a once-over for the hundredth time. He couldn't seem to stop staring at her.

She pulled Peyton's coat tighter around her, feeling more irritated than ever. "Depends on what you mean by 'real' and 'thing'."

McClellan smiled, showing a broad swath of white teeth. "A Bio-roid. A living machine. You look very...human."

"Well, looks can be deceiving."

He flicked a broad thumb in Henry's direction. "Is it true you fixed old iron-ass here in less than a day?" He eyed her dubiously, as if weighing her carmine lipstick and sleek stilettos against the story he'd been told of her technical skill.

"Yes," she admitted with a tired sigh. "I fixed him."

"Peyton must've shit a brick. He's the best we've got for fixing things with his experience as a surgeon. Damn good at it too." The note of pride in his voice spoke volumes of his esteem for his friend. "I bet he was floored when he heard Henry talk."

Floored was perhaps a bit strong. "At first I thought he liked it, but now I'm not so sure." It was hard to tell what to think where Peyton was concerned. He'd shown her so much tenderness yesterday, and given her so much pleasure, it had made her memories of what she'd endured at The Factory seem like a faded nightmare. But today? From the moment their argument had started at lunch, to his little display with his secret lover, he'd been nothing but irritating.

McClellan's bushy brows rose. "Got hot under the collar, did he? Well, he's not the sort who likes surprises." His gaze roamed her body again, as if searching for secrets she might be hiding.

"Surprises? Are you kidding me?" She hadn't hidden a darn thing since meeting Peyton. He knew as much about her as she did. The disguise she currently wore had been his idea, not hers. Peyton was the one keeping surprises. Why hadn't he just told her he was in a relationship? Did he think she would care? He was the Master, the one who set the terms. And if he wanted to see someone else on the side, then he just had to say so. And as his Slave, she'd just have to deal with it. Somehow.

She clenched her jaw, trying to get a handle on the way the idea made her feel like slapping him hard across the face. He'd made her feel special, damnit. Unique. His. Even though she wasn't human. Or a perfect companion.

Was he ashamed of her?

Was that the real reason he'd wanted her to stay locked in his quarters and not come on the trip? It didn't have anything to do with wanting to keep her safe. He wanted to leave her behind so she wouldn't make things more complicated.

Well, if that was his reasoning, he had another think coming. She could be the biggest complication of his entire life.

She smoothed back her dark bob with an angry thrust of her hand. The coat was hot, the wig itched, and the restricting boots and corset made it difficult to sit, even on padded seating. She leaned against the backrest and shifted position. The coat rose, exposing another half inch of bare thigh to McClellan's interest. She sat forward again and pulled the hem down.

"Isn't there something you should be doing?" she asked. Like getting a shave. A bit of scruff on Peyton looked sexy, but on this man it seemed...rough.

"I'm doing it." McClellan's smile broadened. "Peyton's orders are to stay with you and make sure you're comfortable."

"Comfortable. Uh-huh." Right. Including the two robots, three escorts were overkill. "You mean you pulled the short-straw on the, 'keep Hell out of trouble' detail?"

He barked out a loud laugh. "You're a sharp one, no doubting that." His grey, V-necked tunic pulled tight as he folded his arms and sat back, appraising her anew. "More human than 'bot, I think. And pretty beneath all that makeup. No wonder he's so pissed."

"Good to know I bring out the best in people," she drawled. "I think 'pissed' is Peyton's favorite emotion."

"Well, I'll tell ya." The amused gleam in his brown eyes sobered. "I'd rather see him upset than showing nothing at all. And nothing is what he's been showing since...well, you know what, happened, right? With the virus and all?"

His gaze flicked to the view out the window. Ice-rimed scree cluttered a steep ravine, forcing the transport to clamber more cautiously as it descended. She could almost hear its Artificial Intelligence whispering. *Slow down. Move with care.*

Wise advice on all accounts.

She was allowing her thoughts about Peyton to upset her. And the man beside her was not responsible for any of it. She pulled in a deep breath and slowly let it out, forcing herself to relax and focus on McClellan. His withdrawn expression was full of unspoken grief.

"It must have been hard for you all. Losing so much," she said softly. Had McClellan lost family too? A mate? Perhaps children? She reached across and touched his hand.

It was a gesture meant to comfort, but he jerked his fingers away from hers. He peered down and flexed his hand, as if the contact had somehow hurt him. Older than Peyton, but not yet middle aged, the muscles of his bearded jaw tightened as he nodded. His face remained averted while he ran his thumb across his knuckles where she'd touched him.

"Peyton saved us." His deep voice lowered, filled with sadness as well as an edge she hadn't heard in it before. "He found the cure. Kept this place going when we thought we were all dead. He never gave up. Not even after Sarah died." His fingers curled as his gaze snapped to hers, his eyes dark and intense. "So you keep that in mind, when using that soft touch on him. He's no fool." His tone was filled with a warning that matched the one in his heated stare.

"Neither am I," she said. Did he think she was trying to play him? After he'd been studiously ogling her for half an hour?

He held her gaze, assessing her with cool regard. "No. You're something else. The world's first living Doll." He didn't sound like he trusted the idea very much.

She smiled despite the edginess she was feeling. "Listen. Peyton is a good man. He deserves happiness, and I mean to help him find it." It was the truth, as painful as it felt right now with the anger and sense of betrayal that simmered deep inside her. But it was truth, nonetheless. And now it was spoken, it hung in the air between her and McClellan like a dead weight that he assessed for its strength.

He arched his brow. "What if he doesn't want to be happy? Did you ever think of that?"

"I've thought of it," she said with a nod. "And it's a load of crap.

Why do you think he drinks so much whisky?"

McClellan's face broke into an involuntary smile. He shook his head and burst out laughing. "I like you. I don't know exactly what you are, but I do like you."

She supposed she should be pleased with his assessment. But instead, it made the feeling of disillusionment deepen. Humans were so judgmental. Were they ever truly satisfied with anything they had?

Thinking of her own desire to achieve perfection, she frowned. There were many things she needed to learn, gaps in her life to fix before she could ever hope to get rid of the human-sized dose of self-doubt she was experiencing right now.

"Can I ask you something?" At McClellan's nod she added, "You don't happen to know how to cook, do you?"

He opened his mouth to reply, but a loud snort intruded as the cargo pod doorway opened. "Now that sounds like a recipe for disaster," Joanna said, stepping through into the crew cabin.

Jared slipped past her. "What does?"

"Hell just asked if Mac could cook."

"Cook? Him? Hell, no." Jared's easy laughter filled the room. "He'd burn water." He gestured back toward the cargo bay with a jab of his thumb and focused on McClellan. "Stuff's all secured and accounted for, so you can stop staring at Hell's legs and go start calibrating the diagnostic equipment."

McClellan snorted. "Tell Rusty to do it."

A red-haired head poked around the doorway behind Joanna, snub nose smudged with dirt. "Nope. Your turn. I already did the regulators." His green eyes danced as he dusted his hands on his dark brown pants. Younger than the others, his slender freckled face still held the softness of youth. "It's my turn to make sure Hell's comfortable." His russet brows waggled.

"Like hell!" spat McClellan, standing abruptly. "She doesn't need a pup like you trying to hump her leg."

"I think—" interjected Joanna with a curt wave of her hand. "What Helen needs is a bit of space to herself." Her shrewd glance traveled over Hell's wig to her spiked heels. "And a new change of clothes. Why don't you come with me, dear, and we'll see what we can find?"

Grateful for the excuse to leave, Hell stood. "Thank you. These boots are a pain." Numb from being pinched for so long, her right foot twisted as she stepped forward. Jared was there before she hit the floor. He grasped her with his arms and held her close, keeping her upright. McClellan's hands followed a scant second later, grabbing her hips from behind to steady her. Sandwiched between two slabs of male, she tried not to breathe in their unappealing, not-Peyton scents and hissed in pain as blood tingled painfully into her deprived toes.

"I can't leave you alone for a second, can I?" Peyton demanded, his voice dry. In the excitement of falling, she'd missed the sound of the cockpit door opening.

McClellan's hands were gone from her hips in an instant. Jared pulled back but kept her propped up with a tight hold on her shoulders.

"She fell," he said in response to Peyton's unamused glare.

"My boots," Hell explained with a point at her feet. Though why she owed him any type of explanation was beyond her at the moment.

Peyton ignored her as he crossed the room, attention on Jared's lingering hold. "When I asked you to keep a close eye on her, this isn't quite what I had in mind."

Jared snorted. "She'll fall if I let go."

Hell gritted her teeth. What did Peyton think she'd been doing? Entertaining the troops? "You really need to lighten up," she muttered and tested out her feet by wiggling her toes. Tingling pain answered her.

"Do I?" Peyton said. His eyes flashed with anger as she caught his dark gaze.

"Definitely."

Catching hold of her arm, he grabbed her out of Jared's embrace.

She whimpered as her feet protested the sudden return to full gravity. "Give me a minute," she said and sagged toward the seat again. "I just need to get these boots off. Bambi has smaller feet than me."

Peyton growled under his breath and caught her about the middle. Then lifted her up and tossed her over his shoulder as if she weighed nothing. The coat bunched as he did so, dragging her thin panties out of place. Cool air kissed her exposed butt cheeks. She squeaked and tried to pull the coat down again.

"Peyton!" she cried out.

"Stop squirming," he ordered.

She slapped his ass.

His grip tightened, squeezing the corset into her sides. She stopped struggling and gasped for air as he stomped toward the cargo pod. At least she assumed it was the cargo pod. Upside down, the wig flopped over her face. What the others must be thinking, she couldn't see or tell.

"Out!" Peyton ordered, as he stepped through a doorway. Quick footsteps and a snicker passed by—Rusty?—before the door slid shut.

A mechanical hum vibrated the air, along with a strong scent of lubricants, which reminded her of Peyton's workroom. Blood rushed from her head as he righted her on a padded bench. Dizzy, she blinked for a moment before his face came into focus.

His fingers gently brushed the hair from her forehead. "Does your head hurt?"

She stared at him. How could someone sound concerned and grumpy at the same time? She shook her head. "No. It's fine. No thanks to you. Did you have to embarrass me like that?"

"You provoked me." Dark hair fell across his brow. It shadowed his eyes as he squatted and began to unlace the shiny black pleather, which trapped her calves and feet.

She leaned back and dug her fingers into the seat's coarse upholstery. "I provoked you? You tossed me upside down like a...like a Doll."

"You are a Doll."

"I am not!" Well, technically, she was a Doll, a manufactured plaything, but he didn't really think so little of her, did he?

He glanced up, dark eyes glinting in the cargo pod's overhead lights. "Maybe..." he said with a grin, "...you need to lighten up."

The teasing ass! She jerked her foot away. "Everyone could see my ass!"

"And a fine ass it is, too." He grabbed her foot again and continued to ease the tight binding. Relief echoed in the wake of each loosened lace and despite her annoyance, she couldn't resist an appreciative sigh. "Nicely rounded, but not too plump," Peyton added. "I'm sure it'll look even sweeter pinkened by that whip."

16

PUNISHMENT

"WHAT? THAT'S NOT funny," said Hell. Peyton was joking about the whip...wasn't he?

His lips tightened in a dangerous smile.

Oh, hell! She pressed back against the bench. He sat between her and the door, and the rows of floor-to-ceiling shelves of net-clad equipment on either side offered no escape. "Um, Peyton?"

Grasping her heel, he tugged on the boot. It slid off her foot after a moment of wiggling. His fingers caught her flexing toes; his thumb skimmed along the ball of her bare foot and pressed hard. Pain and pleasure mixed in an exquisite jolt that arched her back, clenched her eyes tight, and released as a gasp.

"Did you think I'd forgotten?" His softly spoken question went unanswered as he continued to leach all breath from her body by working magic on her toes. "I did warn you to behave, though. And now you owe me twice. First for the whip..."

She opened her mouth to protest but his fingers trailed along the arch, swirled around her heel, and found a pressure point that sparked a tingle between her thighs. She moaned instead.

"Second," he said. "For slapping my butt."

"I...couldn't...help it," she managed to whimper between gasps. Where had he learned the art of foot massaging? And why couldn't the erotic feeling he now evoked ever be achieved with simple walking? "Ahhhhh."

"I see." With a quick squeeze of her toes, he lowered her heel to the floor and began to unlace the other boot. "Just like you couldn't help turning my home upside down without asking, upgrading my robot—again, without asking—and willfully embarrassing me in front of my aunt?"

"It's more efficient to organize your clothes from smallest to largest, and I didn't embarrass you on purpose."

"Really?" He stopped unlacing her boot and pinned her with a knowing look. "Tell me sweetheart, are you still feeling, you know, kinda *grrrr*?"

Heat flushed her face. In truth, kinda didn't cover it. Her nipples pebbled against the coat, begging to be kissed. Between her legs, moisture gathered in response to his massage. He must know how aroused she was, he could probably detect her scent. "I, well...yes." She folded her arms across her chest. "The clothes make me feel sexy."

"The clothes?" The corners of his lips pulled upward. His eyes smoldered as he pulled the boot off with a quick flick and tossed it aside. "I don't think it's the clothes."

His pheromones were heavy with desire, his pulse beat a rapid rhythm at his throat. She wasn't the only one excited. Strong fingers kneaded the ball of her foot and massaged the blood back into her toes. She sagged against the bench, closed her eyes, and gritted her teeth against the deep moan of pleasure building inside her. She was still irritated with him. For treating her like a potato sack. And for his attraction to Genova.

"Your skin is so soft, even your heels, and here along your ankles and calves." His fingers danced, gentle and insistent, up her leg. "But not as soft as between your thighs."

The moan broke free. She parted her legs as he skimmed the contour where thigh met pelvis. He circled close to her crease, once, twice, but not quite touching her panties, then stroked down her leg again.

"Do you really think I'd mark your beautiful skin with a whip?" he asked.

Flushed and flustered, she opened her eyes.

In the cargo hold light, his brown eyes were shadowed, but she could see his serious expression and the hint of remorse. "I'd never want to hurt you," he said, holding her gaze. "Not in any way."

She kept her arms crossed tight. "Then why didn't you tell me about your lover?"

"She's not my lover. Not anymore."

"Really?" she scoffed. "So that kiss was just a friendly goodbye?"

"For me, yes." He paused, and the warmth radiating from his skin increased.

"But not for her?"

"She'd rather keep things going," he admitted, sounding unhappy.

"You shouldn't have let her kiss you then," she chastised. "It's not nice to be lied to."

"I was protecting you."

"Really? Don't bring me into this. You enjoyed her attention. But you're so caught up in being alone, you'll do just about anything to drive people away. By punishing yourself, you punish the people around you who care about you. Her only crime is in trying to get close to your heart."

"My heart?" He laughed, a flush creeping up his neck. "The only thing she wants from me is my cock, sweetheart."

"Why don't you just give it to her then? She's pretty and willing." *And human.*

His brows rose. "You want me to sleep with her?"

She shrugged. "Don't you want to?"

He shook his head. "No." His expression became hard. "I did once. After Sarah died. When I was very lonely. But Genova isn't what I want."

"What is it that you want then?"

Perched on his knees between her legs, he watched her carefully in silence. The dangerous smile, which touched his lips, lit his eyes with fierce desire. He wanted her but held himself in check with steely control.

Each pulse beat seemed to vibrate the air between them as he studied her face. He slid his thumb slowly across her bottom lip. A thin smear of crimson stained his skin. He frowned.

"Lipstick doesn't suit you."

"No?"

He shook his head and pulled at the pins fastening her dark bob. "Take off the wig."

"I thought you liked brunettes."

He didn't answer as the hot wig pulled free and cool air brushed her scalp. She sighed as she dragged her fingers through her hair, enjoying the freedom of the strands. Fine blond hairs fluffed about her face. He stroked them away from her cheeks.

"Much better," he murmured.

The heat coming off him warmed her skin. She swallowed hard.

"Don't I need to keep the disguise on?"

"Not here." He continued to play with tendrils of her hair, as if the silky texture mesmerized him. "Not now we're away from the Dome. You're under my protection. The others respect that." His tone spoke of dire consequences if anyone dared defy his claim, and she remembered the jealous heat in his eyes when he'd seen Jared and Mac holding her. She couldn't help smiling a bit at that. His possessiveness was intoxicating.

His fingers moved to where her jacket was held closed at her throat.

"Ohh," she sighed, as it pulled open, leaving her exposed to his scrutiny. He pushed the heavy coat from her shoulders and stared at her chest. The corset's design plumped her small breasts. They strained toward him, prominent nipples poking over the top, ready to be soothed by his tongue. He touched one taut bud with his finger and circled the extruded areola. She shuddered and arched, unable to stifle a gasp.

"Very beautiful," he said. "I love the sounds you make." He kneaded both breasts and used his thumbs to further harden her nipples. "And the easy way you react to me."

She had no breath to comment. Sensation warmed her skin, tightened her abdomen, made her thighs flex as he massaged her with his palms.

His hands moved lower to unfasten the laces pulled tight in a bow across her ribs. Gently, he eased apart the constricting material until it loosened enough to slip over her torso and onto the floor. The coat slid off her arms with it. Naked, except for the black lace panties, she dug her fingers into the soft seat as a wave of arousal flushed her body at his intent stare.

Still kneeling between her legs, he leaned close and kissed her belly. "So hot," he murmured. Cool air puffed across her skin as he blew a line up toward her breasts. She shivered and gripped the seat harder. "It wasn't the clothes that made you aroused, was it?"

"No."

His hands trailed up her sides as he rose to his feet. "You enjoy my touch so much, don't you?"

She arched into his palms as his hands found her breasts again. "Yes."

He pinched both nipples.

She bit her lip and turned her face away as pleasure shot straight to her belly. Her legs spasmed, rubbing her sensitive thighs against his legs. "Oooh!"

His spicy scent filled her senses as he leaned close to her ear.

"Turn over," he whispered. He moved back to give her room.

Limbs shaking, she managed to twist around and comply. Resting her forehead on the padded backrest, she placed her palms on the seat and waited. His hands smoothed across her buttocks, squeezing the presented globes.

"Did you know you have a perfect heart-shaped ass?"

She shook her head, unable to speak as his fingers continued to stroke and caress and pull down her panties.

"Cute dimples here at the top, and then the most delicious seam." His finger traveled the length of her cleft to the edge of the lips below. She tensed, startled by the intrusion.

He slapped her buttocks hard enough to make the muscles constrict. "I think you're ready for your punishment now."

She gasped and tried to turn.

But his lips kissed the stinging skin and shock transformed to erotic pleasure. His hands found her dangling breasts. His mouth swirled over each butt cheek, dipping closer to the seam with each pass.

They'd discovered the night before how much she enjoyed being licked down there. If this was punishment, she could take it forever. She dug her nails into the upholstery and tried to remain upright as her legs turned to rubber.

His tongue swirled low, licked along the cleft, and down around her engorged folds. His fingers squeezed and stroked her nipples. Feeling the tingling bite of pleasure teasing through her, she trembled, completely at his mercy.

Covering her sex with his mouth, he circled her exposed sheath with the tip of his tongue.

"Mmmmm," she moaned as a knot of anticipation lodged deep in her belly. She spread her thighs wider to give him better access.

He pulled back and kissed her ass cheek again. "Do you want me inside you?"

Was he kidding? "Yes," she hissed between clenched teeth.

"Are you going to behave from now on?" Husky and hoarse, his voice demanded obedience.

Behave? What? Nerves jangled, she tensed. His tongue dipped around her folds again and licked the wetness between. She wanted him. Oh, yes, she wanted him to enter, to feel him deep inside. But this was blackmail, this was torture, this was—

The spasm caught her by surprise. It clenched her whole body tight in a hot, breathless gasp. She shook as he continued to lick her sensitive sex. Unable to support her body anymore, her arms gave out. She sagged against the cushioned seat and pressed her cheek to the coarse fabric.

Breath filled her lungs after a few heaving attempts. She opened her eyes to find Peyton standing nearby, wiping his face with a cloth. He watched her with flushed cheeks and a supremely smug expression in place of a smile.

"Promise me you'll behave from now on." His fingers moved to the fastening of his pants, then paused as he waited for her response.

What was this? Was his "punishment" the denial of further pleasure? An attempt to show her he was in control? That he could make her writhe and scream on command? That he didn't need the pleasure in return?

If nothing else, the bulge in his trousers proved him wrong.

"Know what?" she said, holding his fierce gaze. "I think you were right. I should have stayed behind at the Dome. We could both use some space." Her arms felt like rubber as she propped herself upright on the bench again.

He frowned. "What's that supposed to mean?"

"It means, you can forget about having sex on this trip. You wanted a break? I'll give you a break." She stood on shaky legs and pulled up her panties again. It's not like there was anywhere on the transport that they could really be alone anyway. The door separating the cabins wasn't particularly thick and his family and friends were right on the other side. "Where can I find some proper clothes?" His shirt would have been nice, but then again it would have reminded her of him.

And she didn't want to think about him. Not when desire and anger surged through her veins.

"*Bullshit*," he shouted. "Bull. Fucking. Shit." He was on her in an instant, pushing her back down. His body made a cage around her as he pressed his palms against the back of the seat. His heated stare pinned her, his face looming close to hers. "You wanted to be my slave, remember?"

She nodded, her mouth having gone dry at the primal power radiating off him as he asserted his dominance.

"It's time you learned what that means," he murmured, and the low throaty promise of pleasure made her body flare with heat.

CLAIMING

PEYTON STARED AT Hell. The fevered brightness of her eyes matched the heat coming off her skin and that intoxicating sweet scent, which had become so ingrained in his mind he'd begun to dream about it.

She was angry with him, but at the same time daring him to take her.

Claim her.

Dominate her.

She wanted him to fuck her without mercy.

Who was he to deny her that?

The others could wait. The whole fucking world could wait.

She wasn't leaving this room until they'd sorted this shit out.

He quickly locked the cargo pod door and came back to where she sat on the seat, naked except for those black lacy panties, which cupped her sex and hid it from his avid stare.

"Take them off. Now," he ordered.

Her gaze flicked to the door. "Peyton—"

"Did I say you could talk, slave?"

She swallowed hard. "No..."

"Then take off your panties."

It was wrong, so wrong, to dominate a woman who'd been imprisoned all her life. But staring into her eyes, he saw her need to be given boundaries. To be cherished. Loved. Held. And fucked within an inch of her life. All the things it would be so dangerous to do, and yet at the same time so right.

His pulse thudded through his veins as she slowly stood and lowered her panties, baring herself to him. She kept her gaze trained on his as she bent forward and slid them over her feet. Her breasts swayed with the movement. Christ, they were perfect. He fisted his hands to stop from reaching out and stroking them.

"Sit on the bench and tuck your legs up. Spread your knees wide."

There was no bed, not even a decent seat where they could do this right. Just this narrow bench with a cargo rack on either side and crates stacked up high behind him. But he knew he was sure as all fuck going to as she silently did as he instructed—arranged herself on the bench with her feet on the edge and her knees pulled up and spread wide. He felt her attention trained on his face, absorbing his expression as he absorbed the sight presented before him.

He dropped to his knees, not caring about the hard metal floor. His focus was on her perfectly symmetrical sex and the way her lips pulled open, revealing her glistening center. Fuck, she was gorgeous. Her aroused scent rose off her in a cloud of sweet warmth, which raced through his blood and hardened his already stiff cock.

"God, you are beautiful. Pink. Hot. Perfection." He leaned forward and placed a gentle kiss on her mound.

She jerked, air hissing between her teeth, but she kept her knees spread wide.

Resisting the urge to deepen the kiss and tongue her core, he pulled back to catch her heated gaze. "You want me to fuck you, don't you, slave?" Her need was obvious, but she had to say it.

Her gaze skittered away from his. "You're the master. You decide."

He sat back on his heels, denying the instinct clawing through him to grasp her by the hips and slam balls deep inside her. "That's not how it works. I need your permission, always."

"Why?" His heart twisted at the look of genuine puzzlement she gave him.

"Because being my slave," he said, managing to keep his voice gentle despite the deep-seated rage that burned inside him for all the atrocities she'd endured, "means allowing me to give you pleasure whenever you want it. But you have to tell me you want it. And you do want it right now, don't you, Helen?"

"Yes."

He straightened and began to undo his fly. "Then no more of this 'no-sex-during-the-trip' crap. I know I hurt you earlier. For what you saw with Genova. I promise I'll make it up to you. But denying yourself to try to hurt me, only hurts you."

Her eyes misted over as she stared at him. "You wanted to leave me behind," she whispered.

His chest tightened. She sounded so lost, so hurt. Like a child trying to make sense of an incomprehensible world. She wasn't alone in feeling that way. The same confusion ate at him too. And he suddenly realized her anger wasn't about Genova at all. She'd thought he was rejecting her by wanting to leave her in the safety of his quarters back at the Dome.

And hadn't he been? Hadn't he been searching for an escape? A way to put some distance between himself and the emotions Hell brought to life. The torment sizzled through his veins. He didn't want to need her, didn't want to want her, but he hungered for her with an almost shameful thirst that made his soul shake.

"It's all...so fast," he said. Her attention focused on his fingers as he unzipped his fly. "You...this...connection we share." He fumbled for the words that would make sense of what he was feeling. "I'm...used to being alone. And every second we're together, I can't stop wanting to fuck you." Every time he came, all he wanted to do was to sink back into her hot, wet sheath. Feel her shudder and moan and clasp him tight. So tight, he had no choice but to fill her with his seed. Over and over again. In the short time he'd known her, it had become an obsession.

"And that's bad?" she asked as he pulled down his pants and boxers in one quick movement, freeing his stiff cock.

"I want to keep you safe. Not use you like a fuck doll." But he was going to fuck her, right here, right now until she screamed his name, and he didn't care who the hell heard.

Her eyes rose from admiring his hard-on and met his gaze. "I think you're afraid of being hurt again. I won't hurt you, Peyton."

He shook his head, stifling a bitter laugh. How could this sweet girl who'd been so badly used be trying to protect him?

"Come here," he said and sat down on the bench beside her. Taking her from behind would work, given the space they had, but he wanted to be able to see her eyes widen with pleasure when she came. Her beauty in that moment was an image burned into his mind forever.

She didn't resist as he helped her straddle his lap with her knees on either side of his hips. Her hands gripped his shoulders. Her breasts hung close to his face. She smelled like fucking heaven and felt even better, her skin hot and soft where he clutched her hips.

Her breathing came in uneven pants as she steadied herself above his cock. Her eyes met his and locked as she stilled, waiting for permission to move.

"Tell me what you want, slave."

Her pink tongue darted out to wet her lips. "You," she said, her voice husky. "All of you. Inside me."

"Show me."

Using her fingers, she parted her slit and slowly began to lower herself onto his stiff shaft. She bit her lip, her eyes closing at the first touch of her sex meeting his tip. He tightened his grip on her hips, stopping her from descending any further.

"No. Keep your eyes open. Watch me. Look at what you do to me."

Her eyelids flashed open, her aroused gaze finding his.

Her hips lowered, enveloping him in hot, tight silk. He sucked in a sharp breath as his entire body flushed with the pleasure rushing through his veins. A harsh groan hissed between his lips. "So...fucking...perfect." Too perfect. Just like the first time he'd entered her, he was consumed by the unique pleasure that was Hell. The way she wrapped around him, grasping him so completely, he'd never experienced anything quite like it, not even with Sarah. And the knowledge was as exhilarating as it was damning.

He lifted her up and then slammed her down on his cock again, making her breasts bounce with the force.

She gasped, her eyes widening, her pupils becoming large. Her body trembled from the pleasure he could feel rippling in spasms around his cock.

Oh, fuck. He needed to slam into her and make her come so hard.

She pushed herself up and down, milking his cock. Her breasts bounced before his face. But he kept his eyes locked on hers. "Do you see what you do to me, baby?"

"Peyton," she whimpered as he tightened his hold on her hips.

He slammed her down against his groin and thrust his hips. "You make me so fucking hard. With your perfect tits, and your perfect little clit." Shifting his hand from one of her hips, he brushed his thumb over her sensitive nub.

She cried out, her eyes blinking shut for a brief moment. A full body shudder rippled through her as she grasped his shoulders tight.

He kept his thumb in place so that every time she thrust down on his shaft, his thumb made connection with her clit.

She moaned and keened, her breaths coming in unsteady puffs which matched his own.

"Oh fuck, oh fuck," he hissed.

Christ, the expression on her face was exquisite, full of undisguised need. It made him want to grind himself into her even more, give her so much pleasure she would never want for anything. Except him.

"God, you're beautiful, Helen."

She kept her eyes trained on his, wide open just like he liked. Her raw desire clear to see in her shimmering amber eyes. "Say it," she moaned as she bucked against his thumb, her insides massaging him tight. "Say I'm your slave."

She sounded almost desperate to hear it, to have him claim her right now in that way. She quivered on the edge, needing the words to trigger her release.

She belonged to him.

She was his in every sense of the word.

But as he buried his face into her neck, his balls aching to fill her with his seed, he whispered, "Yes, baby, I'm your slave."

And as she arched back and screamed his name, clenching his cock so tight he could do nothing except let loose his own orgasm, he knew deep in his soul it was true.

JUDGEMENT

"FEELING BETTER?" JARED asked.

"What?" Peyton smoothed his shirt and ignored the sidelong glances as he took a seat beside his brother-in-law. Except for Hell, everyone was gathered for a meeting in the crew quarters to discuss business at the Dome. His little dalliance in the cargo hold had made him late. Not that he gave a fuck. Actually, he had given a fuck, he realized with a grin, and my God, had it been worth it.

"When you went into the bathroom, you looked a little, er...flushed." Jared leaned back in his chair and raised a brow.

"I, uh, ate something that didn't agree," Peyton said, deciding to downplay the obvious fact he'd just fucked Hell like a king, and see how far it went. Everyone must have heard the sex which had happened in the cargo hold. Hell's pleasure-screams still rang in his ears. He'd tried to avoid the stares as he'd quickly ducked into the bathroom afterward, in order to clean himself up as best he could and wipe off her lipstick stains. But who the hell was he kidding?

"I guess that explains why you were clutching your, ah, stomach?"

"I thought it was his tool belt," snickered Rusty.

"What are you laughing at, asswipe?" McClellan cuffed the red-haired man lightly in the shoulder. "At least Peyton's got a tool."

Rusty grinned and started to stand, gesturing at his groin. "You wanna see a tool? I'll show you a tool."

"Ha!" McClellan snorted. "That's more like a one-inch nail."

"Yeah? It's a fuckin' two-hundred-pound hammer." He grabbed his groin through his pants and shook it at McClellan.

"If you two are finished..." Aunty Jo placed her palms on the small table and leaned forward, pinning both of them with her intent scowl. "We need to get back to business."

With a smirk, Rusty resumed his seat. Still red-faced, McClellan crossed his arms and ignored the younger man. The room became quiet as attention at the circular table focused on Joanna.

Satisfied, she nodded. "Since you've finally decided to join us, Peyton." He became the next victim of her hard glare. "Perhaps you'd like to explain why you didn't come forward about Helen when you first realized there was a problem?"

"Problem? There's no problem." Nope, no problem at all. Everything was under complete control where Hell was concerned. A few quick pumps of his cock and she was back to being all smiles again.

Aunt Joanna pursed her lips. "No problem?"

"Nope." He held her disbelieving stare as sweat began to bead on his brow.

"Have you gone insane?"

"Quite possibly." An insane man obsessed with fucking a more-real-than-real android.

"This is serious." Joanna's eyes narrowed. "I can understand your reluctance to tell the Domers about her, but what about us? Your family. You couldn't tell us you were harboring a fugitive?" She sounded genuinely hurt, which, of course, inspired guilt; a controlling ploy that had worked like a charm since he was a child. His simmering arousal cooled.

"You were safer not being involved," he explained.

Joanna shook her head. "Stop being so dramatic. Why do you always think you have to do everything the hard way?"

"Helen's existence does pose a curious question," Lee Palmer interjected. His calm, stoic presence was one of the few things capable of soothing Joanna's bluster. He reached toward the center of the table and grasped a flask of water, his weathered hands strong and sure as he poured a glassful. "Her origin and purpose have yet to be determined."

"Her purpose?" Joanna's green eyes flashed as she sat back in her chair. "I think her purpose is abundantly clear." The mocking glance she shot his way set Peyton's teeth on edge. "Can you blame her for running away from The Factory after everything she's been through?"

"Do we know for sure she ran away?" Jared accepted the flask from his father, poured a glass and passed it to Joanna before pouring one for himself. "The neo-genesis program was developed to facilitate the continuation of human life. If you wanted to see how the latest experiment in genetic engineering fared outside the laboratory, what better place to test a subject's adaptability than an environment such as this?"

Peyton stared hard at his brother-in-law. Since Hell was unable to remember what had happened, the facts concerning her escape were based on conjecture, he had to admit. What Jared proposed was possible, but it didn't sit right in Peyton's mind. And why was Jared bringing the idea up now?

He glanced between Jared and his father with a prickling sensation of unease. Lee had remained silent the entire time Peyton had privately filled him in about the details concerning Hell. He'd simply listened, his face a blank mask of studied interest as he absorbed the particulars of the situation, his only outward reaction a slight raise of his brow when Peyton had discussed Hell's critical memory situation and what he'd done to fix it.

Lee raised the same curious brow at his son now. Blue eyes studied blue eyes. "You think she's been planted by The Factory?"

"It's a possibility," Jared said.

"No." Peyton dismissed the idea without hesitation.

"Maybe they created a situation to see how effective she is in stirring human attachment?" Rusty asked.

"No," Peyton insisted. "It's a clear-cut case of abuse of power. They made her suffer, just because they could." Memories of Hell's horrendous treatment pierced his thoughts, clear and sharp as the knife that had cut her skin. He slammed his fist on the table, drawing everyone's attention. "She hacked her own programming to disable her tracking device and escape. But it doesn't matter if she ran away or was sent here. They beat the fuck out of her on purpose. Repeatedly. And we can't let that go unchecked. Her mind was so broken I didn't know if she'd even remember her name when she woke from surgery. I did my best to repair what I could, but with so much memory loss...whatever she was before yesterday morning, isn't who she is now."

"She could still be recording data about everything she experiences and sending it back to The Factory whether she knows it or not. Did you check for a Neural Network implant?" Rusty asked.

Peyton shook his head. "Her uplink is direct connection only. There's no way she could send information across the world without using an external messaging system just like the rest of us."

"You're sure she doesn't have any new-fangled gadgets hidden anywhere, ready to pop out and surprise us? How thoroughly did you check her out, Peyton?" McClellan's dark brows waggled, eyes twinkling.

"Yeah." Rusty grinned. "Did you give her a complete examination?"

Beside him, Jared snickered. "In and out, in and out..."

Laughter broke out around the table, except from Joanna, who choked on her water.

"Listen." Despite the need to remain in control, heat crept up Peyton's neck. In the past twenty-four hours there wasn't a micron on Hell's body he hadn't explored in detail. "She's not a typical android, or even what you'd expect for the idea of a Bio-roid. She's been grown in a lab, not manufactured like a droid."

"Yeah, but grown from what?" Rusty asked. He broke off as the door opened and Hell stepped from the bathroom into the crew quarters. His jaw dropped so fast it nearly hit the table. "You're a blonde?"

More like an amber goddess, Peyton thought. Without the dark wig to cover it, Hell's fair hair caught the light and everyone's attention. She paused when her eyes found his, and she brightened like a ray of sunshine in a cloudy gloom.

His ray of sunshine. Those glorious golden strands looked just fine draped across his pillow, thank you very much. *When did I become such a sucker for blondes?*

A clasp at her nape held her hair back from her face, all except for a sexy tendril that curled down her cheek. Her hand strayed upward and tucked the wayward wisp behind her ear in a self-conscious gesture that caused his breath to hitch. She'd wiped off the makeup and her naturally pretty skin glowed pale and perfect with the deep blush that had crept into her cheeks. With a shy smile, she broke eye contact with him and peered around the table at the ring of gaping faces, seeming suddenly embarrassed.

"Am I interrupting something?"

"Oh, my dear!" Aunty Jo quickly stood, her seamed face breaking into a rare smile as she beckoned to Hell. "Come sit with us," she added as she made room for Hell between herself and Lee. "We were just about to eat an early dinner."

Hell glanced between Peyton and Joanna, as if reluctant to be seated away from him in the cramped space, but then gave a small shrug. "Um, okay."

Joanna settled again and nodded, satisfaction brightening her face. "I'm glad you found something that fit. Feel free to use anything else of mine that you need."

Now clad in the same kind of gray, serviceable one-piece jumpsuit that Joanna wore, Hell cinched her makeshift rope belt tighter, and nodded with a demure smile. "Thank you. These clothes are much more comfortable."

Comfortable was not how Peyton would put it, delicious maybe, ravishing definitely. The fit was baggy, but if she thought the plain clothes hid her appeal better than the sex-bot outfit, she was mistaken. He knew exactly what perfection was hidden beneath, and the pull of the fabric as she bent forward slightly to take her seat opposite him granted him a quick view of her chest.

No bra. Of course she wore no bra. Where would she have found one her size? Her small, perfect breasts didn't need support anyway. No, no, they jiggled quite nicely as she adjusted her seat. Unfortunately, he wasn't the only one noticing. He shot a glare around the circle of male eyes transfixed by her nipples, which tightened as the fabric rubbed against them.

McClellan smoothed a hand across his dark stubble as his ears pinkened. The others quickly turned their attention to fiddling with their glasses of water and making room on the table for food to be served. All except Lee, who stared at Hell with open fascination, examining her face closely as she settled in beside him. She smiled politely at the grey-haired man as she caught his glance. But he didn't return the gesture; if anything, the puzzled knot of his brow deepened as he watched her. His almost obsessive interest was disconcerting, but could Peyton blame him?

When was the last time any of the guys here had been around a pretty, new member of the opposite sex? The lack of access to new sexual partners at the Dome was another reason Peyton hadn't wanted Hell to come along on this trip. The guys were trustworthy—he'd known them most of his life—but temptation might strain even the strongest bonds of friendship. Jared had seemed just a little too eager to prop her up earlier when her boot-failure had happened. And seeing another man's hands on her had made Peyton's blood boil. It was simmering again now.

She belongs to me. The words hissed through his mind with primal urgency. He gripped his glass instead of reaching across the table and pulling her into his lap and away from the others. *I am not jealous!* But the protest echoed with a distinct lack of conviction. *And now I'm arguing with myself again.* He really was insane.

He frowned at the cause of his insanity.

Hell had her hands tucked in her lap, looking sexy and sweet. Sweet enough to devour. *Get a grip, man.* His need to taste her again was so strong it was like he hadn't just fucked her.

"Would you like some water, dear? Or perhaps some tea?" Aunt Joanna shot Peyton an impatient frown, as if he'd been derelict in his manners, before smiling again at Hell and gesturing at the pitcher of water.

Hell grasped the remaining empty cup on the table and turned it around, examining it. "I don't know. I've never had tea. At least, I don't think I have?" She shot Peyton a questioning glance.

He gave a non-committal shrug as he dutifully reached forward and poured some water in her empty glass. Not being much of a tea-drinker himself, he'd never thought to ask what she preferred. The topic had never come up. When had there been time for questions like that?

Joanna's smile slipped for a fraction of a second. "I see. Well," she reached over and patted Hell's fingers, "we'll have some with dinner. It's exciting discovering your tastes in things, isn't it? Bambi..."

At the sound of her name, Jared's sex-bot stirred where she was sitting by the window beside Henry. Her emotionless eyes blinked and focused on Joanna.

"It's time to serve the food," Aunty Jo said.

Instruction given, Bambi rose and sauntered to the opposite wall where a panel opened to reveal a small galley. Designed to entice the eye, her sleek hips balanced a diminutive waist and full breasts that didn't just jiggle when she moved, they caused the flimsy wrap covering her body to ripple. Her long dark, synthetic hair swayed down her back in a glossy wave; her pale synthetic skin was flawless. Too flawless. Just as her lips were too plump, too artificially red. *And her eyes never flash with anger or pleasure.* Next to Hell's vibrancy, Bambi seemed a cheap, over-sexualized knockoff of femininity. And creepy.

Metal squeaked as Hell pushed back her chair. "I can help her with that."

Peyton reached across and put his hand over hers, stopping her mid-rise. "No. I told you before, you don't have to wait on me. Or anyone else." Her fingers tightened beneath his as her gaze snapped round to meet his. Uncertainty played across her features.

"That's right, dear. Let the robot take care of it. You look a little pale. You aren't feeling ill too, are you? Peyton apparently ate something that upset his stomach, which is surprising as he's quite a good cook, you know. At least, he used to be before he decided to live like a hermit in that that tiny box he calls an apartment."

Peyton bit off a groan. *Jesus Christ, Joanna strikes again!* She'd obviously latched onto his earlier joking comment about what—or rather who—he'd been eating and decided to make a point of it.

Hell's eyes widened as she glanced at Peyton. "I made you sick?"

"What? No!" *Oh, dear God!*

Snickers erupted around the table as his face flushed. In truth, eating her out had not made him ill—unless one considered being aroused beyond sanity a kind of sickness.

Hell snatched her hand free from his and covered her mouth. Her bottom hit the seat with a thump. "It—it was that bad?"

"Hell, no!" He tried to catch her hand again, but she kept it fisted in her lap. "Yours is the best I've ever tasted," he insisted. With a start, he realized it was true. Hell's pussy was the best he'd ever tasted. Her slick juices were an addictive combination of honey-sweetness and woman that still lingered on his tongue.

"You're lying." Her eyes narrowed. "I tasted it too."

"You did?" Her taste must have been on his mouth when he'd kissed her.

"It was horrible. And I just wanted to please you after such a wonderful night together." She pressed her fingers to her temples and shut her eyes. "I feel so stupid not remembering how to cook."

"Cook?" *Er, what?*

"Even a low-functioning sex-bot like her knows how to fix a meal." She pointed at Bambi who was busy chopping up vegetables. "And I can't even make soy-scramble."

Soy-scramble? Shit! The pain and frustration in her voice made his chest constrict, and the room suddenly became quiet except for the sounds of Bambi preparing their evening meal. "It's not your fault, sweetheart," he said. She was still hung up on the breakfast fiasco. He should have paid more attention to her feelings this morning. Her lack of memory hurt her more than he'd thought. He reached for her, but Joanna got there first. She wrapped her arm about Hell's shoulders in a tight hug.

"It's fine, dear. Nothing a bit of time can't fix."

Jared coughed discreetly. "Er, Bambi came with a selection of tutorial data cubes. You can borrow the one on 'cooking for pleasure' if you want. Just upload it to your cortex and presto—expert chef in thirty seconds."

"Really?" Hell pulled back from Joanna's embrace and studied him with hope in her eyes.

Peyton shook his head, hating to put a dampener on it. "It's not that simple. Maybe in a few weeks, when your synapses have had time to heal, we can try some uploads and other mnemonic treatments. But for now, it's best if you take things easy and learn things on your own. An instantaneous upload of information might do more harm than good."

"I don't understand." McClellan rubbed his jaw. "She can fix machines like a whiz, but she can't remember how to cook?"

"Selective memory damage," Lee said. He studied Hell, thoughtful interest still bright in his eyes. "I wonder what else you can't remember."

"If you're implying I'm choosing to forget certain things on purpose—"

"No one's implying anything," Joanna interjected with a frown at Lee. "You've been through a terrible ordeal, Helen. We all understand how difficult this must be for you." She gave her shoulders a squeeze and studied her face. "You seem tired. I hope my ungrateful nephew didn't keep you up all night."

Hell's brows rose. "I, um—"

"She slept just fine, thank you very much Aunty Jo." Peyton speared her with his best glare. Come to think of it, though, Hell did seem unusually quiet. "How's your head, Hell? Does it ache at all?" Maybe the sex in the cargo hold had been too much for her.

"Will you stop calling her that?" Aunty Jo snapped. "It's insulting. Her name is Helen."

"It's fine," Hell said. "It's just a nickname."

He glared at Joanna for reminding him of the snap decision he'd made when choosing the name. It'd seemed appropriate at the time. A joke. But now? "Do you want me to call you Helen?"

She sucked in a breath and shrugged, but he couldn't ignore the flash of pleasure which had filled her eyes when he'd said her full name. "It's fine," she repeated. "I'm fine. It's just..." She broke off and pinched her lips together as if trying to decide what to say as her gaze roamed the group and then settled back on Peyton. "This might sound odd, but I feel...disconnected inside."

"Disconnected?"

"Yes." She paused and frowned, her gaze becoming distant as

her thoughts turned inward. "There used to be a voice, helping me make decisions, but now when I ask myself questions…sometimes I get a flicker of an answer, like a memory, but it's so indistinct. I can't quite grasp what is said before it's gone."

She'd been hearing voices in her head? Not surprising considering the state of decay her brain was in before surgery.

Lee leaned toward her, blue eyes intent. "What kind of voice?"

Hell shifted in her chair. "It's hard to explain, but a woman sometimes answers when I ask certain things. Like when I need to run a diagnostic it will answer the command. Or when I don't understand something Peyton does, it will offer a suggestion. But a lot of the time it's just a fragment of a conversation. It's very frustrating."

McClellan snickered. "Don't worry. None of the rest of us understand why Peyton acts the way he does either."

Even Lee, usually reserved, laughed at that comment. Dickheads. But the old man quickly sobered again as he studied Hell. "You said the voice is a woman's. It's different than your own voice?" he asked.

"Yes. But I don't know who she is. I feel like I should, though. I feel like I should know her."

Bambi sauntered over and placed a large tray of finger foods on the table. Peyton selected a carrot stick and focused on Hell. "It's probably a bridging program that helps link the gap between your computer and human selves. A way for you to make sense of things." Which would explain her confusion and sense of disconnection if the program was damaged and not doing its job properly.

"Trace memory of whoever programmed her at The Factory?" Rusty suggested.

"The program might take on that persona in her mind," Peyton said with a nod. "An avatar to guide her. Like a conscience."

He studied her for a moment. The uncertainty in her expression was so human it was easy to forget she was part machine too. "I've got a portable scanner onboard. It's not very sophisticated, but I'll do a scan later while you're sleeping to see if I can isolate this program," he said to try and reassure her.

She nodded and smiled, but there was a troubled flicker in her eyes.

"Do you remember what this woman who talks to you looks like?" Lee asked.

Hell blinked for a moment as if the question troubled her. She glanced at her water glass where it rested on the table. Her grip on it tightened. "She's...like me, but not like me at all." Her brows pulled together, and her eyes shut as she struggled to focus her mind. "Blue eyes. Her hair is dark. She's...pretty."

"A young woman?"

"Yes."

"Do you see her now?"

"No. She's gone again." Her hand on the glass shook with the effort she was using to concentrate.

"How old are you, Helen?" Lee asked, his tone quiet, his gaze piercing.

Hell's eyes flashed open. She stared at Lee. In physical appearance she was a young adult in her prime, but she'd been grown in a lab using accelerated means like a clone. Peyton had never thought to check her inception date, though it probably would be recorded in her cell structure. His main concern had been keeping her alive. But now, as he watched the expression on Lee's face change from one of intense curiosity to one of hope, his heart began to race. The old man knew something he wasn't saying. Something about Hell.

"According to my internal chronometer, I came online three years, two months and twelve hours ago," Hell said. "Why?"

"Because," Lee said, and his hand shook slightly as he raised his palm and gently cupped her cheek, "I believe you may be all that remains of my daughter."

REMEMBERING

"*WHAT?*" HELL SAID with a gasp, her eyes wide with shock.

"Jesus Christ. Jesus *fucking* Christ. What did you just say?" Peyton asked. He stared at Lee, his mind filling with a buzzing sound that was making it hard to understand what he'd just heard.

"I think Sarah created Helen, Peyton, and that avatar program is an echo of her."

"An echo..." he said, his voice full of disbelief, "of my wife. Who's been dead for nearly two years." At Lee's nod and unwavering stare, he added, "Why would you think that?"

Icy suspicion crept down his spine, his pulse thudded through his veins as his gaze flicked to Aunt Joanna and took in the way her hand covered her mouth. But the look in her eyes was filled with sympathy rather than shock as she kept her gaze carefully focused on Lee.

"Because she was working on a prototype for the Bio-roid project three years ago," Lee said quietly. "And seeing it succeed was very important to her."

"*Fuck,*" Peyton shouted. He rose from his chair, not caring that it banged hard against the backs of his legs. He raked his fingers through his hair and glanced at Hell and back at Lee. "You really think she'd do something like this without telling me?"

"Peyton. Calm down, son," Lee said in a steady voice. He exchanged a quick glance with Joanna.

"Go to hell." He didn't want to calm down. He paced back and forth, his pulse racing faster with each heartbeat. "Three years?" Peyton cried, his mind spinning. Three fucking years. "You've been online for *three years*?" he asked Hell.

She nodded, her amber eyes wide and filled with confusion as she pushed back from the table and stood. "What's going on?" she asked, her voice barely audible.

He'd assumed Hell had been created recently. But if that assumption was wrong...

Sarah had died two years ago. Which meant it was possible that what Lee suspected was true. That Sarah had created Hell. Or at least that she'd participated in her creation when she'd worked at The Factory three years ago. She'd talked about the Bio-roid project. Her dream. Her burning ambition to save the world from extinction. But if she'd created Hell, why hadn't she told him about it when she'd told him about so much of her other work? Why had she kept him in the dark about her little secret project? And why had she thought it was okay to tell her father instead?

He glanced around at the ring of faces gaping at him. His friends. His family. The people who he trusted, who had watched him struggle with the loss and grief he'd been consumed by since Sarah's death. The people who were having a hard time holding his gaze as he scrutinized them now.

Had all of them known about Sarah's little secret and suspected it might be Hell?

"I need to get the fuck out of here," he said. He strode to the wall by the main door and slapped a panel, which opened a storage compartment full of outer gear. Grabbing his heavy winter jacket, he called out to the A.I. computer guiding the transport, "ANT? Execute emergency shutdown of the propulsion systems."

The transport lurched to a halt as the computer instantly obeyed.

The hiss of the main door opening sounded loud in the sudden silence. As the crisp outside air flooded the crew cabin, he glanced backward at the group still seated at the table. They watched him with a mixture of shock and concern, all except Hell, who appeared panicked.

"Peyton?" she called. She started to move, as if intending to come after him.

But Lee stopped her by putting a hand on her arm. He shook his head, keeping his gaze on Peyton. "You stay here," he said to her with a quick smile that didn't reach his eyes. He rose to his feet, the motion slow, yet sure. "Peyton and I need to talk in private."

**

"What the hell is going on, Lee?" Peyton asked. The snow crunched beneath his boots as he paced within a copse of fir trees the transport had stopped not far from. The bracing air chilled his cheeks and made his hot breath mist in an angry puff. He stopped and turned to face the older man who'd followed closely behind him when exiting the transport.

Lee Palmer nodded as he met Peyton's gaze, his expression somber. "I understand your confusion, son. I can't be certain myself, of course, but seeing Helen in the flesh, certain things do make sense now."

Peyton folded his arms and leaned against a thick birch tree. "What things?" he said, not bothering to hide his frustration. "Do they all know too?" He gestured back the way he'd come at the transport.

Lee shook his head. "No, son. You're getting it all wrong. Joanna was there when Jared first told me about Hell. And I voiced my thoughts with her. That's all."

"Yeah? That's not fucking all. Why the hell didn't you tell me?"

Why hadn't Sarah?

She'd not always been close to her father; they were too much alike. Stubborn. Proud. Not until she was a teenager when her mother had died in a fall while exploring city ruins and the shared grief of the experience had drawn her, Lee, and Jared together.

But she'd always enjoyed the power that keeping secrets had given her. The control. The ability to surprise him at random with things and show how much she cared. A little note tucked in his pocket. A special birthday dinner. Or when they were teenagers and feeling the burn, organizing a secret rendezvous in the greenhouse at midnight so they could be alone.

He'd liked the unexpectedness, the intensity of her cleverness. It had kept their relationship exciting and alive. But this type of secrecy where she kept him from something important in her life—it twisted the grief he felt and brought up old insecure frustrations where he wondered if he'd ever really known his wife.

Lee shoved his hands in his pockets and blew out a breath of mist. "I wasn't sure, until I saw Hell with my own eyes. Until then, I didn't see the point in telling you something that could have been nothing more than an old man's delusional hope."

Peyton studied his seamed face; the lines grief had etched deep.

They seemed bottomless in the late afternoon lighting. Peyton wasn't the only one who missed Sarah. "You really think she created Hell?"

"She was obsessed with finding the solution. Winning the game. You know that," Lee said, his voice clear in the cold air. "It's what drove her to work on the neo-genesis project at The Factory in the first place."

Peyton stared at him, waiting for him to go on.

"One day when messaging, she seemed especially preoccupied. Tired. Distracted. Like she was struggling with something. I questioned her, of course. She shrugged off my concern at first. Said she'd been working too hard. But before she signed off, she said something that made me wonder if everything was all right. She said she wished she could make the project she was working on go faster so she could come home. To you."

Peyton stared at him, his gaze blurring as guilt and the loss of his dreams smashed his heart all over again. Maybe it had been selfish of him, but he'd never wanted her to leave Deliverance and work at The Factory. But it was what Sarah had wanted. What she'd said made her happy. Or so it had seemed at the time. But that hadn't stopped him from missing her every second she was away or telling her so every chance he'd gotten.

"It was shortly after that, when she came back for her next visit that she started talking about the progress she'd made in the Bioroid project. This time she was excited. She swore me to secrecy because it was still in its planning stage, but she thought she might have found a way to bring it to life earlier than projected. And that when it was finished, we were all going to be so surprised."

"Surprised? How?"

"I'm not sure, but I sure as hell am surprised to see how lifelike Helen is."

Yeah, Peyton had been pretty shocked by that fact himself.

"And here she is showing up out of the blue, like she knew exactly where to go for help," Lee said.

"You think Sarah gave her the information through the avatar program?"

"I'm not sure what I think about Helen. But I do know my daughter. And if she'd gotten herself in over her head with something because she'd taken a risk, I know she'd find a way to try and put it right. What is Helen's DNA made from?"

Peyton shrugged, his mind racing in time with his heart. The cold outside air wasn't helping to clear his thoughts like he'd hoped it would. "She's a hybrid of human and machine."

"Which human?" Lee probed, his blue eyes bright and intense.

"A cross section of DNA samples taken from the colony."

"Not Sarah?"

"Not hers alone, anyway. I didn't check to see whose DNA had been used for the mix."

"You might want to check that out, son." Lee's gaze remained on his, steady and sure.

"You think she used her own as the base?" Peyton asked, though he already knew the answer deep in his heart.

"If she was desperate enough and couldn't find an answer to a problem any other way? Yes."

"Oh, God. Oh, my God. Sarah." Agony lanced through Peyton. That kind of experimentation went against every rule in the book. What if she'd really done it? Compromised her professional integrity to try and wrap up her work faster, so she could save the world and come back to him as quickly as possible? "My God, baby, what did you do?" he whispered into the icy breeze.

He closed his eyes and shook his head, a sinking sensation settling in the pit of his stomach. He could see Sarah; he could see her doing it. Her brilliant mind. So quick, and always trying to find the perfect solution.

"She never said anything about it before she died," Lee said softly. "But I think we need to check it out now."

Peyton pressed the heels of his palms to his eyes. "She wouldn't have been able to once she was infected." A bitter laugh suddenly filled his chest and escaped as a hollow moan. "The Kareeza virus destroys memory first. We weren't there when she came home the last time. We arrived a few days later, remember, from the trip to the New York ruins? And by then the virus had already taken hold of her. Even if she'd wanted to, she couldn't have said anything about Hell then. So who the hell knows what happened at The Factory." He pushed away from the tree, angry fire racing though him. "*Those fucking bastards!*"

A bird cawed, disturbed by his rage as it echoed through forest. "They killed my wife. Stole her work. And tortured the fuck out of Hell. Because why? Because she wasn't supposed to exist anyway? So why not have a little fucking fun? Goddamnit!" If only he'd known, he could have stopped it. Could have rescued them both.

"Son," Lee's hand pressed his shoulder. "We don't know that's true."

"Bullshit."

He beat his fist against the tree trunk, not caring if the rough bark shredded the glove. He needed to punch the shit out of something. To fix the injustice that had been done. To give him the answer he desperately needed to the question pounding though his mind, *Why, Why, Why didn't you trust me, Sarah? Why?*

He should never have let her work at that damn Factory. He should have put his foot down and told her no. Kept her safe. Loved her more. Loved her so much she never died.

"Son," Lee said again, his voice full of emotion. "It's not your fault. Not any of it."

Peyton didn't say anything. Couldn't. Or he might choke on the grief blurring his eyes and piercing his chest with stabs of guilt. Because he knew damn well it was his fault for not protecting his wife. For not loving her enough she could trust him with all her innermost secrets, whether she'd done wrong or right. And now she was dead, gone, except for the legacy of her life.

Which he'd just spent the past two days fucking.

And maybe, just maybe, beginning to more than like.

He shook off Lee's hand and punched the tree trunk again, enjoying the ache that ricocheted through his hand. It was better than the one which consumed his heart.

"Think, Peyton. If Sarah knew she was in trouble, what do you think she'd do?" Lee asked.

"Obviously not trust me enough to tell me," Peyton said and punched the tree again.

"If she wanted to protect us, and couldn't say anything, what would she do?"

"She'd leave a message somehow."

"My thoughts exactly."

Breath panting in a cloud of mist, Peyton turned to face Lee, the man who'd been like his father ever since his own had died, who'd mentored him, and grieved with him. Who'd given him the space he needed to deal with Sarah's loss for the past two years. Who stood before him now, his eyes filled with a fierce, determined light.

"If Sarah is inside of Hell somewhere as that avatar program, we need to help her come alive. To find out what really happened."

Peyton nodded, the realization taking root that all the answers he sought might literally lie within Hell as the digital ghost of the woman he'd loved most of his life, a ghost that might have been trying for the past two years to find him.

Was that why he felt so drawn to Hell?

Because Sarah had designed her and left a piece of herself behind?

The part of him that would give anything to have Sarah back leapt forward with a savage growl. But the part of him that had gotten him through the grief of the past two years looked at the problem with a practical eye. It was possible Sarah existed somewhere inside Hell, except for one thing.

"Hell knows what Sarah looks like. She saw an image of her in my mind when we were connected through the scanner before her surgery. But she doesn't recognize the image of the avatar."

Lee paused for a long minute. "You said yourself that who she was before the surgery isn't who she is now. It's possible her memory of what Sarah looks like was damaged or removed during the operation. Or maybe Sarah's image of herself is different than what you remembered. Maybe if we show Hell a picture, it will activate that part of her memory?"

Peyton closed his eyes, wishing he could go back to the moment he'd woken this morning with the warmth of Hell's body beside his and her scent filling his mind. For a second before he'd blinked his eyes open, he'd been at peace. A far cry from what he was now.

He glanced at Lee again. "I can try that. But her mind is still recovering from the trauma she's been through. I don't want to upset her more or have anything else happen to her. She's been through enough."

"I'm not suggesting we do anything drastic," Lee said. "But over the next few days if we talk about Sarah and show Hell the things Sarah used to like, it might bring back the connection she's lost to the avatar."

"And if the avatar isn't Sarah?"

"Then we still need to figure out who it is and if it can communicate with us. Because if what you suspect is true about the criminal activity going on at The Factory, then we need to shut it all down for good. No one else should suffer like this. And we need to clear the name of Deliverance Colony and my daughter."

BAGGAGE

THE SOUND OF bootfalls in the snow made Peyton turn. Hesitant steps followed by more sure ones. His heart leapt in recognition; it knew who he'd find before he saw her.

Jared walked beside Hell, his arm wrapped about her shoulders as he helped her gingerly follow the trail of boot prints Peyton and Lee had made earlier. She stepped carefully into each hollow, as if uncertain of her footing. Her gaze caught Peyton's as she chanced a glance upward, her eyes full of determination.

Stopping by Peyton and Lee, she turned to Jared. "Thank you for your help. I'll be okay now," she said with a bright smile.

Jared paused and glanced at Peyton, his gaze full of reluctance, as if apologizing for bringing her out to him. But knowing how stubborn Hell could be, she probably hadn't left him any choice. "If you're sure...?"

Peyton answered Jared's raised brow with a reassuring nod.

"Well," Lee said, filling the awkward moment. "I'll leave you both alone, then." He smiled at Hell and glanced at Peyton with a meaningful look which appeared to wish him luck. Then he clasped Jared's shoulder and followed his son back to the transport.

Hell wiggled her boots in the footprint hollows she stood in, as if fascinated by the slipperiness and squeaking sound the snow made. "I've never experienced snow before. It's...different."

"Yes," was all he could manage as reality kicked him hard in the chest again. Of course, she wouldn't have been outside before. She'd been held captive for at least two years.

She seemed so small, so fragile, and blindingly beautiful standing there in one of Aunt Joanna's bulky parkas, her sunshine hair escaping in long waves from beneath her snug-fitting hat, and her amber eyes soft as they studied him.

She reached for his gloved hand and lifted it, examining the torn material where the rough bark had shredded it. "You're self-harming again." Her lips pulled into a frown. "You shouldn't do that."

Tugging his glove off of his fingers, she pressed her lips to his bruised knuckles. Then quickly slipped the glove back into place and caught his hand in hers. The simple intimate gesture almost made him lose his footing as she stepped forward into the undisturbed snow and tugged him along with her.

"Let's walk," she said. "I've never been outside like this before. It's pretty."

He nodded and wrapped his arm about her shoulders, pressing her side against his. So slight, even with the bulky coat she wore. "Are you sure you aren't too cold?"

"I'm fine," she said.

They walked a few steps in silence, she carefully stepping into the soft snow and smiling as her boots disappeared, and he enjoying her joy in this new experience even as it was bittersweet.

He didn't know where to begin this conversation. Or even what the hell he should think.

How could he ask her about Sarah? About whether or not his dead wife currently occupied space in her head? Did he really want to talk to Sarah? Even if she was inside Hell, what the hell would he say to her?

Hey, baby, I miss you. But I wish you'd told me about your experiment. She's amazing and stubborn, just as you were brilliant and stubborn. I've been fucking her, by the way. You did a fantastic job of making her so real I think I might be falling in love with her.

"I don't know anything, you know," Hell said suddenly. "About me, or you or Sarah. Or even this world," she added after a pause, her attention trained on the snow and how it fluffed into a spray of sparkling crystals when she kicked it into the air. "What happened to everything? Why did all the people die?" She stopped playing with the snow and turned to face him, her expression full of curiosity and a hint of sadness. "Why was I made?"

He cleared his throat. "You were meant to save us." It was the simplest explanation, but as her expression shifted from curiosity to confusion, he glanced at the nearby range of hills and decided to start at the beginning. "Do you see those structures that look like broken trees? That used to be a city."

Enormous spires twisted from the landscape, like gnarled fingers grasping the sky. Powder-white rime frosted each beam, creating a skeletal forest of metal, stark in contrast to the green conifers which dotted the hills.

"A city?"

"A northern metropolis once ten times the size of the Arkopolis, housing several million people. All that's left are a few supports from the central buildings."

"Why are they all twisted about like that?"

"Fire," Peyton said, and wrapped his arm around her shoulders tighter. "Even perma-steel warps under extreme heat." When she didn't say anything, he added, "Can you imagine how it once looked, though? A millennia ago, these buildings were a testament to mankind's success, shining towers meant to last forever that reached high into the sky." Ice crunched under his boots as he shifted a nearby chunk of frost-covered stonework with his toe. "Now it's all turned to rubble and dust."

The wind puffed cold against his face and swirled wisps of snow around the shafts of ancient metal. Nothing grew in the base of the icy cityscape. Scrub and conifers ended on the hillside where rubble began. Eroded by relentless centuries of weather, broken brickwork had settled into snow-swept hillocks surrounding the defeated supports. The rest of what had made the place a city was now gone. Incinerated maybe or buried beneath the frozen rubble. Much like he'd often wished his heart had been buried when Sarah had died. But feeling Hell's warm body nestled against his, he knew it was strong and alive.

"So much for the permanence of man's monumental erections," she said.

"What?" An unexpected laugh escaped him.

"I was talking about the buildings," she said and gestured at the twisted beams, but there was a distinct twinkle in her eyes.

"Uh-huh." Peyton grinned. He pulled her in front of him, so he could wrap his arms around her and feel her ass pressed against his groin. "If you're interested in erections, I've got one you can take a closer look at," he murmured beside her ear. Even now, when his heart ached and his soul bled, he craved her.

She giggled. "Yours isn't monumental."

"Keep wiggling like that, sweetheart, and it will be."

"Mmmm," she murmured and snuggled closer against him, sliding her arms over his. "What happened here? You said there was a fire. Was there a war?"

He tucked her head beneath his chin. "The fire happened because no one was left to keep the city maintained. Probably took a few years for corrosion to do its work, but without anyone to repair things—like the gas pipelines running beneath the streets— it was only a matter of time before explosions happened. The failsafe devices basically...failed."

"Where did the people go?"

"Do you remember anything about the Arkology mission?"

"No," she said softly, all of the laughter gone from her voice.

He caressed her gloved fingers with his own. "A thousand years ago, Earth was very different from now. Overpopulated. Polluted. On the brink of annihilation." He gestured at the frozen hill and its wasteland of skeletal towers. Silence filled the crisp air, broken by the occasional bird call and gust of wind rattling through bracken and trees. "With global famine and war raging and the planet's resources stretched beyond sustainability, there were only two clear choices for survival. Curb the population growth or leave to explore new planets to colonize. My ancestors chose option two. They hoped the answers to our problems lay amongst the stars, while others felt it existed here on earth through genetic modification. Both plans were put into effect. And ultimately both failed." A bitter smile twisted his lips. "Who knew we'd end up using the terraforming technology to recolonize Earth."

"Is that why you came back? To help out here?"

Peyton shook his head. "Not exactly. The Arkology mission didn't work out as planned. The idea was to collect a cross sample of humanity from all the continents. The best and brightest, healthiest, and, of course, wealthiest, were offered a chance to build a new life on a new world." He shifted his feet in the snow, enjoying the warmth of her pressed against him. It seemed to calm his raging soul. "It was a desperate gamble at best, setting out untested to find a new home. Very risky, considering extra-solar space travel hadn't been attempted before, and how little we knew for certain about the nearby planets similar to Earth. But still, the expectation was to find something out there we could make into a new home. Three ships left. Only one survived. The others lost contact and were presumed destroyed."

Hell stiffened within the cage of his arms. "Only one? That's not good odds."

"No. It was one problem after another: unstable plate tectonics, an atmosphere rich in gasses other than oxygen." He waved his hand at the list in his mind. "Turns out Earth is quite unique in terms of supporting human life. After centuries without finding a successful match, the A.I. running the mission decided the best choice for our survival was back on Earth, so it set course for home and awakened the crew as the ship entered the outer Sol system. Problem is humans hadn't traveled so far and for so long in space before. The long-term effects of micro-gravity and inter-stellar radiation weren't known."

"I take it they are known, now?"

Peyton caressed her arms as he nodded. "Half the passengers died in cryo-sleep. Most of the survivors, like my aunt, found they were sterile."

"Wait a minute. Your aunt? And Lee Palmer? They're part of the original crew?" She turned in his arms to stare at him, her eyes wide with shock.

"Yes."

"That makes them..." Her gaze became unfocussed as she did the math.

"Over a thousand Earth-years old, due to the cryo-sleep and time distortion of FTL space travel. Look good for their age, don't they?"

She blew out a long breath. "Definitely. But that makes you..."

"Part of a new generation conceived through in vitro fertilization. I was born as the ship passed Venus on its way back to Earth."

Her brows drew together. "You...weren't born on Earth?"

"No." Peyton studied her thoughtfully. "In that respect, you're officially more native to this planet than me."

"I think you're forgetting I wasn't actually born. I didn't have a mother."

"Maybe not in the conventional sense, but you were grown from cell tissue derived from a cross-section of humanity. This entire world is your mother if you want to think of it that way. And you represent a real breakthrough in our goal to facilitate human life."

Her expression became shadowed. "How very...clinical."

He stroked her cheek with his gloved finger. "We had hoped to find people living here, to mix our genes with, but that wasn't the case. You really are very important, Hell."

"How many humans are left?"

"In the seven Domes settled across the continents, including what remains of Deliverance…barely three thousand people.”

“That’s…that’s not nearly enough for natural genetic diversity, is it?”

“No,” he said, his voice somber, riveting her attention. “Without genetic engineering, in less than five thousand years, there won’t be anyone left to tell whether a bear shits in the woods.”

She squeezed her eyes shut tight and shook her head as if the importance of what he’d just revealed was too large to bear. “That’s why you need me. Because I’m adaptable. I can be programmed to live in any environment…and propagate.” Her gloved hand slipped down to rest above her uterus.

“Yes.”

“So the genetic research didn’t fail then. Because I exist.”

“Not exactly. Genetic research to better the species has been going on for millennia. A little snip here, a little addition there, and people can run faster, breathe deeper despite polluted air, and fight off diseases without ever getting sick. But it’s a game of give and take. With each change, the pattern alters, sometimes in ways no one can determine until generations later.”

“And then it’s too late to go back?”

“Or attempts to fix the problems end up making things worse. We know the people living on Earth did some heavy genetic experimentation during the years we were gone. There are interesting mutations in some of the plants and animals that have happened far quicker than a few thousand years of natural selection can account for. Which is why we have to be careful what comes into the Dome. The air we breathe is fine, but much of the landscape, especially around the cities, is still contaminated.”

“Contaminated? With what?”

Peyton ran his hand along her arms and pulled her close again as he followed her alarmed gaze to the dead city. “Don’t worry, we’re fine here. But traces of a virus, well intended, but gone wrong, were found in the desiccated remains of humans around the globe. The infection probably happened fast, traveling the planet in a matter of months, burning through the population, and burning out itself as a result. To be safe, we created an antigen to protect ourselves from exposure, but…things have slipped through the cracks.”

“What do you mean?”

“The viral signature is a cousin to the Kareeza Idiopathic Syndrome.”

“A genetically tailored virus destroyed humanity and you’re

telling me a mutation is what devastated your Dome? No wonder everyone is afraid to have anything to do with Deliverance!"

"I suspect it's not a natural mutation."

"What? After all that's happened, someone deliberately tampered with the virus and created a new one?"

"It's never been proven, but I think so."

She turned to face him fully again, horror clear in her expression. "Why would someone do such a thing?"

"The virus which destroyed humanity was designed to solve the overpopulation problem by curbing reproduction." He kept her gaze glued to his. "I can only assume someone at The Factory thought to manipulate the strain and produce an altered version that would enhance reproduction instead. A very dangerous gamble with predictable results."

"Oh. Oh, Peyton!" She wrapped her arms about his waist and pulled him close, pressing her cheek against his chest.

His gloved fingers smoothed her cold hair. "Not everyone believes in the neo-genesis project. It wasn't a unanimous vote. Some people think that there's still a chance to fix our reproductive problems by manipulating the human genome itself and that creating life using bio-robotics is an abomination."

She jerked. "Is that what I am? An abomination?"

He shook his head. "Not to me."

She pushed away from him and started pacing. "It sounds to me like you're all still busy fighting amongst yourselves about what to do and haven't learned anything from the past. A once mighty race, brought to its knees by its own stupidity. How very sad."

Peyton nodded, but couldn't help the edge of anger which flared inside him. "You're right. It is sad. This whole hellish situation is fucking unbearable." *And we've put you right into the middle of it.*

"I'm not her, you know," she said, suddenly turning to face him. "I know you're wondering if I am because of what Lee said, but I'm not Sarah." She tapped her chest, her eyes flashing with hurt and anger. "I'm the girl on the other side of the glass. The one that was left behind."

The angry ache in his chest expanded until he thought it might burst. He caught her and clutched her to him tightly, trying to make up for the years of her torture and captivity with his closeness now. "Shit, baby. Oh, shit. If I'd known, I'd have come rescue you. I'd have killed those motherfuckers before they had a chance with that knife."

She studied him, her gaze somber. "But you want me to be, don't you? You want me to be Sarah, deep down inside."

"I don't know what I want anymore," he said, truthfully. The lines had become blurred. Was it possible to love Sarah and Hell at the same time? And what the fuck did he want to love anyone for, anyway? That path led straight to insanity and a broken heart all over again.

"It's okay, you don't need to lie. I'm designed to adapt, to become what you most want. My roots are already coming in darker because I know you like brown hair. See?" She tugged off her hat and showed him the dark edges of her hair that were beginning to grow in. "And my breasts." She tossed her hat to the ground and cupped them through her coat. "Maybe you can't tell yet, but they're growing larger. Just the way you like them. Just like hers, right?"

"You're physically changing to be more like Sarah?" Icy horror twisted inside him.

"It's what you want, isn't it?"

"No," he said and let go of her abruptly.

"But you still love her." She seemed genuinely puzzled.

He grabbed her arms again and shook her slightly until she held his gaze. "Listen. Whether you're a clone of her or not, or have her avatar trapped inside, it doesn't make a difference to me. You don't have to change to be more like her to please me. That's the last thing I want." He couldn't imagine living the rest of his life with an imitation of his dead wife. He caressed a strand of her pale hair and let it fall through his gloved fingers. "You're unique. Special. Just the way you are." He swallowed hard at the way her eyes glistened. Maybe it was from the cold, but maybe something more. And he needed her to understand. "But if Sarah is inside of you somewhere, we need you to help us find her. It's very important, Hell."

"Of course it is," she said her voice a bare whisper, but clear in the crisp winter air. She swallowed hard. Her gaze slid from his.

He pulled his tablet out of his pocket and accessed his pictures file. Selecting which ones he needed, he set it to carousel the album. His hand shook slightly as he handed the device to Hell.

"Is this the person who speaks to you? The woman you've been seeing?"

She stared at the images as they cycled by on the screen. Pictures of Sarah that he liked best. Favorites from the life they'd shared.

Her face twisted, her lips pulling into a pained smile. "You were so happy together."

Her expression didn't change as she handed back the tablet to him, but he saw the answer in the tears filling her eyes even before she licked her lips and nodded.

"Yes," she choked out. "I think so." She covered her face with her hands but couldn't hide the sob that shook her.

"Oh, fuck." He pulled her close, wrapping her shaking body tight in his arms. "Oh, shit, I'm sorry. You don't have to cry, baby." He'd done it again. Hurt her, just like he'd never wanted to, but it seemed it was impossible for him to be around Hell without causing her some kind of pain.

"I don't know who I am anymore," she sobbed into his chest, clutching him tight. "I don't know what I am."

"Shhh," he whispered, stroking her hair, dotting gentle kisses to the top of her hair, willing the pain that bled out of her and into him to stop. *Please, stop.* "I'm sorry, love. So sorry."

"Tell me who I am. Please," she begged.

"You're mine," he said over and over, kissing her face and her hair, her soul, until finally the tears subsided, and they stood in the cold breeze together, sheltered in each other's warmth. "You're mine. And I'm never letting you go."

RECLAIMING

"WHY AM I in here?" Hell asked, only her name wasn't Hell. It was...she struggled to remember as she pressed her hand to the glass.

The woman on the other side of the wall looked up from the computer screen where she sat at her worktable. She smiled that distracted, pretty smile she always smiled whenever Hell asked a question these days. Only this time the little lines between her brows deepened and the smile didn't reach her blue eyes.

"Don't you like your room, Elf?"

Elf, yes, that was her name. She'd seen it written on a report once, ELf-3. She glanced around her room. Brightly lit, with a monitor on the wall that she used for her lessons. The bed where she slept, covers neatly folded in place like she'd been taught, a sink and shower where she could keep herself clean, and the toilet where she took care of other necessary things. It was a nice room, but she had the feeling that more existed in the world than a room made of glass walls kept inside a dark place.

"Yes, but why do I have to be in here? Why can't I go with you when you leave each day?"

"Because you're very special, Elf. So special I need to keep you safe."

"Is it dangerous outside my room?" That thought made her pause and replaced curiosity with fear.

"Yes."

"Why?" She ran her hand along the glass, feeling the familiar cold smoothness caress her skin. If the doctor said it was dangerous outside her room, then it must be something bad. The doctor was her only friend in the world, and she never lied.

The doctor sighed and Hell knew she'd asked one of those questions that was the kind her friend found difficult to answer, the kind that made her seem anxious. Hell didn't like to make her anxious, it made her pretty blue eyes seem sad, and the tiny lines at the corners of her mouth pull down.

"It's complicated to explain," the doctor said. "But we have to keep you in here for a little while longer. It's for your own good. One day, when it's safe, you'll come live with me until we can find a proper place of your own. You'd like that, wouldn't you, Elf?" She pushed back her long brown hair with her hands, refastening the clasp which held it in place at her nape.

"Yes." Hell mimicked the action, pulling her own pale hair back from her face and pretending to fix it in a clasp, but when she let go, it fell back around her face. Disappointed, she frowned, but the doctor had already turned back to her work at the computer and Hell didn't want to disturb her again over something as silly as a pretty clasp.

The door opened at the far end of the room on the other side of the glass, the door which led to the outside that the doctor said was dangerous. A red-haired woman walked in wearing a white outfit similar to what the doctor wore. She was the only other person Hell remembered seeing. She didn't like this one as much. Her dark green eyes never sparkled when she smiled, and she poked Hell with needles and always stared at her when she cleaned herself in the shower. But she ignored Hell now as she shut the door again and walked over to the doctor.

"The new test results are back, Dr. Chase," she said and handed the doctor a tablet.

The doctor took it with barely a glance and set it on the table, her attention transfixed by whatever she was working on at her computer.

The thin, red-haired woman stared at Hell now, her bold gaze assessing from the top of her head, down her skin-hugging outfit, to her slipper-covered feet. "It really is amazing," she said cocking her head to the side. "You used your own DNA as a base to clone from, but she doesn't look anything like you."

"She isn't supposed to," the doctor said absentmindedly. "She's designed to be blank. A basic form to build on. She can be adapted to whatever the circumstance requires. That's where the extra gene hybridization comes in, to allow diversification."

"She'll be worth a fortune on the market."

"Perhaps. But she isn't for sale, Clarissa, and she never will be." The doctor glanced up from her computer. "She's meant for much bigger things, aren't you, Elf?" And the proud smile she gave Hell filled her with such pleasure, it chased away any concern over what those 'bigger things' might be.

Clarissa glanced at Hell and back at the doctor. "Really," she said and sounded unimpressed. She crossed her arms over her chest and sat on the desk, disrupting the doctor's view of the computer screen with her body. "Willbright is going to take her away from you as soon as he knows what you've done." She shook her head. "Using your own ova—"

"I wouldn't have had to if he'd given me permission to use a sample from the genetics bank. He forced my hand. But look at her. She's perfect!"

Dr. Chase rose from her chair and walked to the glass smiling at Hell, her expression filled with pride, but there was a wildness to her eyes, as if she was forcing the happiness she felt. Hell pressed her hands to the glass, suddenly wishing she could pull her friend through and inside her room where it was safe.

The doctor's hands were so like hers, resting on the opposite side of the glass. Same size, same shape, except she had that pretty ring and Hell had no prettiness at all.

"You *are* perfect," the doctor whispered, studying Hell's face. "The most perfect creature that ever lived."

Hell wanted to say yes, she was perfect, because it seemed so important to the doctor that she was right. But she couldn't speak the lie. How could she be perfect and not be able to keep the anxiety from filling her friend's eyes? Surely a perfect creature would be able to do something like that.

Clarissa moved from the desk to stand behind the doctor. She put her hands on her shoulders and began to massage them lightly.

"You know you could have used one of my eggs," she said with a soft smile. "I wouldn't have minded."

"The risk was mine to take," the doctor said. She closed her eyes and rested her forehead on the glass wall.

"I love how protective you are," Clarissa said. "Well, you know your secret's safe with me...all your secrets are." The red-haired woman placed a gentle kiss on her cheek. "No one has to know anything we don't want them to."

A frown crossed the doctor's face, but she didn't pull away as the kisses continued, soft by her ear and up the side of her face. Clarissa stopped the gentle massage and ran her hands along the doctor's arms, leaning against her body until Dr. Chase's breasts were pressed against the glass and their fingers were linked.

"You seem tense today. What's wrong? Your husband hasn't found out about us, has he?" Clarissa asked softly, her brows drawn.

The doctor shook her head, but kept her eyes shut tight. "No."

"Good," Clarissa murmured. "I know you love him, but... I love what we have together too. You're so damn hot."

Watching Hell through the glass, she moved one of her hands down the tight-fitting outfit which covered the doctor's body, over her stomach and touched the place between her legs the doctor said no one was ever to touch. Not unless permission was given, and with the way the frown on the doctor's face deepened, Hell was sure permission hadn't been given. Or had it?

As Clarissa's fingers moved, Dr. Chase's expression softened, and she gave a little gasp that made the red-haired woman smile. "Damn, girl. I love the sounds you make. I bet he does too. Maybe one day he can join us when he's ready to understand. What do you think? Two pussies, one cock. I can show him how you really like it, and he can—"

"Not here," the doctor said her tone pleading. "Not in front of her." Her eyes flashed open, and the look she gave Hell was full of so much desperation, Hell covered her mouth to stop from screaming.

"Why not? She's curious. Aren't you, Elf?"

Hell shook her head and backed away, confused about what was going on, and why it made her pulse race and her nipples hard and filled her with mixed feelings. This wasn't what her friend wanted, was it? Clarissa was touching Dr. Chase in secret places, that made her eyes clench tight, and her pulse race, and her fingertips whiten where they pressed hard against the glass.

"Anywhere, anytime I want, that's what you said, Sarah. What we both agreed to, right? You aren't going back on your word now, are you?"

Dr. Chase shook her head. "No."

"No, what?" Clarissa pressed, nipping her earlobe.

The doctor gasped, her cheeks reddening. But her voice didn't waver as she said, "No, I'm not going back on my word. You can do whatever you want with me."

"Mmmm, yes." Clarissa smiled. "Yes, I can, can't I? And you

love it so much. Is it the playing hard to get or how good it feels to submit that turns you on more? You're always so damn wet."

Dr. Chase's gaze found Hell's, full of desperation, and shame, and things Elf couldn't quite understand. "Look away, now, Elf," she begged. "Look away."

Look away!

Hell sat bolt upright on her makeshift bed, ripping away the wires and electrodes that connected her head to the portable medical scanner beside her.

"Oh, fuck," she said and clutched her hands to her face.

"What is it? What's wrong, baby?" Beside her on the narrow cot, Peyton wrapped his arms around her, but she didn't dare take her hands away from her face.

"Hell?" The anxiety in his voice brought tears to her eyes. She wiped them with the heels of her hands and slowly lowered them, taking a few shaky breaths.

"It was a dream. Just a bad dream," she managed to say.

"It must have been," he said. "I've never heard you swear like that before." He was trying to make her smile. But she felt too sick inside, too shaken to do more than grimace.

In the dim lighting of the cargo hold, she could just make out the furrowing of his brow as he gently touched her temple with his fingers.

"You're shaking, Hell. Tell me what's wrong. Is it your head?"

She shook it. "It's fine, I just... Can you get me some water, please?"

He nodded, still studying her closely. Then left the compartment by opening the door as softly as possible and quietly entering the darkened crew quarters to find a glass from the galley.

It must be still nighttime. And the others asleep.

She grasped the moment to try and calm her breaths, but quicker than she could reflect on what she'd just witnessed in her dream, Peyton was back and closing the door again, glass of water in hand.

"Thank you," she said as she took it from him.

He settled back onto the cot beside her while she took a sip. There was barely enough room for the two of them, hemmed in between the bench and the racks of gear, but at least it afforded them a bit more privacy than the pull-down bunks the others were sleeping on in the crew cabin.

Peyton picked up the portable scanner from the bench and

studied the readout. "You were in deep REM sleep, which is good because it means your mind is healing. But I wish we had access to my scanner at home. This little one doesn't record your dreams, just your neuro activity."

Thank the Maker for that, thought Hell.

She couldn't imagine how Peyton would react if he'd seen what she'd just seen. Actually, she could imagine how he'd react. Seeing his beloved, pristine wife with another woman and how much she enjoyed it was the last thing he needed right now.

"Did you see the avatar?"

She shook her head. "No, it was just a dream."

He seemed disappointed by that. He and the others desperately wanted to speak with Sarah. To know what had happened at The Factory before she'd died. But Hell was certain that some truths were best left buried, especially this one. Sarah had loved Peyton, she was sure of that. But Clarissa hadn't seemed to be cruel. Had Sarah loved her too?

"What was it about?" he prompted. He wore only boxers, his fit arms and chest illuminated by the shadowy light. She ran her eyes over the contrast between dark and light and the play of his muscles, finding comfort in his familiar beauty and warm, masculine scent.

"I was at The Factory," was all she said, hoping he wouldn't press any further. She couldn't lie to him, but she also didn't want to hurt him with the truth.

"Aww, baby," he said and pulled her against him. "No wonder you woke up scared like that. That wasn't a dream, it was a nightmare."

"Yes." She had no problem agreeing to that.

He rocked her gently, stroking his hand up and down her back. Like usual, she was naked except for one of his shirts. Taking the glass from her hand and setting it on the bench, he kissed her forehead, her cheek, her mouth. Softly at first, then more insistently as the heat of his body warmed her.

Pulling back, he tugged her down onto the cot beside him, his hand wandering over her thigh. "Come on, sweetheart. I'll give you something better to think about."

His mouth found hers again as he held her close, and his hand slid to the junction of her thighs. It felt so good to be touched and held by him, she wanted to lose herself in the closeness forever.

But it was too soon, too close to what she'd just seen in her dream. The sickness she'd felt at witnessing Sarah's attack still had her in its grasp. It twisted inside her, making her pull away when she'd rather be giving back.

"Hell?" Peyton asked, confusion clear in his voice.

"Can we just...cuddle, for a little while?" she asked, feeling like the world had stopped spinning and a hole had opened up inside.

"Sure, baby. Whatever you would like."

God. He was so gentle, so perfect. She couldn't help the tears that prickled her eyes as he readjusted her so her back was against his front and he wrapped her tight in the safe warm cage of his arms.

She played with the hairs on his arms, and snuggled back against his erection, knowing that even though he wanted her, he'd never take her that way unless she asked. Which was more than she could say anyone else had ever done for her in her life. Or Sarah's.

"I love you, Peyton," she whispered, so softly she half-hoped he wouldn't hear her. But by the slight shift of his breath against her ear, she knew he had.

It didn't matter that he didn't answer.

Because she knew deep in her soul that time wasn't on their side. She could only put off the inevitable questions about Sarah and her involvement at The Factory for so long. Eventually they'd return to Deliverance, and that scanner, and Peyton would learn the truth about her.

She was the cause of every last ounce of grief in his life where Sarah was concerned.

So it didn't matter that he didn't love her.

Because he was going to hate her with every inch of his heart.

WHERE THERE'S SMOKE

"I'LL TAKE CARE of it as soon as I get back." Peyton's tired voice drifted across the crew quarters in the small transport.

It was at least the hundredth time Hell had heard him utter the phrase in the past twenty minutes. She snuck a peek at him over Joanna's shoulder as she placed a wrapped rectangle of soy protein onto the galley countertop. Seated at the table with his back turned toward them, Peyton spoke via his tablet to his 'friend' Genova at Deliverance Dome.

"Yes, I understand." He scrubbed his fingers through his dark hair. "Try auto-calibrating the pressure sensors on the sprayer intake valves. It should increase the water flow. But I'll take a look at it when I get back." He shifted in his seat, long legs stretching, and Hell caught a glimpse of the pretty woman on the screen. Genova's full lips pulled upward into a pleased smile as she moved the conversation to yet more problems in the greenhouse that'd crept up at the Dome—difficulties it seemed only Peyton could fix.

Hell drummed her fingers against the hard countertop.

Three days.

It had been three days since the revelation about her connection with Sarah.

Three days full of sideways glances from the crew, whispered conversations the others thought she couldn't hear, and fractured sleep where she lay awake beside Peyton on the cot, fearing that if she closed her eyes another nightmare memory might surface.

Three days since they'd last had sex.

Not that either of them had been avoiding the subject. The desire remained the same, but neither of them had made a point to act on it. Not even when they were alone at night in their makeshift room in the cargo hold. Peyton would kiss her, soft and sweet and full of toe-curling desire that made her heart race...and then she'd turn away. Shy, awkward, afraid to move within the cage of his arms until his breathing changed and he'd fallen asleep.

Something had changed.

And she was pretty sure it was her and the secret she held in her heart.

Frowning, she poked at the squishy package of soy and glanced at Joanna.

"Isn't there anyone else at the Dome who can fix things while he's gone?"

"Humm?" Aunty Jo looked up from the box of food containers they were sorting through. "Oh, of course there is, dear. Peyton just has a knack for finding solutions."

"Genova seems to need a lot of solutions found," Hell muttered, then instantly regretted it as Joanna's perceptive gaze narrowed on her accompanied by a knowing smirk.

"Put her out of your mind, dear. She just enjoys attention. Peyton has you now. And if there's one thing my nephew stands behind, it's commitment."

Commitment. The image of Sarah with her lab assistant flashed through Hell's mind, making her stomach clench tight again.

Hell had been worried that in the close proximity of the transport Peyton might confront her over whether or not she remembered anything yet about Sarah. He hadn't, however, tried to push her into recalling details of her life at The Factory. If anything, he and the others had been nice. Too nice. Including her in every aspect of their lives, from the superfluous argument of whether The Chase was rigged and Vassino had lost the last race on purpose, to deciding the best course of action needed to fix the Reclaimer once they found it.

They were trying hard to help her fit in and show her that she belonged with them. Help her remember all about their beloved Sarah Palmer Chase by bringing that part of herself to life with patience and understanding.

But how the hell was she supposed to tell them the truth? That she didn't want to be Sarah Chase because Sarah had done things that would break their hearts? Wasn't it better to keep that information from them and save them the pain?

Peyton had tried to protect her after her surgery by denying her access to the truths stored on the data cube. He'd wanted to save her from the pain the truth would bring. She was doing the same now, protecting him. And that was the right thing to do, wasn't it? What you did when you loved someone? You protected them?

But didn't you argue that knowing the truth, no matter how painful it might be, was better than living a lie? Sarah's voice whispered through her mind.

Is that what you want me to do? she asked the ghost. *Tell him you cheated?*

But like all her conversations with Sarah Chase, the ghost faded away as suddenly as she'd arrived, leaving the question unanswered.

It didn't matter. Hell knew the answer anyway. She was living on borrowed time. She couldn't lie to Peyton, and she couldn't hide the truth from him once back at Deliverance Dome and hooked up to that medical scanner.

The only thing she could do was decide how best to break the news to him.

And then embrace the inevitable pain the truth would bring.

Trouble was, she couldn't bring herself to embrace the pain, not when it meant Peyton would be tossed into a deeper pit of despair than the one she'd originally found him in.

"Do you think Peyton will ever want to move back to the main part of the Dome?" she asked Joanna quietly.

The older woman's lips pressed into a thin line as she darted a glance at her nephew. "I hope so. He took it hard when everyone died. I think he thought he could always win. The virus taught him a difficult lesson." The light from the galley lit the sadness in her green eyes. "No one blamed him for what happened. But he's beginning to open up again now that you're here. So there's hope." A smile flitted across her features. "Now..." She squinted at the label on the cream-colored cylinder and nodded. "We'll need this and...this." Selecting a small box, she offered it to Hell, who accepted the container automatically as her aching heart ached even more.

Joanna hoped Peyton was going to be okay now that Hell was there to bring Sarah back into his life.

And here Hell was, poised to destroy the little happiness he had left.

"Helen?" Joanna prompted.

"Umm? Oh...." She avoided Aunty Jo's scrutiny by lifting the lid on the container and making a show of breathing in the fragrant aroma of spices that tickled her nostrils. "This smells wonderful."

Joanna's smile brightened. "Basil, oregano, a bit of dried red bell pepper, some salt, dried garlic, and a touch of sage. Just the thing to add some zing to boring old soy protein cubes."

"Not pickles?" Hell joked.

Joanna patted her hand. "Pickles are a food best served as a condiment, dear."

"Not a mistake Sarah would've made, I'm sure," she said, unable to keep irritation from creeping into her voice.

The older woman's brow flicked as she peeled the crinkly wrapping from the large rectangle of fresh soy curd. "Actually, Sarah didn't like to cook. She relied on service-bots, or Peyton, to do it. She was always busy working, planning the eco-reclamation projects or working on the neo-genesis project at The Factory."

Yeah, she was busy, all right. Busy destroying her marriage.

Because as much as Hell believed that Sarah had initially been coerced into a relationship with her assistant, Sarah had also enjoyed it. And reciprocated the attention. The long pleasure-filled moans that Hell couldn't stop from echoing in her memory were proof of that.

Look away now, Elf. Look away!

She'd looked away as instructed. But that hadn't blocked out the sounds the two lovers had made. And although she couldn't remember anything else, she was sure it wasn't the only time they had enjoyed each other like that.

Avoiding Joanna's gaze, Hell put down the spices and reached for the glistening soy slab. "I can mash that."

Joanna handed her a bowl. "Just press it with the fork until it crumbles. Yes, that's the way. Like that."

Satisfyingly pliant, the cream-colored substance gave way to the tines of the metal fork with ease. "I like the way this feels when I squish it. It's satisfying." *Like I'm mashing Sarah's face,* she thought to herself as anger over what her predecessor had done flashed through her. *Peyton loved you! How could you do it? HOW?*

"Slow down, dear," Aunt Joanna said, taking the bowl from Hell. "We don't need it pureed."

"Oh...." Hell put down the fork as heat flushed her cheeks. "I'm sorry."

"Don't be sorry. You've done nothing wrong," Joanna said. She placed her arm around Hell's shoulders and gave them a small squeeze. "You seem agitated today. What's troubling you, dear?"

she asked quietly.

"I'm...I'm just trying to figure out this whole thing with Sarah," Hell said, unable to deny the truth.

Joanna nodded as if she'd expected that response. "It must be very confusing having part of her in here." The ceases in her face deepened as she smiled and tapped her finger to the middle of Hell's forehead. "Do you want to talk about it?"

Yes. No. Definitely no. Yes.

Hell glanced at Peyton still engrossed in his conversation with Genova. "I don't know," she said as she wiped her hands on a cloth and steadied them on the cool countertop. She closed her eyes, trying to settle the turmoil swirling inside her and keep it from spilling out, but her lips parted as if they had a mind of their own. "What was Sarah like? Before she went to The Factory?"

"Brilliant. Inventive. Driven to heal the rift between the planet and humanity. Maybe too driven. The idea of having a family came late in her plans. But who knows, it could be things would have turned out the same anyway."

Hell's eyes flashed open. "Peyton wanted children?"

"Oh, yes. Sarah kept putting it off, though. Her work was very important to her, but Peyton kept pressuring her to make a choice. My understanding is that she agreed to try once she was done with her research at The Factory."

"But then she died."

"Yes."

Taking all his dreams for the future with her.

She stared at Peyton, her pulse hammering. Why hadn't it occurred to her before that those dreams might have included offspring? A handsome, intelligent man like Peyton would of course want a family. And he'd want a mate who could satisfy all his needs, not just his sexual whims. Which meant he needed a *real* woman, with *real* ova, and a *real* chance at a new beginning. Someone like Genova. Not someone like Hell. She was just holding him back from moving on.

"I can't have children," she whispered.

"I'm sorry." Joanna gave her shoulders a tight squeeze, undisguised pity in her eyes. "I suppose the technology hasn't advanced that far yet?"

Hell managed a stiff shake of her head. "No. I *could* have had children. Maybe. Or at least there was the possibility, I think. But Peyton said my ova were missing when he examined me with the scanner. I'm sterile."

Joanna studied her thoughtfully. "How interesting. I'm sterile, too. A lot of us 'originals' are, thanks to the effects of long term cryo-sleep during space travel. But if all you need is some reproductive DNA, my dear, there's an entire cross section of the colonists' genes stored at The Factory."

"There is?"

"It could be where your ova are stored too. Genetic samples are collected for hybridization research. It still seems odd to me, making children using DNA from multiple parents, not just two. No offense dear, but when I was a girl, most babies were created the old-fashioned way. Not in Petri dishes."

Hell's mind raced as her heart pounded a new rhythm. "Can anyone access this fertility bank?"

"No. You need permission to use it. But since we intend to bring your abuse case before the High Council anyway, I'm sure we can put in a bid to have what genetic material was taken from you returned. If that's what you'd like to do," she added with a soft smile.

From the recesses of her secret hopes, the image of Peyton caressing her very pregnant belly swelled in Hell's mind, almost bringing her to tears with the vividness of the image.

Would that be something *he'd* want? A child? With her?

He'd never talked about it.

"How important is having children to Peyton now?" she asked Joanna quietly.

"I don't know, dear. That's something you'll have to ask him yourself."

Hell nodded. But if she could give him a child...maybe...maybe it might help him forget the past and everything yet to come with what she had to tell him about Sarah. Maybe it was a way to a new future for them.

All she had to do was retrieve her ova from The Factory, either with permission or without.

Can I go back there? They tried to kill me there. A shiver of fear caught her as it rippled down her spine. Memories of pain that made her body flush. The cruel edge of that knife... Her fingers gripped the edge of the counter.

I could do it for our future, she said to herself with a certainty which rose above the fear. *I could face anything for that chance.*

Yes... The word whispered through her mind like a pleased sigh from whatever recess of her brain Sarah occupied, bringing with it a sense of hope. A dangerous sense of hope. But hope was hope, nonetheless.

"You know," Joanna stared at her quizzically, "I wasn't sure at first what to make of you. But I like you, Helen. And if you're worried about how you fit in with the others, don't be. To be honest, I can't tell the difference. I wouldn't have guessed you were a Bio-roid unless I'd been told. But I suppose that's the point, isn't it?" She nodded toward the far side of the crew pod where Bambi sat out of the way beside Henry, brushing her long synthetic hair with a comb. "On the other hand, Dolls like Bambi are quite obvious. They are meant to serve a very specific need." Her eyes twinkled as she leaned closer and lowered her voice. "I've heard you can order male Dolls with a variety of, er...tools."

"Male Dolls? Really?" Hell scanned Joanna's expression for any signs of deception and found none. "I've never heard of a male Doll before. Why would anyone order one with different tools?"

"Hummm, well...a man you can program to please you in many ways has its merit, don't you think? And then there's the variable speed vibration..."

Variable speed vibration?

Joanna couldn't mean what Hell thought she meant, could she? Hell's gaze slid to Peyton. Then away again as certain lower body parts ached to feel the rhythmic 'vibrations' of *his* 'tool'.

"But I suppose you don't have any trouble in that department," Joanna said. "Peyton seems to keep you happy."

Oh, the Maker. I am so not going to discuss my sex life with Peyton's aunt.

"Um, well..." She picked up the fork and began to slowly stir the soy again. "He makes me angry with his rude remarks," she said changing the subject slightly, "but at the same time, I can't stop thinking about him. It's insane. I'd blame my damaged cortex, but I guess I'm programmed to like him no matter what."

"That sounds like love to me, dear. It doesn't always make sense who we fall for, but try as we might, we can't resist when it happens."

The cockpit door opened and Lee entered the crew pod on his way through to the cargo hold. As he passed by, Joanna's gaze lingered on him before flicking back to the bowl of mashed soy.

Uh-huh! It wasn't the first time Hell had noticed Joanna looking at Lee. Did Aunty Jo have an interest in him that she wanted to hide? Hell did her best to hide a smile. "Looks like I'm not the only one who's got love on the mind."

Joanna inhaled sharply. She studied Hell, face impassive. After a moment she looked toward the closed door through which Lee had disappeared. She clicked her tongue. "Love has nothing to do with it. We're old friends. And you can keep your opinions to yourself, thank you very much."

Hell bit back the urge to growl. Really? After all the opinions Joanna had tossed her way? Hell tossed down the fork and folded her arms. "Why won't you tell Lee you love him?"

"Excuse me?"

"If you love him, you should tell him."

Joanna's eyes flashed. "I thought I asked you to keep your opinions to yourself. The soy is mashed enough. You can turn on the grill while I add spices to the scramble." Color dotted Joanna's cheeks as she picked up the fork and focused on the pale paste inside the bowl. Her pinched expression indicated the subject was closed.

Hell turned the grill on to high and closed the lid to let it heat up. If Joanna thought it was okay to pry into other people's love lives but not open up about her own, she was dead wrong. "Lee is very handsome and intelligent. I can see why you're attracted to him."

Joanna made a disgusted noise. "You mashed this soy too much. It should still have some texture to it. We'll have to make burgers now." She tossed in some more spices, a splash of the creamy liquid from the jug, and busied herself mixing.

Ignoring the barb about her cooking ability, Hell leaned against the counter. "You're not the only one who's got complicated feelings for other crew members on this trip, you know."

Joanna gave her a sideways glance as she put down the fork. "What do you mean?"

"McClellan and Rusty," she whispered.

"*What?*" Joanna's gaze darted to the back of the crew compartment where the two men in question rested up for the hard work ahead, on separate cots. "You can't be serious."

"Oh, yes. There are very physical reactions in both their bodies when near each other, just like you and Lee. Accelerated pulse, enhanced pheromones, erectile—"

"Well, I'll be...I had no idea. I wonder if anyone else knows. Not that it matters. I mean, it's not uncommon to have multiple lovers, and not all men like only women, or women only men, or know what they really like until they experiment a bit..." Joanna shook her head as if to clear it. "Rusty likes to flirt with anyone in a skirt if given the chance. I've not seen him do so with men, but who knows, right? Mac, though. That's a shocker. He was married for several years to a lovely woman who was a friend of mine, and I never suspected he had other desires. But monogamy is sometimes more of a choice, I think. Mates come in all different shapes, genders, and sizes."

"Well, it looks like he's found a new mate."

Joanna smiled. "Well, if that's so, then I'm happy for both of them. We need more happy young-folk around this place."

Hell closed her eyes and concentrated on picking up the traces of pheromones dancing through the room. Joanna, so determined not to show her attraction, tried to reign hers in with a will as strong as perma-steel. The subtle perfume was there, however, attached to thoughts of Lee Palmer. On the cot, Rusty's young, virile scent called to McClellan in his sleep, inspiring a hard-on as well as uncertainty about the new direction his arousal had taken. Beside the window, Jared sat reading. Alone. His body sated by artificial love, but oh, so alone. And Peyton—

His aroused scent slammed into her like a fist, taking her breath away.

She gasped, eyes flashing open, as answering desire pumped through her veins and caused her nipples to tighten.

"What's wrong?" Joanna peered at her. "Your skin is flushed."

"Nothing." Hell turned away, clenching her thighs together to ease the intense throbbing there. "It's nothing." *Nothing some vibrating action couldn't fix, ha, ha.* She smiled and waved her hand over her face in an attempt to cool her racing pulse. "Whew, is it hot in here or what? For a group of people who claim you aren't attracted to each other, there sure is a lot of sexual tension flying around."

Joanna's laughter barked long and loud through the compartment. "Oh, my dear...you are a treasure."

Hell smirked. "Lee is attracted to you, too, you know."

"He's not." Humor slipped away as Joanna's expression became serious. "Lee and I have been friends a long time, since before the Arkopolis mission began. There has never been anything more between us."

"Oh, no? I can't believe that. You're both widowed. It's a logical choice."

Her expression hardened. "Believe what you will. On the romantic spectrum, he's never seen me as anything more than an annoyance."

"Funny, that's the way Peyton sees me," Hell said and matched Aunty Jo's implacable expression with one of her own. She was going to have to state the obvious in order to drive the point home. "But I also know he's got a hard-on the size of a fist right now," she added, "and it isn't for that woman he's talking to from the Dome. He's attracted to me, despite everything. And I think if you were to check in Lee's pants the next time you're both alone, you'd find—"

"I'm quite aware of what I'd find!" Joanna's face reddened. She pulled in a breath and gestured at the grill. "Put some sliced bread on that and make toast while I ready my panties, I mean, patties. Ready *the patties*," she corrected quickly.

Hell smirked and did as asked in silence, allowing Joanna a reprieve. Hot air warmed her fingers as she placed pieces of bread on the grill and closed the lid.

Joanna's strong hands worked, scooping up palmfuls of the soy mixture, rolling them into balls and then flattening them into thin disks. She stacked each on a plate to await grilling.

Without looking away from her task, Aunty Jo cleared her throat. "Thank the Lord we aren't making sausages," she said and choked on a giggle. "What I might find in Lee's pants, indeed."

Hell joined in the giggling. "But that won't be soy. That'll be some real meat," she couldn't resist saying.

Joanna gasped. "Oh! You are so bad!" But she was laughing, eyes bright and full of happiness. "To tell you the truth, I haven't eaten real meat in over a thousand years. I've forgotten what it tastes like." She sank against the counter, chuckling.

"A millennium without real meat?" It was Hell's turn to gasp. "That's long enough to declare yourself legally dead a hundred times over. Wait a minute, you haven't been ordering 'meal service' from one of those male Dolls, have you?"

Joanna raised her brows, her eyes sparkling mischievously.

"You have!"

Joanna put her hand over Hell's mouth to stifle her loud squeal. "Don't tell Peyton!" she hissed while grinning, "Or anyone else for that matter. They don't know I have one, and they'll never let me live it down. I have a reputation to uphold, you know." Astonishment must have shown on Hell's face, because Joanna added, "I might be old dear, but I'm not dead."

"Danger!" Henry suddenly shouted from where he sat beside the window. "Danger, danger!"

Arms waving, he headed in the direction of the galley as the scent of scorched bread tickled Hell's nostrils seconds before an alarm began to wail.

"Oh, my God!" Joanna reached for the grill and opened the lid, cursing. A plume of smoke rose into the air.

Coughing, Hell snatched the grill's cord from the outlet and stepped away as Henry activated a fire extinguisher built into his body. With a thick white whoosh of propellant, the burnt slices of bread ceased to smoke.

"What the hell's going on?" Peyton leapt to his feet.

"Hell's learning to cook," answered Jared, staring at her in horror.

Lee burst through the door and into the compartment. "Where's the fire?"

"There isn't one," Joanna said. "The toast just got a bit overdone." She turned to the ring of anxious male faces and raised her hands in a calming manner. "It's okay, everyone. Just a little accident. Everything's under control."

"Under control, my ass," muttered Peyton. "ANT, discontinue the emergency alarm and open the air vents," he requested of the transport. As the blaring klaxon ceased, he turned to the tablet where Genova's anxious voice could be heard asking what was happening. "It's nothing. I'll call you back." He flicked the screen off and fixed Hell with a hard stare.

Her face burned hotter than the charred toast. "I'm sorry," she whispered. "I'm so sorry, everyone." If the floor could have opened up and swallowed her, she would have welcomed it.

Lee eyed the lumps of blackened bread swimming in the foamy mess left behind by the extinguisher. "How did this happen?"

Hell cleared her throat. "I put the bread on to cook. We got talking, and..."

"What were you talking about?"

She shared a glance with Joanna. "Um...sausages?"

"Sausages? I could do with some sausages," Rusty said, pushing his way through to blearily peer at the mess on the counter. "But, uh...I think I'll pass on the buns." He backed away again, nose wrinkled. The stench of scorched bread hung thick in the air, despite the environmental controls at maximum.

Joanna's lips twitched. She made a choking sound, then burst into laughter. Pressing her hand to her stomach, she smoothed her shirt and blew out a long breath. "Oh, what a mess. I think I could use a drink."

"It's the smoke. I'll get you some water." Lee reached for a panel on the wall.

Joanna placed her hand over his, stopping him. "Make it whisky and you can join me." At his startled expression, Joanna grinned and gave his fingers a small squeeze before letting go. "I'll meet you in the cargo pod. We need to discuss some...dietary changes." She winked at Hell. "Don't worry about the mess, dear. One of the bots will clean it up." Turning on her heel, she headed for the hold.

Brow wrinkled, Lee grabbed two glasses and a bottle of amber liquid. "This better not be about eating more spinach."

A hysterical giggle escaped Hell. "I think you'll be excited with this change."

"Really?" He glanced at the burnt food, frowned, and headed after Joanna.

Hell pressed the heels of her hands to her eyes and groaned. Could things get any more screwed up? She'd practically burnt down the transport. At the very least the grill must be ruined. Dinner certainly was and… "Oh, shit. I really can't cook, can I?"

"Not unless charcoal is a new delicacy." Peyton's warm, strong arm wrapped about her shoulders and gave a small squeeze. She glanced up and caught him chuckling and shaking his head.

"You think this is funny?"

His brows flicked. "Don't you?"

"No."

He sighed and rolled his eyes heavenward, as if asking the Maker for patience. "Was it an accident?"

"Yes."

"Then don't worry about it."

Don't worry about it? They stared in silence at the charred remains of yet another disastrous attempt at her cooking. His arm felt way too comforting across her shoulders, his scent warm and inviting. She tried to shrug him off, well aware that she still needed to find a way to explain about Sarah. And until she did, despite the desire burning through her veins, being intimate didn't seem right. "I'd better clean this up," she said with a sigh.

But he tightened his hold and shook his head. "I'll take care of it," he said, his voice sounding weary, but deep in his eyes a smile glowed. "And then you can show me what you know about…sausages," he added with a wink.

"Um, sausages?" she asked, her heart beating wildly. Had he overheard her conversation with Aunty Jo?

He opened his mouth to speak, a mischievous look in his brown eyes, but that was when the transport interrupted with,

"Destination achieved. Reclaimer number twenty-four in the northern sector."

SIZE DOES MATTER

"OH, THE MAKER! It's so...huge!" Hell's mouth gaped open as she leaned against the cockpit's console and looked through the main window. "When you said you'd made the worms bigger, I didn't think you meant large enough to swallow a transport pod whole."

"*Lumbricus terrestris*," Peyton said with a smile. "Otherwise known as a Nightcrawler. With some important modifications, of course."

A steady blip on the console's scanner insisted the creature still clung to life, yet as the transport scuttled closer to the motionless worm, what could be seen of its grayish skin in the thickening swirl of afternoon flurries gave no outward appearance of health. Hopefully, once they freed the annelid of its icy prison and transported it back to the worm nest, it could be salvaged. Good thing they'd recharged the anti-gravity load lifters in the cargo hold. The twenty-two-foot-long worm's inflated proportions gave new meaning to the term megadrile. Half frozen it would weigh more than the transport.

Peyton pressed his body against Hell's as he bent close to her ear. "It looks like an enormous *sausage*, don't you think?" he teased in reference to the conversation he'd overheard between her and Aunty Jo.

He was rewarded by her strangled cough as she inched away.

She'd done her best to evade-him-without-evading-him during the clean up after the near-fire, which she'd insisted on taking care of rather than order the robots to do. Naturally, he'd insisted on helping, but when their hands had touched while they'd washed the counter and grill, she'd jerked away from him and avoided his eye contact as much as possible.

He was tempted to call her out on it. She was supposed to act on her desire for him, not try to hide it. But she'd been skittish for the last few days.

Things had gotten weird.

The whole Sarah-gate situation had knocked them both off kilter. It was difficult and confusing for her to have the digital ghost of his deceased wife taking up space in her head. Christ, it was difficult and confusing for him to have a part of Sarah existing inside Hell.

But he'd been thinking a lot over the past three days, especially when he held her close at night and pretended to be asleep so that she might fall asleep.

Thinking about those words she'd said after waking up from her nightmare about The Factory.

Those scary, impossible, precious words.

I love you, Peyton.

Truth was, Hell might be the best gift he'd ever received in his life. She certainly was the most complicated, intelligent, and stubborn...and heart-aching beautiful. The fact Sarah occupied a portion of her was unusual, he had to admit. But did it change the way Hell made him feel?

Hell, no. He was just as insane for her as before the revelation. Maybe even more now.

And he really needed to fuck her hard and tell her so.

Right fucking now.

But she inched a little bit further away as she turned to Jared, who stood beside them looking out the window, and asked, "Why worms?"

"They're perfect for reclaiming the land." Jared nodded toward the steady blip on the scanner. "They break up the soil while cleaning it. We altered these, made them able to eat just about anything as food. Concrete, metal, toxic waste. Some of the landscape is so polluted plants won't grow even after half a millennium of abandonment by people. We're fixing that with the Reclaimers."

"Why so big, though? Wouldn't it make sense to keep them small and have a few million of them swarm the area?"

"Sweetheart." Peyton slid his hand over Hell's hip and pulled her against his side. "You know it's not true when they say size doesn't matter."

She turned her face toward him, the ghost of a smile caressing her lips. "Bigger isn't always better."

"Ahh, but I know how much you like bigger."

"Really? You really had to go there?" She shook her head, and turned back to Jared, but Peyton wasn't falling for her attempt at distancing herself from him. She burned for him. He could feel her heat through their clothing.

What was it he'd overheard her tell Aunty Jo? Something about how she couldn't stop thinking about him? Well damn. He couldn't stop thinking about her either. And the moment they were alone, he'd do more than just think. He'd make her pant and scream and moan. He'd make her pay for distracting him and giving him a permanent hard-on for the last three days while they worked through this weird shit they were going through.

He was done with being patient.

Lord only knew what he'd agreed to do at the Dome for Genova the Diva. That whole conversation had been a blur, with him nodding and saying, "Yes, yes, I'll take care of it," while Hell's sensual voice and sweet laughter had drifted across the compartment and filled his mind with thoughts about every sexy thing he'd like to be taking care of with her. She didn't get to just invade his life, make him have fucking feelings, and then back off because things got weird. Oh, hell no. She was going to pay for turning him into a gibbering idiot.

"Well, in this case, bigger wins," Jared said with a wink at Hell. "We need the worms large enough to completely process whatever toxins they eat. Think of their bodies as really big-ass filters. Bad stuff in, good stuff out." He pretended to fill his mouth with food, swallow it, and then gestured with his hands behind his ass.

Hell shook her head at his display but couldn't seem to help laughing. "I bet a worm that size would make a huge amount of, um... reclaimed soil?"

"Worm shit," Jared said.

"Worm shit," she conceded with a smile.

"And, yeah, there's a lot of it," he added. "Just one worm makes enough good, clean soil for our greenhouses to use with plenty to spare. The twelve Reclaimers we have in service for this northern sector alone are going to have the worst of the land cleaned up in just a few years."

"Bottom line is small worms just aren't big enough for the job."

Peyton said. "The pollutants build up in their bodies too quickly, which leaves the problem of poisoned worms when they die. Let them decompose in the soil? The toxins are released back into the landscape. Burn them? The air becomes polluted."

"So, these really are...Reclaimers."

"Exactly."

As the transport slowed to a stop, the worm's body filled their view like a wall, signaling the end of their journey. Partly submerged in a drift at the base of a windswept hill, snow concealed the creature's head as well as whatever had drawn it out of the cozy nesting cave during winter. Had it woken early by mistake and become hungry? It was a problem they'd had before. Though genetically hardened against cold temperatures, the Reclaimers were programmed to rest until spring when debris was easier to ingest. But sometimes they had a mind of their own.

Hell craned her neck closer to the window to get a better look. "Those black spiky things, are they some kind of protection?" Dark spiny bristles, each a hand span in length, stuck out of the creature's tapering back end in sparse clusters.

Jared smiled. "Those are setae. They're kind of like hairs, a natural adaptation worms have, except in this case they're on a large scale. They're very useful when tunneling to nest and hunt."

"Hunt?" she asked, and Peyton felt her body tense. "I thought they just ate dirt and concrete and stuff."

"Don't worry," he said and moved his hand in a soothing motion across the base of her spine. "They can move pretty fast, but they prefer food they don't have to chase. Wait 'til you get a look at this one's mouth. The digestive enzymes it secretes can melt perma-steel."

"Perma-steel! That's impressive," she said, her voice soft with admiration. She leaned sideways against the console and craned her neck again, trying to see more of the worm. The window misted as she blew out a breath and shook her head. "And Sarah helped think this up?"

Peyton's fingers tightened as he slid them around her hip and pulled her back to his side. Hell hadn't talked about Sarah very much and he hadn't prompted her to, despite what Lee wanted. He wasn't certain he was ready to hear anything she had to say about the time she'd spent with Sarah at The Factory. The fact she had a connection with his wife that went beyond what he had known was disturbing on a level he couldn't quite identify. Maybe it was because Sarah hadn't trusted him enough to tell him herself that made the subject a difficult one for him. But there was something in the way Hell said Sarah's name now that made him wonder if talking about her creator was just as difficult for her, if not more so.

Jared cleared his throat. "My sister didn't just think up the idea for the Reclaimers, she engineered it. Helped design the bio-robotic matrix which allows us to control the worms while letting them exist as independent life forms."

"Bio-robotic matrix? You mean the worms are like me?" Her wide-eyed amber gaze turned from the window to dance between him and Peyton with a mix of surprise and concern.

Peyton shook his head. "Not exactly. They're much more primitive."

"But this is where she got the idea from to create me?"

"I suppose so, yes."

Her pale cheeks and rose-bud lips were as unlike the thick spongy hide of a worm as could be. A faint smudge of soot dotted her nose. With the tip of his finger, he brushed the dirt off her skin. Her breath brushed his palm in return, causing a thrill to pass along his nerves.

What was he to do with her?

She appeared to be healing well. Once they'd fixed the Reclaimer, they'd head back to Deliverance where he'd use the scanner to be sure she was okay, and Lee would proceed with the legal issues of her abuse at the hands of The Factory and confirm her status of belonging to him. Because, without a doubt she did belong to him.

And then what?

Having her underfoot night and day was driving him insane with her constant meddling and sexy, well...sexy *everything*. But he also couldn't imagine his life without her in it now. The idea of anyone else having her was...intolerable.

It's lust born of circumstance, that's all.

But he knew that wasn't all. Not anymore. Not by a long shot.

She stared up at him, silent and pensive, her lips a quick kiss away. They parted slightly as her tongue darted out to lick them, a nervous gesture by the wary look in her eyes, but just as effective an invitation. Her gaze remained locked with his, her breaths quick. With arousal, or was it anger? Did it matter? She seemed either unwilling or unable to move, and in a moment, he would bend forward and kiss her, press his lips against her soft ones, and give in to his will.

His will?

Wasn't his will to be left alone?

Maybe once, but not now. Now he wanted her to stop being skittish and get naked so he could make her forget all her worries and scream his name in pleasure.

Except Jared was standing there watching, and they had work to do, and she wasn't tearing her clothes off, she was still being skittish.

With a sigh, he settled for stroking her jaw and pressing a soft kiss to her forehead. "I'm glad she created you," he said and meant it. "You're much sexier than a worm."

Her eyes went wide. And he could see instantly that what he'd meant as a joke wasn't how she'd taken it.

"Yeah, three cheers for Sarah, right?" she said and pushed away from him.

"I didn't mean—"

"You never do," she said as she stormed past Jared and through the door to the crew pod.

He let her go and drew in a steadying breath.

What the hell had just happened?

"Sexier than a worm? That was the best you could do?" Jared said.

"Well, she is, isn't she?"

Jared crossed his arms over his chest. "Given that she's a partial clone of my sister, I decline to answer that. And speaking as her sort-of-brother, you'd better treat her nice or you'll have to answer to me."

"Are you fucking serious?"

"Yep. Helen's a sweet girl. She doesn't look like Sarah, but sometimes I think in the way she smiles, I can maybe see it."

Peyton stared at his brother-in-law at a complete loss of words. Jesus Christ. Was everyone on this transport going crazy? Next thing Jared would be asking him what his intentions were.

"So, what are your long-term plans for Hell?"

"Oh, for fuck's sake." Peyton shook his head. "Let's just go get that damn worm."

Head down, he turned and started toward the crew cabin. Time to get the equipment unloaded from the cargo hold. Henry could handle the load lifters but not the snow outside. So it was up to the crew to—

Something warm and soft and scented like Hell plowed into him with a startled squeak as he rounded the doorway. His arms instinctively went out to steady her, but she righted herself, holding the heavy parka she held clenched in her hands like a shield.

He raised his own hands in apology. "You okay?"

"Fine. I'm perfectly fine."

"Um-hum." She looked as 'fine' as a trapped fox, angled in a defensive posture and eyeing him warily. Her hair clip had come loose, and strands of her fair hair clouded about her face. The sudden urge to set the rest free made his fingers twitch.

She raised the parka higher. "I suppose you're going to tell me I'm supposed to stay inside while you and the others go out to the worm?"

He sighed and crossed his arms over his chest, praying for strength and patience. "And I suppose you're going to insist on coming with us anyway?"

She lowered the parka and nodded. "You need me."

"You'd be safer inside. It's cold out there. And if the worm wakes up while we try to move it, there could be trouble."

"Which is why I need to go along." She darted a glance out the window toward the Reclaimer, and the nervousness he'd been sensing about her for days seemed to increase. "I think...I think I can talk to it."

REDSHIFT

A GUST OF wind tugged at Peyton's clothing as the team stepped out of the transport and into the icy twilight. Snowflakes skittered along the waterproof outer shell of their protective gear but seemed more than happy to stick to everything else. Already, a fringe of white outlined Hell's brow where the soft lining of her hat met her goggles. The exposed tip of her nose was turning as rosy as her lips.

Seeming oblivious to the weather, however, she stepped carefully through the calf-deep drifts, her attention riveted upon the worm, 'listening' for sounds of it becoming conscious, or however it was she expected to communicate with it. She hadn't been able to explain it very well, other than she could 'feel' the worm's presence in her mind, much the way she could hear the transport's Artificial Intelligence, if she concentrated hard enough, making decisions while it operated the ship.

Which was something he hadn't known she could do, and it gave him pause as he watched her now. She was recovering more each day, which he was glad to see. But what exactly would she be capable of once she was fully healed?

The rest of the team fanned out behind her, carrying the equipment needed for securing and transporting the Reclaimer. Peyton let drop his end of the case he shared with Jared as they neared the tail end of the worm. "Here's good enough."

Jared grunted and let his end fall as well. The case sank several inches into the drifted snow and stopped. With surprisingly deft fingers for the thick gloves she had on, Aunty Jo undid the latches and opened the lid. Snow immediately swirled inside and tried to cling to the load lifter's metal plates. She brushed it off and began unfastening the straps which secured the lifters in place.

A quick glance at Hell saw her standing as still as a statue beside the worm. Light from the transport caught the tilt of her goggles as she concentrated on listening to the worm's A.I.

"Hear anything?"

She shook her head, disturbing the snow which tried, despite gusts of wind, to gather on her shoulders and hood. "No. It's just cold, poor thing. So cold...numb."

"It's programmed to go into low power mode and wait for help if it ever gets into serious trouble. Let's hope it stays that way until we've got it secured." Once the lifters were in place, they could erect a proper stasis field around the worm and secure it for the trip back to its den.

He checked the readouts on his portable scanner. The worm's pulse rate was so low that it barely seemed alive. Which wasn't necessarily bad. It reduced the risk of the giant annelid flailing about as it suddenly regained consciousness, which it might if it mistook their efforts to move it as an attack.

The wind shifted and blew a twister of flakes about them so thick that, for a moment, Hell's silhouette seemed to become one with the worm's. The sooner he had the worm secured for transport and everyone back inside, the better.

"The weather's worsening. Let's get this worm saddled."

Aunty Jo snorted. "It's just a bit of snow, Peyton. Nothing we've not been out in before."

"But no reason to delay either," Lee said. He took the lifter from her hands as she struggled to release its bulky mechanism from the case. "Wouldn't you rather be getting warm and cozy inside?"

It was hard to tell with her thick hood casting shadows in the uncertain light, but Peyton could have sworn she blushed.

"What do you think, Peyton?" Lee asked. "One lifter for the tail and two on each side? We'll have to dig the head out of that drift before we can place more."

"Yeah." Peyton looked toward Mac and Rusty, who unpacked a case of their own. "Better break out the shovels."

"Already on it." Mac hauled a flattened rectangle from his case and, pressing a button on its side, ejected a long cylindrical handle. Another press of a button and a low hum emitted from the unit. The air around the rectangle began to waver and distort as heat radiated off of it in a beam. Snow hissed in protest, billowing into a cloud of steam as he set to work on the drift pinning the worm's head.

"Do you think it's hung up on something?" Rusty asked, unpacking his own shovel unit. "I mean, why'd it end up here of all places? There's nothing but snow, rocks and a few scrubby trees. The nearest city-wreck is miles away. Not exactly good eating, if you know what I mean."

Peyton glanced at the scanner strapped to his wrist. A three-dimensional image of the worm revolved on the small screen, orange for its body, blue for the surrounding snow and ice, and different hues of green for the underlying hillside. He focused on the head section. The mouth was wedged around a portion of rock, part of which appeared dissolved. He shook his head. "Hard to tell. It appears to have been trying to feed when it initiated shutdown. I'll have to run a more in-depth diagnostic of all its systems once we get it back to the nest. Might be a problem with its logic subroutines."

"Could it have been trying to dig a new home?" Hell asked.

"Out here? In the middle of nowhere?" Rusty shook his head. "That doesn't make sense."

"Maybe it didn't like where it was." She ran her gloved hand over the Reclaimer's flank, brushing off the crust of snow in an almost affectionate gesture. "Maybe it was running away."

"Running away? From what?"

"Maybe it wanted to be free."

The wistful tone of her voice gave Peyton the feeling she was talking about more than just the worm. "The Reclaimers aren't slaves, Hell. We don't keep them chained up."

She turned to face him. "Have you ever asked them how they feel?"

"No. How could I? They aren't sentient like you. Their A.I is designed to act on impulses derived from programmed responses. A very simple system. Their root purpose is to eat and breed and that's about it."

Her stance stiffened. "Just like Henry was supposed to be a service bot without any say in how he might do his service. But look at how happy he is now he has a choice."

"That's only because you changed him."

"Is it?" Her gaze was accusatory. "Or did I just bring to life what was already there?"

"What would you have the worms do? Sit around drinking tea and discussing philosophy?"

"They deserve the freedom to make their own choices."

"Choices?" He moved closer to her. Was whatever connection she shared with the worm messing with her brain? "They get plenty of choices. Eat. Don't eat. Sleep. Don't sleep. Anything more complicated would confuse them. So don't get any ideas about 'upgrading' their abilities."

Her goggles hid the expression in her eyes, but by the firm line of her lips and the way her hand trembled slightly as she reached out and placed her gloved palm against the worm, anger brewed hot and deep within her.

"Henry deserved to be able to talk. Why don't these worms deserve the same?"

"Did you ever consider that giving a simple robot ability beyond its specifications might actually be cruel? If I'd thought Henry should talk, I'd have made him that way myself."

"This isn't about *you*, Peyton!" Hell shouted, her frustration clear as she slapped her hand against the slide of the giant worm. "It's about what's right! It's about treating things with respect, even if they're just a robot, or a giant worm, or a Doll—"

A low moan rumbled through the wind and seemed to vibrate upward through his boots. Hell snatched her hand away from the worm as its body began to shiver and tiny avalanches of snow spiraled down off the long back.

"Everyone get back!" Peyton ordered. He grabbed Hell's arm and bolted backward as the moaning deepened. They vaulted over the packing case and skidded, falling awkwardly in the snow. Rolling over in a tangle of limbs, he pulled her behind the case and held her close.

"What just happened?" Her voice quavered, hot breath tickling his cheek.

"What's it look like, sweetheart?" Anger mixed with fear, making his voice harsh. "Your little hissy fit woke up the goddamned worm!"

She stiffened beneath him on the snow. "I did not! All I did was—" The rest of what she was going to say was muffled as he pressed himself over her, protecting her while the worm shuddered hard enough to make the ground shake. It was waking up, trying to get free of the ice it was partially buried in.

"Shit," he said. "Come on." He rolled sideways away from the crate, taking Hell with him, trying to create some distance between them at the worm's tail section, which was starting to move. He needed to get her back inside the transport where she would be safe.

As he came to the top of the roll, he glanced sideways, looking for the others.

Mac and Rusty were already hurrying their way back through the snow to the transport, Jared not far behind, each carrying a shovel. Lee and Aunty Jo were by the head of the worm, a load lifter between them as they worked quickly to fix the metal panels into place before the worm broke free.

"Leave it!" Peyton shouted. "Get back to the transport!"

The elderly couple staggered, one of the panels falling as another shudder moved though the ground, making the snow and ice underfoot even more slippery. Joanna went down hard onto her knees with a soft cry.

Peyton leapt to his feet, yanking Hell to hers. "Get inside," he yelled, pushing her in the direction of the transport as he started in the opposite direction towards Aunty Jo and Lee.

His father-in-law had a hand on Aunty Jo's arm, helping her to her feet as best he could on the uncertain surface without losing his own footing. Her lips were a thin line, and she shook her head angrily as she tried to get up, probably annoyed with herself for falling in the first place.

The worm's body was moving now. Rippling and shuddering as it struggled in the snow. Peyton ran faster, pulse racing. If anything happened to his aunt, he'd never forgive himself.

"Come on," he shouted as he reached her side. He grabbed her free arm, helping Lee pull her upright. The surface of her coat was slick in the thickly falling snow, making his grip fumble in his haste to get her and Lee to safety.

With a loud crack that he felt in his bones, the worm broke free of the ice, the force knocking them all off their feet. Its head swung high, shards of ice and stone falling like jagged rain about them. Peyton looked up. Through the swirling snow, the worm began to descend, its gaping mouth letting out a bellow of pain and rage.

He tensed for the impact, covering Aunty Jo as best he could. Counting the seconds until they were crushed beneath the Reclaimer's weight.

"NO!" He heard Hell scream.

Boom.

A cloud of snow erupted, covering him in a wave of icy crystals like the surf on a stormy sea as the worm's head slammed sideways, narrowly missing them.

Then everything stopped, the shaking ground, the worm, his heart as he wiped snow from his goggles and saw Hell.

She stood between them and the worm, her hands spread wide in the air, using some invisible force to make the creature roll away from them as it bucked and struggled against whatever mental hold she had on it.

"Hell!" he called out, fear for her thumping wildly in his chest. "What are you doing?"

"Stop!" she shouted at the worm, ignoring him. "You must stop."

Snow swirled around her in a gust of wind. She pushed her hands outwards in the air towards the worm, oblivious to the weather and everything else around her. The worm moved back away from her, twisting and writhing, its tail section digging into the ground as a deep rumbling moan issued from its mouth.

Peyton knew that sound. It was a sound a worm made when it was getting ready to eat. *Shit. SHIT! "Hell!"* he shouted, rising to get to her as the worm's mouth opened, revealing a triple ring of sharp, triangular teeth. Its throat flexed, forcing up digestive acids with a bellow of anger.

Still in control of the worm, Hell twisted her hands in the air, a second before Lee leapt up from beside her and knocked her aside into the snow. The worm twisted with the movement Hell made, slamming back against the rock wall behind it with a crack that sent shockwaves trembling though the ground. The spray of digestive vomit went wide, a sizzling arc that cut through the air like an acid blade. Then the worm stopped moving, stunned by the force of the impact and maybe whatever Hell had done to it.

The digestive acid hissed where it hit the snow, causing acrid-scented mist to fill the air. The bulk of it went wide of its mark, missing them.

And then Joanna screamed.

"Lee!" she cried out. "Oh, God. Lee!"

He lay on top of Hell, shielding her with his body. Tendrils of smoke wisping from his back where the acid spray had hit him.

Neither of them were moving.

Oh, God. OH, GOD. Not Hell. Don't take her from me now.

"Jared! Get my med-kit!" Peyton yelled into the communication device strapped to his wrist.

"Sweet mother fucking Jesus!" he cried as he skidded to his knees beside Hell and Lee. How hurt were they? Had they both been hit by the acid? He couldn't go through this again. The loss. The grief.

Hell moaned, which he took as a good sign, and the tight knot in his chest released in a harsh breath. Her hand rose to reach for Lee, who had landed on top of her midsection crossways, pinning her in the snow.

"No," Peyton said, "don't move him yet, baby," he cautioned as she grabbed Lee's shoulder, trying to push him off. Peyton ripped off his glove, ignoring the cold, and checked for a pulse in Lee's neck. A steady beat fluttered beneath his fingers. "He's alive." But he needed to work fast to stop the acid from burning deeper.

He grabbed a handful of snow and began pressing it to the open wounds, hoping the wetness and cold would dilute the acid until the med-kit arrived.

Hell pushed herself up onto her elbow, her attention fixed on Lee.

"He shouldn't have done that," she said softly.

"Done what? Saved your life? What the hell were you thinking, standing in front of it like that." Peyton's hand shook as he placed more snow on the wounds, now clearly visible through Lee's thick outerwear and the shirt beneath. "Help me get this jacket off him."

"I was saving you," she said but there didn't seem to be any emotion left in her voice, just flat words that blew away in the wind.

They turned Lee on his side so they could undo his jacket and shirt and peel the fabric off of him. Even in the uncertain evening light, the red welts on Lee's back were starkly visible, the skin bubbling slightly and blood oozing. Peyton removed his own coat. Hell cradled Lee's head as they lay him face down onto the coat and covered and him back up as best they could to keep in this body heat, while leaving the wounds free so Peyton could tend to them.

"Shit. Where the hell is that med-kit?" The icy wind whipped at Peyton, threatening to tear his shirt from his back. His hands shook as he applied more snow, melting it with his palms so it would wash the acid away from Lee's skin.

"Damn that Jar-head," Aunty Jo said, putting her arm around Peyton in an attempt to keep him warm. "Where is he?"

Peyton darted a glance toward the transport. Jared was on his way through the door, running, the others following closely. As soon as the burning was stabilized, they'd get Lee inside and out of the cold. The old man was shivering, his body going into shock. Thank God he was unconscious so he wasn't aware of the pain.

Hell took off her glove and placed her palm against Lee's back as if testing his skin, her lips a thin line of concern.

"Do you have a knife?" she asked.

"What?"

"A knife."

Aunty Jo looked at her sharply. She knelt beside them, seeming oblivious to the fact she was covered from head to toe in a dusting of snow. "Come on, you old faker," she said as she placed a gloved palm on Lee's forehead. "Don't give up on me now."

Peyton grabbed the med-kit from Jared as soon as his brother-in-law arrived.

"Dad!" Jared cried out. "Oh, shit, what happened?"

Peyton ignored the question as he rooted through his instruments and found a scalpel and a syringe. He could use the first to incise the wounds and the second to apply a topical inhibitor to stop further tissue damage from the acid.

"Give it to me," Hell said.

He hesitated. "What? We don't have a lot of time—"

"Trust me," she insisted and grabbed the scalpel from him. But instead of cutting into Lee as he expected, she cut her palm open. An inch-long slice that parted her skin in a clean wound and made her bleed freely.

Aunty Jo sucked in a startled breath. "Oh, my God! What are you doing?"

Hell quickly pressed her palm to the worst of Lee's wounds, wincing.

Peyton grasped her hand, intending to stop her, but she stopped him instead with a shake of her head. "Don't. My blood will heal him better than you can," she said. "He's Sarah's father, which makes him partly mine too. We share a portion of DNA. My nanites will recognize him and help fix the damage."

"You sure about that?" McClellan asked, not sounding very sure.

"No," Hell admitted spreading her blood over Lee's back and making sure it entered each of the wounds. "But it won't hurt him to try. And these are very deep. Almost to the bone."

"Well, holy shit," Jared said, staring at Lee's wounds in disbelief.

The skin had stopped bubbling as Hell's blood caused the burning to cease and the bleeding was running less freely.

"You should get him inside now," she said, rising unsteadily to her feet. She clutched her wounded hand tight to her body. "He's still in shock and very cold. And so are you," she said to Peyton.

"What about the worm?" asked Rusty as he, Jared, and Mac bent to lift Lee, using Peyton's jacket as a make-shift stretcher.

"You don't have to worry about that anymore," Hell said and turned toward the transport. Her foot slipped on the ice and she staggered but righted herself before Peyton could reach her. "It's asleep and won't wake again until I let it. You can attach the lifters whenever you want to." Her voice was flat, dead, barely a whisper on the wind.

The snow swirled around them in a gust of fat, cold flakes, causing Peyton to shiver. But his numb limbs didn't stop him from catching Hell as she slipped again. He lifted her in his arms as she sagged, holding her body against him. So light and seemingly fragile, yet at the same time strong. And brave. Almost frighteningly so. He had no idea how she'd done the incredible things she had just done.

Her head rested against his shoulder, her goggles cold against his skin.

"You can let me go," she said, she but didn't struggle against his hold as he held her close and carried her through the snow to the safety and warmth of the transport.

"No, I can't, baby," he whispered by her ear. "No, I can't."

He was pretty sure that despite the alien territory their relationship had entered, he was never going to let her go.

Ever.

HEALING

"IT'S JUST A little prick," Sarah said. She sat beside Hell in the glass-walled room, using a syringe to extract blood from her arm. "See? Over in just a second. Did you feel anything?"

"A little bit," Hell said.

"Well, the wound's already closed. You heal so fast I don't even need to put on a bandage." There was pride in her voice, but her eyes were downcast as she put the vial of blood in a container and closed up her kit. She'd been quiet lately, more so than usual and it made Hell nervous. She rubbed at the spot on her arm where the blood had been drawn, but the mark was already gone. The pain lingered, however.

"Have I been bad?" she asked.

"What? Why would you think that?" Sarah said, sounding surprised. She placed the kit down on the table and turned in her chair to face Hell.

"You seem upset. Your pulse is fast and your body tense. Did I do something bad?"

"No, ELf." Sarah reached out and took her hand, giving it a tight squeeze. "I'm not upset. You haven't been bad. You're so special, ELf. So important. You can do so much that I can't. You're my most important creation."

"Why am I so important?"

"Because you are going to give everyone a new chance. This

world is dying, but you can give it new life." She gave Hell's fingers another tight squeeze then let go and rose, collecting the kit again. "I have to go away for a little while now. Clarissa will look after you while I'm gone."

Hell frowned. "Do you have to go?"

"Yes."

Hell darted a glance towards the doorway where the red-haired woman stood, watching everything with an unhappy frown. "I don't like her," Hell whispered to Sarah.

"Who? Clarissa?" Sarah turned and exchanged a glance with her assistant. "Why not?"

The doctor seemed surprised. Hell wasn't. "She doesn't like me."

"That's not true." Sarah closed her eyes and shook her head. "It's me she doesn't like right now. She doesn't want me leaving either."

"She loves you," Hell said.

"I know."

"Do you love her?"

"Yes." Sarah's voice was a soft whisper.

"Then why do you have to go?"

"It's complicated."

Clarissa gave a soft laugh. When Hell glanced toward her, the doorway was empty and the door swinging closed.

"You love your husband more?"

Sarah's brow creased. "It's not a competition. But when I get back, you'll be able to come home with me. You'll like that, won't you, ELf?"

"Yes." She didn't like the idea of Sarah being away. Or being left alone with Clarissa. Clarissa loved Sarah. But Clarissa didn't love Elf. And Clarissa didn't like the man Sarah talked about. The one who made the smile bright in Sarah's blue eyes. "Am I going to live with you and your husband?"

"That's right. Do you remember his name?"

"Peyton. Peyton Chase. He's a doctor like you, who lives at Deliverance Dome," she said, reciting what she'd been told before.

"Yes, that's right. Very good," Sarah said with a nod, her eyes losing the tiredness that had been haunting them for weeks. "Listen, ELf. Listen very closely now. I want you to remember Peyton. If anything ever happens to me and I don't come back, I want you to remember him. He's the only person who ever made me feel truly safe. Remember that. If nothing else, I want you to remember him."

"Peyton Chase," Hell said, memorizing the name and locking it deep inside her heart. "But you are coming back, right?" she asked, panic taking root that maybe that might not happen. Sarah was her everything. Her creator. Her friend. Her lifeline to the world. If she wasn't there, what would happen?

"I will always come back for you," Sarah said and pressed a gentle kiss to her forehead. "I'll be gone for four weeks at the most, I promise," she said as she walked out the glass door, closing it behind her.

But she hadn't come back.

She hadn't ever come back.

**

Hell awoke with a feeling of deep sadness tight in her chest as she thought about Sarah. About how she hadn't ever returned. And the horror that had happened afterwards. Things were becoming clearer now, the memories less broken. But did she want to remember them all?

She lay on a bed in a darkened room. Light filtered through the cracked open door, illuminating the fact that she was alone. The soft, cool breeze of atmospheric controls the only appreciable sound.

They'd arrived at the facility where the Worms were monitored the day before, wounded and exhausted. But alive. Yes, very much alive, even though she'd slept a good portion of the last two days since the battle with the worm.

The poor thing. But it had survived, too. And was also healing. She could feel it at the back of her mind, its pulse steady, its mind at rest while it slept in the company of its brethren.

Rising, she went in search of her own.

"Peyton?" she called out as she pushed open the door of her room and entered the main lab area. The room was empty except for Lee, who sat at a monitor, watching whatever was on the screen. He looked up with a smile as she paused and blinked, her eyes adjusting to the brightness.

"Hello, Helen. Did you sleep well?" His voice was warm and deep.

She nodded. "Yes, I think so." Controlling the worm with her mind had left her exhausted, but other than a stiffness in her body from sleeping so much, she was fine.

"How is your hand?"

She flexed her palm, tracing the shiny pink scar that ran the length of it with her finger, remembering how close she had come to losing him, how close she'd come to losing them all when the worm had awoken in the snow and attacked.

She pulled out the seat next to him and sat. "It's almost healed. How is your back?"

He stretched his shoulders and winced. "Tender," he admitted, "but far better than I should be. Peyton tells me the muscles have already grown back and I'll be fine in a few days. Thanks to you, and your quick thinking."

"I'm sorry you got hurt."

He shook his head, a soft smile lighting his eyes and pulling his moustache upward. "You have nothing to be sorry for. I did what I did, and I'd do it again if I thought it would save you."

She flexed her palm, making the scar ripple. It would be gone in a few days. "But I heal so much faster than you. I would have been fine."

"But I wouldn't have been if I'd stood by and done nothing while you got hurt. We care about you, Helen. All of us."

She heard the affection of that statement but couldn't hold his gaze. His blue eyes reminded her so much of Sarah's.

Instead, she traced her scar again and remembered her dream, the ache in her chest tightening. "She should have taken me with her when she left," she whispered after a moment. "My blood could have saved her."

He paused. "You're starting to remember things about Sarah?"

She nodded and chanced a quick glance at his face. The seamed lines around his eyes deepened as he studied her. His bushy white brows drew together slightly as he waited for her to continue. But there was no judgement in his familiar face, only a willingness to listen that she desperately needed right now.

"She was going to bring me home, to live at Deliverance. I think she was coming back that last time, to tell you about me first. About what she'd done. Because she'd had to do things that were...not right...in order to create me. And she was afraid about what would happen. But she was going to bring me home. That's what she wanted. To come home. With me."

Lee's eyes misted, but he remained silent.

"But she didn't come back." The ache expanded until it filled her whole body, filling it with the sadness she hadn't truly felt until now, when she was confiding it to the man who she wanted to call father. "She didn't come back for me. She broke her promise. And I could have saved her. I could have saved us all this pain. If she'd just taken me with her." Tears filled her eyes, burned her throat. So many people had died because of the virus that had infected the Dome, but if she'd cured Sarah with her blood before the virus had spread, they would be alive today and the sadness, the deep sadness would never have claimed Peyton.

"It wasn't your fault," Lee said and took her hand, the one with the scar. Bringing it to his lips, he kissed it. "You brave girl. None of it was your fault."

She couldn't help the sob that escaped her.

Because that's exactly what she'd thought when Sarah had never returned. That somehow it had been her fault. That she'd done something to make her go away forever. That maybe she'd deserved the punishment that had come next in the cruel words and sharp knives and all the endless days of pain.

"Come here." Lee gathered her in his arms and held her tight. It felt so good to be held like that, like a father comforting his daughter. It was something she'd never had, and it made the tears come hard and fast while he gently rocked her, making soothing pats with his hands on her hair.

But she also felt like she was taking something that didn't belong to her. Because he missed his daughter, and she wasn't Sarah no matter how much everyone wanted her to be.

"I loved her," she confessed. And it was true. She had loved Sarah. It had hurt so bad when she'd never come back. "She created me, and I loved her. She wasn't perfect. She made mistakes. But I loved her. And now she's gone except the pieces left in me. But I don't know if I want to be that girl anymore. The one she left trapped back at The Factory." Tears slipped silently down her cheeks. Lee wiped them away with his elderly fingers.

"People change. Everyone changes. It's how we grow. You don't have to be anyone you don't want to be," he said. "I know that you aren't Sarah. My daughter died. I accepted that long ago. But you are a most precious gift. Like a child I didn't know I had."

The tears rushed out of Hell with renewed force. She felt Lee's love. His open heart. The trembling of his hand as he cupped her cheek, the depth of his grief and loss.

She wanted to embrace his love. But she knew things about Sarah that would break his heart.

"I know everything is very confusing still," he said. "But I want you to know that as far as I'm concerned, you are part of our family. And no matter what happens, you will always have a place here with us."

She doubted that would be true once the truth of Sarah's secrets got out. She wiped at her cheeks, embarrassed for her emotional display. He was such a kind man. But his kindness was breaking her heart.

"I think I'd better go check on the worm," she said and gently pushed away.

"Helen," Lee said before she could escape his hold, "whatever it is that you think I can't handle, there isn't anything about my daughter that would make me hate her. Or you."

She doubted that, but after a moment she said, "Maybe. But, what about Peyton?"

"I've known him all his life. He's stronger than you think. Their marriage wasn't perfect. No relationship ever is. Think about what you want yours to be and then give it a chance. He's happier now than I've seen him in a long time, but he's not a stupid man."

Meaning, Peyton knew she was keeping something and was waiting for her to tell him? Probably. Lee's expression didn't change, but the look in his eyes suggested he could see right through her.

"Thank you," she said and meant it. In an odd way she felt better now, like a weight had been lifted from her and the ache that had been so tight in her chest had loosened. Enough that she could breathe again.

"Come on," he said rising from his chair with a smile. He held out his hand for her to take. "Let's go see what the others are up to down at the worm den. If I know Mac, he's cracked open the home-stilled whisky and is trying to get everyone to sing *Molly Malone* around the fire pit."

FAMILY MATTERS

HELL PAUSED AS she stood at the top of a short flight of roughhewn stone stairs and surveyed the scene before her. The subterranean cavern that the Reclaimer facility had been built inside was unremarkable in its structure. Floor, ceiling, and walls were made of grey rock, lit by panels of lighting. A pathway from the main lab and habitat led down to a flat level of rock, along the far side of which a floor to ceiling glass barrier had been erected. The wall-sized window looked down on the worm den below, allowing for observation of the twelve worms in residence, including the recent escapee now safely returned home. They were all sleeping peacefully in the semi-darkened enclosure, their long tubular bodies curled over and around each other for warmth, and perhaps comfort, if Hell understood their primitive dreams correctly.

But what was far more interesting to Hell, and that which had caused her to pause mid-step, was the fire that had been lit in a small stone circle near the center of the observation area. More specifically, the two grown men who were currently on their hands and boot tips beside the fire, racing each other to see who could do the most push-ups.

Laughter echoed around the chamber, magnified as it bounced off the walls, accompanied by cheers from the onlookers egging

Peyton and Jared on.

"Thirty-five seconds left," Aunty Jo called out overtop the ruckus that Mac and Rusty were making. Mac appeared to be on Peyton's team and was berating him for not doing the push-ups faster, while Rusty was doing the same for Jared.

The two combatants heaved themselves up and down, biceps bulging, and gazes locked as they battled to see who could out-do the other. Henry stood between the two, officially keeping count.

"Come on, you lazy bastard, my grandma could do better than that," Mac cajoled. "Teach that skinny shit a lesson!"

"Screw that!" Rusty shouted, laughing. "You got him, Jared. He's old. Look how much he's sweating!"

Lee started chuckling at Hell's side. "Old? Age means nothing. I could beat all your asses," he called out.

She stared at him in open-mouthed shock. She'd never heard him say anything so playful before. The arm he had around her shoulders shook with fatigue as she helped him to descend the stairs, a very real reminder that he was far from healed. But his smile was wide, and his eyes shone bright, taking years off his seamed face.

"Lee! What are you doing up? You're supposed to be resting," Joanna said, rising from her chair by the fire. She dropped her tablet on the seat, indicating the contest was over. Her focus was now on Lee as she hurried to greet him, a stern frown on her face.

"I'm fine," he said downplaying his weakness, "better than I've been in years." And maybe it was true. It certainly did seem to be so as he drew Joanna close and gave her a soft peck on the cheek, turning her stern expression into a shocked gasp.

She pulled back and gave him a confused look. "What's gotten into you?"

"Helen," he said with a laugh. He shook his head as he let Joanna lead him to a chair and help him sit. "She has remarkable healing powers in that blood of hers."

"Really?" Joanna shot her a wary glance as if wondering what Hell had done now.

"Don't fuss. I'm fine," Lee insisted as Joanna sat in the chair next to him. "In fact..." He leaned toward Joanna's ear with a grin. Hell caught him whisper something about sausages that made Joanna's cheeks redden. The old woman broke out in a soft, embarrassed laugh, but she didn't pull away when he laced his fingers through hers.

Hell smiled, pleased and simultaneously self-conscious about Lee's sudden open affection with Joanna. Perhaps her nanites had cured more than just his obvious wounds.

"Well, if it isn't sleeping beauty," Mac called out to Hell, grinning, "finally awake."

"Good to see you up, Helen," Rusty added.

Jared waved, too winded to speak from where he lay panting on the hard floor.

Peyton studied her, his chest heaving from exertion. Sweat dampened his skin, outlining the fit form of his muscles beneath his shirt where he lay propped up on one elbow by the fire. But by the look in his dark eyes, she couldn't tell if he wanted to kiss her or kill her.

"What are you doing out of bed?" he asked, his voice gruff and winded from the exercise. Or maybe it was just gruff and winded from looking at her. Avoiding his gaze, she searched for a drink to give him. Several cups and two bottles of whisky, one empty and one partly drank, stood on a table nearby, as well as several other containers of liquids and a selection of finger foods. She grabbed a pitcher of what she hoped to be water and quickly poured him a glassful.

"I woke up," she said as she handed him the drink. "And I wanted to see where everyone was."

He raised his brow at her as he took an appreciative sip, then downed the glass. She had the impression he'd been there while she'd rested. Watching over her during the past couple of days since the worm incident. Checking to make certain she was okay. It had brought her comfort as she'd slept off and on, knowing he was there, while her mind tried to make sense of everything, and her body healed. And maybe that's why she'd woken up feeling so anxious. Not just because of her dream about Sarah, but because she'd sensed he wasn't there. Because despite the uncertainty of where they stood now in their relationship, being around him felt right. And sexy. Yeah, definitely that.

"Waaaterrrrr..." Jared gasped, as he pretended to be dying from thirst.

Bambi rose from her seat by the fire, but Hell laughed and beat her to it, handing him a cup of water.

He accepted it with a playful grin.

"Who won?" she asked, looking between the two men.

"Jared," Henry said in his monotone voice. He pointed one of his spindly arms at him. "By two."

Rusty hooted with laughter. "You owe me twenty credits," he said to Mac and slapped him on the back.

"Shit," the older man said with an annoyed grimace. "You suck,

Chase."

"It wasn't a fair contest," said Peyton, rising to his feet. "I was distracted at the end." He looked pointedly at Hell as he put his empty glass on the table.

"Yeah, well, you owe me, you lovesick pup," Mac said. "I'm out twenty because of you and your 'distraction'." He pressed his thumbprint to Rusty's tablet, signing the transaction. "So you know what you're going to do?" he asked with a grin as he picked up his half full glass of whisky and took a long swig.

"Oh, shit…" Peyton said with a groan and closed his eyes.

"Oh, yeah." Mac raised his glass in the air, his mouth pulled in a broad grin. "You're going to perform a little song for me. And you can dance it, too."

Peyton shook his head in protest, but Mac slapped him hard on the back, clearly not accepting anything other than yes for an answer.

"C'mon, sing it now! *In Dublin's fair city, where the girls are so pretty I first set my eyes on sweet Molly Malone* … Not like that, you laggard," he said as Peyton barely mouthed the words, "sing it *loud!*" He gave Peyton a hard shove, forcing him into the center of attention by the fire. "And get your feet moving, too."

"Damn," Peyton said, then with a bemused glance at Hell, he added his deep baritone to his clearly drunk friend's.

Hell watched, taken by surprise with how well Peyton could sing, and enjoying the fact he humored his friend, even though it was clear he'd rather not do the little dance steps he was doing to the chorus of the song. Had he been drinking too? He hadn't had a sip of whisky in days.

The others were clapping and keeping the beat, so Hell took an available seat and joined them, laughing at Mac's and Peyton's performance. His eyes were shining, and he was clearly enjoying himself, despite his initial reluctance to be singled out by his friend.

In moments, they were all singing, even the robots, Henry waving his arms to the beat as Mac pranced around the fire with Peyton, the two of them belting out his favorite tune.

As the song wound down, McClellan stopped before Hell. "You're next, lassie," he said with a wink and grabbed her hand, pulling her into the middle of the circle of chairs by the fire.

"What? No!" She'd never sung or danced in her life.

"Not this time," Peyton said, rescuing her from McClellan. He pulled her down onto his lap as he sat in the chair. "Doctor's orders. This one still needs rest."

"Oy, you're no fun," Mac said.

"Shut up and take a break," Rusty rumbled. He refilled Mac's empty whisky glass, topped up his own, and shoved him into the chair beside him.

"You doing okay?" Peyton whispered by Hell's ear.

She nodded. There hadn't been much time for talking since the worm attack, beyond her groggy murmurs while she'd been half asleep that yes, she was fine, just tired. She pressed close to him, enjoying the feel of his strong body and the protectiveness of his arms wrapped around her.

The cavern was warm enough that they didn't require any bulky coats and winter gear. His body heat radiated through his pants and shirt, along with the gentle rumble of his chest as he laughed and joked with the others. As the conversation swirled around her, she settled into the rhythm, enjoying the happiness the group had created and the crackling fire. She'd never experienced anything like it in her short life. The carefree friendship and sense of belonging. Was this what it was like to have a family?

Smoke spiraled lazily upwards into the darkness high overhead where phosphoric lichens decorated the rocky ceiling like glittering stars. She considered them as she thought about that, about family, and the one thing that seemed missing from the group—children. There were no children here. Not that it would have been appropriate to bring any along on a trip like this, but she'd never seen any at the Dome either. Or heard anyone talk about them outside of her brief conversation with Joanna. Had they all died in the viral outbreak, or was the struggle to create human life that real?

It's real, Sarah whispered in her mind. *So real. But you can fix it, ELf.*

The sadness and hope in Sarah's voice settled deep into Hell's bones. The sense that she needed to have a child of her own became so strong she shivered and closed her eyes tight. It was what Peyton wanted. A child. Deep down in his secret wishes where he didn't let himself hope, the dream rested there, asleep, waiting for her to awaken it into reality. She could feel it radiating from him, saw it in his subconscious desires, a lost little bubble he'd never forgotten about, but set adrift. She cupped it carefully in her mind's eye and kissed it gently. *Your wish is now my own*, she vowed, and tucked it safely within her heart as her fingers slipped down to rest over Peyton's. His hand covered her belly protectively. Did he even know he was doing that?

"Hell?" Peyton asked.

"Yeah?"

"What's wrong? You're shaking."

She realized then that the conversation had stopped, and that everyone was watching her. Embarrassed, and not wanting to give away what she'd been thinking, she smoothed her hair over her shoulder as her mind raced to focus on what they'd been talking about. Oh, the worms, they'd been joking about the worms. She laughed awkwardly.

"Do you want to know why that one ran away?" she asked, looking toward the glass that separated them from the sleeping megadriles.

They looked at her expectantly.

"It couldn't find its mate," she said. "The others had all achieved offspring. But it hadn't. And it decided to look for a new den where it might find a compatible mate."

"Worms don't have mates," Peyton said.

"That one wants one. The others rejected it. So it left. But I think I've convinced it to stay now. And the others to give it a chance."

It wanted to belong. To reproduce. It wasn't very different from the group of people sitting around the fire staring at her with a mixture of awe and confusion. Or her.

"How does that work, exactly?" Jared asked. "That you can talk to them without a direct link?"

"It's just...something I can do." It was a lame reply, but there were no words to properly describe the relationship she had with the world around her. The things she could hear and feel that they could not. "Just like I can hear the transport talking, though its language is a bit different."

"Can you hear people's thoughts?"

"No, but I pick up on your emotions."

"What am I feeling right now?" Mac asked, banging his glass onto the table as he set it down hard.

"Like you need to relieve yourself something fierce," she answered, trying hard not to laugh.

"Oy! The girl's got a witchy talent, that's a fact!" He nodded, admiration clear in his voice as he spoke sideways to Rusty. "I've gotta piss so hard I'm gonna burst."

The others laughed as he rose from his seat and staggered off into the darkness, looking for a place to relieve his bladder.

"Um, I'd better go make sure he doesn't trip over a rock or something," Rusty said and rose to go after his friend.

Hell smiled. If what she sensed from him was accurate, it was quite likely neither would be back for a while. The need to pee wasn't the only one he and Mac had.

"Weeeelllll.... I think it's time for some music," Jared said with a polite cough.

"And a toast," Lee added, raising his glass. "To Helen, our newest family member. May you always be as happy as you are loved."

Cups were filled and quickly passed around so that everyone present could join in.

"To Helen," they said in unison.

"And to all of you," she whispered, dazed by the moment of incredible warmth. "My, my...family." She tripped over the unfamiliar word. Her eyes blurred as she lifted her drink to her lips and took a sip. The whisky burned, making her cough. She'd never tasted it before and couldn't say she liked it. Peyton's hold on her tightened as he wrapped his arm about her waist and gently kissed her temple.

My family.

It was both precious and overwhelming to be included in something that intimate and beautiful. But she felt like a stranger peeking through a window, catching a glimpse of something she craved, yet didn't really own. She belonged, but didn't. She was like them, but different. And then there was the whole issue of Sarah, and the secret life she'd led.

So as Jared clicked on his tablet, starting up some dancing music, she nodded gratefully when Peyton bent forward and whispered by her ear, "I'm going for a shower. You coming?"

**

"You had a good talk with Lee?" Peyton asked Hell as they walked slowly back up the stone steps towards the habitat and his much-needed shower. He had his arm wrapped about her waist, holding her close to his side, enjoying the feeling of her slight body moving with his.

He wanted to keep her close these days. It was the only way he knew he could make sure she was safe. What she'd done to save them from the worm had scared the piss out of him. When it had pounced, he'd thought he'd lost her. And now he could tell she'd been crying. She had that look about her eyes. He just hoped to God it was from something nice this time instead of something shitty.

Not that he'd ever think Lee would do something to hurt her on purpose. But it didn't make him feel any better when she shrugged off his question and simply said, "Do you always do this kind of thing?"

"What? Ask questions to try and figure out what the hell goes on in your head? You should know by now that's a definite 'yes'."

She rolled her eyes and stopped walking. "No, I mean *this*." She turned and pointed back at the group around the fire. "The party."

He smiled. "It's tradition whenever we're out on excursions. Helps everyone blow off steam."

She studied the group as if trying to figure it out. "It's so...unexpected. But it's fun. I like how everyone's laughing. And dancing. That looks like fun too."

Jared was twirling Bambi around to the fast beat, while Lee and Aunty Jo were swaying together gently, not seeming to care about keeping time to the music. Which was an interesting turn of events. He'd never seen them do that before.

He eyed Hell. "You've never danced, have you?"

"I've never done a lot of things."

When was the last time he'd danced? Sarah had often cut the fire-pit fun short and gone back to the lab to work while he stayed and drank with the others. But they had danced sometimes, closely, together. And he'd enjoyed it. He just couldn't think of when.

"Come on," he said. He pulled Hell in front of him on the wide flat stone step and wrapped his arms around her waist. She tentatively placed hers about his shoulders in turn. "Now just follow me," he instructed.

She moved awkwardly, her bottom lip caught between her teeth as she concentrated on following his lead. "Aren't we supposed to be keeping the beat?" she asked. Her breath was warm and sweet, scented with a touch of whisky as it fanned across his cheek.

"Doesn't matter," he said. "It's more about how the music makes you feel in here." He tapped her chest between her breasts. Her nipples were erect and pointing at him. Her hips pressed against his. The muscles of her back unyielding beneath his hands. "Relax."

"I'm trying to."

"No you're not. You're caught up in whatever's going on in your head."

She tensed. "Maybe I just can't dance. Just like I can't cook."

"Nobody's perfect, Hell." He spun her in a slow circle.

"But I should be, shouldn't I? Wasn't that why I was made? To be a perfect companion?" She stopped moving to the music, forcing him to as well.

"You are," he said, and held her gaze, willing her to believe him. "You're *my* perfect companion. And you scared the crap out of me, standing there in front of that worm. I thought you were going to die." And then when she was lying there in the snow beneath Lee, he'd thought for an instant that she *had* died.

Her lips pulled into a firm line. "Peyton, I've been burned, stabbed, poisoned and broken more times than I can count. If you cut things off of me, they just grow back. It's very hard to kill me. Sarah did a great job of making sure of that."

He flinched inwardly, trying hard not to picture what she'd endured at The Factory, but the abuse he'd witnessed during her surgery flared bright and raw in his mind. "You're remembering more?" he asked.

"I remember too much," she whispered.

She pushed away from him abruptly and hurried up the steps to go into the lab.

"Hell!" he called out to her. "Talk to me, baby. Don't shut me out."

She paused at the doorway, and he swore he could see those damned tears glistening in her eyes again.

"There isn't anything I can say that you want to hear, Peyton," she tossed at him. "There isn't any of it that's good. Not about me. Not about Sarah."

TAKING CONTROL

HE FOUND HELL in the lab, sitting at one of the consoles. Her shoulders hunched and her lips pinched together as she pretended to be engrossed in whatever was on the screen rather than notice him. Screw that. He was done with being shut out.

"Come on," Peyton said, grabbing her hand and yanking her to her feet. "First we're going to shower. Then we're going to fuck. Then we're going to talk." *And maybe we'll skip the shower*, he thought. But then decided fucking her while in the shower would be even better.

"Peyton, stop. *Peyton...*" she said, struggling to get her hand from his grip as he tugged her across the room and into the bathroom.

He closed the door and locked it behind him, barring her from escaping. She stood between him and the shower stall, her eyes wide, her cheeks flushed, and her nipples tenting her shirt, giving him a double thumbs-up.

"Strip," he commanded.

"What?"

"Strip!" he shouted, pulling his own shirt over his head.

She stared at his naked chest, her gaze traveling over his pecs and abs. Her mouth opened as if to say something, but no sound came out.

"Fine, I'll do it." He grabbed the edge of her shirt and pulled it up over her head and arms, tossing it to the ground. No bra, of course.

"Goddamnit," he said, staring at the perfection before him. "You have the most beautiful tits I've ever seen."

She looked down at them, as if bewildered, then back up at him. She took a step back towards the shower, her hands clenching and unclenching at her sides. "Peyton?" she said a question in her voice and her eyes.

"Don't think, baby. Just help me get the rest of your clothes off and let's get in that shower." He couldn't wait to soap her body. His already hard cock was pressed tight against his pants just thinking about it. He freed it as fast as he could and kicked his clothing into a pile on the floor, then helped her do the same with her own.

Naked. God. Naked. And it had been five days since he'd heard her little pleasure-filled gasps and moans—and screams, oh, Christ, the screams—she made while he pumped her hard and fast. And slow. And then fast again. And, oh shit, he was going to blow his load like some fucking horny kid if he kept thinking about it. But that's what Hell did to him. Made him hard and crazy. So crazy he could barely think.

The water poured down as she turned on the faucet. Cold at first, then misty warm. She turned to him as she walked beneath the spray. Rivulets ran in streams down her body, caressing her pale, flawless skin.

He followed her and reached for the container of soap which rested on a shelf. But she shook her head and grabbed it instead.

"Let me," she whispered, her breath warm as the watery mist. The look in her eyes changed from wariness to something deeper, hotter, more primal as she embraced the obvious need they both had for this connection.

She poured soap into her palm, then pressed it against his skin. The touch made his cock jerk. She glanced down at it and smiled. "Yes, you'll get your turn." She caught his gaze, the look in her own reminding him that she was attuned to his pleasure, his wants and needs like no other person could ever be. "Put your hands on the walls and keep them there," she said.

"Hell," he hissed between clenched teeth, but did as she wanted. Giving up control to her made his pulse race, an excited drum beat beneath his skin. This was the Hell he loved. The one who confidently took what pleasure she wanted from him. Not the skittish girl filled with uncertainty and fear he'd been walking on eggshells around for the last few days.

She soaped his chest and arms, creating a lather of the almond scented cleanser with her efficient movements. Her palms swept up and down, teasing his skin. Her soft fingers played with the hair on his chest, lingered on his nipples.

He clenched his teeth against the intense pleasure the sensation caused. "I can't—" He groaned, his fingers pressed hard against the shower walls as he tried to resist reaching for her. He needed to pull her close, fuck her.

She lowered her palms to his stomach. "You're so strong," She played her fingers over his abs, making his muscles flex. "Your skin is hot and smooth. I love the feel of it."

His knees shook as blood left his head and pooled in his groin. He was hot, hard, and aching to be touched there. But she took her time, sinking onto her knees, and washing his legs and thighs.

The water rained down on her back as she knelt there, cleansing him. It was the most arousing sight he'd ever seen. His beautiful Helen. Her lips pressed together as she concentrated on exploring him with her soapy hands. Up and down his calves, over and over, making his muscles flex as she moved to his thighs, the inside of which quivered as she gently washed him. Fuck. It was agony; it was bliss. She soaped up to the edge of his groin, then reached between his legs to soap his ass, before finally—finally—bringing her touch to where he wanted it most.

He shook with the strain of not blowing his load while she stroked his cock, spreading soapy foam all over it, up and down, slow and precise, paying careful attention to the tip. He hadn't touched her or even given himself a hand job in days, and now this exquisite torture had him right on the edge.

"Baby," he said as she rinsed him off. "You're so fucking beautiful."

She looked up at him with her amber eyes, full of heat and a flicker of doubt, even as she licked her lips.

His heart twisted. She didn't believe him?

Her hair was dark from the water, dark blonde with darker roots. It hung in wet strands about her face, the water running down her cheeks like tears. She thought he wanted her to be Sarah. Wanted his wife back. But Sarah was gone, and it wasn't his dead wife that had him so desperate right now. So insane with lust and so much more that it made him ache inside.

She bent forward to take him in her mouth. He stopped her with his hands in her hair.

"No," he said, and shook his head, despite the screaming of his cock to please, please let him come in her mouth.

Her eyes widened, filled with confusion.

"You didn't do anything wrong," he said before she could think he was rejecting her. "I just want to pleasure you first."

He wanted blonde hair, not dark, not on her. He wanted her to be here with him because she wanted it, not because she thought it would please him.

"You *are* beautiful," he insisted. "The most beautiful person I've ever known." It was true, and it wasn't just the physical beauty. It was her kindness and strength too. Sarah had filled him with excitement and love, but it had never made him feel quite like this insane, ravenous, *need*, he was filled with when around Hell. And he'd almost lost her. She could have been eaten by that worm, despite what she thought. She wasn't invulnerable. And the fear he'd felt then still shook in his core. He'd lost Sarah. He couldn't lose Hell too.

She closed her eyes. "Please stop saying that I'm beautiful."

"Never." He soaped her neck with gentle strokes, then moved south and focused on her gorgeous breasts. "God, you're perfect." Soft and firm, her breasts filled his hands as he moved the soap over and around them. Her nipples were hard and tight, growing tighter as he focused on washing them.

She bit her lip. "It's what Sarah used to say. That I was perfect and precious. The most perfect creature ever created."

"She was right. You are." He turned her around and soaped her back. Her skin was flawless, ivory silk. He couldn't get enough of touching her.

She shook her head. "No. If I was perfect, I should have saved her. For you."

The ache inside him expanded. "Hell, my sweet angel." He pulled her back against him, wrapping his arms around her so she couldn't pull away. "It was me who failed. I pushed her into making a choice between me and her work, and in doing so I pushed her away. She didn't trust me to tell me about you or what she'd done or why. She didn't trust me to love her enough to understand. And because of that, I failed to protect you both." It was a hard truth to admit, but he owed her that truth.

She shook her head frantically, trying to deny it. "She loved you. I know she did—"

"And now, I love you." There. He'd said it. The scary real words he'd been denying since the first time he'd held her in his arms and known that she was a living, breathing complication that had invaded his life. A complication that had brought hope for a new future without endless days of loneliness and pain. He hadn't wanted that hope then. It was scary as all hell to want it now. But he did want it. He wanted her.

She turned sideways in his arms and stared at him in disbelief, bordering on horror. "You can't."

"I can. I didn't want to at first. But I can't imagine spending my life without you now. So, yeah, it's a done deal. I love you, Helen. So do me a favor and don't ever take a stupid risk again like you did with that worm. I can't handle it."

"Oh, Peyton," she whispered, her eyes filling with tears. "I didn't mean to scare you." Her hand trembled as she gently stroked his cheek.

Tears and guilt could go to hell. He clutched her to him. She was beautiful. His. He needed to make her understand what that meant.

"Listen to me carefully." He held her gaze, keeping it on his by grasping her jaw so she couldn't turn away. "I know things have been weird between us because of Sarah. But I want you to understand. I don't care that she is part of you. Or that she created you. It doesn't change how I feel. You are the bravest, most caring, and beautiful person I've ever known. I love you and nothing will ever change that."

Her eyes glistened as she held his gaze. And he saw the painful fear and doubt, shadowing them. "She...she did things... To protect me. She did things that will make you hate me." Her eyes squeezed shut as tears slipped down her cheeks.

He wiped them away with his thumbs and held her tight against him. She shook like a leaf in the wind. A precious leaf he wanted to protect and cherish forever.

"I will never hate you, Helen. Whatever Sarah did..." He paused as the ache in his heart flared into anger that made it momentarily impossible to speak. It was just as he'd suspected. Hell had been keeping something from him. Ever since that nightmare she'd had about The Factory. Something she was afraid to tell him. About Sarah. Had Hell seen what had happened to her? Did she know how Sarah had been infected by the virus that had killed her and so many others?

He burned to know the truth, but seeing how it tormented Hell, maybe he didn't. He couldn't ask her to tell him, not until she was ready, not if it caused her this much pain. He crushed her to him, trying to still the trembling of fear that ran through her body. Was she afraid of what had happened or what he might think?

"It's not your fault," he whispered, kissing her closed lashes. "It was that place. The Factory. I'm going to burn it to the ground and make every last one of those sick motherfuckers pay."

The Factory had done this. Broken his dreams. Broken his wife. Killed her. And he'd let it happen. The guilt that had shadowed his thoughts and haunted his dreams for the past two years clawed hard at his insides, threatening to drown him in blackness.

Hell's trembling fingers tightened in his hair. Her warm body shifted against his, anchoring him. Reminding him that she needed him. Despite the odds, he had a new chance. Sarah had done that. Gifted her to him. No matter what else had happened, she'd done that. And he was never the fuck ever going to give Hell back. "You can tell me what happened when you're ready, but it won't change how I feel about you. I love you, Helen. You. Just you."

He kissed her lips, catching her sob, wanting to distract her, and wanting even more to show her how much he truly cared. Because now he'd said the 'L' word, it burned inside him like a torch, filling him with heat. He needed to share that fire with her. To imprint it on her skin and let it fill her soul until she burned with it too.

She moaned against his mouth, her sobs quickly becoming consumed by his kisses and the desire pulsing though them both. She tasted so good, her tongue rubbing against his as he explored her body with his hands. Her beautiful breasts, her smooth ass. God, she was perfect. So perfect and his. His blood pounded, his breath coming in pants.

"Oh...I need..." she said with a gasp and gripped his ass with her hands.

"I need it too, baby." He shook with it. The desire to be inside her. To be one with her. His fingers trembled with the fierce need to join with her fully as he slipped his hand down between them and touched the soft lips between her legs.

She came alive in his arms, as if he'd charged her with electricity, writhing her wet body against his. Her hands grasped his shoulders, his back, his ass. Her breath warmed his lips as she licked and nibbled them between kisses.

Fuck. He could fuck her right here. With the water raining down on them.

He turned her to face the shower head and nestled the length of his cock between her firm ass cheeks. Her perfect fucking ass, slick and wet with water. He added more of the creamy almond scented soap and let her cheeks cup him as he moved his hips back and forth. It felt so damn hot to be with her like that. Sliding his dick up and down her crack while he gripped her hips. He'd never been much into ass play, but with Hell it was hard to hold anything back.

"Mmmm," she moaned as she curled her arm backward around his neck. The other hand clutched his thigh. She turned her face to reach his lips with her own. Then devoured him with fierce, hot little licks and kisses that told him she burned for him too.

He gripped her breast and cupped her mound. He wanted her to come before he did. He pressed his finger inside her entrance. She was hot and slick, so ready.

"Peyton," she breathed against his mouth.

"My love," he said and rubbed her clit with his thumb as he stroked her from the inside with his finger. "My beautiful Helen."

She whimpered, her hands clutching his thigh and gripping his hair as a shudder passed through her. She was close, so close to coming.

He wanted to hear those beautiful sounds. The ones she made when the pleasure took over and she gave herself to it. He wanted to hear them every second of every fucking day for the rest of his life.

He adjusted his hand on her sex, touched her deeper as the water rained down on her hard nipples and firm breasts. Shit, they were perfect. Bigger now than when he'd first met her. Perky and full. Her nipples were like thick thumbs. He pulled at one, tugging it between his thumb and forefinger.

"Harder," she moaned and arched back against him. Her fingers dug into his thigh.

He gyrated his hips, rubbing his cock against her. It felt so good. Too good.

"Damn, I'm going to come all over your hot little ass." He gave her nipple a slight pinch and rubbed his hand against her clit.

She sucked in a breath. Then let it out in a beautiful keening wail as her body jerked against his. The sound of her pleasure made his spine tingle and his heart beat wildly. There was no greater gift than hearing her surrender.

As her tight sheath clutched his finger, he couldn't hold back and joined her, the sound of her pleasure triggering his own. He struggled to stay standing as his orgasm ripped through him like a blinding, white hot brand.

"Fuck, you're beautiful. So fucking beautiful," he said over and over again in ragged breaths by her ear as she trembled in his arms. "I'm going to fuck you forever tonight." Fuck her until she understood what his love meant. Fuck her until *he* understood what it meant. Fuck her until the ravenous need for her pushed away the fear lurking deep inside. The fear that loving her somehow meant losing her. That he'd fallen for her too fast.

"Yes," she said, "forever, my love." Her lips found his, the touch urgent, the fire still burning bright inside.

He quickly rinsed her clean between increasingly burning kisses, then wrapped her in a soft towel and carried her to their room.

MESSAGE IN A BOTTLE

HELL LAY ON the middle of the bed where Peyton gently placed her. In the semi-darkness of the room, he loomed over her, his strong body wet from the shower, naked and breathtaking.

He loved her.

Peyton Chase loved her.

It was almost too wonderful to be true. But the vulnerable way he looked at her as he lay down on his side facing her and gently cupped her cheek with his palm...she couldn't deny his sincerity. He trusted her. Adored her.

Loved her.

The beauty of the gift filled her, a warm glow that spread from her chest to her toes and pushed the guilt nagging at her to the edges of her mind. The persistent anxiety that it was wrong to claim these feelings when she was the reason Sarah had done what she'd done prickled her conscience.

She needed to tell him everything she remembered. She *would* tell him.

But she wanted this more than anything, this feeling of completeness. Of belonging. Of being accepted and desired. It felt so good to be kissed by him, to be caressed by his gentle, strong hands. She wasn't going to give him up for anything.

She wanted to give Peyton everything he'd ever dreamed of. Every pleasure he'd ever wanted. He loved her. He needed her.

She could give him the future he desired deep down inside. The one he was too afraid to even think of.

All she needed to do was get her ova back. And she would do that. She would find a way soon. But right now, she needed him to make the sweetest love to her. No, not sweet. She ached for him to fuck her hard. Make her burst into flames with his love.

He whispered soft words about 'silky' and 'beautiful' as he trailed his lips down her neck. It was hard not to believe him when he said it like that. She did feel beautiful when he touched her. He made her shine inside, like a glittering star.

His lips settled on her breast, covering her nipple. She grasped the sheet beneath her as he did that wonderful thing with his tongue and lips that made the tingling ache in her breasts spread through her whole body. They were so tight and sensitive now. Fuller than ever. And he knew just how she liked to be touched there. It was exhilarating.

It wasn't enough.

"Ahhh," she gasped as she arched her back.

The orgasm he'd given her in the shower still hummed through her veins, and it surged into an impatient roar as he kissed and suckled her breasts. She dug her fingers into the hard muscles of his shoulder.

He angled his gaze to catch hers.

"More. Now. *More*," she managed to say as the desire to have him completely nearly took her breath away. She ached with it. Writhed with it. She spread her legs wide as he moved his strong, commanding body over hers.

"Yes, love." He was hard and ready again, his thighs spreading hers, the tip of his cock nudging against her sex. He stared at her exposed center where every beat of her desire for him pulsed.

His gaze rose and found hers. "My beautiful, Hell." He was backlit, but even in the dimness she could make out the burning truth in his eyes. "I love you," he said as he grasped her hips, lifted them, and pushed forward.

As his hard heat filled her, stretching her, she cried out from the indescribable pleasure that was Peyton Chase. This was better than she'd ever felt before. More intimate. More everything. Is that what being loved did? Made everything magical?

He sucked in a sharp breath and glanced down at their joined bodies, as if he, too, was caught off guard by the incredible feeling of being one. "Shit. Oh, shit." He hissed, altering the tempo of his thrust, slowing it down. "You're so hot, baby. You feel amazing."

She tightened her abs as he pulled out, increasing the closeness and pleasure as he thrust back in again.

His muscles were taut, his body straining to keep control. His thighs quivered as she wrapped hers around him, clasping him to her, forcing him deeper.

He groaned through clenched teeth and lowered himself, resting his weight on his arms. "Hell. So tight. Perfect. God." His mouth met hers in a hot wet kiss.

She writhed with him as he thrust his hips. Fast. Hard. She couldn't resist. The sounds he made. He needed this. They both did. And it was all so much better. So much more than anything before. She felt his fierce desire for her with every movement of his body. His longing for release. His fight to hold back and build the moment.

His love. His impossible love.

It was like an opened door that she'd stepped through and on the other side was the most incredible feeling of warmth. It bathed her, filled her with a brilliant ecstatic joy.

She was hot inside, her belly tingling and fluttery where his cock rubbed her. She slipped her hand between their bodies and placed her palm on the spot where she felt him thrusting, in and out, beneath her skin.

It felt so good. Wild. Electric. But at the same time not quite enough. She needed him to release his pleasure and drown her with it.

"Peyton," she said between panting breaths. "Fuck me harder. Make me come." She pressed the heel of her palm down on the spot where the tip of his cock touched her inside. The heat spread out from there. The burning, which seemed to seep through her skin.

"God, Hell. My God."

His thrusts increased, slamming her against the bed.

Oh, Peyton. Peyton.

"I love you," she cried out.

Forever.

"Hell," he shouted as he arched against her.

He filled her with his seed. Thrust after jerky thrust. His fingers tight in her hair. His breath hot against her cheek.

She welcomed it. All of it. The pleasure and the heat. The feeling of electricity that rushed through her as her body spasmed from the bliss. So much bliss, like a white light that had no beginning or ending. An eternity of pleasure.

That he filled her with again. And again.

And again.

**

It was dark in the room when she opened her eyes. The flat-screen monitor on the far wall the only faint light, the readout indicating 4:01 AM. She blinked and made out the form tangled in the sheets beside her. Tall and strong and snoring gently. Peyton.

She smiled.

She was deliciously sore in all the right places, thoroughly ravished, and slightly disoriented by the exhaustion she felt. Her head pounded like she had a hangover. Intoxicated by his love? Her smile broadened. He'd made love to her like there was no tomorrow. No wonder he slept so deeply.

Careful not to wake him as she slipped out of bed, she went in search of a drink.

And paused.

Something didn't feel right. A whisper at the back of her mind that called to her softly, beneath the pounding of her pulse.

The worms? Maybe. They slept restlessly. Perhaps disturbed by the same thing that had woken her. She pulled on one of Peyton's shirts draped over a chair and opened the door into the lab.

It was quiet in there and just as dark. Her eyes had adjusted to the dimness now. The monitors sat idle, the chairs empty. The others would be sleeping.

Just like she should be. Except, something had woken her.

She made her way through and outside into the cavern, drawn by the prickling sensation that something wasn't quite right.

The fire pit sat empty, the embers black. Not a breath stirred the air.

She went down the steps and pressed her hands to the glass wall separating the cavern from the worm pen below.

They were all there but dreaming fitfully. She closed her eyes and tried to see what they were seeing but caught only a glimpse of the sensation of being stalked and trying to run away from danger.

It was so eerily similar to the disturbed feeling she'd had when coming out of stasis the first time Peyton had woken her in that shipping container, she jerked her hands from the glass and broke the connection.

She looked around her, staring into the darkness of the cavern, her heart and mind racing. She half expected to see someone waiting there, ready to attack her. But the darkness remained empty. The only sound the heavy beating of her heart.

Everything was as it should be. And yet, it felt as if everything had changed. She placed her hand over her belly, remembering her excitement a few hours past. It was still there, fluttering inside her. But different.

Now it was urgent. Insistent.

A warning?

Look away now, ELf. Look away!

Sarah? She called to the invisible presence inside her. The avatar that had been with her since the beginning. Guiding her. Protecting her. As Sarah had promised she always would. No matter what.

Yes, that's right.

Hell covered her ears and winced at the volume of that voice inside her mind. It was as if Sarah were speaking right beside her in the darkness, not the usual soft whisper.

Come to the transport.

Again, the piercing loudness. She kept her hands locked over her ears as she shook her head. She didn't want to go to the transport, but her feet seemed possessed by a different idea and moved her in that direction.

Don't scream, was the next command. Her voice locked up, the ability to utter a sound suddenly silenced.

Don't be afraid.

But that was one thing they didn't have control of. The one thing they'd *never* had control of. Her feelings. And right now, she was terrified. More frightened than she'd ever been at The Factory, strapped to that table in the darkness. They'd left her feelings alone so she could make them her own.

So she could be human.

And fall in love.

And be loved.

And...

She let out a strangled gasp, despite the control forbidding her to make a sound, as everything fell into place and she remembered. Memories flooded her brain about why they'd tortured her for two years. Why they'd almost killed her, cracking her mind. Why they'd sent her on this risky mission. And why, oh why, she should have never fallen in love with Peyton Chase. Silent tears streamed down her cheeks as the horror of the realization filled her.

Love.

That was the key. The one she had resisted for so long. The one she had refused to give in to. Not even when they'd killed Sarah, her beloved creator, trying to get her to cooperate with their plan. It was the one trap Hell had told herself over and over through the years of torture to never fall into. Love was a dangerous thing. She remembered that now. It opened up the doors inside her and let people use her for terrible things.

But now it was too late. They'd tricked her. Their plan had been to fool her into thinking she'd escaped. But she hadn't escaped. She's fulfilled their plan. She'd betrayed herself. And they'd won.

The transport doors hissed open, the sound ominously loud in the quiet cavern. Warm light flickered on as she entered, too afraid to silently scream, too filled with despair not to.

Her limbs felt heavy as she made her way to the cockpit area and sat in the operations seat. The one no one ever used because the ship guided itself. All it needed was instructions.

The engines fired up, a gentle rumble she felt in her bones.

Shut down, she silently, desperately willed it.

But she wasn't the one in control.

The console screen to her left glowed, showing the image of a smiling woman's face. The dark hair. Blue eyes. An exact replica of Sarah Palmer Chase in every detail, except this cloned creature had never had her soul.

"Thank you, ELf. You've done excellently. Even better than we'd hoped," the Sarah-clone said with a genuine smile. "It's time for you to come home now."

Hell shook her head frantically.

Please, let me go. She didn't want to go back. She couldn't go back to The Factory. Not now, not like this. But if begging for freedom had never worked before, why would it work now?

"Are you certain she's carrying his child?" Markus Willbright asked. He stood beside the Sarah-clone on the screen, peering at a tablet in his hand with a frown. "I'm seeing only a slight rise in her hCG levels."

"Yes. I've been monitoring her closely through the link provided by the avatar program. It was just as you suspected. It was about that bond of trust. Her body responded to Peyton's instinctual need for a child and grew new ova. She unlocked them when she realized she loved him." The Sarah-clone took the tablet from him and nodded. "It's very early on, but yes, she's pregnant."

Hell stared at the monitor in horror as her hand slid protectively over her belly.

Pregnant.

It was true.

Everything they'd said.

The fluttering inside. The difference in her awareness.

Tears flooded her cheeks, blurring the images before her. She would have wiped them away, but she couldn't seem to lift her hands now.

"Destroy her ova we harvested earlier," the Sarah-clone instructed. "We don't need them now. This child will give us everything we need. Congratulations, ELf," she said, smiling at her again. "You're going to give birth to a new generation of humans. Ones we'll control properly. Unlike you. So willful and stubborn. Sarah thought you were perfect. But I'll make sure your children truly are."

No, no, nooooo! Not my baby. Leave my baby alone.

"It's not yours, ELf. It belongs to the human race. And me." Her smile twisted, showing her perfect teeth. "Peyton always wanted a child. Sarah never gave him one. But now, thanks to you, I have. Do you think he'll love me for it?" Her eyes glittered, bright blue on the screen.

Never, screamed Hell, *NEVER*, as the desperate rage filled her.

Images flashed through her mind. Memories that filled the gaps in her life, even as they burst with dark terror.

This clone of Sarah had done so much harm, almost as soon as she'd been born. She'd killed her creator in the name of science. Killed so many people with the KIS virus. Kept Hell captive for nearly two years and tortured her mercilessly. All so she could fulfill the dream of creating a superior human race. She'd inherited Sarah's ambition and intelligence, the drive to succeed. Which was what Sarah had wanted. A clone to take her place at The Factory and continue the research, while she went back to her life with Peyton at Deliverance Dome.

But the clone hadn't inherited her conscience. Her soul. Her respect for life.

Hell had vowed to die before giving this creature what she'd wanted—viable hybrid ova with which to experiment on further.

Hell's fingers twitched where they lay protectively across her abdomen as she reaffirmed that vow. She'd find a way to save her baby. A way to save Peyton and them all or die trying.

But as the transport moved out of the cavern and into the swirling, snow-filled darkness, carrying her away from the safety of her new-found family, the Sarah-clone laughed loud. It was the victorious song of a hunter mocking her prey.

And Hell knew it was only a matter of time before she moved in for the kill.

GONE

THUMP.

Thump, thump.

"Peyton, wake up. *Peyton!*"

At the sound of Aunty Jo's familiar voice, Peyton groaned as he opened his eyes and stared blearily into the darkened room.

"Yeah?" he called out, groggy from the exhaustion that wanted to drag him back down into the blissfully deep sleep he'd been jerked out of. What the hell time was it? He blinked and tried to focus on the monitor on the wall, but he couldn't make out the time.

"Wake up and come to the lab," Aunty Jo insisted, her voice slightly muffled by the closed door. "And bring Helen with you. The worms have gone crazy!"

Helen. The mention of her name caused him to smile. His beautiful, sexy Hell. She was the reason he'd been so deeply asleep. She'd worn him out last night.

He rubbed his hands against his eyes. It would be nice to curl up with her, maybe let her wear him out some more, and pretend he hadn't heard his aunt's voice or her pounding on his bedroom door. But he knew better than that. If they didn't get up and see what had Aunty Jo's panties in a twist, she'd probably break down the door and drag them out of bed with her bare hands.

Could they not, for the love of all things holy, even have a night

253

alone together without being disturbed?

Apparently not.

The door cracked open an inch, letting in a beam of bright light. "Peyton? Did you hear me?"

"Yeah, yeah. We're coming. Just give me a minute. Jesus Christ."

"Well, hurry up. And don't swear at me. I brought you up better than that." The door closed again with a sharp click.

Right. "Jesus *fucking* Christ," he muttered. He reached over and patted the rumpled pile of sheets next to him on the double bed. "Come on, love. We'd better get up. Aunty Jo's on a warpath. Hell?"

The sheets beside him were cold. The space empty of Hell's warmth. But her scent lingered, sweet and full of memories of the intimacy they'd shared. It chased away the momentary disquiet of not finding her in his bed and filled him with impatient need to see her again. She was likely up already and in the bathroom. Maybe he'd join her for another shower. That thought made him grin, despite the protesting of his muscles as he pushed away the covers and got dressed.

The lab was bright and smelled like fresh-brewed coffee when he opened the door and exited his bedroom. Aunty Jo and Lee were crowded around one of the monitors, staring intently at the screen. The concern on both their faces made his yawn die mid-exhale.

"What's going on?" he asked and moved to stare at the screen with them.

"It's the worms," Aunt Joanna said. "Something's woken them. All of them."

They writhed about each other in the enclosure, clearly agitated, as if something had disturbed them and continued to do so. Peyton had seen similar behavior when the worms were woken from hibernation and entered a mating state. But he'd never seen them quite so aggressive and restless before. They curled around and over each other, their bristled tails rasping against the rock walls and flooring, creating grooves in the stone and score marks on their skin. It appeared as if they were rooting around, searching for an escape.

"Shit. When did this start?"

"Sometime in the middle of the night. Number twenty-four's the worst. It's stirring up the others. Look." She pointed at the screen.

One of the worms reared up high, its mouth gaping wide as it bellowed a sound that echoed like an angry roar off the cavern walls. The noise caused the other worms to groan uneasily and wriggle faster, seeking escape from the confined space. But without an opened exit, the nearest Reclaimers couldn't avoid the impact as the errant worm descended with a loud bang. It smashed hard against two of the others, the spines on its tail digging in deep and tearing long gashes into their flesh. The worms screamed as if in pain. Enraged, they thrashed about, twisting around and over each other, trying to get away.

"It's starting to get ugly. Do you think we should let them out?" Mac asked, peering at Joanna and Lee through the surveillance camera. He and Jared both wore protective gear, ready to go into the enclosure if needed.

"Hold on," she said to Mac. "We don't know what woke them in the first place. No telling what they'll do in the tunnels." She glanced at Peyton with a frown, peeking behind him at his bedroom. "Where's Helen? We need her to talk to them and find out what's going on."

Peyton darted a look toward the bathroom. The door stood open, the room inside empty of occupants. "Isn't she already up?"

"If she is, I haven't seen her."

A feeling of unease gripped Peyton's spine. He spoke into the com link to Mac and Rusty. "Have either of you seen Hell this morning?" He checked the time. Yes, it was morning, just past six a.m., though it always looked the same inside the cavern no matter the time of day or night.

They looked at each other and shook their heads. "No. Isn't she with you?"

The door to the main entry hissed open and Jared hurried into the lab. "Transport's gone," he announced, slightly out of breath as if he'd hurried to bring that news in person.

"What?"

"Gone? How can it be gone?" Aunty Jo asked.

Jared waved the tablet he carried in this hand. "Looks like it left around three fifteen a.m. or so. There's a visual of it exiting through the exterior cavern door."

"Christ!" Peyton shouted, dark panic flashing through his veins. "It must have been Hell." Though he couldn't imagine why she'd take off in the transport in the middle of the night. At least, he couldn't imagine any good reasons why she'd leave in the middle of the night. On her own. Without telling him. After he'd told her he loved her. And fucked her until they were both raw. Was she upset about that? Or was it something else? She hadn't been herself the past few days.

Using the monitor at the workstation, he opened a communication link with the transport. "Hell? You okay, love?" Silence greeted him. "Hell?"

"Maybe she's not on it?" Jared said.

"Then who's driving the transport? It wouldn't just leave on its own." And neither would she. He tried contacting her again, anxiety slicing through him. "Hell? If you're on the transport, please respond." Silence continued to answer him. Something was wrong.

"Peyton. Look at the worms," Lee said his gaze fixed on the screen. "Watch them and call her name again."

"Hell?" Peyton said into the open link to the transport, his gaze trained on the worms.

Reclaimer number twenty-four, the one Hell had connected with earlier, reared up and started bellowing. The other worms hurried to get out of its way as it thrashed around the pen.

"Every time you call to her, it does that," Lee said. He stood and started to pace restlessly. "I knew something was wrong. I could feel it." He gripped the back of his chair with both hands and stared at the screen, his bushy white brows pulled down in a frown. "I woke up in the middle of the night, but I couldn't find anything wrong. And then when the worms started acting up, I thought it was them. But it was Hell, wasn't it? It was her." He shook his head. "I think she's still connected somehow and trying to tell us she's in trouble."

Aunty Jo caressed his back, her gaze full of concern. "Don't you start blaming yourself. Whatever's happened here, it's not your fault, Lee."

"It makes perfect sense," Peyton said, watching the worms through the monitor. "She was talking to them using some kind of remote link, remember? Maybe that's possible even over long distance. Hell?" he said into the link to the transport. "If you're connected to that worm, answer me."

Reclaimer twenty-four reared up and bellowed loudly.

"Goddamnit, there it is. That is you, isn't it, baby? Why can't you speak? Are you in trouble?"

The Reclaimer twisted and bellowed, this time violently smashing itself into the exit portal, as if desperate to escape.

"Oh, my God," Aunty Jo said. "It's going to crush the others if it keeps doing that."

"Do you want us to sedate them?" Mac asked.

"No," Peyton said, his mind racing. "Get Henry down there and see if he can talk to them. Maybe the machine language Hell used to reprogram him is the same as the worms'. It might be our only chance to communicate with her directly." Whatever had happened, Hell was definitely in trouble.

He raced to the exit where his outer gear hung and grabbed his coat. "I'm going after her in the CAT." Three hours. She'd had about a three-hour start. The Climate Accessible Transport was smaller and more mobile than the larger unit. He should be able to track the transport and catch up to wherever it was headed.

"I'm coming with you," Jared said. He grabbed his coat from the hook beside Peyton's.

"Be careful." Aunty Jo gave them both a quick hug. "Something's very wrong here. She wouldn't just leave on her own like this."

"No, she wouldn't," Lee said quietly. The expression on his face was implacable as he stared at the writhing mass of worms. "Not unless she was forced to." He glanced up and caught Peyton's gaze. The look in his eyes confirmed the suspicion screaming in Peyton's mind.

It could be the transport had malfunctioned, rendering the com link unusable. And it could be Hell was being creative and using her connection with the worms as an alternate means of calling for help. But there was no way she'd leave in the middle of the night without telling anyone. Not willingly anyway. She was so desperately afraid of going back to The Factory that she hadn't wanted to be away from him since the moment he'd rescued her from that damn box.

And now she was gone.

Unexpectedly, mysteriously gone.

The obvious explanation burned like a hot coal inside his heart, igniting fury.

"She didn't leave on her own," Peyton said. His hands shook with as he grabbed his gloves and headed out the door. "The assholes at the fucking Factory took her."

**

Snow streamed past the curved windshield of the CAT in a thick wall of flakes that seemed to have no beginning or end. In the near-blizzard conditions, visibility was so poor that the morning light barely brightened the view outside to a dull grey.

Not that Peyton cared what the hell the weather did. His concentration was on the navigation screen, and the fact that after an hour and a half of travelling at steadily reducing speed due to the worsening storm, they were finally about to catch up to the transport and Hell.

"This is taking too fucking long," Peyton said, frustrated with the slow progress despite their imminent arrival.

"We'll be there in less than a minute," said Jared. His voice was calm and probably meant to be encouraging. But nothing would convince Peyton that Hell was okay. Not until he saw her again and felt the steady, reassuring pulse of her heartbeat when he wrapped her in his arms and held her close.

"It's a fucking minute too late."

"Peyton, chill man. The transport hasn't moved in the last hour. Hell's probably got everything under control and is just waiting for us to get there."

"Yeah? So why isn't she still answering any calls?"

"Well...that could be any number of things."

"Like what?"

"Like the communication system is still down and she can't repair it."

"When have you ever known Hell to not be able to repair anything mechanical?"

Jared remained silent and shook his head as the CAT lurched in the wake of another deep drift.

"My point, exactly," Peyton said.

They hadn't spoken much during the trip. Both of them lost in their own dark, anxious thoughts about what had happened to Hell and not wanting to voice them. Peyton was trying hard not to think about the icy fear, which lodged like a hard lump his soul, that whatever had made Hell leave in the transport couldn't be good. Not when The Factory was involved.

Images of the torture she'd endured while held captive crashed through his mind again and again. He couldn't stop thinking about it or hearing her screams echo in his thoughts. Couldn't stop the sick feeling that had him in a tight grip that she might not be alive. That he'd lost her like he'd lost Sarah.

He couldn't go through this again.

Not again.

"Fucking Christ." He banged the throttle hard with his gloved fist, as if brute force might make the machine go faster.

"It's redlined, Peyton. We're already killing the batteries."

"Fuck the batteries."

"You think I don't want to get there fast too? She's like my sister—"

The small transport lurched to a sudden halt in the drift, tossing them both forward against their seat restraints. The beacon on the navigation screen flashed green.

"We're here," Peyton said. His gut tightened as the outline of the ANT transport loomed directly ahead of them, a shadowy grey shape in the thick swirling snow.

He quickly activated the hatch, not caring that the wind whipped inside the small pod and coated everything with a dusting of flurries. Ice crystals stung his cheeks as he launched himself outside into the snow. Knee deep, the drift slowed him down, increasing the desperate beating of his heart to make it through the few feet to the transport.

"*Hell*!" he shouted, his voice lost in the howling wind. "I'm coming baby, I'm coming."

It seemed to take an eternity to step through the drift, but he reached the side of the large transport in seconds and activated the main entryway. It slid open without delay, allowing him and Jared to enter the crew quarters and shut the door behind them. The sudden silence was deafening after the screaming wind.

"Hell?" Peyton called out again. But the relief he felt at having finally caught up with the transport was overshadowed by a renewed flood of fear when his question was left unanswered.

"I'll check the cockpit," Jared said. "You try the cargo hold."

Peyton nodded. Maybe she was in the bed? His boots rang on the metal flooring as he raced through the empty crew cabin and into the cargo pod.

"Hell?" The cot they'd shared lay empty, nestled between the racks of equipment secured to the walls. Everything was just as he'd left it last time he'd been in there a few days ago. Nothing had been disturbed, not even the blankets.

She wasn't in there.

"Where the hell are you, baby?" His heart hammered in his chest as he made his way back through the crew cabin and into the cockpit area. Was she hurt? Unconscious? Lost in the snow? Dead?

God, please. Please. Not again.

"She's gone," Jared said, his gaze averted as he focused on reading a display log on the main console. His lips were a firm line, his expression tight.

Peyton's heart lurched in his chest. "Gone? What do you mean by gone?"

Jared caught his gaze and held it. "An air transport picked her up. Looks like it was arranged to meet her at these coordinates."

"*Sonofafuckingbitch.*"

Peyton smashed his fist against the console, causing it to shake with the force of his rage. The sense of loss and impotence to do anything about it charged through him. It flooded his body, bleeding from his soul. While The Factory had the resources to access an air transport, he didn't. Unless Lee could pull some weight with the High Council, the next air transport available would be from Deliverance Dome on its regularly scheduled run. And if they left now, it would take five days to get back there.

Five fucking days.

The bastards had taken Hell and there wasn't a single thing he could do about it.

He gripped the edge of the console hard and stared at it, unable breathe, unable to think.

"Fuck this shit. We'll get her back, Peyton," Jared said, his voice deadly serious. He punched in the coordinates on the navigation screen, setting a course for the worm den. "Dad will file a formal complaint. The Factory won't be allowed to get away with this. I'm sure she didn't want to leave."

"She didn't," Peyton whispered.

He couldn't take his eyes from the console. Next to where his own fingers gripped the edge, tiny grooves had been scratched into the opaque black surface. Marks in the otherwise pristine surface like someone's nails had clawed into it. Faint marks, but as he studied them, they seemed to form a pattern...letters... F...A...C...T...

His blood ran cold.

"Oh, sweet Jesus."

"What's wrong?" Jared asked.

Peyton shook his head, squeezing his eyes shut tight. Every nightmare he'd ever envisioned about Hell at The Factory raced through his mind. He pulled off his gloves and traced the marks with his fingers, envisioning the terror that had caused her to make them, her desperation. Her need to tell them where she was. Her hope that they would follow.

"Does that say Factory?" Jared asked.

"Yeah." Tears misted Peyton's eyes as his heart beat strong and bitter within him, and full of so much rage he could barely breathe.

Twice in his life now, The Factory had stolen the precious center of his heart.

He'd let it die the first time. He wasn't going to let it happen again. Hell was alive, he was sure of it, and strong. She'd always been strong.

"Fucking son-of-a-bitch." Jared snarled. "I'm going to kill him. I'm going to kill every last one of them."

"You'll have to get in line," Peyton said.

With an angry thump he sat in the pilot's chair and manually engaged the drive to full throttle. The transport lurched forward at the sudden thrust, jolting them until the stabilizers kicked in a second later.

"Hang on, baby. I'm coming to get you," he promised Hell, his heart full of the need inside him, burning to make that happen.

But deep within, doubt whispered.

It trembled with a fear that wouldn't be silenced.

He would rescue Hell from Willbright. That he was sure of.

But will I be too late?

THE FACTORY

HELL LAY ON her back on the all-too-familiar padded bed. The glass walls of the room were the same, the lighting, the sharp smell of whatever antiseptic cleanser they used to clean everything in this lab. Even the scanning array was the same, perched above her like an old familiar lover, knowing every detail of her inside and out.

But the tiny little blip on the image of her uterus that had the two scientists in the room entranced, that was different. It floated above her in the holographic display, a red dot against the blue of her womb.

Her child was real and growing inside her. So small. Just a tiny pinpoint of life. But real. She wanted to cry with happiness. Scream it to the world. She'd given Peyton his dream. She'd achieved what Sarah had wanted. Proven humanity wasn't doomed to be extinct. People could be designed from the cellular level up to be better, stronger, adaptable to any circumstance. A hybrid of human and machine that had passed the final test—they could breed independently.

It was a miracle.

The ultimate in scientific achievement.

But instead of happiness, she wept silent tears of horror. They slipped from the corners of her eyes and down her cheeks, unimpeded by the semi-stasis field that held her frozen in place on the scanner bed.

Her child wasn't her own. *She* wasn't her own. Not if she believed what these people wanted her to believe.

'The greater good', they'd reminded her on the flight back to her 'home' at The Factory. It was all for the greater good. And they were so happy she'd finally agreed to cooperate.

Except she hadn't.

They'd tricked her. She thought they'd let her escape, but she'd been a rat in a maze. And Peyton. Poor Peyton.

I'm so sorry I dragged you into this. I didn't know. I don't know...

But now she was pregnant, and she needed to find a way to escape for real this time.

Because the type of 'greater good' these scientists preached felt like death. The end of freedom. The beginning of a new human race of slaves where choices were made before people were even born, about who they'd be and how they'd behave.

And they wanted it all to start with her baby. Her innocent child, who had been created out of love.

"We should remove it now," the clone of Sarah Palmer Chase said. She turned to Markus Willbright, who stood beside her, admiring the holographic image of conception that floated between Hell and them. "We can grow it in the gestation chamber. The longer it's in her, the less control we have over it."

Markus shook his head. "No. I told you before, it's too risky. We have no idea how it will react to being removed from its mother. We can't afford to lose it by being over-confident."

The clone sneered. "Over-confident? Is it over-confident to want to continue the experiment in a sterile environment where it can be controlled completely?"

Willbright turned off the scanner. The holographic image disappeared and so did the semi-stasis field, but Hell lay on the bed just the same as when she'd been instructed to not move by the Sarah-clone.

He collected his tablet as he studied the clone, his lips set in a hard line. "How many attempts did your predecessor make before achieving success in creating an Enhanced Lifeform? Twelve? And out of those twelve ELfs, three survived to maturation, only one of which—the one lying right here—ended up being a viable hybrid. And despite two years of trying, we haven't been able to replicate the same level of success. So yes, I do believe it is being over-confident to try removing the child before it's viable. We can't take the risk. We may never get a second chance at this." He looked at

Hell, his dark, almond-shaped eyes cold as they assessed her. A look she'd seen a thousand times from him. "This opportunity is...too precious."

"Precious?" the clone scoffed. "You've lost your nerve, doctor."

Willbright's expression never changed as he studied the clone, but the temperature in the room seemed to drop ten degrees. Goose bumps rippled along Hell's arms.

"Need I remind you that the reason I tolerate your existence is because you are useful to me? Do not make me question that usefulness." He turned and left the room without waiting for a response, his ever-present tablet clutched beneath his arm.

The clone stared after him in silence, the expression in her blue eyes a mixture of frustration, resentment, and hate. Hell forced herself to ignore the chill that gripped her body at the coldness in that expression. The complete lack of compassion that the clone exhibited never ceased to take her breath away. It passed through the constricted muscles of her throat with a squeak.

"You think that was funny?" the clone asked. Her gaze narrowed as she glanced at Hell sharply. "I assure you he does need me. Because I'm the one who controls you. And I do control you, don't I?" She let out a soft sigh. "Or have you forgotten the things I can make you do? All the games we've played over the years?"

Her head tipped to the side in a thoughtful gesture as she gently stroked Hell's hair. "Precious. Everyone thinks you're *soooo* precious." Her lips twisted into a parody of a smile. "But I know the truth, don't I? You're just an aborted bundle of coding that got lucky and survived."

She settled down onto the edge of the scanner bed, her hip pressing against Hell's thigh. "Tell me, did you feel precious when Peyton said he loved you?" She wiped at the tears leaking from the corners of Hell's eyes with the tip of her finger. "Awww, look at you, crying like a child. Do you miss him? Do you think he really does love you?" The look in the clone's eyes changed, became something hotter and harder as it swept over Hell with a sneer. "Or is it something else that you miss, humm? Like when he touched you here?" The clone's fingers brushed over Hell's lips in a feather-light caress. They stroked downward over Hell's jaw and neck and stopped between her breasts. The thin fabric of her gown didn't hide the reaction of her nipples. "Oh, look at that. I think it is," the clone crooned. "It's the sex doll programming in you. You're a dirty little whore at heart." Her smile twisted as she moved her fingers to Hell's left nipple. "You loved how he played with these so much. Sucking them, pinching them. Like this?" She tweaked Hell's nipple between her thumb and finger, rubbing it the way Peyton had. The skin reacted to the stimulus, becoming thick and hard.

Hell wanted to shut her eyes, to block out the sensations she was feeling as the clone mimicked the way Peyton had touched her. But she couldn't. She could only lie there and try not to remember how pleasurable it felt to be stroked by him. Her nipples were so sensitive, especially now she was pregnant. But being touched by this creature made her stomach twist.

"You came so hard for him," the clone said and gave Hell's nipple a hard pinch. "I enjoyed watching you through the avatar link. It was quite...exciting. Especially when he touched you here." Her fingers left Hell's nipple and trailed down over her stomach to her groin.

Hell's heartbeat roared in her ears as the clone lightly rested her fingers where no one had permission to touch, not without her consent. And she'd given that to only one person—Peyton.

"I loved the moans you made for him." The clone's gaze found Hell's again, hot and demanding, but still empty of compassion. "Do you remember the moans you made for me the first time I taught you how to fuck?" Her tongue darted out to wet her bottom lip. "Didn't it make you feel precious when I showed you what your vagina was meant for?" She blinked, once, twice, her fingers soft and unmoving over Hell's mound. "Answer me."

"No," Hell said as her vocal cords released from the hold the clone had over them. She'd been hurt and broken after she'd been violated that first of many, many times. Bleeding. Torn. The memory of the pain twisted her insides. But she bit back on the urge to scream. Screaming was what the clone liked—her fear. She wouldn't give her that. Not until she had to.

"Then I need to remind you," the clone said and patted Hell's sex. "You're a horny little slut that likes it hard. Lift your knees and spread them wide."

Hell did as instructed, unable to resist, even while the urge to vomit knotted her stomach so bad it hurt. The control over her through the avatar program was too strong to deny.

The real Sarah Palmer Chase had designed the program as a diagnostic tool and a way to monitor Hell's development. Her friend and beloved creator had never abused it in any way. In fact, it had been a comfort to have a digital version of Sarah inside her mind, helping her to make sense of the complexity of being a biological machine. And it had been designed to be shut down, she remembered Sarah had said, when it wasn't needed anymore, when Hell was grown up enough to live on her own.

Well, Hell was pretty damn sure she didn't need it anymore, but this clone...this clone...being genetically identical to Sarah in every way, it gave her direct access to Hell. It allowed her to twist her, break her, fuck with her brain. But it had never controlled her feelings. Those remained hers in every sacred way. And right now, she chose to remain calm and detached as the clone pushed the bottom of Hell's examination gown up her thighs, exposing her groin.

"Just like I remember it," the clone said with a pleased sigh, her gaze lingering on the exposed, naked area between Hell's legs. The force of that gaze crawled over Hell's skin along with the touch of the clone's fingers, examining the contours of her folds in an almost loving way. "With all the fucking Peyton's been doing, it's a wonder," the clone said, her voice full of contempt. "But I suppose that's what we wanted, wasn't it? For you to be irresistible to him. A perfect little whore. So loving and full of trust. You opened yourself right up to him, didn't you? Oopsie." She patted Hell's belly over the place where the baby grew, a smug smile on her face. "And to think you'd vowed you'd never fall in love and unlock the access to your reproductive subroutines. Tsk-tsk. I told you I'd find a way. You should have believed me two years ago. It would have saved you so much pain."

Hell stared up at the ceiling, concentrating on breathing calmly as she tried not to think about what was coming. About how this version of Sarah loved to punish her in the so-called name of science. More often than not strapping her down rather than commanding her not to move, so Hell could moan or writhe or scream freely. She'd explained it was so she could tell how real Hell's reaction was to whatever stimulus she was exposed to.

But Hell knew it had more to do with the fact the clone detested her.

When had the hatred first begun? It was hard to say. Hell had tried to like her and be friends in the beginning. It was what Sarah had wanted when she'd first introduced Hell to her new 'sister'. But even on that first day, the clone had looked at Hell with cool dislike clear in her blue eyes, and maybe jealousy too, though Hell hadn't recognized it at the time. Sarah had never hidden how pleased she was with Hell, how important and perfect she was, whereas the clone was a means to an end, created to help with the workload.

And the deadliest mistake Sarah Palmer Chase had ever made.

The clone pressed her fingers into Hell's mound and spread her slit wide, exposing the center of her. "Time to open up for your inspection, little slut," the clone said, and softly tapped Hell's clit, making Hell flinch inside. She was identical to Dr. Sarah Palmer Chase in every way, from her voice to her mannerisms, except her soul...her twisted, compassionless soul. "Do you remember how much you enjoyed being inspected? When I put my fingers inside you—"

The clone's hand jerked back as a pulse of electricity discharged from Hell's body. She gripped her fingers as if they'd been burnt. "*You fucking bitch.*" She rubbed her hand. "You did that on purpose." She loomed over Hell, glaring.

Hell wanted to smile at the shocked expression on her face but couldn't. "No. I imprinted on Peyton. I belong to him. Not you. Not anymore."

"That damn sex doll security system. No matter. I disabled it once. I'll do it again."

"You can't. Not without Peyton's permission. He's my master."

The clone laughed. "You think a little bit of programming has ever stopped me?"

"But you'd have to hurt me to do it. And that might harm the baby. Do you really want to take that chance? Willbright said no unnecessary risks. If something happens to my baby, he'll take it out on you."

"We'll see about that." The clone bent close to Hell, her breath hot against her face. "As soon as that baby is viable, it's mine. Willbright is an idiot. It's going to be a pleasure killing him. Just like I killed Sarah. Weak-minded fools. Getting in my way and trying to hold me back. They have no vision of the future."

"You'll have to kill me too," Hell said. "Because I'll never let you have my baby."

"Kill you?" The clone laughed. "Oh no, my dear *precious* ELf. I'm going to break you. Dissect you into a thousand pieces. Just like I did before. You *are* mine. Until I'm ready to be done with you. And when I'm done, Peyton will never want you again. In fact, he's going to hate you for being the little slutty whore that you are."

And the way she said it, Hell knew the clone was going to enjoy every bit of the breaking process, just like she'd done the first time.

"He's going to come for me. He loves me," Hell said, putting all the defiance that burned inside her into her voice as much as she could. "And he's going to love this baby."

"Oh, I'm counting on it. I want him to come here. But he won't want to rescue you. Not once he's seen me." She batted her dark lashes and her expression changed in a flash, becoming innocent and vulnerable, the beginnings of tears rimming her eyes. "His poor beloved wife." She sniffled dramatically. "Held captive here for two years. Unable to contact him. To tell him that Willbright lied. It was an illegally made clone of Sarah that died, not me. I've been forced to work here all this time, missing him, while you—you little slutty abomination—plotted to take my place at his side."

"That's not true. That's a lie!"

"Is it? When Willbright is dead and your mind is in bits, who's going to be left to tell the difference?"

"Clarissa—"

"I'm afraid she had a little accident while you were gone. Shame, really. She knew how to make me come so hard. I'm going to miss that. But tell me...is Peyton's cock really that large?" She brushed the fake tears from her eyes. "No, on second thought, don't answer. I'll enjoy it more finding out for myself." She patted Hell's belly as she pulled the gown back down over her thighs. "Just lie there and gestate like a good little incubator. I want that baby to be healthy when I present it to Peyton. Can't have him thinking I might be bad at my job or the High Council will never let me stay here and oversee this facility when Willbright's gone. And I have so much work to do. So many plans for the future of humanity."

With a cruel laugh, she left Hell lying on the scanner bed and headed for the exit.

Oh, the Maker.

How many days did she have? How many hours before the clone put her plan in play to steal her baby from her and take Dr. Sarah Palmer Chase's place? A few months? A few days? Hours?

The clone had already killed Sarah's lab assistant Clarissa, apparently. And Willbright was next.

Hell had to figure out a way to escape before then. Find a way to warn Peyton.

Where was Peyton? Was he on his way to The Factory even now?

He would come and get her if he could, she was sure of that. He'd promised to protect her, and one thing she knew about Peyton Chase was he'd never break a promise like that. That's what loving someone meant, didn't it? Never giving up on them?

Like he'd never given up on his love for Sarah. Not even after she'd died.

Was it possible the clone could convince him? Make him believe that she was his wife?

Hell thought of the drunken wreck he'd been when she'd first met him. His loss, his loneliness. It was quite possible he'd want Sarah back so badly, he'd believe just about anything, including a lie.

Shit. Shit. Shit. Shit.

She closed her eyes, seeking focus.

She needed to get out of here, and fast. Before Peyton arrived.

For her child's sake, and everyone else's.

But if she'd never managed to escape The Factory in the past two years until they'd set her free as a trap, how much hope did she have of escaping now?

MEETINGS

"ARE YOU FUCKING kidding me?" Peyton shouted at the ring of faces peering at him from the wall monitors at Deliverance Dome's conference room. Six representatives, one from each of the other Domes, which comprised the governing council of New Earth, stared back at him, clearly unamused by his outburst. But he hadn't raced back home through crap weather and five days of little sleep to be stopped from rescuing Hell now.

"Peyton..." Lee said in a cautioning tone and shook his head almost imperceptibly. He put a hand on Peyton's in an attempt to calm him down. But nothing would calm Peyton. Not in the face of this bureaucratic bullshit.

"Listen. Hell's activation sequence was coded to me." He glared at Markus Willbright, who studied him dispassionately through the communication system. "Whether or not she was the right model, you sent her to me, and I accepted the package by signing with my thumbprint. She's my property. I named her. I claimed her. You can't just decide you want her back and steal her in the middle of the night."

"My apologies for the deception, Dr. Chase," Willbright said. "But we released, ELf-3, or rather Hell as you say, into your care for the purposes of undergoing a test to determine her compatibility with humans. And now that she has passed that test, she has been recalled back into our care." He turned his gaze to

Irena Osceola, chairwoman of the High Council, whose clear, blue-eyed gaze studied them all from her office at The Arkopolis. "It was the Turing test, madam chair. The final test to see if she could be accepted by humans. She was never Dr. Chase's property in any true legal capacity."

"A test? Bull-SHIT!" Peyton shouted and slammed his hand down hard on the table in front of him. "She belongs with me. You stole her back so you could use her for your fucked up experiments again."

"Dr. Chase," the chairwoman said. "You will be civil and respectful during this meeting or you will leave. Do I make myself clear?"

She waited until Peyton had managed a nod. It took several deep breaths and his jaw felt like it might snap from the pressure of clamping his mouth shut. But he managed one after a moment. He needed to get Hell back. Pissing off the chairwoman of the New Earth High Council wasn't going to do that.

"Yes, Chairwoman Osceola," he said.

She nodded and turned her cool gaze on Willbright.

"This experimental Bio-roid, ELf-3, otherwise called Helen, is not known to us. Given that it is your responsibility to maintain full disclosure of your projects with the High Council at all times, how do you account for this, Dr. Willbright?"

"It was an oversight, Madam Chair. One I intended to correct as soon as I had the final data to relay about the ELf project's performance."

"And do you have that data now?"

"Yes. In regards to the Turing test, which was the last test we subjected her to, she is fully capable of integrating with the population and is indistinguishable from humans. That test would not have been possible had we disclosed our objective to Dr. Chase when we released her into his temporary care."

"Released?" Jared interjected in a calm tone before the volatile energy beating through Peyton could erupt again. "According to Helen, she escaped."

Willbright nodded. "We allowed her to believe that in order for the parameters of the test to be established."

"And what other tests have you performed on Helen?" the chairwoman asked.

"Standard practice, with mixed success, thus our desire to remove her from Dr. Chase's company as soon as the validity of the Turning test had been established."

"Madam Chair," Lee said. "We have reason to believe Helen

was repeatedly abused while at the bio-robotics factory during the past two years. The information on this data cube was collected during an operation Dr. Chase performed on Helen when she initially arrived at Deliverance Dome in need of acute medical care."

He placed the cube into a holographic projector on the conference room table. Peyton stared at the images of pain and horror that came to life in three dimensions for everyone present to witness. Pain he'd experienced through Hell's eyes. Screams he'd heard with his own ears. Her blood spilling as his own as it ran in streams down her body— Unable to take anymore, he grabbed the controls and stopped the holographic playback, silencing Hell's shrieks, his own scream caught in his chest as he struggled to breathe. He shut his eyes tight, blinking away the tears that threatened to burn holes into his skull and leak like acid from his soul. His love, his sweet Hell, had been through so much already. And for the past five days she'd been back in the clutches of the monsters at The Factory, without any contact or word to know if she was okay.

"Merciful Jesus," Jared murmured, breaking the silence that filled the room as the echoes of Hell's screams faded away.

All eyes of the assembled bodies turned to Willbright.

This meeting had been arranged at the insistence of Lee as the first step in launching an investigation and formal complaint. Willbright appeared to be cooperating, just like he also appeared to have an answer for everything. Lee had assured Peyton that justice would happen as long as they allowed the process to be obeyed. But bureaucracy was not something Peyton had ever had faith in. He just wanted Hell back, right now, safe in his arms, and Willbright behind bars so he could never hurt her again.

"Rape and torture are not part of standardized testing, Dr. Willbright. And they are certainly not actions tolerated by the people of New Earth. How do you account for what we have just witnessed?" Chairwoman Osceola asked in her cool, crisp tone.

Willbright shook his head, seeming unaffected by what he'd seen on the data cube. "The abuse never happened. But ELf-3 was made to believe it had. The degraded memory engrams and cosmetic injuries were provided to her in order to establish an emotional connection with the subject for the Turing test. That subject of course, being Dr. Chase."

"No," Peyton interjected, his voice ragged from the strain of trying to keep silent in the face of the injustice Hell had endured and the unbelievable crock of shit Willbright was trying to peddle.

"Those injuries were real. You can't fake the kind of wounds her body had recovered from. The marks were there. Real fractures. She was forcibly restrained multiple times. It wasn't just all in her head."

"No, it wasn't," Willbright agreed. "Which brings me to the reason we decided to recall ELf-3 once she'd passed the Turing test." He shifted his gaze to look at the assembled members of the council. "She is unstable and prone to emotional outbursts, sometimes requiring restraint— "

"*Bullshit!*" Peyton cried out, his anger a palpable force as it echoed through the room.

"Dr. Chase," the chairwoman interjected. "This is your final warning. You will be removed from the proceedings if you cannot control your outbursts. Dr. Willbright, do you have proof of these unstable episodes concerning ELf-3?"

"Yes, Chairman Osceola, I do. Following the unexpected death of her creator, Dr. Sarah Palmer Chase, ELf-3 attacked one of my assistants who relayed the information to her. She has difficulty in processing extreme emotions, which impedes her ability to follow instructions."

Willbright produced his own data cube. He inserted it into the holographic display on his communications console. A three-dimensional image of Hell appeared, along with a red-haired woman in a lab outfit, who Peyton recognized as Sarah's assistant, Clarissa. They stood together in a glass-walled room, which contained a small bed, metal table and chair, and a wall monitor. The recording appeared to be from a camera positioned in the ceiling of the room.

Hell was visibly agitated; she pulled at the examination gown she wore as she roamed the room like a trapped animal in a cage.

"No, no, NO," she repeated, over and over. By the wetness on her cheeks, which she wiped at intermittently, she appeared to be crying.

"Calm down, ELf," Clarissa said in a warning tone. She held her hands palm up towards Hell in a pacifying gesture.

"Can't you see?" Hell said, ignoring Clarissa's instructions completely. She tugged her fingers roughly through her long blond hair, her mind clearly occupied with working through the problem agitating her rather than on Clarissa. "It was her. She did it. It was *her*."

"You need to calm down, ELf. Now. Or I'll have to lock you up again." She reached out to grab Hell.

"NO!" Hell screamed at the top of her lungs, dodging Clarissa's hold. "*It was her!*" She picked up the chair and threw it at Clarissa, striking her hard with it.

Protecting her head with her hands, Clarissa fell against the wall with a startled cry.

Hell jumped onto the bed and looked straight at the camera. "It was *her*," she shrieked, her eyes wide and red from crying. The agonized look in them pierced Peyton's heart. "*It was her!*"

"She's hysterical," Clarissa shouted into the communication unit strapped to her wrist as she crawled to the door of the room. She hit the exit button and closed the opening behind her as soon as she was through. "Gas her."

As the room quickly filled with a white mist, obscuring Hell from view, the recording cut off.

The chairwoman studied Willbright for a moment. "Who is the 'her' Helen is referring to in this recording?"

"Another assistant of mine, with whom ELf-3 has had a difficult time working due to her sometimes volatile nature."

"Chairwoman Osceola," Lee said. "During the admittedly brief time I have known Helen, she has demonstrated a mixture of emotions under a variety of circumstances. But I have never witnessed her act in a manner that might be considered volatile or remotely harmful to another human being. She healed me with her own blood when we were attacked by a Reclaimer nearly two weeks ago. She put her own life at risk to do so."

"Healed you with her blood? Explain."

"As a partial clone of my daughter, the nanite DNA Helen carries recognized mine as being genetically compatible and repaired my wounds at a far greater rate than otherwise possible. I have the scars on my back to prove it, if you would like to see them."

The chairwoman nodded.

Lee removed his shirt and turned his back to the monitor, showing the assembled bodies the shiny pink scars that marred his skin.

"Those are two-week-old scars?" one of the other Dome representatives asked, his voice full of surprise.

"Yes. Less than that, actually. The wounds were down to the bone. By rights I should be still wrapped in bandages and enduring painful muscle re-growth treatment. But as you can see, I am nearly healed."

"My God," Osceola said, voicing the murmur of approval coming from the leaders of the other Domes. "That's impressive. The implications for health science are tremendous."

"Yes," Willbright agreed. "ELf-3's remarkable regeneration and adaptability are her two greatest strengths. The practical application for humanity is the reason we decided to go ahead with the Turing test despite our concerns about the stability of her overall emotional state. And the reason she has been recalled to the lab now that the test is conclusive. It is where she is safest and best monitored."

"She's safest with me," Peyton declared. "She's my property, not yours."

"In a temporary manner, yes, she was. But only for the purpose of research and now that—"

"Chairwoman Osceola," Peyton said, dismissing Willbright. "Please. When I first met Helen, she was afraid. Deathly afraid of being returned to The Factory. And that fear did not change during the weeks I knew her. If anything, it grew. Five days ago, she was stolen from me and returned without warning back to The Factory, the place she feared most in this world. Isn't that act alone proof that the fear she felt was real? Please. I just want to see her, to know that she's okay." He wanted more than that but seeing her would be a start.

"Dr. Willbright, do you have proof that Helen is unharmed?"

"Of course," he said and nodded off screen to someone else in the room. The image on his monitor split to show both Willbright in his office, and also Hell, lying on a bed in what appeared to be the same glass-walled room as she'd been in from the recording on the data cube.

"Hell?" Peyton said, leaping to his feet. He reached instinctively toward the monitor as if he could touch her through the image.

She blinked but didn't move.

"Hell, baby, are you okay?"

She blinked again but didn't show any sign of recognition that he was talking to her. Peyton turned on Willbright. "What are you doing to her? Why won't she answer me?"

"The audio feed is disabled. She is unaware that you are contacting her, Dr. Chase. But as you can see, she is perfectly healthy and unharmed."

"Why is the audio disabled?" Osceola asked.

"It's important that we keep her as calm and stable as possible during this time. For her safety as well as her child's."

"Child?" Lee said, giving voice to the confusion buzzing through Peyton's mind as he sat there trying to process the word.

Child.

"What child?" Jared asked.

"She's pregnant?" one of the Dome representatives asked, his voice carrying above the shocked gasps and murmurs of the others.

"That's incredible," Osceola said and sat back in her chair.

"That's impossible," Peyton managed after several attempts to form coherent words.

"I assure you it is not impossible," Willbright said. "It is, in fact, our greatest hope for humanity made real." He pulled up on the display, scans from Hell in real time. Her heart beat a steady rhythm, her respiration was even and calm, and yes, there on the bottom of the chart, elevated hCG levels indicating a positive pregnancy, and the image of a tiny dot on the lining of her uterus where a fertilized egg had become attached.

Christ in heaven, it was true. "Oh, my God. How...? She was sterile. You implanted a fertilized ovum?"

"No. This child was conceived naturally. It was you, Dr. Chase." Willbright nodded his head. "Your desires. ELf-3 constructed new ova for you. And now we have what we've always wished for. What Sarah worked so tirelessly towards—a new hybrid human race, completely viable in every way. Adaptable. Strong. Perfect. And able to reproduce at will."

It was possible what Willbright said was true, that Hell had regenerated her ova. Her ability to heal and adapt was remarkable. But the fact she'd done it in response to his own desires...that news was steadily cracking Peyton's mind. He'd wanted a child, yes. With Sarah. But when she'd died, that desire had died too. He'd put it out of his mind. Or so he'd thought. But now with Hell...the idea that she was pregnant with his baby—his soul trembled as the old dream came screaming awake.

My child. That's my child.

MY CHILD.

His heart pounded in his ears. "I need...I need to see her. Talk to her. Let me talk to her, right now." *Oh God. Oh God, Hell.*

"That isn't advisable," Willbright said. "Any excitement could jeopardize the baby and you might—"

"I don't fucking care what you think. If that child is mine, then I have every right to see it and its mother. But you took her away from me before I could find out—"

"Dr. Chase," Osceola said, interrupting him.

"My God. You can't let that bastard take this from me, too. You can't." He lunged at the monitor, ready to shatter it and the indifferent expression on Willbright's face.

"Dr. Chase!"

Jared and Lee grasped him in a firm hold, stopping him. He trembled in their strong hands as they helped him back into his seat and held him there. "Hold on, son," Lee said. "You need to be calm and think."

But Peyton was past being calm. "I can't, I can't..." he repeated as his body shook.

Fuck. His mind couldn't process anything beyond the intense shock of emotions charging through him. Anger, joy, fear, frustration, love. They churned inside him, forming a white-hot coal that burned in the pit of his stomach like molten lead, making it hard to sit, to listen, to breathe to think. *Fuck.*

"This is greater than you, Dr. Chase," Chairwoman Osceola said. "In the interests of ELf-3, known as Helen, and the safekeeping of her child for the future of the human race, she will remain at the bio-robotics laboratory under the care of Dr. Willbright and his team, pending further investigation."

"But—" Peyton said as his heart stopped in his chest and then stuttered to life again with a roar.

"Pending further investigation, Dr. Chase," the chairwoman repeated, her tone sharp and implacable, "by the High Council, during which time she will be carefully monitored and all records regarding her inception and governance will be made open and available to us. Dr. Willbright, this matter is of extreme importance to the inhabitants of New Earth. Disobedience will not be tolerated."

Willbright nodded his understanding. "As you wish, Chairwoman Osceola."

"She belongs with me," Peyton said, ignoring Lee's sharp warning look. "Please," he begged, not caring how desperate he sounded. The truth burned in his heart. And he needed it to save Hell. "I love her. She's all I have in this world."

And she's having my child.

My child.

"That may prove true, Dr. Chase. But she will remain where she is until the validity of her situation can be ascertained."

"As the family involved, we ask permission to visit Helen at The Factory, Chairwoman Osceola," Lee said. "To ensure the safekeeping of both her and the child."

Her clear, assessing gaze flicked between Lee and Jared and landed on Peyton.

"Permission granted with the understanding that you do not interfere with this investigation in any way. We appreciate your stake in this matter, Dr. Chase. But the interest of the human race is a greater one."

"Thank you, Madam Chair," Lee said.

"An air transport will arrive tomorrow to convey you to the Arkopolis with official representation."

"Thank you again, Chairwoman Osceola," said Jared. He quickly cut the feed as the chairwoman nodded dismissal and her screen went black.

**

"They can't fucking keep her there," Peyton said as he paced back and forth inside the small conference room.

"They can and they will if they think it's necessary. And right now, it's necessary while they investigate the facts," Lee explained, his voice calm, yet weary.

"It's not goddamn rocket science. Willbright is a bastard that can't be fucking trusted. And now he has Hell and my baby."

"Is that even real?" Jared asked.

"You saw the scans, just like I did."

"But is it yours? Do we know that for a fact?"

"Jesus. Who else's would it be?" Peyton asked.

"I don't know. She's at a research facility full of DNA samples. It could belong to anyone. Willbright has had her there for nearly five full days. That's plenty of time to implant an embryo," Jared said.

"You know that isn't how it happened."

"Do we? Do you see what I mean, Peyton?" said Lee. "There's too much conjecture right now and not enough facts. And unless we allow the proper process to be followed, we stand very little chance of getting Helen back. Possession is nine tenths of the law. She was developed at The Factory as an experiment in human-android cross-hybridization. And whether we like it or not, that's a pretty convincing argument in their favor for ownership of her and any offspring she has, no matter what part you may have unknowingly played in making that happen."

The main screen on the wall brightened, interrupting the conversation with an incoming message alert from Joanna Chase. Lee accepted, and the familiar, wrinkled face of Aunty Jo eclipsed the screen. She sat in the lab at the worm den where she'd stayed behind with McClellan and Rusty to take care of the Reclaimers.

Her gaze darted between Lee, Jared, and Peyton, taking in the tense scene before her. "I take it the meeting didn't go well? What's going on?"

"Well—" Lee began.

"Willbright is a fucking asshole," Peyton said. "Oh, and Hell's pregnant."

"Well, we knew the first part. But, Christ, Peyton," Aunty Jo said, the alarm in her voice clear even through the transmission. "Did you just say that Helen is pregnant?" She stared at him, the look in her green eyes mirroring the disbelief he still felt.

"Yes."

Her hand lifted to cover her mouth. "Sweet Mother of God. A baby? You're going to be a father?"

"See?" He pointed at Joanna while looking at Lee. "She gets it."

"But that's just so...incredible," Aunty Jo said. "She was sterile. Wasn't she?"

"I thought she was. But apparently, I was wrong."

"Peyton! Oh, my good Lord. I'm going to be a great aunt." Her voice trembled with the emotion she was experiencing. She brushed at her eyes and closed them, her elderly fingers shaking. "After all this damn time."

"Can I ask a question?" McClellan asked, his face appearing over Joanna's shoulder.

"Go for it," Jared said as he slowly spun his chair around.

"What the fuck is going on? How can Hell be pregnant?"

"Well, it's like the birds and the bees and the flowers and the trees—" Rusty said beside him with a wicked grin that didn't disappear when Mac gave him a playful shove and scowled.

"I'm being serious, you butthead."

"So am I." Rusty laughed.

"According to Willbright, Hell didn't run away from The Factory. She was sent to Peyton on purpose instead of the Doll I ordered. Her memories were faked to make us believe she'd been abused so that we'd form an attachment to her. Willbright couldn't let anyone know, otherwise it would compromise the Turing test before it was completed. Which it is now, so they recalled her back. Somehow. Not quite sure how that worked. But it looks like they've been monitoring her all this time," Jared explained.

"Well, shit. And now she just happens to be pregnant?"

"Yeah."

"I need a fucking drink."

"No kidding."

"So all of this was some kind of test? To see if Hell could live with people?" Rusty said, the grin gone from his face.

"That's what Willbright wants us to believe," Jared said. "But I think there's more to it. The things Helen remembers at The

Factory…I find it hard to believe they faked all that."

"It wasn't faked," Peyton said. "That shit was real. They almost fucking killed her."

"Lee," Aunty Jo said. "Oh, my God, Lee. We need to get Helen back. There's no telling what they'll do to her at the lab. And now that she's pregnant—"

"There's a transport coming to pick us up tomorrow, Jo. We'll be at The Factory as soon as we can."

"But what about between now and then?"

"The High Council has ordered an investigation of the entire facility. Willbright has promised full cooperation."

"Yeah, big whoopidy-do. That's really great of him," Peyton said. "He fucking killed Sarah and now he's fucking got Hell and my fucking kid. Why don't I just bend over and offer him my fucking ass too?"

"Peyton—love. I know you're upset, but that's not helping." Joanna's gaze flicked back to Lee. "I hate to say it, Lee, but I don't trust it either. Peyton's right. There has to be something more we can do."

"What about the worms?" Jared asked.

"They're calm for the most part, but still agitated. I haven't initiated a full hibernation lockdown. It would keep them safe from each other, but it might disrupt their connection with Helen if it's still there, and I don't want to take the risk. I'm working with Henry to try and talk with them, so we can use the link to contact her. But without her here to act as a bridge between their programming languages, it's a shot in the dark."

"So we still can't talk with Helen directly?"

"No. Not yet."

"Keep trying."

"I am." She pulled in an unsteady breath. "Oh, my God, the poor girl. I just want to hug her so tight."

"I know. It's going to be all right," Lee said. "We'll get her back, Jo. I promise. But we have to do it the right way. Going in with all guns blazing will make it seem like Willbright is right and she's better off with him than us."

She shook her head, her expression pinched and her eyes glistening with a flash of tears. "I'm going to check on Henry and the worms again," she said. "Let me know how it goes on your end, boys. Love you." The screen went blank as she terminated the connection.

"Shit," Jared said and spun his chair around again. "This really fucking sucks. I vote for getting piss-eyed drunk. You with me?"

Peyton stared at the blank screen. When was the last time he'd lost himself in a bottle of whisky? He'd had a few sips at the party, but not enough to lose his head. Maybe he should grab a bottle or two of the home brew from the mess hall to share with Jared. Just like old times. But the desire to get drunk and numb his pain was no longer there. Nothing was going to calm the intense fury he had burning inside.

Hell was being held captive by the biggest son-of-a-bitch in all of New Earth. But that anger didn't even come close to the searing rage he felt, knowing she was pregnant with his child and there was nothing he could do help her or the baby except wait until tomorrow when the transport to the Arkopolis arrived.

Fuck it.

How was a guy supposed to even process that?

"No," he said. He pushed away from the table and headed for the door as Jared and Lee stood. "I need to get ready for tomorrow."

"You should get some rest, son. You haven't slept in four days." Lee placed a comforting hand on his back.

"Can't," Peyton said, shaking him off. Every time he closed his eyes, he saw Hell, lying still as death at The Factory, waiting for God knew what to happen to her. And the baby.

"She needs you to be strong. You can't do that exhausted."

"Peyton!" Genova called out, hurrying up to them as they emerged from the conference room. "There you are. I was hoping to run into you."

"Hey, Genova," Jared said, filling the awkward pause that had descended, bringing them to a halt.

A smile tipped her lips as her gaze flicked between the three of them and stopped on Peyton. "I heard what happened with your, um, Doll. I'm sorry that—"

"You heard, did you?" They'd been back for only a few hours at most and already the gossip mongers were busy spreading rumors. Part of him was curious to know what was being said. But most of him wasn't. Just like he wasn't in the mood to deal with Genova. In fact, seeing her right now was the last thing he wanted.

"Yeah." Her smile broadened, a look of hope flashing in her eyes. "I just wanted to see if there was anything I could do to help?"

"You can leave me the fuck alone, is what you can do."

"Peyton?" her eyes widened in shock and more than a little hurt. But he'd long since lost the brain space to care.

Ignoring Genova, he nodded at Lee and Jared. "I'll see you

tomorrow," he said and headed for the stairway up to the empty place he called home. Empty, except for the memories, which clung to every nook cranny and surface. Memories of Hell's scent, her laughter, her tears, and the promise that he'd made to protect her.

A promise he had every intention of keeping.

He was going to get her back tomorrow; he'd make damn sure of that.

And Willbright was going to pay for every second of torment he'd inflicted on their lives. Every fucking second.

HELL OR HIGH WATER

IT WAS THE only way.

The only way to escape. The only way to survive.

But Hell still couldn't shake the sick feeling that what she was doing was morally wrong. That there had to be another way.

Except there wasn't. She'd been over it in her mind again and again, seeking a better answer, while at the same time careful to keep her thoughts quiet enough to not raise any alarms with the clone, who might be listening.

It's the only way to save the baby. The only way. The only way, Sarah whispered in Hell's mind—the real avatar-Sarah, not the clone. The clone was busy arguing with Willbright and distracted, which was the only time Hell could really think alone. Luckily, it'd been happening a lot these past few hours, and she'd been able to seek answers without being noticed.

It's the only way to get free and warn Peyton, Sarah said.

Unable to do more than breathe and blink, Hell stared up at the ceiling of the room she knew so well, with its glass walls and familiar antiseptic scent. Gestating like a good little incubator, just as she'd been told to do, while precious time ticked away.

She needed to escape. Now. If she was going to be able to stop the tragedy the clone had planned.

It was one thing to do it to protect herself. But with the baby and Peyton and the whole population of New Earth hanging in the balance, there really was no choice at all.

She had to do it.

Had to break the link with the clone. But the only way to do that was to kill the avatar program. Once it was removed, she could take charge of the situation, send a message to Peyton and free them all.

She had to do it.

Had already done it, in a way. Already instructed her nanites to seek and destroy the part of her which needed removal. All that was left was the final word and they would do it. Reprogramming her nanites was easy. But the actual killing off of the avatar...that was another matter.

She'd resisted this choice for two years. Two years of torture, degradation, and horror. Even though it would have ended the pain, it would also have ended what was left of Sarah. And that was something she'd never been able to do, even at her own detriment.

The avatar of Sarah had always been there. Always. Closer to her than a sister. The thought of killing her hurt as if she were taking a knife to her own heart. Death was final. There were no second chances, not even in the digital world. Once removed, the program would be gone for good. There would be no more questions answered. No more comforting chats.

No more captivity, Sarah whispered in her mind.

Yes, that too.

You don't need me anymore, ELf. It's time to let me go.

I know. I know. But who will I be when you're gone?

You'll be you. And you'll be free.

Hell closed her eyes. *I'll miss you*, she said in her mind, her heart feeling heavy and full.

Maybe for a little while. But you'll have Peyton and the baby. I'm so proud of you, my perfect, precious ELf. You proved my theories right. But you have to let me go now. You don't need me anymore. It's time to end this.

In truth, it was past time, but that didn't make it any easier. Under normal circumstances it wouldn't have seemed so devastatingly final. The real Sarah Chase would have been there after the avatar of her was removed. But Sarah was dead. All that remained was the digital version of her, which existed within Hell. A fail-safe program that had run its course.

It's the only way. The ONLY way.

I know. Hell blinked away the tears that stung her eyes.

Saying goodbye to this remnant of Sarah was the last thing she ever wanted to do, especially for Peyton's sake. But when it came to a choice between her child's life and a digital ghost, there really was no choice at all, no matter how painful the action might be.

The door to her room opened and Willbright and the clone walked in.

It's nearly time, Sarah whispered. *When she's fully distracted by him, that's when you strike. You need to do it when she can't intervene and stop you.*

Hell would have nodded if she could. Instead, she opened her eyes as Willbright and the clone walked toward her, their footfalls sharp with tension.

"You're sure that's it?" the clone asked Willbright as she checked the most recent scans of Hell's pregnancy. "Just Peyton, Lee, Jared and a delegation of representatives from the High Council? Not the entire population of New Earth, too? Christ. You didn't do a very good job downplaying things at the meeting yesterday, did you?"

"I said what was necessary," was Willbright's terse reply. "But once we recalled ELf-3, did you think Chase would let her go without a fight?"

The clone shook her head. "We should remove the embryo now and wipe ELf's memory of its existence. The numbers are strong. It can survive transplantation to a gestation unit."

"I'm afraid that's not possible."

"Why?"

"They already know about the child."

She stared at him. "You told them?" Her blue eyes flashed with anger. "How could you be so stupid?"

"They would have found out soon enough anyway. The bigger issue is what to do about your overzealous handling of ELf-3? Chase had a data cube filled with rather damning evidence of your so-called experiments. I did what I could to downplay the situation, but I'm afraid it's only a short-term solution."

"Then let's destroy everything here and run," she said, waving her hands at the monitor. "Take the embryo with us and disappear to where none of the rules apply."

"Abandon my life's work? Absolutely not."

"Then what are we going to do?"

"You, my dear, are going to take the fall for this mess. And I will finish what was started by your brilliant predecessor."

Is he going to kill her? Hell thought. *After all this time?* The idea took root in a mixture of horror and hope. With the clone dead, the control over Hell would be broken. Maybe she wouldn't have to kill the avatar program after all.

Perhaps he intends to try, Sarah said. *But that's what she wants, so she can defend herself and kill him instead. For her plan to work, she needs him to be the bad one. But to make it seem real, it needs to be self defence. She's already prepared. Look beside you if you can.*

Hell shifted her eyes to the left. There. On a tray with other medical instruments. A syringe lay, uncapped and ready.

The clone backed away from Willbright, her hip nudging against Hell as she bumped into the scanner bed. "Everything I have done—everything—has been with your full consent. If you had issue with my methods, you could have intervened. But you didn't. You let me make the choices you couldn't. Because you never had the guts."

Willbright's expression tightened. "You are an illegal clone, created without my knowledge or consent. I realize, now, that I should never have tolerated your existence. An error in judgement I will shortly rectify." He reached into the pocket of his lab suit and pulled out a data cube. "This record clearly shows your erratic behavior and cruel experiments were never sanctioned by this facility."

"Are you serious?" she asked. "You knew exactly what was going on for the past two years. No one will ever believe you didn't."

"They will if you say it's the truth." Putting the data cube back in his pocket, he pulled out a different device. It was palm length and slender like a pen, but Hell knew it all too well, and the sight of it caused a shiver of fear to ripple down her spine. "It's time for mental reconditioning," he said, "for you and for her." He waved the tip of the memory device between the clone and Hell. "We all need to have our stories straight, don't we?"

"Don't you dare touch me with that thing," the clone yelled and slapped Willbright's hand away.

He slapped her back, so hard she fell sideways against Hell. The clone clutched her cheek, her eyes wide with shock. She reached for the tray of instruments, but before she could touch them, he grabbed her by the hair and yanked her to him.

Tears shimmered in her eyes as he twisted her long dark hair about his hand. He pulled her head back until she shrieked, her arms and hands flailing outward, seeking purchase but not finding anything.

"You brought this upon yourself," he said, his voice cold with fury. "If you don't struggle, it won't hurt. And in a few minutes, you won't remember a thing."

"Fuck you, asshole." She bucked against him and twisted, trying to get away, but the hold he had on her was stronger.

"Stop struggling!" he shouted. He pushed her hard against the glass wall with a bang, flattening her to the smooth surface with his body. He twisted her hair in his hand until her cheek was pressed against the glass and her right temple exposed.

"Go to hell, you arrogant bastard," she said, wild panic in her eyes. She reached for the tray of instruments again, her fingers splayed wide, but unable to grab it.

I can't let this happen, Hell realized, panic ripping through her. *Once he's through with her, he'll come after me. I can't go through that again. I can't. I can't.*

Do it now, ELf. Do it now.

She closed her eyes. This would be the last time. The last conversation they ever had. *I love you, Sarah.* Her heart thudded in her chest, threatening to break.

I love you too, ELf. You and Peyton and the baby.

The clone was struggling against Willbright's hold on her, gasping for breath. Her hand reached for the syringe again and missed. He placed the tip of the memory device against her temple.

Now, ELf, do it NOW.

Sarah! She cried out as she executed the command to terminate the avatar.

A buzzing sound filled Hell's mind, accompanied by a sharp burning pain, which ended almost as quickly as it began.

Then came silence, overwhelming, suffocating silence, and a painful rush of despair over what had been lost and could never be found again.

But she could move.

She was free.

She leapt off the bed, startling both the clone and Willbright. They froze mid-struggle and stared at her.

"*No!*" the clone cried out, her voice full of disbelief. Her startled expression quickly shifted from one of shock to one of anger. Taking advantage of Willbright's distraction, she kneed him hard in the groin.

Willbright groaned, his hold on her hair loosening. She slipped away from him and lunged for the syringe.

Hell snatched it before the clone's fingers could grasp it.

"No. You don't get to do that. Neither of you get to do that," she said, anger pumping through her veins. She held the syringe up, brandishing it between her and the two scientists like a deadly weapon. Which it was. There was no telling what liquid filled it. But knowing the clone, it was something fast and effective at killing.

"Help me," the clone shouted, keeping a careful distance away from the tip of the syringe "I've lost control over her."

"Then get it back, you idiot," Willbright snarled. He stopped clutching his groin and straightened.

"I can't. She's done something. The link is gone." The clone shook her head, shutting her eyes as if the movement pained her.

Good, Hell thought. Then immediately lost any sense of satisfaction the thought had brought as she remembered the avatar of Sarah wasn't there to share it with.

The emptiness, the silence was enough to make her curl up in a ball and cry. But she was done with crying. She was done with everything. And these two so-called scientists would not be allowed to hurt her or anyone else anymore.

She smashed the syringe against the floor, shattering it.

The clone lunged for her, Willbright right behind. But Hell grasped them both by the throat and thrust them backward against the wall so hard the glass shook, threatening to crack. She tightened her grip, cutting off their airways before either of them could recover enough to fight back. The memory-altering device slipped from Willbright's grasp and clattered on the floor.

"I should kill you. I should kill you both. For everything you've done. For everything you've made me do," she sobbed, her grip tightening.

"Stop," the clone whimpered, trying to loosen Hell's grip. "You can't."

"Shut up," Hell spat out, silencing the clone with a flex of her fingers on her slender throat. "You made me kill her, the last thing that was left of her. She was my friend..." A sob choked her.

Adrenaline and hatred burned through her, filling her with strength. The bones beneath her hands felt so weak compared to her own. They wouldn't regenerate like hers had after they'd been broken. Humans were frail creatures. And these two were selfish, vicious, and cruel. They didn't deserve to live.

Willbright's eyes bulged, his face turning red. He reached for her, trying to loosen her grip, but his own was weak. Ineffectual. Just like the rest of him. The urge to finish the job and kill him pumped through her veins. Never once had he stepped in to help her. Not even when she'd begged. He'd just recorded her reactions, his cold eyes never changing, no matter how hard she screamed. She tightened her grip on his throat until his eyes rolled back in his head.

"I should kill you. But I won't. It would be too kind." They deserved to suffer as much as she had. To be exposed for the monsters they were.

She let him fall forward onto the bed, unconscious but still breathing.

Raising the clone until her feet didn't touch the floor, Hell slammed her hard against the wall again, knocking the wind from her. The clone slid down the glass, stunned senseless by the force of the blow.

Sobbing hard and shaking, Hell quickly exited the glass room and locked it behind her. Moving to the control panel on the wall, she accessed the security system. Seconds later the sleeping gas, which they'd used to knock her out so very often when she'd 'misbehaved', filled the glass cell.

Willbright was still slumped forward on the bed, unmoving. But against the wall, the clone turned her head to look at Hell, intense hatred clear to see in her eyes before they drifted shut.

"Sweet dreams, bitch," Hell said. She knew from bitter experience the gas would keep them unconscious for hours and from hurting each other until she got help to apprehend them. Awake they'd turn on each other like the rats they were, and she needed them alive so justice could be made. The world needed to see them for who they were and what they'd done.

All the horrific things they'd done.

Her heartbeat thudded in her ears as she sagged against the wall, limbs trembling. The effects of adrenaline and all the emotions pounding in her veins was taking its toll. She'd never choked anyone in her life. Her hands ached; her arms hurt. She was free, free at last. But at what cost? She didn't feel happy. She didn't feel sad. She felt exhausted. And almost afraid to embrace the relief she felt in case it might shatter.

She slid her hand over her belly, and the life growing there.

You're safe now, baby. Mommy saved you. The bad people will never hurt us again, she thought, and part of her paused as if still expecting a response. Some affirmation from the avatar, that what she said was true, that what she'd done was right.

But there was no familiar comforting reply. There never would be again.

Despair sickening her victory, she pushed away from the wall. "I need to find Peyton," she said.

"I'm right here, baby."

She quickly turned, startled by the familiar sound of his voice. A group of people looked back at her from the doorway of the main entry to the lab, a ring of faces, some familiar: Lee, Jared and, yes—

"*Peyton!*" Her heart leapt with renewed relief.

"Thank God, you're okay," he said, his voice hitching as he raced to her.

His arms were warm and strong as he wrapped them tight around her, lifting her off her feet. She clutched him close, burying herself in him until the strong beat of his heart drowned out her own. Tears slid down her cheeks. His scent, his familiar spicy scent—the first thing she'd ever discovered about him when he'd rescued her from that box she'd been shipped in. She knew it, she knew him, and oh, the Maker how she'd missed him. There were so many things she wanted to say—so many things she needed to say—but they were all trapped in her throat, caught on the sobs that shook her and didn't seem to have any end.

"Hell, love," he said and placed gentle kisses on the top of her head. "Hush, baby. I'm here, I'm here. You're safe now. I'm so sorry it took so long."

She looked up when she felt his body tense.

His eyes were wide with shock, his gaze looking past her. It was frozen on the dark-haired woman who was visible through the glass as the remnants of the gas dissipated.

"Sarah?" he said.

NIGHTMARE

THREE HOURS LATER, Peyton found himself walking through the labyrinth structure of the bio-robotics lab in a daze. It couldn't be real. None of this could be real. And yet it was. A living nightmare.

And Hell had been trapped in it for over two years.

He checked the live video feed on his tablet. She was sleeping, the sunlight steaming through the window of the main hospital facility at the Arkopolis causing her pale gold hair to shimmer like a halo. Her face was relaxed, her beautiful lips slightly parted. A far cry from the tormented woman she'd been until she'd finally fallen asleep in his arms.

Lee sat with her, his hand holding hers as he watched her sleep. He'd promised to stay with her and contact Peyton as soon as she stirred. It was the only way Peyton had been able to force himself from her side. She and the baby were healthy and safe, but she was far from fine.

Her tears, her pain...they cut at him deep inside.

Almost as much as seeing the horrors his wife had created. Especially the clone, who looked so much like Sarah, his heart had died a second death and was now a numb lump, beating erratically in his chest.

"Do you think Hell's seen any of this?" Jared said quietly beside him.

"I fucking hope not."

They walked amongst the team of investigators who were documenting everything in the lab, allowed to witness but not touch. The room they were in was part of an underground lab, comprised of various rooms and hallways and levels. It was dark, it smelled like stale antibacterial cleanser, and was not part of the main facility of the Lumacore Industries Bio-robotics Factory, which existed above. No, this area had been created out of old storage rooms in the basement, accessed by a door that he'd broken open when he'd discovered the delegation from the High Council and been unable to find Hell.

The bewildered Lumacore staff had led them here, saying there was another lab that no one entered, except Dr. Willbright, and his assistant Clarissa, who apparently hadn't been seen in days.

Did anyone else have the passcode for the door? No.

They'd promptly cut that shit open with an acetylene torch knife, raced down a hallway and opened another set of doors. And there had been Hell, his beautiful Hell, so traumatized she'd not stopped crying except to say his name, over and over, and clutch at him like he might disappear.

Christ almighty.

He stared blankly about him, barely able to take it all in. A gestation chamber stood at the ready, filled with artificial amniotic fluid. That had been meant for the baby—his child—once it was viable enough to be removed from Hell. Anger over what they'd planned burned through him, but it was swallowed by the horror, which stared at him from multiple glass containers lining the walls. Fetuses in various stages of development, some almost human, others in bizarre contortions of limbs that were barely recognizable. But the two which caught his eye were the fully grown specimens floating in glass coffins. One bald and misshapen, its features twisted, but its body otherwise intact and slender. But the other—the wisps of fair hair were unmistakable, the amber eyes, and the slightly parted lips—it was Hell.

"Enhanced Lifeform One and Enhanced Lifeform Two," Jared said, reading the labels on the containers. "Non-viable matrix mix." He turned to Peyton. "Looks like Hell won the genetic lottery."

"Yeah," Peyton said. He turned away, unable to keep looking at the lifeless, eternally staring amber eyes of the hybrid attempt that hadn't made it.

He caught the nearest investigator by the elbow. "Make sure you destroy this when you're done cataloging everything or I'm going to lose my fucking shit."

The investigator nodded, his face grim. "We'll need some of it for evidence, Dr. Chase, but after that—"

From a console at a workstation where another investigator sat, a holographic image of Sarah suddenly appeared. Her long hair was pulled back in a ponytail, her blue eyes tired but bright with enthusiasm, just like he'd seen her in her last message from The Factory, saying she was finally, finally coming home.

"The Enhanced Lifeform project is an attempt to fuse genetically hybridized human DNA with robotic controls via nanites. The purpose of this experiment is to strengthen the human genome, and make it adaptable to any environment, thereby increasing the viability of reproduction. My experiments so far to create a stable matrix have been limited, but the addition of diversified cloned tissues has now shown success. ELf-3 is completely formed and breathing on her own. My task now is to teach her diverse human and robotic selves to grow together, so that she may operate and interact on a human level, while at the same time maintaining the advantages her robotic half affords...." The investigator turned off the holographic journal entry and Sarah disappeared.

She turned to Peyton. "Um, we can review this at a later time."

"Send me a copy of everything," he said, somehow managing to keep breathing. "I want to see it all."

She nodded, seeming shaken. Probably by his harsh tone. But there was only so much a guy could take and he was way over his limit. Problem was, this nightmare from hell wasn't done yet. Sarah's intentions to create a new hybridized human lifeform may have been good, but they had become twisted and misshapen, just like the aborted fetuses floating in their glass cases.

Somehow the clone of Sarah had been made, Sarah herself had died, and Willbright hadn't intervened to stop any of this illegal shit from happening. Peyton needed to find out how and why, and how to heal Hell's bleeding soul. It seemed that by being back in The Factory, her memories had returned in full, but she couldn't or wouldn't speak of them. They cut her too deep inside.

"It's going to take some time," the doctor at the Arkopolis hospital had said. "She appears to have been through a great deal of emotional trauma."

"I know," had been his only response.

And although all the scans had come back fine and everything looked right, he knew in his heart that the answer to her eventual healing lay in his ability to understand what it was that she couldn't say.

So he left the illegal lab his wife had created in a desperate attempt to save humanity from extinction, and went back to the room he'd found Hell in.

The team of investigators looked up from the console they were at as he and Jared entered.

"They attempted to alter and erase the data, but we've managed to access the original streams, Dr. Chase. It's just like you said. She was being tortured."

"Give me a copy of everything you have," Peyton said and held out his tablet. "All the files. Everything."

The investigator hesitated. "Are you sure? Some of this is...hard to watch."

"Yes, I'm fucking sure," he snarled. His patience was at an end. The numbness around his heart had faded. Instead, it was bruised and angry, a hot coal of pain. "I want to know what happened." He glanced at the glass cell Hell had been kept in. The clone had been moved to an interrogation chamber elsewhere already. But Willbright was finally waking up.

Two enforcement officers were cuffing the scientist's wrists behind his back. Willbright staggered slightly as they forced him to rise, but he managed to stay on his feet. Bruises ringed his throat, purple and black marks, which looked swollen and painful.

God, I hope so, you bastard.

Peyton walked through the open door and into the chamber. Willbright's eyes were heavy lidded but he seemed aware of his surroundings.

"We're moving him to incarceration for further questioning," one of the officers said.

"Is he lucid?" Peyton asked.

"Yes."

"Good. I want him to remember this."

He swung hard with his fists. The first smashed into Willbright's gut, causing him to bend forward sharply. The second connected with the hard ridge of his nose.

Bone crunched. Blood splattered.

Willbright screamed.

"Dr. Chase!" One of the investigators cried out.

Strong arms latched onto Peyton and pulled him back.

"How's it feel, you fucker?" He glared at Willbright, breathing heavily. His knuckles ached. But it was a good ache. It almost throbbed enough to feel satisfying. Except Willbright was still alive and moaning like a pathetic piece of shit. "What's that?" Peyton asked. "You want more?" He kicked out and caught

Willbright in the knee, twisting it sharply sideways.

Willbright cried out in pain and sagged heavily against the two officers. They helped him down onto the bed again. Blood streamed from his nose and onto his face and clothes. He moaned pitifully, unable to stop it.

The officers watched him, seeming unaffected.

"Damn. Looks like he might need a stretcher."

"Yeah, better call for a med team." But neither moved quickly to do it. The nearest one raised a brow at Peyton. "Are you done questioning him, Dr. Chase?"

"Hell, no." The desire to kill Willbright burned through him. It was the least the bastard deserved for everything he'd done.

Jared kept a tight hold on his arms. "Come on, Peyton," he said, shaking him slightly. "If you kill him, you'll go to prison. Maybe face the death penalty."

"Fuck it."

"I know, dude. But Hell needs you. Let this asshole rot."

Peyton shut his eyes and forced the murderous rage pounding in his veins to subside. Hell did need him. And this sack of shit wasn't going to keep them apart anymore. Enough harm had already been done.

But, by God. If he could have throttled him, he would have. If they'd been alone.

"Come on, buddy." Jared handed him his tablet, now fully loaded with data from the lab files. "Let's deal with the rest of this shit so we can go the hell home."

Peyton studied the tablet. Hell was still sleeping peacefully with Lee at her side. "Yeah," he said and stroked the image of her with his fingers. Hell would do better, the sooner he got her away from this place and back home. He nodded at Jared and turned his back on Willbright.

He needed to get back to Hell.

But first things first, he needed to talk to the clone.

**

So much loss.
So much pain.
So many lies.
Peyton looked from the tablet filled with file upon endless file of damning evidence and at the woman sitting before him who

looked like Sarah—exactly like his beloved Sarah—and yet, was not.

She watched him through the glass separating them in her incarceration room. Her hands were tied behind her back as she sat on the edge of the bed, her posture relaxed, her long legs crossed, and her full lips tipped with a soft smile.

It was hard to look at her, those lips, those eyes, that smile. So familiar it hurt. So beautiful it made the lump of pain his heart had become want to explode in his chest. Hadn't he dreamed of seeing Sarah alive again? Endless nights of troubled sleep where he'd begged for divine intervention to make her death just a nightmare from which he'd awaken.

And now here she was, just as if she'd never died. Sensual, brilliant...and completely lacking any semblance of a soul.

His prayers hadn't been answered. The nightmare hadn't ended. It had just gotten fucking real.

This clone, this shell, this mockery of everything his beloved wife had been...she was a living nightmare. There were no words to process the grief that spilled from the fresh wound in his soul.

His fingers ached from clutching the tablet tightly while he'd read the reports of the experiments she'd run. His eyes were raw from the tears he'd shed while watching the recordings of the horror she'd inflicted, over and over again on Hell. Torture. Rape. Things Sarah was incapable of doing. Would never have allowed to happen. Had tried to stop. And been killed for.

The things this clone had done...the many things she had done...and had been planning to do, to him, to Hell, to everyone— Peyton stared at her, trying to make sense of how the woman he'd loved more than his own life could have given birth to such a monster.

He cleared his throat. "I'd like to speak to her alone for a few minutes, if you don't mind." His voice was a dry rasp, the result of a body pushed past its limit and a mind so full of emotions it had become a dead weight.

The official sitting next to him studied him. "Are you sure, Dr. Chase?"

Peyton nodded. As much as he wanted to forget she existed and walk away, he couldn't. He needed answers, and he needed privacy to find them.

"I'll be right outside if you need anything." The official glanced at his tablet as he picked it up from the table. "Just so you know, there's more than enough evidence here to suggest that neither she nor Willbright will ever be allowed freedom again. But their ultimate fate will depend on the outcome of the public trial." He rose from the seat and exited the room. The door slid shut behind him with a soft hiss.

"Well…" the clone said, her voice sensual, husky, and identical to Sarah's. It travelled over him, causing his skin to prickle. "Alone at last. I knew you'd come to see me."

He swallowed hard and wet his lips, trying to find the moisture to form words.

She re-crossed her legs and shook the manacles that clasped her wrists together behind her back. "Of course, I didn't think it would be like this. I know you like it kinky, but I didn't realize you were into forced bondage." Her smile was soft and smooth, reminding him of a cat he'd once seen in the wild when it had caught its prey.

He ignored her attempt to play him. He was definitely not the prey in this situation.

"Why?" he managed after a moment. It was the word screaming the loudest in the maelstrom chaos that had become his mind.

"Why?" She sounded incredulous. "Why not?"

He shook his head and glanced down at the tablet, and the damning facts it contained. "Sarah created you. And then you killed her." His long-time hunch, that Sarah had been deliberately infected before she'd left The Factory on what would be her final trip home, had been validated. The truth sat caged before him. He'd found his proof at last, but at what cost? He should feel vindicated. Instead, he felt as though he were made of soot and ashes. Any pleasure over discovering the answer was gone.

"Oh, I see." She tossed her head, causing her hair to flip over her shoulder. It was long and loose and shimmered like dark satin in the lights of her cell. "You want to talk about that, do you? Well, if you must know, I did her a favor, actually. I put an end to her misery. The fact that doing so tested the new fertility retro-virus we'd been working on was just being efficient."

"Efficient?" He stared at her, unable to comprehend her lack of remorse. "Over half of Deliverance Dome's population died, including most of the children."

She shrugged. "Is it my fault the retro-virus had unfortunate side effects? Poor Sarah wanted to have a baby with you *au natural*, but her body wasn't cooperating. Imagine what would have happened if it had turned out the other way? You'd probably have two or three of the little brats by now. And the colony would be over-run with them."

He did his best to block that image from his mind. "Did she know you had injected her?"

She laughed. "No. I gave her a little gift while she was sleeping. She never felt a thing. I did you a favor too, you know. I got rid of a tricky situation you were about to have. The least you can do is thank me for it." She shook the manacles meaningfully.

"What do you mean?"

"Well, let's see. Sarah was going to take sweet innocent ELf home with her to live with you. I honestly don't know how she thought that would work out. She wasn't going to be able to hide her pet freak from the High Council forever. And the little slut's based on a sex doll. She likes to fuck. But you know that already, of course." She snickered. Her expression turned serious, almost pitying. "You weren't having marital difficulties, by any chance, were you? Was Sarah trying to spice things up by bringing you a treat to share? She swung both ways between the sheets, you know. Maybe your dick wasn't enough for her?"

"That's a lie."

"Oh no. It's quite true. Sarah passed that part of herself on to me, as well as her brains and her fucking hot body. I like a good thick cock, not that Willbright actually has one, but I'll take a pussy lick by a pair of awesome tits anytime."

Breathe in. Breathe out. Breathe in. Breathe out. That's it, Peyton, hold it together. She's goading you, trying to get a rise. Don't let her win.

Except it was hard when he'd seen the recorded evidence. Of Sarah having sex with her assistant, Clarissa. Multiple times in the lab. And even though it had clearly been a coerced affair started by Clarissa, part of him wondered if Sarah hadn't enjoyed it a bit. Because her moans had been just like he remembered them when he'd made her come.

Who the hell knew? Maybe there had been something missing in their marriage. Maybe a secret part of her had been attracted to women too. He was willing to admit that possibility. But he could never think she'd willfully cheat on him. That was not the Sarah he'd known since birth.

"Cat got your tongue, darling?" the clone said with a distinct purr of pleasure in her voice.

He looked her straight in the eye. "I don't really care about your sexual tastes. But I've seen the recordings. Sarah never initiated a single thing. She was protecting Hell."

She shook her head. "You keep telling yourself that, sugar, if it'll help you sleep at night." She re-crossed her legs and flexed her shoulders, causing the bodysuit she was wearing to pull tight against her full breasts. Her erect nipples tented the fabric. "Tell you what. Why don't you take out your cock and show me how big and hard it can be? Play with it. I bet I can make you come, just by watching." She licked her full, red lips and stared at his crotch. "It'll be my gift to you. One last bang with the old wife. I know you've been thinking about it since you walked in here."

Despite himself, his cock jerked against his pants from the horror her words inspired.

She laughed, long and hard, clearly amused by his lack of control and mistaking it for desire. "Oh, God. Men are all the same. And you say you love that little whore, ELf. Just like you said you'd always love Sarah. But you couldn't get enough of her, could you, the little sex bot with her tight cunt. I was there, you know, watching through the avatar program. Every time you sucked her little tits and fucked her hard...you were really fucking me too."

"Christ," Peyton said. He hadn't known the avatar program had worked quite like *that*.

"Could you feel it? Could you feel me watching? In the back of your mind when you imagined it was your wife? I trained the slut well, didn't I? Taught her how to suck cock like a pro. You never stood a chance." She shook her head, a pitying look in her eyes. "Now don't feel bad. She's meant to be fucked hard. And the fact you fell for each other in the process, well that's just the best thing ever, isn't it? Because she needed that to get herself knocked up. She wouldn't do it any other way, no matter how many times I took her apart and put her back together again." She was ranting, her blue eyes bright as she talked, her breasts bouncing slightly in her excitement as she shifted on the edge of the bed. "God, how I loved that part, seeing what made her tick. But this baby, now that's a special thing. Something new that's never been dissected before. I was going to share it with you." She focused on him, her expression full of regret. "But now all we have is this cell and your fucking hard cock to entertain ourselves with. Come on the glass for me, Peyton. Come on the glass and I'll pretend to lick it off."

He stared at her, at a loss for words. He'd seen her behavior on the recordings, and thought he was prepared. But this? He shook his head, disgust mixing with anger.

Sarah had always been his ideal body type. Luscious. Invigorating. But the look in the clone's eyes as she eagerly scooted forward onto her knees, pressed her breasts against the glass wall separating them and began to lick it suggestively...that was something he'd never expected to see. It was something Sarah might have done in a kinky mood when they were alone together in the greenhouse.

But this wasn't Sarah. And it certainly wasn't Hell, for whom he'd endure every indignity he could imagine, if it would make her well again. But this...this was where he was going to draw the line.

"Did you get all that?" he asked, speaking into his tablet.

"Yes, thank you, Dr. Chase. The recorded evidence we had was good, but her confession will go far in bringing swift justice to this matter."

Peyton rose. He looked at his tablet, at the live image of Hell, her pale face asleep, her lips soft and inviting. He was going to kiss those lips and never stop kissing them until she understood how much he loved her.

"Don't you dare leave!" shrieked the clone. The insane remnant of his brilliant wife. Created out of a desire to maintain the two halves of her life—the scientific work she loved at The Factory and her need to have a family with him.

He'd insisted he couldn't live at the Arkopolis. That he hated it there. Which was true, but perhaps if he'd listened to Sarah more carefully, he'd have heard how important her research was to her.

He should have compromised.

Instead, he'd made her choose.

Yeah, he had a lot to answer for there. He couldn't escape his part in this disaster. He'd live with the guilt for the rest of his days.

But he didn't look back as he left the room, despite the clone screaming obscenities and banging on the glass. His mind was fully engaged on the mother of his child and how he was never again going to take for granted the wonderful gift she'd been, and the precious love she brought to his life.

HEAVEN

HELL AWOKE TO sunshine streaming in the room and the sound of birds chirping. She turned her head to the left and looked out the window. A tree grew on the other side, its full leaves casting a shadow over the bird perched on the branch. It must have a nest nearby, because she'd seen that bird, or one just like it, most times when she'd woken. It was sometimes twittering, sometimes not, but almost always there to greet her when she opened her eyes.

"Hello, little friend," she murmured with a smile.

The bird twittered back, returning her greeting, then spread its wings and took off into the blue sky. It sang again, as if calling her to follow.

"Sure. You make it look so easy," she said with a sigh.

Her body resisted as she tried to sit up, wanting her to rest in the soft bed. But she'd been sleeping so much she wanted to move. After days of being forcibly imprisoned, it wasn't fair to still be lying in a bed. In a hospital. Far away from home.

But the birds were nice, and the bed was soft, and the breeze coming in the window warm and full of nice smells that reminded her of flowers, though she couldn't for the life of her remember what kind. Desert Pee? Something very odd sounding, or so the staff at the Arkopolis hospital had informed her.

The door to her room opened, and Peyton peeked inside. A relieved smile crossed his face when he saw her struggling to sit up.

"You're awake!" he said and came into the room. "Glad to see you up, gorgeous." He hurried to her side to help her.

"I can manage," she said, forcing her body to do what she wanted no matter how much it protested. *It's just sitting up straight for the love of all things, not running a marathon.*

"I know, I know," he said. "But it's easier this way."

She smiled and relented, allowing him to fuss over her until she was propped up with pillows and her blankets straightened again. If it made him feel better to help, then she'd let him.

There were dark circles beneath his gorgeous brown eyes that hadn't been there before. He was thinner, too, as if he'd lost weight, the stubble on his chin thicker. All clear signs that the last few days had taken its toll on them both. She was certain that while she'd spent so much time sleeping, he'd barely gotten a wink.

She brushed her fingers across the scruffy bristles covering his chin as he sat down on the bed beside her. "How long have I been out of it this time?" she asked.

It seemed that every time she exerted herself and went through some kind of life-threatening ordeal lately, she needed to sleep for days. Which was weird because she'd never had to do that before. She'd always recovered from her beatings at The Factory quite quickly. But of course, she hadn't been pregnant then.

"Three weeks," he said. His body was warm as he wrapped his arm around her and snuggled her into his side. His heartbeat was strong, familiar, comforting.

"That long?" she whispered, shocked that so much time had passed.

"Yep. And you're not ready to leave yet either." His fingers stroked her hair. "The High Council won't let you go until they're sure that you'll be fine." He didn't sound particularly happy about that. Probably because it meant they were stuck here at the Arkopolis. She knew how much he hated this place and The Factory. But he'd come for her just the same. And stayed. "Got at least another week and then maybe you'll be good for the ride back home," he added.

Home.

Tears sprang to her eyes. He'd been here beside her most of the days, either him or Lee or Jared. Always someone close by to make certain she wasn't alone. She remembered hearing them talking softly, feeling them holding her hands while she slept, in between the tweets of the bird calling to her to wake up. Connections that filled her empty places, so she didn't have to think of the silence.

She pulled his hand over her belly and laced her fingers with his, bewildered at how much effort it took to do something so simple.

She frowned. "I crashed really hard, didn't I?"

His thumb caressed her palm. "Choking two people at the same time will do that to you, I guess," he drawled, but the guilt and sadness that haunted him was clear in his eyes. He wrapped his arms around her, pulling her tight to his chest, as if afraid she might disappear again. "Goddamnit, I should have known that they'd try to take you. I should have been prepared. I'm so sorry, Helen." He placed a kiss on the top of her head. "You were so brave, baby. So brave."

She squeezed her eyes shut tight and listened to his heart beating like a drum by her ear. She didn't feel brave. She felt hollow inside and twisted with guilt. "I'm so sorry," she whispered. "I never meant to hurt you. I didn't want to leave."

"I know that, love. I know that they made you. I've seen the recordings of what they did. Two years. Two fucking years full of shit. I don't know how you survived." His voice hitched, full of agony. His hand trembled as it stroked her hair, his comforting touch making her die a little more inside.

"I didn't..." Tears slipped down her cheeks. She hadn't yet had a chance to tell him what she'd done to escape. Or maybe avoiding that conversation was why she'd slept for so many days. She kept her eyes shut tight. "They broke me so many times. They would have broken me again. But I couldn't let them hurt the baby."

His palm covered her belly. "God help me," he said, "Just when I think I can't love you more, you go and prove me wrong."

A deep sob shook her, escaping her control.

He lifted her chin, forcing her to look at him, and wiped her cheeks with his fingers.

But she closed her eyes. It was impossible to hold his gaze. Full of love and tenderness that she wasn't sure she deserved right now. Not when she'd killed what was left of his wife.

"I talked to the clone," he said softly.

Her eyes flashed open, her heart racing. "Oh, Peyton." It must have been absolute pure torture, seeing Sarah alive again. "I wanted to warn you, before you saw her. But there wasn't a way. I didn't remember until they trapped me again. And then it all came back. Everything. But she wouldn't let me move, or speak, or do anything unless she said. I tried to send a message through the worms, while I could still hear them. But I don't think it worked.

Their language is so different."

Peyton closed his eyes and shook his head. "It's not your fault, Hell," he said softly. When he looked at her again, his gaze was warm and tender. "I know what happened and how she controlled you through the avatar program."

"You know?"

He nodded. "You broke the link in order to escape, didn't you?" His gaze was steady, calm. Everything she wasn't.

She nodded, unable to say anything.

"I thought so. It's the only thing that made sense."

She'd expected him to be as devastated as she was about it. Instead, he just seemed tired. And maybe a little bit tense. "Why aren't you upset?" Maybe he didn't understand what breaking the link meant?

"You think I'm not upset?" An edge clipped his voice that hadn't been there earlier. Or maybe it had been, but she hadn't heard it. Because now his body practically vibrated with strain. "I'm beyond upset. *I'm fucking pissed the hell off*," he shouted.

She flinched from the force of his sudden rage, but he didn't seem to see it.

"When I think of everything you've been through over the past two years. And then those bastards tried to do it again. To you and my child. Holy Christ. How the hell did you not kill them? That's what I want to know. Because I sure as hell would have." His cheeks were flushed, his eyes bright, his grip tight on her arms.

She could see he meant it. That given the chance it's what he would have done. The need to protect and defend was that strong. Part of her loved him for it. But another part was horrified. Who would he have been afterwards? When the murderous rage was gone and he'd had to live out the rest of his days, knowing he'd taken a life? Especially the clone of his wife?

She didn't want to think about what that guilt would have done to him.

Her own guilt was bad enough.

"I wanted to," she admitted, remembering the feeling of her hands on their throats and the burning need to end it. "But killing is wrong," she whispered. And yet she'd done it. Killed the avatar. Her best friend.

"It isn't always," he said, his jaw tight. "Not when it's in self-defense."

She shook her head. "It still makes you feel sick inside, even then."

He stilled, his expression turning wary.

"That avatar program was part of me," she snapped, her own anger rising. "My last connection to Sarah. The only friend I ever had. And I killed it. I cut it out and killed it. How do you think that feels? Huh? Well, I'll tell you. *It feels like fucking shit!*"

The door to the room suddenly opened and a nurse peered in. "Is everything all right? I heard shouting."

"Yes," Peyton said, his voice gruff. "We're fine."

The nurse didn't look convinced.

He gently stroked Hell's hair, pulling it back away from her face. It seemed to have grown longer while she slept and was definitely in need of a brush. She must look a complete mess with her hair in knots and her eyes puffy and red.

"We're just...discussing things," she said and managed a nod and a tight smile.

"Well, if you need anything, just ask," the nurse said to Hell. She gave Peyton a stern, warning glance as she disappeared behind the door, closing it again.

"Fuck," he said, breaking the sudden silence left by the nurse's absence. He caught her gaze and shook his head. "Is this what's been eating you up inside?" he asked, his anger gone.

"Yes." She sighed and grasped his hand, his long fingers with broad palms, prefect for fixing things. Except he couldn't fix this. No one could. "There wasn't any other way. It was Sarah or the baby and the baby needed me more."

"Of course, it does." Peyton's fingers tightened on hers. She looked up at him. A soft smile lifted his lips. "Baby, I'm so sorry for what you went through," he said, and blinked away the wetness glistening in his eyes. "But what you did was right. You broke free."

"But I killed Sarah."

"Hell...Sarah's been dead for over two years. That part of her inside of you was a program. If you really wanted to, I'm sure you could make another one. You're a robotics genius, for Christ's sake."

"I can't undo this," she whispered, her throat tightening. "This was final."

He gathered her in his arms again. "Ah, my sweet love. It's hard to let go, isn't it? It hurts like a sonofabitch."

"I feel so alone."

"Everyone does. It's part of being human. We're alone inside here with our thoughts from the moment we're born." He gently stroked her temple. "That's why love is so important. It keeps us connected and fills us up, so we don't go insane from the emptiness." He smiled softly and snickered as if something funny had come to mind. "You know, before I opened that box and activated you, I was so busy being empty, I'd forgotten that. But you reminded me."

"Oh? I seem to remember you didn't want me," she said, trying unsuccessfully not to smile.

He smirked, seeming amused, and dried her cheeks with his shirt sleeve. It was the same type of shirt he'd worn when they'd first met, she realized. Blue, long sleeved. A bit looser now around his pecs, but she could change that with some decent meals. She winced inside. If she could ever learn how to cook.

"Maybe not then," he admitted. "But I can't live without you now. I love you, Helen. You are the strongest, bravest, most loving person I've ever met. I'm the luckiest man alive that you chose me to create a life with."

His fingers slid from her grasp and covered her belly.

"Are you happy about the baby?" she asked, feeling self-conscious, but enjoying the possessive warmth of his palm that seeped through the blankets. "I didn't exactly realize that was going to happen," she admitted. "I mean, I knew you wanted a baby, and I wanted a baby, but I didn't know I could make it happen like that. I think my nanites have a mind of their own sometimes."

The news about her pregnancy must have come as a huge shock to him. But maybe not less than the shock she felt now. The emptiness was a bit less, the silence inside her mind less damning, now she'd told him what she'd done. It was like a weight had been lifted, taking the sadness away, and leaving room for the love, which shone clearly from his eyes.

He was right. And she'd been wrong.

He could fix this. But only if she let him.

"Happy? Are you kidding me?" He smiled wide, and it was like a thousand suns lit up the sky. "I don't care how it happened or that it wasn't planned. I'm fucking ecstatic, Hell. You've given me Heaven."

He reached into his pocket and pulled out a tiny bracelet. The silver-colored metal flashed in the light. It was beautiful, delicate, precious. A tiny gift to fit the wrist of a beloved child.

"Oh, the Maker." She traced the inscription with the tip of her finger as tears choked her all over again. "Heaven? You want to name the baby Heaven?"

"Why not? I named her mother Hell," he said with a teasing wink.

"You're terrible," she said and broke into laughter.

"Yeah, but you love me anyway."

"Yes, I do. I love you so much it hurts, Peyton Chase." She cupped the bracelet in her palm. She couldn't get over how beautiful it was. How thoughtful Peyton had been to get it made.

"It hurts? Where? Here?" he said and gently stroked her breast. "Or here?" he said running his fingers down over her belly. "What about here—"

"Stop!" she ordered and caught his hand before it went any farther south. "We can't do that in a hospital."

"No?" he said, looking crestfallen, an expression completely ruined by the teasing twinkle in his eyes. "But I'm a doctor. My job is to make you feel better." He waggled his brows suggestively.

"No," she insisted and glanced at the door. "The nurses will hear."

"Then hurry up and get stronger so I can take you home." His hand snuck out of her grip and cupped her breast again, gently squeezing it. His fingers played with the tip, just the way she liked so much. She let out a loud gasp and tipped her head back against the pillow as stars exploded before her eyes.

Shit, shit, shit, shit. I've really missed this.

"I'll be ready tomorrow," she said and captured his mouth for a long, hungry kiss.

Outside the window, a bird sang as it flew high in the sky.

But the only thing Hell heard was the pounding of her pulse as the love she felt for the man cherishing her with his body and his soul, soared free.

A NEW BEGINNING

"YOU AND YOUR family have our deepest apologies, Dr. Chase," Chairwoman Osceola said. Her hair blew softly in the recycled afternoon breeze outside the air transport hanger. "It grieves us to know such atrocities happened right here in our own city, and we at the High Council never suspected a thing."

Peyton doubted that. He wasn't buying the whole 'we knew nothing' crap. But at least he was being allowed to bring Hell back to Deliverance and away from this rat's nest.

Hell had made good on her promise to get better fast. Even so, it had taken nearly two more weeks to convince the High Council she was well enough to travel, and to negotiate the terms of her return home. Now that they had the future of humanity in their grasp, the government was reluctant to let her go. No one like Hell had ever existed before. Did she belong to the people of New Earth, or did she have individual rights like everyone else? And then there was the child to consider.

Peyton had re-asserted his legal claim of ownership in order to keep her and the baby safe from being considered government property. And Lee was pressuring for new legislation, which would incorporate future generations as well as Hell, and recognize human-bio-roid offspring as citizens.

But, Christ, that would take months, if not years, to put in place. And after all the weeks of worry, and waiting, and bureaucratic bullshit, and waiting, and delays, and waiting, and waiting and fucking waiting...he really just wanted to get Hell home.

He managed a polite nod at Osceola. Anything to get them on the ship and out of the Arkopolis before the High Council changed its mind and forced them to stay. "Thank you, Madam Chair," he said.

"You will keep us updated with the child's progress?"

"Of course," Hell said before Peyton could say anything different. "I understand the importance of Dr. Sarah Palmer Chase's research and its implications for the human race. It is my greatest wish to see her dreams to fruition."

The chairwoman studied her for a moment. Probably as amazed as everyone always was with how human Hell seemed, rather than 'droid. "Your willingness to cooperate is greatly appreciated and a tribute to Sarah's memory."

"Thank you," Hell said.

Peyton linked his fingers through her hers, feeling the same sadness he heard in her voice. Wishes and regrets. Things that each of them would never forget.

Osceola nodded toward the Administrative center in the near distance. "Your assailants have been found guilty of the crimes they committed. I assure you they will be held accountable during sentencing."

"Are they going to be executed?" Hell asked.

"It's not yet been decided."

"Please don't," Hell said. She grasped Osceola by the arm, her expression earnest. "It's important they remain alive as an example to others. The people of New Earth need to remember that ambition unchecked leads to madness, not victory. And that the means do not always justify the end. If executed, they will quickly be forgotten."

"How very insightful and well said."

Peyton stared at Hell, barely managing to keep his jaw from dropping. When had she become so good at the whole political speech thing? But there were lots of things different about Hell now.

She'd always been beautiful, but in the sunlight streaming through the transparent domed roof that contained the city, she looked radiant. Confident. Alive. Her flawless skin seemed to glow with renewed energy. Her amber eyes clear and bright. Her hair was a darker shade of blond, now that her roots were growing in. Honey gold with mocha streaks that flowed over her shoulders and halfway down her back and stirred in the warm breeze. Her breasts jiggled full and firm beneath her shirt. He couldn't tell if that was the result of her pregnancy, or if it was an adaptation she'd acquired because she knew he liked it.

Either way, he really did like it.

She smiled at Osceola and gestured at the gardens around them. "The Arkopolis is beautiful. So many trees and flowers and birds. I've never seen it before, you know. Even though I lived here for two years. I was never allowed outside." She looked up at the protective ultraviolet barrier that artificially maintained the optimum environment for humans to survive. "One day, we must all learn to escape our cages."

"Yes," Osceola said, seeming taken aback. "Yes, we must."

Lee leaned forward and grasped Osceola's hand in a farewell gesture. "I look forward to the shipment of new medical equipment that you promised, as well as the increase in trade between all the colonies." He and Jared hadn't lost any time taking advantage of the situation to barter improvements for Deliverance.

"We will have the three new Reclaimers you requested ready by next month," Jared added.

Osceola smiled. "Together, we forge a new future."

"But not if we don't get on that ship," Peyton interjected, managing to avoid rolling his eyes. Maybe. He started to walk toward the transport, tugging Hell along with him. He'd more than maxed out his limit of political double-speak bullshit. "We have a long flight ahead of us and Helen needs to rest. Doctor's orders."

"Doctor's orders?" Hell said. She quirked a brow but didn't try to pull away.

God. Was she actually cooperating for a change?

"Does that include enforced bedrest?" she asked with a sexy wink that made his pulse jack and his groin surge with heat.

"Yeah. And frequent examinations." Oh, Christ. He really needed to get the fuck on the ship and somewhere private. He hurried his steps. They hadn't had proper sex in weeks.

Osceola laughed.

Peyton turned at the unexpected sound. He'd never known her to be anything but cool as ice.

"Well, then by all means you must see to your patient, Dr. Chase." She waved them all on their way with a smile. "Enjoy your flight."

Peyton grinned. Now that was politics he could get behind one hundred percent.

**

Sixteen hours later, they arrived back in snow and cold, but Hell had never been more relieved to see it. The metallic grey dome surrounded by fir trees, with the greenhouses nestled nearby and that pretty river...it was home.

Deliverance Dome

A place she'd thought she might never see again.

"Thank fuck," Peyton grumbled as the ship rolled to a halt inside the transport bay. "Let's go." He stood and grabbed her hand, yanking her to her feet.

Not that she could blame him for being grumpy and anxious. She was feeling that way herself. The flight had been long, tiring, and cramped. With Jared, Lee, the pilot, a full-to-bursting compliment of supplies aboard, and a tiny bathroom, which could barely fit one person...there hadn't been any room for privacy.

No wonder the chairwoman had been laughing.

'Enjoy your flight', indeed.

"First thing I'm going to do is have a shower," Jared said with a sigh as he stretched and grabbed his things. "And then I'm going to have a stiff drink."

"You do that," Peyton said. He charged for the exit as the door unlatched. "First thing I'm going to do is—"

"Take a mean shit?" Rusty asked, peering in the door and blocking the way out.

Mac laughed from behind him. "We heard you brought a full load." He pushed Rusty out of the way and craned his neck to see into the transport. "Christ. Look at all this stuff."

"Will you two jackoffs get out of our way?" Peyton said, and tried to push his way through.

"Well, about that..." said Mac, and crossed his arms, not budging. "We came to warn you."

"Warn?" Hell asked. What chaos had happened now?

Mac spread his arms and pulled her in for a tight hug. "Good to see you again, Helen."

"What the fuck is going on?" shouted Peyton.

"It's Aunty Jo. She's...made you a surprise," Rusty answered, and gave Hell a tight hug too.

"And if either of you ruin it by blabbing, she'll be spitting mad," warned Lee. He stood in the aisle with Jared, waiting to leave.

"You know what it is?" asked Peyton, looking back at Lee. "Of course, you know. Why would that even shock me?" He shook his head wearily. "Come on, let's go see what's she's done. It's been a long few weeks."

They made their way through the surprisingly empty transport bay, considering they'd just gotten back from being away for over a month, and into the main chamber of the Dome.

"Gotta close your eyes now," Mac said.

"Are you shitting me?" said Peyton. "Forget the cloak and dagger shit. I'm going up to my place to crash."

"Yeah, you'll get there in a few minutes," Rusty insisted. "But you gotta close your eyes first."

"Come on, Peyton. Don't be a pain," Hell snapped. "Just close your eyes and let them surprise us."

"Fine," he huffed. "But if I get tea-bagged by these jerkwads, I'm holding you responsible."

Hell shook her head and closed her eyes. She let Rusty lead her further into the Dome, listening for any signs of whatever Aunty Jo had planned. But other than the normal mechanical noises of machinery working in the background, she couldn't detect anything else. Which in itself was unusual, because there should be the murmurs of people going about their business.

They stopped after a few minutes of walking filled with Peyton's grumbling mutters.

"Okay... We're here," Mac said. A door hissed open.

"Surprise!" a crowd of people shouted.

"What the hell?" Peyton said.

"Oh, the Maker." Hell opened her eyes.

They stood in a part of the Dome she'd never been to before, where the colonists lived. The main hallway was bright and filled with people. Lots of people. Some she recognized, like Genova, and many she didn't. Everyone who lived at Deliverance must have gathered to see them. Their cheers and clapping were almost deafening.

"Welcome home," Aunty Jo said above the noise, her face beaming. She rushed forward and gave them both a crushing hug. "Oh, my dear child. I'm so happy to see you again." Her eyes glistened. She planted a kiss on Hell's cheek and gave her another tight hug. She looked at Peyton and grinned, her green eyes flashing with excitement and more than a hint of impishness. "We've been busy while you've been off lounging in the sun."

Peyton's brows drew together. "Lounging?"

She laughed. Grabbing their hands, she pulled them through the crowd and said, "Come see, come see!"

She pressed her hand against a panel beside one of the many

doorways. It hissed open and she tugged them inside, practically bursting with excitement. "Well, what do you think?" She gestured around the room.

Hell was too stunned to reply.

The apartment was beautiful. White and silver and warm. Brightly lit, with morning light streaming in two large triangular windows along the outside wall, which offered a view of fir trees and melting spring snow. A metal and glass table was in the center of the room, with plenty of comfy seating placed around it, enough to host friends, or fit a growing family. A monitor was positioned on the opposite wall, a tablet on the table. Trays of finger foods had been prepared, along with several glasses and bottles of beverages, and a cake. Bambi was in the process of setting it on the table. The inscription read, 'Welcome home Peyton and Helen.'

Hell covered her mouth with her hand. "This is for us?"

Aunty Jo nodded. "You can put up pictures when you're ready. There's a kitchen through there." She gestured off to the left. "Bathroom's here, workroom's over there—"

"You moved my stuff?" Peyton said, not sounding particularly happy about the idea.

She gave him a withering look. "Yes, and I organized it all just the way you had it. Some of it, anyway," she added and grinned. "Bedrooms are here. Master, guest, and...well, I have to admit, this one's my favorite."

The room they entered was smallish, but again brightly lit with a window. Recessed panels lined one wall where clothes could be put. A shelf for trinkets and a table with drawers occupied another. But it was the crib that stood in the middle of the room, which made her breath catch. Made of dark wood, it had already been outfitted with soft yellow blankets. Henry was placing a stuffed bear inside it. He turned when he saw them and held the bear out to Peyton instead.

"No squeaks," he said.

Hell burst into tears.

She couldn't help it. Couldn't stop it.

"Oh, Helen, dear. Oh, oh!" Aunty Jo put her arms around her and hugged her tight. She peered at her, looking crestfallen. "It's not what you wanted?"

Hell shook her head. "No, no. It's beautiful. Perfect. Thank you." Wetness burned her eyes. She wiped it away and cupped the elderly woman's worried face. "I just...I didn't think I was coming back." She looked around the room. A pretty, perfect baby's room.

Something she'd never thought she'd have. "And now you've done all this." A sob caught her throat and then burst free. It was overwhelming to be this loved and part of something so special. She threw her arms around Aunty Jo and gave her a big kiss on the cheek.

The older woman grabbed Hell's hand and gave it a quick squeeze. "Well, I just thought with the baby coming, you would need a bit more space. That bat cave upstairs would have gotten pretty small pretty fast. And I'm right down the hall whenever you need a hand."

Hell nodded and kissed her again. It was time to make a change and move forward. Create a home for their new family. "Thank you." She glanced at the doorway and the people crowding it, Lee, Jared, Mac and Rusty. And so many more behind them. People she barely knew but accepted her as one of them. "I love you so much. All of you." Hell patted Henry on the head and turned to Peyton.

He was staring at the bear, his eyes wet and glistening. "Where did you find this?" he said. He stroked the bear's raggedy, uneven ears. It looked well used and hand stitched, the brown fabric worn in places. But its little red vest and black button eyes appeared shiny and new.

"Mr. Boobles?" Aunty Jo smiled softly. "I packed him away. Kept him safe for you. Thought he might be needed again one day."

"I thought he was lost." He blinked, his eyes shining in the light. "Aunty Jo made him for me. When my parents died," he explained to Hell. His expression reflected the little boy he'd been, lost, and lonely and scared. The heart of the man he'd become, strong, loyal and caring. And handsome. So breathtakingly handsome.

Hell brushed the tears from the corners of his eyes, certain her own were leaking again. "You're a lucky man. He's the sweetest, softest bear a guy could have."

"Shit," he said and put the bear in the crib. "He's not sweet. He's badass. He'll kick butt on all your nightmares, Heaven."

He pulled Hell close, placed his hand on her belly and a kiss on her temple. The touch was soft, but she felt it deep inside, like a tiny fluttering bird taking flight.

"Heaven?" Aunty Jo smiled. "You're happy then? With everything?"

Peyton looked around the room and back at her. He grinned, his eyes bright. "Hell, yeah. Love you, you crazy woman. Even if you did move my shit without asking." He captured her in a tight hug that lingered for several moments. "Thank you for everything," he whispered. "But for the love of all things holy..." He darted a meaningful glance at the open doorway and the curious onlookers milling about. "Please get all these people out of my house."

She laughed and tweaked his nose. "You're such a bossy grouch. Can't imagine where you get that from." Grinning, she marched into the main room. "All right everybody. Time to go. Peyton needs a nap."

But there were toasts to drink and cake to have and congratulations to give and receive. So it took two hours or more before they were finally alone, just Hell and Peyton, in their new bedroom.

"I can't find anything," he said, shutting a panel on the wall. "Where's all my shirts?"

Perched on the bed, she watched him fuss. He was so cute when he frowned like that. "Probably next to your pants."

His hair glistened, wet from the quick shower they'd taken. His whole body did, gorgeous and naked except for the towel wrapped around his hips. His pecs flexed as he opened another drawer and peeked inside. "I can't find those either."

"Then I guess you'll just have to wear nothing." *What a shame*, she thought with a grin. After all the hours of travel and then the impromptu welcome home party, she should be exhausted. Instead, she was far from it.

Keeping her gaze on him, she let her own towel fall away and leaned back on the bed.

"Mmmm," he said. His irritation at not finding his clothes melted into a lazy grin. He dropped his towel. "Matching outfits. I can get behind that."

Holy sweet everything, so could she. His cock was hard and getting harder. Long and thick. She couldn't take her eyes off him as he pranced to the bed. It had been too long since they'd been alone, safe from the world. They'd been through so much since the last time they'd made love, it seemed like a whole other lifetime. Her need to be with him, skin to skin, made her toes curl and her breasts ache, not to mention what it was doing to her insides. Oh, the Maker, how she loved every inch of this man, body and soul. But as he lounged beside her on the bed, there was something she'd been meaning to ask.

"You called your bear Mr. Boobles?"

"Eh..." Peyton shrugged. "They've always been my favorite

thing." He stroked hers. Lovingly. Longingly. Paying special attention to the tips.

"Fair enough. Just...oooooh, please keep doing that."

"You like that do you? What about this?" He sucked her nipple between his lips and gently licked it over and over again until it tingled and ached.

She twisted her fingers in his hair. "Oh, yes!"

"And this?" He kissed his way downward between her breasts, giving her skin little nips and licks.

She shivered, goose bumps rippling her skin. "Yeah," she squeaked. Damn, he was sexy. Muscular and strong. His shoulders flexed as he crept down the bed and spread her thighs with his weight.

His mouth was warm and wet as it settled over her sex.

"Peyton." She tensed and caught his gaze. Heat rushed through her at the intense need she saw there.

"Relax, baby. Enjoy. I've been dying to taste you for days."

He stroked her with his tongue and sucked her with his lips. Each movement sensual, soft. Warm, so warm. She writhed against the sheets, tangling them in her hands.

"Ahhhhh," she gasped.

He moaned as he lapped at her wetness. The sound vibrated through her, making her clit throb.

It wouldn't take long. It never did when he pleasured her like this. It was so intense, but at the same time not enough. She needed to feel his thickness, stretching and filling her, hot and hard when he came.

That image tipped her over the edge.

"Peyton!"

She arched and jerked as the storm rushed through her.

"God, you're beautiful. So fucking beautiful."

She moaned, unable to speak.

As her body slowly cooled and stopped trembling, he licked his way back up again, and stopped when he reached her lower abdomen. He gave it a soft kiss. "Hell?"

"Yeah?" She opened her eyes and looked at him, body and mind still tingling.

His gaze was full of so much warmth it made her gasp. Who knew a person could feel intimacy like this?

"Do you know how much I fucking love you? Really, truly love you?" He pressed his lips against her abdomen again. "What you've given me. This little miracle. I...it's something I wanted for so long, but never thought I'd ever have. You're just... The most amazing woman I've ever known. I can't..." He shook his head, struggling to find the right way to say the words he needed to say. "I can't believe how lucky I am. I just want you to know that I adore every part of you. And this baby...I promise to be the best father I can."

She stroked his cheek. "I know that, my love." She felt the fluttering inside, again. The little excited bird. Her pulse spiked as she slid her hand over her belly. "And I think the baby does too."

His eyes went wide. "What? Really?"

"I'm not sure. Maybe. I'm feeling...something."

"It already has a heartbeat," he said, his gaze turning thoughtful. "It's possible there's a deeper connection too."

"Part you, part me." And she could talk to machines without being connected. Maybe she and the baby could communicate that way too.

"Hello, little Heaven. Daddy loves you," he whispered and kissed her belly again.

The fluttering answered. Wordless love. That pushed the silence inside her away. And in that instant, she knew that Peyton had given her the greatest gift he ever could. She would never be alone again.

"Oh, Peyton." She clutched at his hair and pulled him upward, craving a deep kiss. "I need you, now. Please, baby." The desire was urgent, burning hot inside her. She could hardly breathe with the force of it.

He grunted, his pulse racing, his mouth hungry as it claimed hers. "God, I need you so bad..." He breathed the words, hot desire against her skin.

Fuck.

She couldn't get enough of him. Or have him fast enough. She raised her hips and wrapped herself around him. Pulling him close. Closer. *Oh!*

She shuddered as he spread her, stroking her with his tip.

Then he was inside her.

Thick and hard, and it felt so good, so good, *so good*, to be like this again.

"Hell," he whispered by her ear and nipped it.

"Do it. *Oooooh*, fuck me hard, Peyton. God, I need your cock. Fuck me with it. Fuck me hard."

Her words lit a fire in him. It smoldered in his eyes. Burned from his skin.

Scorched her in all the right places.

With a growl, he captured her wrists above her head and did

exactly as she asked.

**

Sometime later, they lay entwined on the bed, satiated and relaxed. She played with the hair on his chest, slick with sweat, and watched his flat nipples tighten. She could keep doing this for hours, loving and fucking and coming hard. But the silence in between while they rested? She liked that best. Because she could hear the steady beat of his heart and the soft way the breath passed between his lips and she knew she'd worn him out. Again. Her Peyton. The only man who'd ever made her feel truly safe.

It was a wonderful thing, being with him and being alive.

"I've been thinking about names," she said, breaking the quiet.

He stirred and sighed. "What about them?" His voice was drowsy as he stroked her arms.

"You only gave me a first name. I'd also like a last one."

He lifted his head off the pillow. His hair was a tousled, sexy mess, his eyes sleepy and relaxed. But a smile twitched his lips as he turned to her and propped himself up on his crooked elbow. "Okay. Hmmmm...what should that be? I know." He grinned. "How about...Peebles."

"Helen *Peebles?*" She laughed. "No."

"Helen Sexyass?"

"No!"

"Helen...Throat-wobbler-mangrove?" he teased, laughing.

"Absolutely not!" She smacked him playfully on the chest with the flat of her palm.

His expression turned serious, his smile deepening. "What about Chase? You'd like to be Helen Chase?"

"Yeah."

His throat moved as he swallowed hard. "It has a nice ring to it."

"Yes, it does."

"I think there's some sort of ceremony we need for that one." His fingers played with her hair.

"Probably. But if you say it now, it will become fact." She wanted to belong to him in every way. Including as his life-partner and wife.

He cupped her cheek and stroked it, the look in his eyes solemn. "Helen Chase," he said. His lips were warm and firm as they pressed against hers.

She closed her eyes. A sense of completeness spread through her, like a happy sigh, as she imprinted the new name. "I am now Helen Chase."

"The sexiest woman alive," he added and kissed her again. "And the smartest. And the only woman who ever made me come three times in two hours."

"Really?"

"Yeah."

"Wanna try for number four?"

He stared at her for a moment, seeming shocked by her boldness.

"I counted at least six for me," she said. "I owe you two back."

He flipped over onto his back and spread his arms wide on the bed. "Do with me what you will, insatiable woman." He laughed. "I think when I opened that box, I became your slave and you, my master."

She cocked her head sideways and gave him a sexy wink. "Took you long enough to realize."

EPILOGUE

"ARE YOU SURE you want to do this?" Peyton asked Jared.

His best friend nodded, his expression solemn as he took a sip of his drink. "Yeah. It's time to make a change."

Peyton nodded in return. He didn't have to like it, but he understood.

They sat together in the clearing they'd made outside the Dome, watching Heaven play. She was fascinated with pine cones. Picking them up and putting them in the little basket she carried in her chubby hands. The look of determination in her dark eyes was the most priceless thing he'd ever seen.

"When are you leaving?"

Jared shrugged. "Probably tomorrow. Or the next day. You'll look after my things?"

"Yeah."

"Thanks. I don't know how long I'll be gone."

"Have you told your dad?"

He shook his head. "Not yet."

"He's going to be upset. He wanted you to take over leading the Dome. Not go off exploring the ruined cities." Lee was going to be more than a bit upset. Jared's mother had died doing the same risky thing. But apparently the need for adventure was a family trait she'd passed on to her son.

Jared smirked. "He doesn't need me to help with politics. He's got Hell for that."

She stood alone on the other side of the glade of fir trees, her hair blowing in the late spring breeze as she spoke into her tablet. She was engrossed in a heated conversation with one of the leaders of the other Domes. Something about her nanite blood and basic human rights. She glanced up sharply and covered the tablet. "Heaven, not in your mouth, love."

The little monkey let the pine cone that was now covered in drool drop onto the ground and rubbed her mouth, as if it tasted bad.

Hell smiled at her and went back to her conversation, her hand sliding over the new little bump growing in her belly. Number two would be born in a few months. And Peyton couldn't help wondering what the hell they were supposed to do then. Because one baby was keeping them busy enough.

Apparently satisfied with her hoard, Heaven toddled over to Peyton and Jared, her dark pigtails dancing like pussy willows stuck on her head.

She stopped beside him and put her basket down. Picking a cone from her collection, she handed it to him.

"Dat," she said.

"Thanks, lovely monkey."

She picked another cone and handed it to Jared. "Nunka Jed." She smiled at him, her dark eyes beaming.

"Thank you," he said and smiled back. "It's the nicest pine cone I've ever had."

She giggled.

She didn't speak much yet, even though she was a-year-and-a-bit old and Aunty Jo was sure she should. But Hell said it was fine. Heaven talked her ears off to her in her head. She'd speak out loud when she was ready. Right now, she was busy being busy and learning.

Heaven left her basket and toddled off again. This time in search of twigs.

"She'll miss you," Peyton said to Jared.

His lips twisted. "She'll be fine."

But Peyton didn't miss the sadness that lingered behind his words. Heaven was part of the reason Jared was leaving. She was a reminder of the life he wanted and probably should have, but he'd never been able to find. At least, not at Deliverance.

"Hell couldn't do anything with Bambi?" he asked softly, taking a sip of his own drink. Black coffee. Hot. Just the way he liked it.

Jared frowned. He looked at the ground and didn't speak for a minute. "She said she could do what she did for Henry. Reprogram her and give her emotions. But she'd never be real, like a Bio-roid. Or be able to have a kid like Hell can."

Peyton studied his friend, his heart aching.

"You're a lucky sonofabitch, you know that?" Jared said.

"Yeah, I am." Should he tell him what he'd learned about Sarah's plan? That Hell had originally been meant for Jared? That she'd wanted to bring her home for her brother? Or would that just make the agitation Jared was feeling worse?

"I'm gonna leave Bambi here. Turn her off and pack her away."

"You sure you want to do that?"

"I won't need her where I'm going."

"Where is that, exactly?"

"Not sure yet. South maybe. Heard there was an expedition going to one of the coastal cities. I might join that."

Peyton nodded. Things had changed so much since he'd synthesized Hell's blood and made it compatible with most of the colonists. And with her nanites to strengthen and protect them against pathogens, a new spirit of exploration had started. Jared wasn't the only one moving out of the Domes and investigating the old ruins.

"Peyton!" Hell shouted.

He jerked, spilling his coffee.

She covered the tablet with her hand and waved angrily at the far side of the clearing. "Heaven's eating leaves again!"

"Fuck," Peyton muttered as he jumped to his feet. There she was, his little monkey, peeking behind a tree and munching away happily, a fist full of birch leaves in her grubby hand.

"Gotta go. Good luck, buddy," he said and raced off after his daughter.

Jared laughed and shook his head. "I think you need it more than me."

The End

DEAR READER...

Thank you for reading *Project Hell*. I hope you enjoyed Peyton and Hell's story.

I love to hear from my readers, so please drop by and leave me a review at the vendor of your choice. You can also email me directly at felicitykates.author@gmail.com

For up-to-date information on my books, including upcoming releases and giveaways, please visit the KC Stories website www.legacyhunter.space where you can also sign up for my newsletter and join my Facebook reader group The Legacy Hunter Guild

More from Felicity Kates
The Little Miss Kick Ass series

More than skin is revealed when costumes come off at a cosplay conference. In this two-book series of unconventional romance stories, four characters discover the secret truths of their identities as well as their hearts.

Cosplay: Casey Jackson thinks she has it all. A sexy job as a promotional model and an even sexier boss who keeps her happy in and out of the bedroom. She doesn't mind the blurred lines of their relationship, until Lucas Haskell gives her the ultimate ultimatum—commit or leave. Love is one thing, but is marriage worth the price of her freedom? Lucas Haskell knows what he wants: Casey Jackson. She's the love of his life and the muse he's always dreamed of. She may have doubts about marriage, but he's ready to do everything in his power to convince her they are meant to be together. When opportunity presents itself at a Fan Expo convention, playing dress-up has never been so steamy...or so much fun.

Secret Identity: Astrid Bitten isn't smitten. All she wants is a night of dress-up adventure to bring some excitement to her lonely life. When she meets the most gorgeous guy she's ever seen at a Fan Expo convention, she jumps at the chance to explore what lies beneath the stretchy Spandex of his superhero suit. But is she ready to discover the truth of her secret cravings? Race Lindstrom wants a second chance. At life, at love, at using the gods-given talents he's been born with for good rather than evil. When he spies the golden-haired goddess across a crowded room, he knows he'll never let her go. But second chances don't come easy. He'll have to confront his deepest secret if he wants to make Astrid his forever.

www.LegacyHunter.space

"Original! Awesome! Steamy! And utterly adorable! For once, a story that is not about a millionaire and a virgin!" –Amazon Review

ABOUT THE AUTHOR

Felicity Kates is the spicier pen name of Canadian science fiction and romance author, Kate Reedwood, notable for the bestselling Project Hell serial (as Felicity Kates) and the Amazon internationally best-selling Legacy Hunter series, (as Kate Reedwood) co-written with Australian author, Chris Heinicke.

A classically trained writer and artist, with a Bachelor of Arts degree in English from the University of Guelph as well as a diploma in Classical Animation from world-renown, Sheridan College, Kate enjoys creating stories that combine humor with strong characters, and adventures which seek to define what it means to be human, no matter the time or place in the universe.

Kate lives off coffee (mmmm coffee), enjoys chilling with Netflix shows such as Altered Carbon, and is an avid fan of all things sci-fi, especially Star Wars. When not dreaming up new worlds and books with Chris Heinicke, she can most often be found writing about them.

Science Fiction   Romance   *Suspense   Urban Fantasy*

Find our exciting stories at:
www.Legacyhunter.space

BOOKS BY FELICITY KATES

LITTLE MISS KICK-ASS SREIES
Sizzling contemporary romance with a paranormal twist

Cosplay
Secret Identity

THE NEW EARTH SERIES
Sexually-charged post-apocalyptic sci-fi romance

Project Hell Parts 1-5
Project Hell the complete novel

BOOKS BY CHRIS HEINICKE

THE PM SERIES
Thrilling suspense with a sexy dark side.

5 PM
7 PM – Brittany
7 PM – Jack
7 PM – Ed and Hannah
7 PM – Talissa
7 PM – Emily
7 PM – Bjorn
7 PM -- Boxed Set
11 PM (coming soon)

THE MAN IN BLACK
Out-of-this-world investigative sci-fi

The Man In Black

COMING SOON...THE ZODIAC SYNDICATE
Urban Fantasy in a MC world
12 book series

BOOKS BY CHRIS HEINICKE AND KATE REEDWOOD

THE LEGACY HUNTER SERIES
Science Fiction Adventure

Queen Killer
Star Keeper
Dark Horizon
Fatal Fortress
Phoenix Rising
Core Shifter (coming soon)
Lost Legacy (coming soon)

COMING SOON...THE GALACTIC MISFITS SERIES
Time travel science fiction adventure set in the Legacy Hunter universe, featuring Shiznit from the Legacy Hunter series.

Book 1 – Microscopic Mayhem available NOW!